About the Authors

Anne Fraser always loved reading and never imagined that one day she would be writing for a living. She started life as a nurse and helpfully, for a writer of medical romances, is married to a hospital doctor! Anne and husband have lived and worked all over the world, including South Africa, Canada and Australia and many of their experiences as well as the settings find their way into her books. Anne lives in Glasgow with her husband and two children.

Joss Wood's passion for putting black letters on a white screen is only matched by her love of books and travelling and her hatred of making school lunches and ironing. Fuelled by coffee and craziness, Joss is a hands on Mum and, after a career in local economic development and business lobbying, she now writes full time. Surrounded by family, friends and books she lives in Kwa-Zulu Natal, South Africa with her husband and two children.

With Love From

COLLECTION

With Love From Cape Town

ANNE FRASER

JOSS WOOD

MILLS & BOON

First Published in Great Britain 2020
By Mills & Boon, an imprint of HarperCollins*Publishers*
1 London Bridge Street, London, SE1 9GF

WITH LOVE FROM CAPE TOWN © 2020 Harlequin Books S.A.

Miracle: Marriage Reunited © 2010 Anne Fraser
She's So Over Him © 2012 Joss Wood
The Last Guy She Should Call © 2014 Joss Wood

ISBN: 978-0-263-28083-8

0220

MIX
Paper from
responsible sources
FSC™ C007454

FSC
www.fsc.org

This book is produced from independently certified FSC™ paper

to ensure responsible forest management.

For more information visit: www.harpercollins.co.uk/green

Printed and bound in Spain
by CPI, Barcelona

MIRACLE: MARRIAGE REUNITED

ANNE FRASER

CHAPTER ONE

DR ROBINA ZONDI studied the austere man addressing the conference delegates and sucked in her breath. Dr Niall Ferguson, the keynote speaker and the man on whom the success of her book depended, was disturbingly good looking and surprisingly sexy. Somehow she had expected someone middle-aged, not this Adonis with a beak of a nose that prevented fine features from being too beautiful. He couldn't be more than thirty—thirty-five tops. Young surely to exude such easy confidence. As he spoke, he pushed a lock of dark hair which kept flopping across his brow aside with impatient fingers.

She had looked him up on the internet, but there had been no photographs accompanying the rather dry but impressively long list of credentials. She certainly hadn't expected to be enthralled—as everyone else in the conference appeared to be—by his presentation. No polite, bored coughing had interrupted the smooth flow of words, as he emphasised key points in his lilting Scottish accent. It was a flawless and professional performance and as soon as the question-and-answer session was over, he was surrounded by journalists and attendees all vying for his attention.

This was going to be harder than she'd anticipated. The butterflies that had been setting up home in her stomach were creating havoc. It was very likely that he would send her away with a flea in her ear, but Robina had never been one to give up without trying. If her easy-to-read guide on infertility were to be taken seriously, she needed someone of his stature to give it his seal of approval. Her publishing company had sent him a copy, but he hadn't even had the decency to acknowledge its receipt. To be fair, he probably had loads of people wanting his views or his endorsement. When she had read on the internet that he was to attend a conference in Cape Town, the opportunity to ask him face to face had seemed too good to miss.

Robina waited until he was finally alone before approaching him.

'Dr Ferguson, may I have a word?' Blue eyes, the colour of the rarest of Kimberley diamonds, looked up. He frowned as if trying to place who she was.

'You don't know me,' she said quickly. 'I'm Dr Robina Zondi. I know you're a busy man, but could I have a minute?'

He stood and Robina was disconcerted to find that he towered over her. Taller than he had appeared at the podium, he had to be at least six feet three. It was all she could do not to take a step back.

'Of course,' he said politely. 'Please have a seat.'

Robina dipped into her briefcase and pulled out a copy of her book.

'I hope you don't mind, Dr Ferguson,' she said quickly before her courage failed her, 'but I have a favour to ask you.' She handed him the book.

'*A Guide to Infertility,*' he said quietly, glancing at the cover. 'How can I help?' He smiled encouragingly and his face relaxed, making him seem more human and even more devastatingly handsome.

But before she could launch into her carefully prepared speech, a short, dark-skinned man appeared and elbowed his way past Robina. 'Dr Ferguson, I'm Professor Lessing, based at Groote Schuur Hospital. I've been trying to get a hold of you for weeks now, and I wondered if I could have a moment?' He glanced at his watch, making it clear that he was a busy man.

'I'm sorry, Professor,' Dr Ferguson said in his deep lilting voice that made Robina think of water rushing over rocks, 'but I'm afraid this lady got here first. Perhaps we could schedule a time later on?'

'Please, go ahead,' Robina interrupted. 'I can wait. Actually, I'm dying for something to drink, so can I get you something while you speak to this gentleman?'

'You wouldn't mind? In that case a glass of iced water would be great.' He grinned and a dimple appeared at the side of his mouth. Robina's heart skipped a beat. She tried to tell herself it was just nervousness about her book that was turning her legs to jelly and her mouth to dust. February in Cape Town was hot enough without being in a crowded room where the air-conditioning had broken down. If Dr Ferguson was feeling the heat, he gave no sign of it.

By the time she fought her way back through the crowds with three glasses of iced water on a tray, it looked as if whatever the professor had been discussing with their guest speaker hadn't made him very happy. Just as Robina approached, the older man leapt to his feet, knocking the tray of drinks from her hands. Robina watched in horror as three glasses spun in the air, spilling ice cubes and water over Dr Ferguson and his companion.

'For God's sake, woman,' Professor Lessing growled, dabbing at his suit. 'How can you be so careless?'

Robina glared back. It hadn't been her fault. If he hadn't jumped to his feet without looking, the drinks would have stayed on the tray. She bit back the words and glanced at Niall. A small smile tugged at the corner of his mouth.

'I don't know about anyone else,' he said slowly, 'but a cool shower was just what I needed.' He looked at Robina and grinned.

'Stupid girl,' the professor muttered irritably, still dabbing at his suit.

All of a sudden the smile left Dr Ferguson's face. 'What did you say?' he asked quietly.

'She should have looked where she was going.'

Dr Ferguson's eyes glittered. 'I think we all know whose fault it was. Now, Professor, if you would excuse us?'

The older man looked as if he were about to protest, but something in Niall's expression stopped him in his tracks. 'I don't see any further need to meet again,' he said tightly. 'You've made your position quite clear.' And with that he turned on his heel and left.

'I'm so sorry,' Robina said.

'Don't be. The man has an over-inflated opinion of himself. And he's a bore—even more unforgivable. You did me a favour, actually. He wants me to put my name to some paper he's presenting, but I told him I'm not interested. I'm afraid he wasn't too happy.' He sat back down in his chair, indicating to Robina that she sit too. 'Now, where were we?'

Robina wiped droplets of water off the front of her book and pushed it across the table. 'I know I have a cheek asking, but I wondered…' She paused. Now it came to actually asking the question it seemed ridiculously forward. But she was here now and she could hardly just get up and leave. 'I wondered if you would read my book and consider writing the foreword?' There, it was out. He could laugh in her face, or send her packing, but at least she had asked.

He turned the book over in his hands. 'As a matter of fact, I have already read it. It was sent to me by your publisher. I've been kind of busy, otherwise I would have replied by now.' He leaned back in his chair and scrutinised her face. Robina felt her pulse kick up a gear. What if he'd hated it?

'I thought it was well written,' he said, to her relief, 'and very accurate. I particularly liked the style—informal without being patronising. I can see the need for a book like this. We specialists aren't always the best people to explain complicated medical issues to the general public.' He grinned and Robina's heart somersaulted.

'But what makes you qualified to write it? I haven't heard your name associated with the sub-specialty, and I know most people,' he continued, his eyes never straying from hers. The way he was looking at her made her feel they were the only two people in the room. Her heart thudded against her ribs.

'I'm a doctor—a GP—but before that I was a journalist.'

'And being a GP makes you qualified to write such a book?' he queried, his eyes drilling into hers, but then his gaze softened. 'Or is there a more personal reason?'

She shook her head. 'Purely professional. I saw loads of women at my surgery who wanted to know about infertility, but didn't know where to go. Often they didn't know if they even needed treatment. Their questions were what gave me the idea for the book.' She stumbled slightly over the words. When she said it like that, it did sound a little simplistic. He wasn't to know about the hours she had spent researching the area and more particularly, talking to women, finding out what they wanted to know rather than what the experts thought they *should* know.

His eyes dropped to the bare fingers of her left hand and then he looked up at her and grinned again. Robina caught her breath. Never in her twenty-eight years had a man had such an effect on her and suddenly, crazy though it was, Robina knew that she was smitten.

Niall looked over her shoulder and Robina turned to see a group of people bearing purposefully down on them. Niall stood suddenly and whispered in her ear.

'Let's get out of here,' he said, 'before I get trapped.'

Robina could no more have refused him than she could have walked across the Atlantic. She tried to pretend to herself that the opportunity to have access to one of the leading lights in infertility was the reason, but gave up that notion the second he gripped her elbow and steered her outside. Suddenly the last thing she wanted to talk about was work. Instead she wanted to know every personal detail about this man, down to the name of his first pet.

He led her to an open-top sports car and helped her into the front seat.

'Where are we going?' she asked, not really caring.

'I thought you could show me a bit of your country. In return for me endorsing your book?'

'So you'll do it, then, Dr Ferguson?' Her heart was still doing its ridiculous pitter-patter and it had nothing to do with the relief she felt at his words. What was the matter with her? She was reacting like some star-struck groupie.

'Yes, but only if we have a deal. And by the way, it's Niall.'

Robina forced herself to breathe normally before she replied. 'Have you been to Cape Town before?'

'Once, but I never got out of the hotel.'

'You are kidding, right?' she said incredulously. 'You came all the way here and didn't see anything? Not Table Mountain, Chapman's Peak, the vineyards? Nothing?'

All of a sudden his smile vanished and his expression turned bleak. 'There wasn't time,' he said shortly. 'I had...' he paused '...only a couple of days. I didn't want to leave my daughter for too long.'

So he was married, Robina thought, aware of a crashing sense of disappointment. He hadn't been wearing a ring, but many men didn't.

'And your wife?' she said lightly. 'Did she come with you?'

'My wife's dead,' he said quietly. 'She died two years ago.'

This time there was no mistaking the raw pain that shadowed his face.

Before she could help herself, she reached across and squeezed his hand. 'I'm so sorry. She must have been very young.'

'Thirty.' He sucked in a breath as if it hurt him to say the words. 'Mairead died just six months before that last conference. Unfortunately, these things are arranged months—even years—in advance. I couldn't get out of it, but I didn't want to leave my daughter for a second longer than I had to. I flew back as soon as the conference finished. I don't think I saw anything apart from the inside of my hotel.'

'But you've got more time this trip?' Robina thought it wise to get the subject onto safer ground.

'I have the rest of the weekend,' he said. 'The first flight back I could get is on Monday. So until then, I'm all yours.' He looked at her and Robina felt the world spin. Never before had she experienced such an instant, overwhelming reaction to a man. 'So where are we going first? What do you recommend?'

'What do you want to see? The tourist Africa or the real Africa?'

'The real Africa, of course, that's why I've kidnapped you.' Her heart lurched. If only that were true! The thought of being kidnapped by this enigmatic man sent all sorts of fantasies spinning around her brain. Stop being ridiculous, she told herself. He wanted a guide in exchange for his help, nothing more. From the expression on his face when he'd mentioned his wife, he must have loved her very much. And he had a daughter. All very good reasons for Robina to run a mile.

'So, where to?' he asked a little later as he put the car into gear and exited the conference car park. They came to a T-junction. 'Left or right?'

'Right.' She paused as a thought struck her. 'You're not afraid of heights, are you?'

'I'm probably going to regret this but, no, I'm not. Why, are you?'

'Terrified!' Robina admitted with a smile. 'But I would never forgive myself if I didn't take you up Table Mountain—especially on a beautifully clear day like today. I know it's a bit touristy, but everyone has to go up at least once in their lifetime. So why don't we start there? And then…'

'Then we'll see,' he finished the sentence for her. There was something in the tone of his voice that sent a shiver up Robina's spine. It was a promise and a warning. She knew that if she wasn't to get in too deep, now was the time to call a halt. But even as the thought formed in her mind, she knew it was too late. She could do nothing except allow this man to pull her along in his wake and enjoy the ride. For once she was going to throw caution to the wind and let life take her where it would.

As they waited in the queue for the cable car, they chatted

easily about work. When their turn came to board, Robina's heart began to race. Although she had made the trip many times before, each time she was swamped by a rush of anxiety. The doors opened and Robina immediately clutched the handrail that encircled the oval cable car. But she knew it would be worth it once they got to the top—the views over Cape Town and the South Atlantic Ocean were breathtaking. Niall would be impressed.

'Are you all right?' he asked quietly, and she could feel his breath on her neck.

'I'm fine, really. Like I told you, I'm just not very good with heights.' She looked up at him and smiled with as much reassurance as she could muster.

'For some reason, I didn't think of you as someone who could be afraid of anything.' He placed a comforting arm on her shoulder and she felt the heat of his fingers burning her bare skin.

And suddenly she wasn't frightened any more. Before she knew it, they had reached the top and were spilling out onto the flat top of Table Mountain.

Two hours stretched into three then four as they explored the trails along the top of the mountain, eventually retreating to the outside restaurant for a late lunch. A cool breeze tickled their skin and Robina thought she had never felt as happy as she did at that moment.

Niall topped up their water glasses. 'So is this where you take all your guests?' he asked.

Robina took a sip of her drink and pointed to an island in the distance. 'Do you see that strip of land over there?'

He nodded.

'That's Robben Island. Where Nelson Mandela was incarcerated.' She felt the tears prickle behind her eyes and she blinked furiously.

But she was too late. Niall touched her hand. 'Hey, are you all right?' he said gently.

'I come here at least once a year,' Robina said.

Niall raised an eyebrow in a silent question. 'On the anniversary of my father's death,' she continued.

'Was he there too?' Niall probed gently.

'For six months. When he was a young man.' She turned to face him. 'It's open to the public now, but I somehow can't bring myself to go there. It would be too painful. So I come up here and pay my respects instead.' Robina took a deep breath.

'You know the prisoners spent their free time teaching each other whatever they knew, so that by the time they were released, they would have the skills and knowledge to lead a government. My parents had to leave South Africa when they got married. At that time it was still illegal for a white woman and a black man to marry. They continued their work in the UK, before returning here in the early eighties. My father said not living in Africa was like not being able to breathe.'

'He sounds like a remarkable man.'

'He was. I've spent my whole life trying to be someone he could be proud of.'

Niall grinned and, taking her hand in his, rubbed her fingers. 'It looks like you succeeded.'

'I don't know. Maybe. Perhaps if he were here to tell me himself...' She shook her head. 'Anyway, enough about me.' Suddenly she was appalled. How had she let herself go on like that? She never discussed her private thoughts with anyone, yet here she was spilling her heart out to a relative stranger. 'I just wanted you to experience Table Mountain—even if you see nothing else,' she added lamely.

'Thank you for showing me. And sharing with me.' Gesturing the waiter over, Niall peeled off a pile of rand notes.

'Where to next?' he asked as they stood up. When he took her hand, it felt like the most natural thing in the world.

'I want you to meet my grandmother,' Robina said impulsively. 'She lives about an hour's drive from Cape Town.'

'I'd like that,' Niall said simply.

As they drove into the township, leaving a flurry of dust in their wake, Niall kept glancing at the woman sitting beside him. It wasn't just that she was the most beautiful creature he had ever seen, with her exotic almond eyes, smooth dark skin and elegant long limbs, but her strange mix of nervousness and passion enchanted him. Every minute he spent with her, he felt himself falling more and more under her spell. Never in a million years had he ever thought he would meet anyone again who made his pulse race the way this woman did.

Now that the heat of the day had passed, people were beginning to emerge from the cool shelter of their houses. Women were returning from the well, balancing enormous pots on their heads, while still others carried long sheaves of firewood in the same way. A number of schoolgirls mimicked the older women, balancing their school books in neat piles on top of their heads. It could have been a different world.

Robina pointed to a mud house with a neat fence and a small verandah where an old woman was rocking gently as she worked with her hands.

As Robina got out of the car, the old woman stood unsteadily, leaning heavily on a stick. When she saw Robina, a smile spread across her broad face. 'Mzukulwana!'

Niall waited as Robina hugged her grandmother. There followed a long stream of words incomprehensible to Niall. Finally Robina stood back and beckoned him forward.

'Niall, I'd like you to meet my grandmother. Makhulu,

this is Dr Niall Ferguson.' She repeated her words in the same language she had used to greet her grandmother and listened carefully to the reply.

'My grandmother says you are welcome to her home and asks if you would sit. I'm afraid she only has a little English—she speaks mainly Xhosa.'

'Could you tell her that I'm honoured to meet her?' Niall said, taking the older woman's hand. The old lady shook his hand warmly.

They sat on the verandah drinking tea as the shadows began to lengthen. Before long there was a group of curious women gathered in front of the house.

'Sisi,' they called. 'Who is this good looking man you have brought to meet your grandmother?' And then they added something in Xhosa that made Robina blush. She replied in the same language and it seemed from the appreciative laughter that she was giving as good as she got.

Niall could have sat there all afternoon just listening to the babble of voices and looking at Robina. He had never met anyone like her before—she was a strange mix of the modern and the traditional. One moment shy, the next joking with her grandmother's neighbours and friends. He was happy, he thought, surprised. He hadn't felt like this since Mairead had died.

Eventually Robina stood. 'I have one more place to show you,' she said as she kissed her grandmother goodbye. 'Unless you want to get back to the hotel?' she added anxiously. 'Perhaps you've had enough for one day?'

Niall shook his head. 'No,' he said quietly. 'Right now there is nowhere I'd rather be than with you.' Robina blushed again at his words and Niall knew she wasn't immune to him either.

By the time they arrived at their next destination, the sun

was beginning to set, casting a rosy hue over the mountains and turning the sea red-gold.

They pulled up outside a house set on its own, almost overhanging a cliff. Niall got out of the car and drank in the views. The front of the house seemed to be almost suspended over the waves that crashed against the rocks, spraying a fine mist. Below was a stretch of beach as far as the eye could see. There were no other houses in sight. They could have been the only people left on the planet. Perfect.

A notice-board outside the house proclaimed that the house was for sale and gave a number for enquiries.

Curious, Niall raised a questioning eyebrow.

'This was my mother's parents' house,' Robina said. 'They lived here up until they retired to Gauteng a couple of years ago. They passed it on to my parents after that to use as a holiday cottage. It's where I spent all my school holidays. Mum and Dad planned to move here when he retired, but then he died. Mum only recently got around to putting it up for sale—she can't bear the thought of living in it without him. I'll miss it when it sells.'

Niall followed her down a steep path by the side of the house onto the beach. Robina looked out at the ocean. 'In spring and summer the whales come in here. When I was a little girl I would sit out here for hours watching them.'

Niall studied her. All of a sudden he had an image of the girl she must have been, sitting on the rocks, her knees pulled to her chest as she dreamed her childhood dreams. He smiled. The image was so different from this cool, elegant woman standing beside him.

'What are you smiling about?' Robina asked.

'I don't know. This, you, everything. It's the first time I've felt…' he struggled to find the right words '…at peace since Mairead died.'

Niall sat on a rock and threw a stone into the sea, where it skidded across the water.

'Tell me about her,' Robina said, finding her own rock close to him to perch on. They sat in silence for a few moments. Then Niall started to speak.

'I'd known her since I was a child. I can't remember a time when she wasn't around. We both grew up in a place called Applecross in the far north-west of Scotland. Our parents were good friends. She was younger than me, and at first she used to irritate me the way she kept hanging around. But eventually, as boys do, I started to notice that she wasn't a pesky kid any more but a pretty teenager with a mind of her own. I went away to university and when I came back after qualifying I discovered that the once irritating tomboy had turned into a beautiful, funny and amazing woman. We fell in love, married and moved to Edinburgh. We tried for kids for years—I guess that's what sparked my interest in fertility—and finally we were blessed with Ella. It seemed as if life couldn't get any better. My career was going well, Mairead loved being a stay-at-home mum, and she seemed content to have only one child. I have never known a woman so satisfied with her lot.'

The familiar ache seeped into his chest. This was the first time he had talked about his wife. He had never been a man to talk about himself and was surprised he could now. Robina, listening in silence, made it easy.

'That's more or less it. Two years ago she started getting bruises. She told me it was nothing, just her being clumsy, and I guess I chose to believe her. But one day the bruising was so bad, I forced her to see a colleague of mine. He diagnosed aplastic anaemia. Three weeks later she was dead. Ella was only two years old.'

He felt a cool hand slip into his. 'I'm so sorry, Niall. It must have been hard.'

But Niall felt he had said more than enough—too much, in fact. Whatever he wanted from this woman, it wasn't pity. Something stirred inside as he looked at her. For the first time since Mairead had died, he wanted another woman. This woman. Before he could stop himself he leaned towards her and found her lips. They were cool under his own and as they parted he groaned and kissed her with a hungry need he'd thought he'd never feel again.

His heart was pounding as she returned his kisses with a passion that matched his own. Eventually they broke apart, both breathing heavily. As Robina looked at him shyly, he stood and pulled her to her feet.

'Come back with me,' he said, knowing that he couldn't bear to leave her.

'What? To your hotel room?' She blushed, the redness darkening her honey skin.

'Yes. There first.'

Robina shook her head, her blush deepening. 'I'm sorry…I can't.'

He froze. It hadn't crossed his mind that she wouldn't be free. But why not? A woman like her was bound to be involved. 'Why?' He forced the words past a throat gone dry. 'Are you in love with someone else?'

'No, it's nothing like that.' Squaring her shoulders, she tilted her chin proudly. 'I know it may be old-fashioned, but I don't believe in sex before marriage,' she said primly.

Niall threw back his head and laughed, pulling her back into his arms at the same time. He kissed the tip of her nose. 'Then we are going to have to spend a lot more time together.' He cupped her face and traced her high cheekbones with the pad of his thumb. 'I'm going to enjoy getting to know everything about you.' Then he remembered they had hardly any time. 'Will you come and see me in Scotland?' he asked urgently.

Robina's lips parted as she turned her face to his. 'Just try and stop me,' she said before he brought his mouth back down on hers.

CHAPTER TWO

'NO WAY! It's out of the question!' Niall slammed his mug down on the desk, noticing but not giving a damn as the coffee splashed across his desk.

'Really?' Robina raised perfectly groomed eyebrows. 'Why not?' she asked, her calm, cool tones underpinning the determination in her dark eyes. Niall leaned back in his chair. The woman he had met a year ago was almost unrecognisable behind the practised, almost cold, façade.

'Why not?' he echoed incredulously before lowering his voice. 'Surely you can see why it's impossible?'

'Let's keep this professional,' she responded calmly, but he flinched inwardly from the reproach in her eyes. How could brown eyes, the colour of acacia honey, which had once sparkled up at him with suppressed laughter, now look so distant? 'Why don't you give me your reasons and I'll respond to each one in turn?'

'For a start, there's patient confidentiality. Then there is the fact that these are a particularly vulnerable group of women, and then finally, if all that weren't enough, how do you expect us to work with cameras in our faces? We'd be tripping over wires, sound recordists and God knows who all else. That's why it's impossible.'

'Quite the opposite.' Robina crossed one slim leg over the other, only the tightening of her lips giving away her determination to have her own way. 'But let's take each of your objections in turn, shall we?' She tapped her pen against her lips. 'Patient confidentiality; we will, naturally, check with the patients whether they are prepared to appear on camera. Only those who are one hundred per cent happy and who our company psychologist thinks can handle it will be asked to participate, and they will be allowed to withdraw their permission at any time. Secondly, yes, they are a particularly vulnerable group of women, I agree. Anyone going through or considering IVF has usually been on a very emotional journey before seeking treatment. However, that is the very reason why making a documentary of this kind is important. It will provide an insight into the process that cannot be gleaned from books on the subject, no matter how detailed or how professional.' She arched an eyebrow at him. 'Even my book on infertility, popular though it is, cannot truly prepare women for what it is really like to undergo treatment. Following the actual experiences of other women, on the other hand, will. That's why this documentary should be made.' She tilted her head, and raised a questioning eyebrow at him, daring him to find a fault in her argument.

Niall started to interrupt, but she held up a manicured hand, stopping him. 'And papers published in medical journals, no matter how worthy or how accurate, simply do not deal properly with the emotional aspect of infertility. And that is the angle we wish to focus on. Women considering IVF will be able to see first hand what a roller-coaster ride it can be, and the effect failed treatment can have on couples, before they decide whether or not to proceed with treatment. Of course we will portray the other side too. The fact that IVF has given so many women—and their partners—the opportunity to have the children they so desperately want.'

He had to admire the way she demolished his arguments. But he had seen her in action before. In front of the camera, faced with an expert from a medical field, she never let them bamboozle her or the audience with science. No, he had to admit, although it pained him, she had a knack of making even the most complicated medical condition understandable to the layperson.

'And as for staff getting in the way, you'll hardly know we're there, I promise you.'

'The answer is still no,' he said. 'This is my unit and as long as I'm in charge, I will decide what is and what isn't allowed.'

Once again the eyebrow was raised. 'I have to say that view sounds a little dictatorial. Is that really how you like to run things?' Her lips twitched. 'And I thought you took pride in being up to date, cutting edge in fact.'

Niall gritted his teeth. It was a sly dig and they both knew it. Just as he opened his mouth to retaliate there was a brief knock on the door and Lucinda Mayfair walked into the room. The unit's general manager was in her early fifties with short grey hair and a wide, determined mouth. Niall had worked with her for a number of years and although they had had their differences of opinion, he had enormous respect for her skills. Without her fighting their corner it was unlikely that the unit would have gained the recognition it had as the foremost centre in the UK, even given his international reputation.

'I'm sorry I had to leave you to get started without me.' Lucinda's smile relaxed the severe contours of her face. Despite her fearsome reputation, and her forbidding exterior, she had a soft heart. More than once he had seen her eyes suspiciously moist when a patient had been given the news they so desperately wanted or sometimes, sadly, dreaded.

Lucinda had shared his dream of making the unit the best in the UK, and so far, working together, with the support of their hand-picked team, they had succeeded. Which, he thought grumpily, they couldn't have done, if it had been anything except cutting edge.

'Don't you think Robina's idea is great, Niall?' Lucinda continued.

Niall frowned. It seemed that they were on opposite sides in this argument. Still, they had been before and he had always managed to talk Lucinda round. He didn't foresee any difficulties this time either.

'I have just been telling Robina that it's impossible. We're a working unit. We certainly don't have time to appear on a TV show. God, is there no aspect of life that reality TV doesn't want to ferret around in?'

'Niall,' Lucinda said warningly, 'you and I need to talk about this. And as for people *ferreting around*, as you so elegantly put it, Robina's a doctor and completely professional. She's not going to go about this in an insensitive manner. You know that.'

Robina stood, flicking an imaginary speck of dust from her beautifully cut Chanel suit. Every inch the professional media woman, Niall thought. Looking as if butter wouldn't melt in her mouth. But there had been times lately when he'd thought he'd seen naked pain in the depths of her deep brown eyes.

'Why don't I leave you two to discuss it? I need to get back to the office. We can speak later.'

As she bent to drop a kiss on Lucinda's cheek, Niall studied Robina surreptitiously. Her closely cropped dark hair, long neck and high cheekbones, along with her chocolate skin, all added to the exotic look known to thousands, if not millions, of viewers. She wasn't just beautiful, she was stunning. At least five-ten, she was slim, recently almost painfully so. If she had chosen a life as a model, Niall had no doubt she would have been equally successful.

Robina walked around to Niall's side of the desk and bending, kissed him on the cheek.

'I'll see you at home, darling. Try not to be too late. You know Ella won't go to sleep unless she can kiss you good-night. Make sure he leaves on time, won't you, Lucinda?'

And with that, Niall watched his wife sweep out the door.

'Robina gets more beautiful every day,' Lucinda said wistfully. 'How she manages it, looking after a young child with a full-time job *and* her writing, is beyond me. She must be some kind of superwoman! I hear she has a new book coming out in the spring.'

The last thing Niall wanted to talk about was his wife and her career, particularly since she hadn't even mentioned until now that her company was thinking of doing a documentary in his unit. There was no doubt in his mind that the two women had been planning the project long before he had been told about it, and he was furious. How had Robina managed to get to Lucinda without him knowing? Robina must have known damn well he would oppose the project, and not just for the reasons he'd outlined earlier. For her even to be thinking about doing the documentary was crazy. It was far too soon and far too close to home. But that was probably why she had gone directly to Lucinda. The unit's general manager didn't know about the baby and even if she did, it wouldn't have crossed her mind that he and Robina hadn't discussed the documentary beforehand. Neither could Lucinda even guess that he and his wife were barely on speaking terms these days, and that the kiss Robina had deposited on his cheek had all been part of the façade they kept up in front of others.

'What in God's name made you think I would agree to this?' he said, trying to keep the anger from his voice. 'We should have discussed it before you set up the meeting with Robina.'

Lucinda looked at him warily. 'Money,' she said flatly. 'Real Life Productions will be paying a lot for this. Money that we could use either for research or to help sponsor more women into the programme.'

Niall hated the funding aspect of the unit, hated anything that took him away from his patients or his research, and was only too happy to leave the finances of the unit in her capable hands.

'I was sure you and Robina had talked about this.' Lucinda's grey eyes were puzzled. 'Otherwise, I wouldn't have gone ahead with the meeting. I assumed when Robina came to me that you must have agreed in principle.'

Niall returned her gaze steadily. The last thing he was prepared to discuss was his personal life.

'Money isn't the only issue here,' he said evasively. 'I see no reason why we should be selling our soul to the devil, and believe me that's exactly what we'd be doing. We'd be exploiting the very women who come to us for help.'

'I'm afraid I don't see it that way. Not at all.' Lucinda regarded him severely and Niall groaned when he saw the determination in her eyes. 'We do need the money, Niall. You are always waiving fees.' She threw up her hands anticipating his protest. 'And I support you. But we can't keep doing it. If we don't generate some extra funding, and soon, we'll have to start turning away all non-paying patients, and neither you nor I want to do that.'

Niall was stunned. He'd had no idea that the unit was in financial difficulty.

'Why didn't you tell me this before?' he demanded. 'You and I are supposed to be partners.'

'I tried to tell you.' Lucinda drew a weary hand across her brow. 'But it is so hard to pin you down these days. You are always so damned preoccupied with one thing or another.'

Niall looked at her sharply. Her eyes looked hollow; her mouth pinched with fatigue. He felt a pang of guilt. Why hadn't he noticed? But even as he thought the question he knew the answer—because he had been too busy trying to block out everything except his work.

'The trouble is, Niall, between your patients and your research, it's almost impossible these days to catch you so we can have a discussion about the business side of things.'

Niall knew she was right. He had little patience for the business side of things, as she put it, at the best of times. And lately, well, he'd had other stuff on his mind. But nevertheless he should have noticed that something was wrong. He shouldn't have let Lucinda carry the burden on her own. The trouble was that he had become used to her taking care of the financial aspects of running the unit and had been only too happy to let her get on with it. He felt a fresh spasm of guilt.

'We can find the extra funding from elsewhere, from my own pocket if necessary.'

Lucinda half smiled. 'I appreciate the sentiment, but your pocket—generous as it's been—isn't enough any more. The kind of money we need has to come from ongoing investment. The kind of investment that would come from a documentary such as the one your wife, or at least the company she represents, is proposing. But,' she continued, 'that aside, I would never even consider it, not even for millions of pounds, if I didn't think it was a good idea. But I have to agree with Robina. Infertility is something so many women suffer from, and I think it is in the public interest to inform a wider audience of the reality. As for your concerns, I'm sure Robina has told you that only patients who are willing to share their experiences on TV will appear and we will, of course, ask them to sign the appropriate waivers. It will be an inconvenience to us, I admit that, but there must be ways we can minimise the disruption. At least say you'll think about it.'

Niall stood and crossed over to the older woman. He placed a hand on her shoulder and squeezed. 'I've been selfish,' he said. 'And I'm sorry. You shouldn't have to worry about funding on your own. Why don't you give me a copy of the latest financial forecast and I'll look at it over the weekend? Then we will talk again,' he promised. 'But in the meantime I have a clinic about to start. Could we discuss this again on Monday?'

Lucinda nodded and then smiled up at him. 'Hey,' she said, 'don't beat yourself up. If you weren't so obsessed with work, the clinic wouldn't have such a fine reputation.'

'You've made your point,' Niall said, smiling. 'The last thing I want to do is turn patients away, knowing that we are their last hope.'

'Like the Dougans?' Lucinda said, referring to a couple Niall had talked to her about the day before. Ineligible for treatment on the NHS, they had paid for one cycle of treatment, which hadn't worked. Mr Dougan had recently lost his job, and there was no way the couple could afford to pay for another cycle of IVF.

'I did tell them we'd only be able to offer them one cycle free—we still have enough in our endowment pot for that, surely?'

Lucinda smiled ruefully. 'Yes, but barely. Without raising more funds, the Dougans might be the last couple we'll be able to subsidise. I know you mean well, Niall, but we have salaries to pay as well as our not inconsiderable overheads. We are a business after all.' She got to her feet. 'You'd better get to your clinic. We'll discuss it again after the weekend. I'm a great believer that, one way or another, things have a habit of working out.'

When she'd left the room Niall closed his eyes for a moment, trying to banish the image of his wife from his mind. If only Lucinda knew the truth she wouldn't be so quick to tell him things had a habit of working out. It was ironic, really. He and his wife spent so much time trying to help others with their lives, yet they couldn't seem to do a thing about the almighty mess they had made of their own.

Robina rushed into the house, glancing at her watch. It was almost seven! She had planned to be home earlier so she could sit with Ella while she had her supper and then read her a story before bed. It was the one time in the day that was precious to her. When she was in the middle of filming, she'd often have to spend the night in London, returning late the following evening. So while her show was off the air, and when she was based at home in Edinburgh, she tried to be home at a decent hour whenever she could—especially when it was unlikely that Niall would be home before her. He often worked late particularly when he knew she was around, so that he could have most of the weekends free to spend with his daughter.

But to her surprise, as she flew into the kitchen discarding her bag and coat in the hall, she saw his dark head bent over Ella as he helped her cut up her fish fingers. Robina's heart squeezed as she paused in the doorway. They were so alike, from the determined mouth to the clear blue eyes. Similar too in temperament. Both equally stubborn. Both so dear to her.

Niall looked up. For a second she thought she saw a flicker

of warmth in his blue eyes, but she knew she was mistaken when the familiar coolness cloaked his expression. Despite herself, her spirits drooped with disappointment. When would she ever truly accept that it was over between them? They were married, but for the last few months in name only. God, they could barely be civil to each other these days.

Niall looked at his watch. 'We expected you home earlier,' he said.

'Sorry, I got caught up at the office.' Robina bent to kiss her stepdaughter, who flung her arms around her neck. She savoured the feel of the little girl's marshmallow-soft skin under her lips and the dear, familiar smell of her. Whatever differences she and Niall had, she couldn't love Ella more had she given birth to her, even if she were a constant reminder of Niall's first wife—and an even more painful reminder of the baby she had lost too early, five short months after their marriage. But all that would have been bearable if only she could be coming home to a husband who loved her. Someone who would want to know about the trivia of her day and would rub the tension from her shoulders, making everything seem all right.

But shoulder rubs and evenings by the fire, sharing the day's stresses, was never going to happen. Had rarely happened even when they had first married, and certainly not these days. The breakdown of her marriage had happened in such little steps she had hardly noticed until—well, until the miscarriage when it had all fallen completely apart.

'Would you like me to read to Ella while you have dinner?' Niall asked formally, as if they were complete strangers, which in a sense she supposed they were. Falling in love, her coming to Scotland for a visit, Niall proposing to her, their marriage, it had all happened so fast they hadn't really had time to get to know each other. They had both thought—*if* they had thought about it at all—that there would be plenty of time later to get to know each other properly. But to her delight and amazement, the book for which Niall had written the foreword had been an immediate run-away success and she'd been asked to appear on a show to talk about it. The producer had been so impressed with the way she had been able to translate medical jargon into simple language he'd asked her to stand in for the presenter of the show, *Life In Focus*, who had to unexpectedly withdraw. The timing hadn't been great, coming right on the heels of their wedding, but she and Niall had both agreed it was too good an opportunity to miss. And that was when it had all started to go wrong.

'No, I'd like to read Ella her story, if that's okay,' she said, realising Niall was waiting for a response. She hated the way her tone was equally formal.

'I told Mrs Tobin that it was okay for her to leave. She's left a casserole in the oven,' Niall continued, referring to their housekeeper, who had stayed on after they had married and also doubled as a childminder for Ella.

'Oh, Daddy.' Ella looked up at him imploringly. 'Can't I stay up later tonight, with you and Robina? I never get to be with both of you at once any more.'

A flash of regret darkened Niall's eyes.

'Not tonight,' he said firmly. 'It's a school night. But why don't I get you ready for bed and then Robina will read to you before lights out? How does that sound?'

Ella pouted, but the little girl knew her father well enough to know he wouldn't budge. She scrambled to her feet. 'Come on, Daddy. Let's hurry up, then.' Taking her father by the hand, she led him upstairs.

Robina sat at the table and picked at the beef casserole.

Most evenings, Niall arrived home after she and Ella had had supper, then one or the other of them would organise Ella for bed. When Niall's daughter was asleep, they would retreat to separate rooms, Niall to his study and Robina to the small sitting room that had, over the last few months, become hers. When the interminable and lonely evening had dragged to an end and they were ready for bed, she would go to the room they had once shared, while Niall slept in the spare room. It was a cold, unhappy home these days and if it hadn't been for Ella, perhaps she would have found the strength to leave— even if it would have shattered her already fractured heart.

Scooping the remains of her half-eaten meal into the dustpan, Robina took her coffee into her sitting room. Before she had left for the night, Mrs Tobin had lit a fire against the cool of the late February evening and Robina warmed her chilled hands. If only she could so easily chase away the chill in her heart, she thought as she picked up the proofs of her latest book. She sighed when she saw the title. *How to keep your relationship happy—in bed and out of it.* If her readers knew the truth, they'd be astonished. She flung the book aside, in no mood to concentrate.

She looked around the room with its tasteful carpets and elegant furnishings. It was beautiful, she admitted, but not really her taste. Perhaps if she hadn't moved into the home Niall had shared with his first wife, things might have been different. But Niall hadn't wanted to unsettle Ella so soon after their marriage, and Robina had wholeheartedly agreed it was the right thing to do. She had been so in love, she would have lived in a cave if Niall had asked her to. What did it matter as long as she and Niall were together? But it had come to matter—a lot. Everywhere she looked she was reminded of the woman who had been the perfect wife and mother. A woman who was as unlike her as it was possible to be.

She became aware of a presence in the doorway and, looking up, found Niall standing there, watching her intently. He hesitated as if unsure he was welcome in her domain.

'Are you okay?' he asked softly, and for a moment Robina could almost make herself believe he still cared. Almost, but not quite.

'Just tired,' she said. 'It's been a long and…' she slid him a look '…difficult day. And I still have the proofs of my book to finish. My editor expects them early next week and…' She bit off the rest of her sentence. Why was she even bothering to tell him? He wasn't remotely interested in her work.

He looked as if he was about to say something, then changed his mind.

'Ella's waiting for you,' was all he said.

Robina's heart felt as heavy as her legs as she slowly mounted the stairs. This wasn't the life her parents—particularly her father—had envisaged for her, surely? Away from her country, her people, her family. Unable to carry a child—and perhaps never able to conceive again. Robina sighed. Perhaps she should end her marriage, even though it went against every grain of what she believed. She could return to Africa and give Niall a chance of one day finding happiness with someone else, even if the thought of leaving him almost tore her in two. Robina blinked hot tears away. They couldn't go on this way, she decided. She had to do the right thing. And ask him for a divorce.

She paused for a moment outside Ella's bedroom and composed herself, wiping away any evidence of her unshed tears. Pushing the door open, she saw that Ella was snuggled under her duvet, her favourite soft toy cuddled in her arms.

'Can we have *Mr Tickle*?' her stepdaughter asked, holding out the well-thumbed book.

Robina smiled as she inwardly suppressed a groan. They had already read *Mr Tickle* three times that week. Surely Ella was tired of it? But it seemed not. Robina climbed onto the bed and waited until Ella made herself comfortable in the crook of her arm.

She read the story as Ella's eyes drooped. When she had finished, she gently eased Ella out of her arms. But as two bright blue eyes fluttered open, it seemed the little girl wasn't quite ready for sleep.

'Robina,' Ella whispered. 'I've been thinking. Would it be okay if I called you Mummy?'

Robina's breath stopped in her throat. 'Of course, darling. If you would like to.' Her heart twisted. Why now? When she had been gathering the strength to leave?

'It's not as if I will ever forget I had another mummy. But I can hardly remember her. I used to ask Daddy about her, but it made him sad to talk about her, so I don't ask any more.'

'I think,' Robina said carefully, 'that you could talk to him now. At first, when somebody dies, it hurts so much that it's difficult to talk about it. But in time it becomes easier. So maybe you should try talking to him again. I'm sure he doesn't want you to forget.' As she said the words her heart ached. She should try taking her own advice! She and Niall had never talked about the loss of their baby either.

'You won't leave me too?' Ella asked. 'I couldn't bear to lose another mummy.' She looked at Ella, her eyes—so like her father's—round with anxiety. Robina squeezed her eyes shut, forcing away the wave of sadness that washed over her as she pulled the little girl into her arms and kissed the top of her head. She chose her words carefully. 'I'll always be here for you, *mntwana*—little one,' she promised. 'For as long as you need me. So whether you like it or not, you're stuck with me. Just like a piece of chewing gum on your shoe. Only much nicer, I hope.'

Ella giggled and snuggled down in bed. 'Okay, Mummy. Night-night.'

Robina stayed on the bed until she was sure Ella had fallen asleep. How could she ask Niall for a divorce now, when she had just promised Ella that she would never leave her? Whatever mess she and Niall had made of things, the little girl had been through enough heartbreak in her short life.

Her head throbbing with unanswered questions, Robina returned downstairs to her sitting room. To her surprise Niall was still there, gazing into the fire, apparently deep in thought.

He flung another couple of logs on the fire. The flames lit the room, chasing the shadows away.

'I told Lucinda I would think about your proposal,' he said. 'We should have an answer for you by Monday.' He stretched. He had changed out of his suit into more casual gear and his T-shirt lifted slightly with the movement, revealing a glimpse of his muscular six-pack. A memory of the sensation of his muscles tightening under her fingertips as she trailed a hand across the dark hairs of his abdomen flashed across Robina's mind. Whatever their difficulties, she knew she still wanted him. Up until the miscarriage, sex had been what had kept them together even as emotionally they had drifted apart. Was it possible, she thought, to still fancy someone like mad even when you weren't sure that you still loved them? Or them you?

Niall crossed the room, placed his hands on her shoulders and looked directly into her eyes. 'Are you sure that doing this documentary is the right thing for you? Isn't it too soon? Too close to home?'

Robina flinched and backed away from him. She could just about cope with anything these days—except his kindness.

She turned her back to him and watched the flames flicker in the fireplace. 'Perhaps my…' she took a breath to steady her voice '…experience makes me the best person to be doing this.'

'Maybe it does,' he said gently. 'I wouldn't know. I don't know how you feel. You've never told me.'

Robina shied away from his words. She had never talked to him about the loss of their baby, because she had refused to let herself think about it. It was still too raw. Every time she thought about the baby that almost was, the pain threatened to crush her. So it was easier, and better, not to think about it at all. But was he right? Should she be doing the documentary when she still felt so wretched? But all she had left right now was her career and she would do nothing to jeopardise it. And she needed to keep busy. It was the only thing that stopped her from going crazy.

'I'm a professional,' she countered. 'I'm still a doctor. My personal feelings don't come into it.'

He made no attempt to hide his disbelief.

'I just wish you had discussed it with me first,' he said tersely.

Robina swung round to face him.

'I would have,' she retorted. 'If we ever spoke these days. I know you don't want to hear about my work. You've made it clear enough that you don't approve of what I do,' she added bitterly.

'That's where you're wrong,' Niall protested. 'I only ever worried that you were doing too much, especially when…' He stopped.

'Especially when I was pregnant and should have known better,' Robina flashed back at him. 'Anyway, I don't want to talk about it right now.'

'When are we going to talk about it? You're never here to talk about anything.' Niall's voice was cold. 'Maybe if you were…'

That was rich, coming from him. Why did he think it was okay for him to work most evenings just because he was a man? It was an old argument. She knew he held her responsible for the miscarriage—and she could hardly blame him. God knew, she blamed herself. He had asked her enough times to slow down. But she'd refused to listen. Her fledgling career had just been taking off and she hadn't wanted to take time off. She had argued that millions of women worked until just before their babies were born. She had thought there would be plenty of time to take it easy after the baby was born. How terribly wrong she had been, and if she could have the time over, she would do it all differently. But thinking like that was pointless. What was done was done.

'It's no use, Niall. Perhaps it's time we both accepted our marriage is over.'

The shock on Niall's face was unmistakeable.

'Divorce—is that what you want? Is life with me so unbearable?'

Yes, she wanted to shout. Living with you, living like this, knowing you don't love me any more—if you ever did—is tearing me apart. But she just looked at him in silence. Perhaps if they had shouted, argued when things had started to go wrong, they might have been able to fashion some sort of life together. As it was, they had barely been speaking when she had miscarried.

'No, I don't want a divorce. Upstairs, just now, I promised Ella I'd never leave her. But we have to find a way of living together—for Ella's sake. You can't be happy either.'

'Why did you marry me, Robina?' Niall ground out. 'I thought you wanted the same things I did. A home and a family.'

'Instead you got landed with a woman who can't have children and whose career *is* important.' Despite her best intentions, Robina felt her voice rise. They stood glaring at each other.

'Daddy, Robina.' A small voice broke into the room. 'Why are you shouting? Why are you angry? Did I do something wrong?'

'No, oh no, Ella,' Robina said, turning to the forlorn figure in the doorway. Niall held out his arms and Ella flew into them, burying her head in his shoulder.

'You could never make me angry, pumpkin,' he said. 'Never, ever. Not in a hundred years. Not unless you don't go to bed when I say so, or hide my newspaper or...' He pretended to look cross.

Unconvinced, Ella lifted her head from his shoulder and looked him straight in the eyes. 'Then you must be angry with Robina. What has she done?' Her face crumpled. 'You're not going to divorce, are you? My friend Tommy's parents are getting a divorce and he has to stay with his mummy during the week and go and live with his daddy at the weekends and he doesn't have any friends where his daddy lives and his mummy is always crying and his daddy is always angry. That's not going to happen to us, is it?' She placed her small hands on either side of her father's face. 'Robina isn't going to go away and leave us, is she, Daddy? Not like Mummy did. Robina *promised* me she would always be here for me.'

Niall looked at Robina across the top of his daughter's head, the anguish in his eyes like a kick to her solar plexus. He was a proud man, and Robina knew he would never beg, but he was pleading with his eyes. Not because he wanted her to stay for himself but because he knew it would break his daughter's heart if she left, and one thing Niall loved more than anything else in the world was Ella. She had thought that she had managed to reassure Ella, but she obviously hadn't.

Ella had taken her words literally. *She'd always be here for her.* And she wouldn't break that promise, no matter how much living with a man who no longer loved her was eating her up inside.

'We are not going to divorce, silly,' Robina said firmly, aware of the relief in Niall's eyes as she said the words. 'Grown-ups argue sometimes, but then they make up and everything's all right again.' She flicked a glance in Niall's direction, knowing he wouldn't fail to notice the irony of her words. 'We are a family and families stay together, just like I told you. Your mummy wouldn't have left you if she'd had any choice and now I am here to look after you and love you for ever. Or at least until you are a big girl and have a family of your own.'

'I'm glad,' Ella said with a tentative smile. 'Cos I'm never going to get married. I'm going to stay with you and Daddy for ever. Because I love Robina very much, Daddy. Not as much as my real mummy, but almost.'

The flash of anguish in Niall's eyes made Robina's heart twist.

'And you love Robina too, don't you, Daddy?' Ella persisted. Robina realised she wasn't going to give up until she had the reassurance she craved.

'I married her, didn't I?' Niall said evasively. He tossed his daughter into the air. 'Remember? You were there.'

Robina's heart cracked a little more as she remembered their wedding day, only three months after they had met. The spring day brilliantly bright, not a cloud in the sky. The pipers, wearing full highland dress, playing them in and out of the small seventeenth-century church; dancing with Niall, who had held her close in his arms as if he couldn't bear to let her go; everyone so happy for them, her silent toast to her absent family, and her dead father the only shadow on an otherwise perfect day. With her new family around her, and her new, exciting career ahead of her, she hadn't thought it was possible to be so happy.

Oh, yes, he had married her. But how quickly it had all gone wrong. Niall had spent so much time at work and her career had taken up so much time that they had barely seen each other after the wedding. Slowly the doubts had started to creep in. Then in one awful series of events, it had all come crashing down. She closed her eyes against the familiar sweep of pain. Would she ever get used to the gut-wrenching sense of loss?

'So why don't we do anything together any more?' It seemed Ella still wasn't convinced. They had completely underestimated how much the sensitive child was picking up of the strain between them.

'Robina and Daddy are busy,' Niall replied. 'But we still have the weekends. Last weekend we went to the zoo. Or have you forgotten?' He wriggled his eyebrows at her in an attempt to make her laugh. But Ella was having none of it.

'No, we don't. Sometimes I have you, like at the zoo, and sometimes I have Robina—I mean Mummy—but I don't have you together. And you just said we were a family.'

Niall's eyes darkened when he heard Ella call Robina Mummy for the first time in his hearing. How did he feel about his daughter's explicit acceptance of Robina? Did it make it that much harder for him to acknowledge their marriage had broken down? Possibly irretrievably? There was no way of knowing. The little girl had picked up on the tension between her parents and it had obviously been worrying her for a while. It shamed Robina that they had been too busy, too wrapped up in their own problems, to notice.

'Then we will have to do something about that,' Niall said

firmly. 'But right now it's bedtime, pumpkin. Come on, let's get you tucked in.' And before Ella could protest further, he carried her out of the room and up the stairs.

Robina sank into her favourite chair and stared into the fire. Whatever she and Niall felt about each other, however angry they were, they needed to make sure Ella was happy. It wasn't fair to let the child sense that they were having problems. And for the little girl to worry it was her fault! That was unforgivable.

In keeping with her mood, the wind hurled rain against the window and Robina wrapped her arms around her body in a bid to draw some warmth into her chilled soul.

'She wants you to go up and say goodnight again.' Niall's voice came from the doorway. Despite his size he moved quietly.

Robina eased herself out of her chair. 'Of course,' she said.

But as she passed him he grabbed her wrist, forcing her to stop. The touch of his hand sent shock waves through her body. How long had it been since he had touched her?

'If you want a divorce, I won't stand in your way.'

'Is that what *you* want?' Robina said tiredly, not knowing if she had the strength to fight him any longer.

'No, you know it isn't.' It sounded as if the words were being dragged from his lips. Her heart lifted. Did he still care? Enough not to want to let her go?

'I don't want my daughter to lose another mother—and you are her mother now. God knows, she's known enough sadness in her short life already. I'd do anything to protect her.'

Robina's heart plummeted. Was that the only reason he wanted her to stay? For his daughter's sake? Not for the first time, she wondered sadly if that was the real reason he had married her. Wasn't that what he had just said? He wanted a home, and by that she assumed he meant someone to run it, and a family. Things hadn't exactly turned out the way he had expected.

'Neither do I want to cause Ella any more pain,' she said sadly. 'As she said, I promised her I would never leave her. You know I love her. So no, we're married and we'll stay married. I made my vows and I'll stick by them. For better or for worse. We've had the better, let's deal with the worse.' She pulled her hand away. 'Goodnight, Niall, I'll see you at breakfast.' Knowing that she was moments away from breaking down and that all she had left was her pride, she hurried away to the sanctuary of her room.

CHAPTER THREE

'MOST of you have met my wife.' Niall indicated Robina with a nod of his head. 'And you all know why she is here.'

There were a number of smiles and nods of recognition from around the room. It was the first day of filming and Robina and her cameraman, John, who would be doubling up as sound recordist, were sitting in on the clinic's regular update meeting. Niall had told her that he was reluctantly—and he had emphasised the word reluctantly—agreeing to let filming go ahead, but he would stop it if he thought it was no longer in his patients' best interests.

'We meet once a week to discuss cases,' Niall explained. 'This gives everyone an opportunity to share any concerns they may have about patients' treatment. It is also where we discuss the more complex cases and agree on a way forward.' Niall folded his hands on the table and leaned forward.

He looks so distant, Robina thought, at least when he looks at me. Dressed in his dark suit, his shirt blindingly white and with a dark blue tie, he was the epitome of the successful doctor and Robina was reminded of the first time she had seen him. He had seemed intimidating then too, at least until she had spent time with him and realised that under that formal, serious demeanour was a man who had a dry sense of humour, who was kind and thoughtful and who could make her pulse race like no other. Where had that man gone?

She glanced around the room. There was an embryologist, whose name she hadn't quite caught, Niall and one of the other doctors, a part-timer called Elaine, two specialist nurses, Sally and Mairi, as well as the nurse manager, Catriona. All the other staff were busy in the lab or seeing patients.

'I would guess that not everyone is happy that we are being filmed, but now that we have agreed to go ahead, I know you will all do your best to make it as smooth as possible,' Niall continued easily.

He knows his staff will do whatever he asks, Robina thought as everyone nodded. They trusted him completely.

'I've contacted all our patients who are either on treatment or scheduled for an appointment, asking whether they wish to take part,' Catriona said. 'And have passed the names of about ten patients to Robina.' The older woman smiled at her. 'For what it's worth, I think it's an excellent idea—as long as the patients are happy and as long as I don't have to appear on camera.'

'I don't mind being filmed,' Sally, the dark haired nurse with an impish grin, said, smoothing her hair, 'I just worry I might say something daft.'

'Don't worry,' Robina reassured her, 'you'll soon forget about the camera, believe me. And if you say something daft, we'll edit it.'

'I'm not appearing, if that's okay,' Mairi chipped in. 'They say the camera puts on ten pounds, and with the extra weight I'm carrying already, I don't think I could face it.'

Everyone laughed and a spate of good-natured teasing broke out.

'Can we move on?' Niall said when everyone had settled again. 'We have a number of cases to discuss before I have to check on my patients in the labour ward.'

On top of his patients at the clinic, Niall still carried a full workload of obstetric cases. No wonder we hardly see each other, Robina thought sadly. Either she was working, or he was, and that included most evenings and weekends.

'Annette is coming in for her seven-week scan this morning,' Sally announced. 'Keep your fingers crossed, everyone.' The mood in the room turned sombre.

'This is Annette's third attempt,' Catriona explained to Robina. 'The first time the embryos didn't implant, the second time, she had a positive pregnancy test, but her seven-week scan, the one we do to determine whether the pregnancy is ongoing, showed no evidence of a heartbeat. As you can imagine, she was distraught. She and her husband have agreed that this will be their last attempt—she was thrilled when this most recent pregnancy test was positive—but they are naturally extremely anxious. I think she might be one of the women who said they'd be happy to talk to you.'

'Who's doing the scan?' Niall asked.

'I am,' replied Sally. 'I looked after her through her other treatments.' She chewed on her lower lip. 'I don't know how she'll cope if we don't find a heartbeat. And I will hate being the one that has to tell her.'

'Let's just wait and see,' Catriona said soothingly. 'There's no point in getting ahead of ourselves.'

'I have a patient I'd like to discuss,' Niall said. 'It is a difficult case and I'd like to know how everybody feels—particularly the embryologists—before I see this lady.'

Everyone turned curious eyes on Niall.

'I have been approached by a woman who wants us to

carry out PGD—pre-implantation genetic diagnosis,' he said to Robina, for the benefit of the camera. 'She has a family history of breast cancer in the family and all the female relatives in her family have either died or have had the disease. As a precaution, she decided to have a prophylactic double mastectomy when she was eighteen, after genetic testing showed that she carried the variant BRCA1 gene.'

There was a sharp intake of breath followed by a murmur of sympathy from around the room.

'Now that Isabel has joined us…' he smiled at the curly-haired embryologist sitting on his right '…we are in a position to offer this service. But I want to know how everyone feels about it.'

'Could you explain what it involves, Niall?' Robina asked, knowing that this was exactly the kind of thing her viewers would be interested in. She only had a vague memory from researching her book of what the procedure involved and progress in this area was rapid.

'I'll let Isabel explain, as she's the one who'd be doing the procedure.'

'I'll try and make it as simple as possible.' Isabel took a sip of water. 'We stimulate the ovaries, in the same way we do for our infertile ladies, and then fertilise the eggs in the lab. Once the eggs are fertilised they start dividing—one cell becomes two, two become four and so on. We wait until we have eight cells, then we remove one and test for the BRCA1 gene. If it's positive, we move on to the next embryo and so on until we find one that doesn't carry the gene. When we do, that is the embryo we replace.'

'Don't some people think this is too close to eugenics?' Robina asked. 'As in designer babies?'

'Not at all,' Niall interrupted quietly. 'This isn't selecting embryos based on hair colour or intelligence or anything like that. This is selection that will prevent someone almost certainly suffering from breast cancer later on in life.'

'I know some people find it distasteful,' Isabel continued, 'but the truth of the matter is that we select embryos anyway to put back.'

Robina was puzzled. 'What do you mean?'

'We add sperm to all the eggs we retrieve. Say we have fourteen. Out of those, sometimes only a proportion will fertilise. We study the ones that are under the microscope and grade them according to specific, recognised criteria. We select the ones with the best grades, and choose one from these to replace. So in a way we are already selecting. PGD only takes it a step further.'

Robina was fascinated and knew viewers would be too. Some might find it controversial, but she had never shied away from controversy. She would present both sides of the argument and leave people to make up their own minds.

'Isn't destroying perfectly healthy embryos wrong?'

'Sometimes we freeze the leftover embryos—the ones that are of good quality, that is—in case the women want further treatment. If they don't, then yes, we dispose of the remainder,' Isabel continued, her face animated. It was clearly a subject that was close to her heart. 'In many ways it's no different to what happens in normal pregnancies. The ovary starts to produce several eggs, but there is always one dominant egg which then releases a hormone that stops the other competing eggs from developing further. In a way we are simply replicating nature.'

'The issue I have is more of a scientific rather than a moral one,' Niall said. 'Not for this gene, which would be present in every cell of the embryo, but when we are testing for other genetic conditions, for example Down's syndrome, there is the risk that out of the eight cells, we test the one cell that doesn't carry the genetic abnormality and are led to falsely believe that the embryo is free of the condition. It is important that anyone considering PGD understands this.'

'She wouldn't be considering it if she weren't desperate,' Mairi interjected. 'And she's already shown how serious she is by having a double mastectomy. I'm not surprised she doesn't want her daughter to go through the same thing.'

Robina leaned back as lively discussion broke out around the table. She wondered how it felt to have to make these kinds of decisions on a daily basis, knowing you held people's dreams in the palm of your hand. Her heart went out to all the couples. The people in this room had such power over their lives. How could so many women bear to put themselves through so much potential disappointment and heartache? She knew she couldn't put herself through it again. Never, ever. She had thought she would never get over the pain of losing one baby. How could she possibly risk doing it all over again?

'Let's take a vote,' Niall said. 'Everyone in favour of my seeing this lady, remembering I intend to make sure she understands the pros and cons before we proceed, raise their hands.'

It seemed that everyone was in agreement.

'Let's move on then,' Niall said, but before he could continue, the receptionist popped her head around the door.

'Annette has arrived for her scan, Sally. I've made her a coffee, but I don't want to keep her waiting—she looks terrified.'

Sally stood. 'Are you coming?' she asked Robina, who immediately got to her feet. 'Keep your fingers crossed, everyone,' she added over her shoulder as Robina and her cameraman, John, followed her out of the room.

Sally showed Annette and her husband into one of the consulting rooms and then left them with Robina and John while she went to set up the scan.

Annette was pale and held on to her husband Mike's hand as if for dear life.

Robina asked the nervous couple if they were sure they were happy to be filmed. 'You can still change your mind,' she told them gently.

'No, we said we'd do it and we will.' Annette raised her chin. 'We want people to know what it's like to go through IVF.'

Robina nodded to John, who focussed the camera on Annette.

'Only people who have been through this know what it's like.' Annette's voice was so soft, Robina had to strain to catch her words.

'At first, every month you hope that this will be the month, but you tell yourself not to get too excited, but you can't help yourself. You just want it so much. And then, when it doesn't happen, it's like a dark cloud descending on top of you. So you ask yourself, why me? What is wrong with me? And then eventually you realise that you have to seek help, because it's not going to happen on its own—no matter how much you want it to. Suddenly, you can't bear seeing babies. Sometimes you'll cross the street so you don't have to look at them, and you even avoid friends and relatives who are pregnant or have young children—even though you know it's wrong and selfish.'

She took a shaky breath. Robina wanted to reach out and put her arm around Annette's shoulders and tell her she knew how she felt, but she forced herself to stay still and let her have her say.

'People tell you to relax, that it will be all right, that there is always adoption, and yes, for some people adoption is the right thing. But although they mean well they just don't know how much it hurts not being able to have children of your own.'

She paused for a moment, her eyes welling up with tears. 'And then, when you decide to go for IVF, you think that this is it. That soon you'll be pregnant. Oh, you know the treatment might be unpleasant, but you don't care. And they tell you it might not work, but you're not really listening, cos you have hope again. So you do everything you are told, and loads of other stuff that you read about on the internet and in magazines—just in case. You go through the injections, do the diets, try the alternative treatments—put up with the hormones making you a little crazy, because you just know that soon you'll be holding a baby in your arms, and you'll do anything to have that feeling. Then when the drugs work, and they take you to Theatre, the hope is almost painful. So you have your eggs collected, but you have to wait again to see if they fertilise, and if they do, and one or two are replaced, you have to wait again to see if they implant. And even if you know there is still a chance you won't fall pregnant, you go out and buy the cot, and start to think of names. And it's the longest two weeks of your life as you wait. You are almost too scared to do anything, even though you know it won't make a difference, and every twinge and niggly pain terrifies you. Then, at last, it's pregnancy test day. And you tell yourself you must be pregnant because you couldn't bear it if you are not.'

Annette took another deep breath. 'But if you are like me, then the first time the test was negative, and I couldn't believe it. I was devastated. But Mike wouldn't let me give up, so we tried again. And this time the test was positive. We were so excited, even though Sally warned us it was only the beginning.'

She paused as Sally re-entered the room. 'We didn't listen, did we? We told everyone and they were so happy for us. But something didn't feel right. I tried to tell myself I was imagining things, but I wasn't. This time we got as far as the seven-week scan—like the one we are having today. But there was no heartbeat. We had lost our baby.'

Robina swallowed the lump in her throat. She also recognised the terrible feeling of loss; even though her baby had been no more than a few centimetres in length. A baby was no less mourned because it was only a tiny embryo.

'C'mon,' Sally said gently. 'Let's get you scanned. I think you've waited long enough for this moment.'

A few minutes later, Annette lay on the bed looking even paler and on the verge of tears. She's expecting bad news, Robina thought. It's written all over her face. Or at least she's preparing herself for the worst.

The room was deathly silent as Sally ran her probe over Annette's abdomen. Annette clutched Mike's hand as if he were a life-raft and if she let go, she would drown.

But a few minutes later a huge smile spread across Sally's face. 'A clear, strong heartbeat.' She swivelled the monitor so the couple could see. 'See just there.'

Robina craned her neck to see where she was pointing and, sure enough, the steady movement of a heartbeat flickered on the screen.

'Are you sure?' Annette whispered.

'One hundred per cent. You can relax, we've got an ongoing pregnancy.'

Annette burst into gut-wrenching sobs and her husband gathered her into his arms. 'I can't believe it,' Annette hiccupped once she had regained her composure. 'We're going to have a baby. Thank you, oh, thank you.'

'Congratulations,' Robina said. 'I'm so happy for you both.' With a bit of luck, in a few months' time this couple would be holding a much longed-for baby in their arms. Robina's throat tightened and she knew that tears weren't far away. Annette's story had brought too many painful memories flooding back.

Leaving the ecstatic couple with Sally, Robina found the staff in Reception gathered around a woman who was proudly showing off a baby, who, judging by its size, was somewhere around two to three months old.

'Isn't he just gorgeous?' Linda was saying. She noticed Robina. 'Dr Zondi, come meet our latest arrival, little Matthew.'

She held out the baby and, before Robina could protest, handed her the tiny bundle as everyone looked on. For a second Robina's heart froze. She hadn't seen, much less held, a baby since her miscarriage. Now she had no choice but to accept the infant.

John was filming, his camera trained on her face. He was one of the few people who knew about the miscarriage, but the thought probably hadn't entered his male head that she would find cuddling a baby difficult. She forced herself to look down at the tiny bundle she held in her arms. His eyes were closed, and impossibly long lashes fanned plump cheeks. She inhaled the baby smell of him and the numbness in her throat spread into her chest, making her feel as if she could hardly breathe. If her baby had lived, she would be due about now. Don't let me cry, she thought. Don't let anyone speak to me, cos there is no way I could force any words past my throat.

She glanced up and over the heads of the nursing staff and saw Niall watching her intently. Without a word, he crossed the room and gently took the baby from her arms.

'Ah, let me see,' he said, holding the baby as if he'd had years of practice, which, of course, he had. 'What a fine-looking lad. You must be very proud of him.'

Robina backed away as Niall diverted attention away from her. She was shaking and desperately needed some time on her own to compose herself. Mumbling something about the Ladies' to no one in particular, she walked as steadily as she could, on legs that had turned to mush, towards the bathroom.

Inside, she slumped to the floor and laid her head on her knees, taking deep, gulping breaths. Her hands were still shaking and she could feel the pressure of tears behind her eyes. It should be *her*, holding *her* baby. She caught her breath as a fresh wave of grief washed over her. She couldn't break down, not here. She needed to regain her composure before she went back out. Maybe Niall was right and she should never have agreed to this programme. She was still too raw, too vulnerable. Thank God, he had seen how close she had been back there to losing it, and had rescued her. How on earth was she going to manage weeks of this? Especially if every time she saw a baby, she thought she would disappear inside herself from the pain of it?

But it was too late for second thoughts. She had made a commitment and she never backed out of anything, regardless of the personal cost. Somehow, although she didn't know how, she would have to lock her feelings back down, deep inside. It was the only way she could continue. She had done it before, and she could do it again. Couldn't she?

CHAPTER FOUR

NIALL sat across the desk from Mr and Mrs Thomas trying, but not quite succeeding, to ignore the cameras. After studying the financial projections, he had been forced to agree with Lucinda. The clinic needed to attract extra funding. So he had agreed to the documentary, but it didn't mean he had to like it. And to add to his discomfort, Real Life Productions had insisted that Niall, given his international reputation, be the one to appear on camera. Mark, the third doctor, and Elaine had made no secret of their relief that they wouldn't have to.

'You're used to appearing in public,' they had teased. 'God knows, your picture has appeared in the press often enough recently.'

They were right, but only because the press wanted pictures of Dr Zondi and her husband, out together and still very much in love. The press hadn't a clue, Niall thought bitterly, and it was just as well. The thought of having his personal life discussed in the papers made him squirm.

Robina had chosen an unobtrusive spot, just to the left of his patients. She was looking drawn, Niall thought with a stab of anxiety. Holding that baby had hurt—she had put her professional face back on, but the way she was nibbling her lip told him she was struggling to hold it together. Damn it! He should never have agreed to this project. Never mind about the finances of the unit, they would manage somehow—but would Robina? He didn't care what she had said about being able to cope—she was more affected than she'd imagined she'd be. But the woman was stubborn. He knew *that* to his cost. He dragged his thoughts away from his wife, concentrating on the anxious man and woman in front of him.

Mrs Thomas, Eilidh, was 38, and her husband already had a child by a previous marriage. Either of these reasons on their own made them ineligible for NHS treatment.

'We only met a year ago,' Eilidh was saying with a fond look at her husband Jim. 'I had more or less given up on meeting the man of my dreams. Then he walked into the room and, bam—just like that. We fell in love.'

Niall couldn't stop himself from sliding another glance at his wife. He knew exactly what Eilidh was talking about.

But if the same thought occurred to Robina there was no sign of it. In the last few moments she seemed to have managed to get her emotions under control. Cool, calm Dr Zondi was back, and she was concentrating intently on what Eilidh was saying.

'We started trying for a family...when was it, love?' Eilidh turned to Jim for confirmation. 'About six months ago. I know it isn't long, but my GP thought that, given my age, we shouldn't wait before we sought expert advice. So here we are.'

She's anxious, Niall thought as Eilidh chewed on her thumbnail. But then again, almost everyone who ever sat in that chair was nervous. They came to him filled with their hopes and dreams, hoping that he'd be able to work some magic that would give them the child they so desperately longed for. And most of the time he did. But not always.

However, he knew there was a good chance he could help the hopeful couple in front of him.

'I have the results of your tests here,' he said.

Eilidh gripped Jim's hands and chewed more fiercely on the thumbnail of her free hand.

'Bill's sperm test is perfectly normal—that's the good news. But the test we did for your ovarian reserve, Eilidh, shows that, as we'd expect from someone your age, your fertility is declining.' Niall kept his voice matter-of-fact.

'What does that mean?' Eilidh asked. Her pale face lightened another shade.

'It means that you are unlikely to conceive naturally, but are a good candidate for IVF,' Niall explained.

Eilidh sank back in her chair and smiled with relief. 'Thank God,' she murmured. 'I was terrified you were going to tell us it was hopeless. That getting pregnant was impossible for me.'

'It doesn't mean I can promise you a pregnancy,' Niall continued. 'Sometimes, no matter what we do, women still fail to conceive. And sometimes they conceive but are unable to carry the pregnancy to term. I don't want to paint a negative picture, but you should be prepared.'

But Niall suspected even as he said the words that Eilidh and Jim weren't really listening. Like so many couples, they couldn't bring themselves to think about the possibility of failure. 'That's why,' he added, 'we suggest you make an appointment with our counsellor. You don't have to see her but I would recommend it. She's excellent and is there should you need to talk to someone neutral at any time through this process.'

Niall couldn't prevent another glance at Robina. Sure enough, her eyes had widened in surprise. When they had first started experiencing problems in their marriage, she had suggested a counsellor. But he had refused. The thought of airing their dirty linen to a stranger was just too much. If she had truly loved him, they should have been able to sort things out themselves. Now he wondered if he should have agreed.

He took the couple through the process; how the clinic would take control of Eilidh's cycle and give her drugs which she would need to inject every day for roughly ten days. In addition, Eilidh would have to come in for regular scans of her ovaries as well as blood tests.

He went on to describe the side effects of the drugs and didn't mince his words when he explained the more unpleasant aspects of the treatment.

'Are you sure you want to put yourself through this, love?' Jim asked his wife. 'I didn't think it would be so…awful for you.'

Eilidh looked her husband straight in the eye. 'What does it matter if we get a baby at the end? I'll be all right. I can do anything as long as I have you!'

They smiled at each other and Niall felt a flash of envy. If only he and Robina could share their troubles in the same way.

'Once your ovaries are producing enough follicles and are at the right stage,' he continued, 'we take you to Theatre and you'll be given a sedative. We remove as many eggs as we can from your follicles and then we will use Jim's sperm to fertilise them in the lab. At that point the fertilised eggs become embryos. Depending on how many fertilise, we will make a decision on when to put one, or two, back. Either day two, three or day five. Are you following me so far?'

Eilidh and Jim nodded mutely.

'How do you decide whether to replace one or two embryos?' Jim asked.

'Essentially it's up to you. The HFEA, the UK regulatory body for fertility clinics, recommends that only one embryo is replaced at a time. That's because twin pregnancies carry a greater risk of complications. However, the chances are smaller of one embryo implanting successfully. We'll go over it again when we get closer to that time but, as I said, the final decision will be yours.'

Jim and Eilidh nodded sombrely. 'I think we'd like to know more before we decide how many embryos to have put back,' Jim answered for them both.

'Good decision. It's a lot to absorb in one go,' Niall said gently, 'but you'll be seeing one of our specialist nurses on a regular basis. They will be only too happy to answer any questions you may have as we go along, and they have stacks of literature that you can take away with you. Does that sound okay?'

'Does it hurt—I mean the bit where you take the eggs?' Eilidh asked.

'It can be uncomfortable,' Niall admitted. 'That's why we sedate you. But, I can promise you, you won't remember a thing about it afterwards. You might be a little sore for a couple of hours, but we'll give you something for the pain.'

He spent a few more minutes going over the same ground with the excited couple before he called in Mairi, who would be co-ordinating their treatment.

'Mairi will answer any other questions you might have,' Niall assured the couple, 'but if you ever want to speak to me, you have my number.'

'Thank you, Dr Ferguson.' Eilidh was beaming and two bright spots of colour stained her cheeks. 'I know there's a chance treatment won't work, but you have given us hope. That's all we can ask for.'

When the couple had accompanied Mairi from the room, John made to follow, but Robina stopped him. 'We'll pick them up later through their treatment,' she said, 'but in the meantime, let's give them some privacy.'

When John left the room in search of some coffee, Robina turned to Niall. 'Thank you,' she said quietly, 'you kept everything very simple. I'm sure our viewers will appreciate that.'

Niall smiled wryly. 'It's the way I speak to all my patients,' he said slowly. 'My God, woman, don't you know me at all?'

And there was the rub. She didn't really know him or, for that matter, he her. Niall had always thought they would have the rest of their lives and had looked forward to years and years of learning about the complicated, complex woman who had agreed to become his wife. Instead, he thought bitterly, it had all started to go wrong almost as soon as they'd married. Truth was, things hadn't being going well even before the miscarriage. He had been so busy at work, and Robina's new career in the media had taken off like a bullet. At first he had shared her excitement about the job, even though it had meant postponing the honeymoon, which had somehow become permanently postponed.

He hadn't realised how little he would see of her. How much her new job would take her away. Then when, to the delight of both of them, she had fallen pregnant, it had seemed that everything was going to work out fine. After the series finished she would take time off to prepare for their child. At last they could begin to be a family. But, boy, had he got that wrong! Whilst he'd assumed she'd spend less time at work, she had worked even harder, determined to establish her career before the baby arrived.

Two days before she had miscarried they had argued bitterly. Robina had returned home from London looking exhausted. She had barely managed to find the energy to eat and Niall was worried that she was losing weight.

'You need to slow down, Robina. You can't keep working at this pace.' He tossed the words down like a gauntlet.

'I will, soon. C'mon, Niall, you and I both know that pregnancy isn't an illness. In Africa, women often keep working until days before the baby is born.' She touched him gently on the cheek, but he grasped her hand and held it in his. He knew if he allowed her to touch him, he'd end up wanting to take her to bed. God knew, that was the one thing that was still okay, more than okay, between them.

'You can't keep burning the candles at both ends. You're working on the show then on your book and they still want you to do public appearances. It's too much.'

'Are you trying to tell me you don't think I should do the show?' she retorted, a dangerous glint in her deep brown eyes.

'Yes, that's what I'm saying. It's all too much. And what about after the baby is born? I thought we agreed you'd be staying at home to look after it and Ella.'

'Did we?' Her eyes deepened and her full, generous mouth tightened. 'Is that why you married me, Niall? To provide a full-time mother for your child and any other children you might want? Because, and let me make this clear, I am not Mairead. I'm not the kind of woman to give up her career just to submit myself to my husband's wishes.'

'Leave Mairead out of this,' he responded furiously.

'But I can't, can I? Not when she's everywhere. I'm living in her house, married to her husband, looking after her child. How can I possibly leave her out of this?' Suddenly a shadow crossed her eyes. 'I know she was a wonderful woman. God knows, everyone tells me, and I can see it for myself.'

'Don't tell me you're jealous of her. She's dead, for God's sake.'

'I'm not jealous of her, Niall,' Robina responded quietly, 'I just can't live up to her any longer. I will never be good at what she was. I can't cook, I can't sew, I'm not good at sports, all I am good at is my job. Please don't take that away from me.'

But he refused to see what she was so desperately trying to tell him. That night they went to bed, but instead of reaching for each other, they lay stiffly side by side, neither prepared to give an inch. Two days later, she went into labour, losing their baby, a little boy, at 12 weeks. The memory of Robina's face, tight with fear and pain, still tormented him. She had looked at him, needing him to do something, anything, to stop her losing the baby—but for the second time in his life, he had been powerless to help. The sadness in his wife's eyes when she had known that there was nothing anyone could do had almost torn him apart. When he had tried to comfort her, she had turned away. Then, a few days later, she had been in ITU with an infection, fighting for her life, and he had been terrified he was about to lose her. Robina's illness had brought back memories of Mairead and the gut-wrenching weeks and days leading up to his first wife's death. He hadn't been able to save Mairead and the thought he was going to lose Robina too had almost driven him mad with fear.

Not once had they spoken about their child or the fact that Robina was probably infertile. They had never shared their grief, or given or taken the slightest amount of comfort from one another, and one way or another their marriage had never recovered. When Robina had come home from hospital she had asked him to move into the spare room, saying that she wanted time and space on her own for a while. After a couple of weeks he had suggested he move back into their bed, but she had shaken her head and asked for more time. He didn't ask her again and that was the way it had been ever since.

Niall dragged a hand through his hair. It was a mess. And for once in his life, he didn't have a clue what to do.

Robina had been watching him in silence. He wondered what she was thinking.

'Our baby would be due in a couple of weeks.' Robina spoke softly, almost to herself. 'Just about the anniversary of the day we met. Seeing baby Matthew just now…' Her voice shook '…was so hard.'

The familiar mask he had become too used to seeing slipped for a moment. Right now she looked so vulnerable, so sad, so different from the public persona which was all he ever saw these days. For the first time in months he glimpsed the Robina he had met and fallen in love with. He wanted to gather her into his arms but he was afraid to break the spell. It was the first time she had mentioned the baby and Niall felt a surge of hope. Perhaps this documentary wasn't such a bad thing after all. Not if it meant they would start talking. He sat in silence, waiting for her to continue, but just then there was a knock and Sally burst into the room.

'Dr Ferguson, I need you to come and see one of our ladies. I think she might have OHSS.'

Niall was torn. He wanted to comfort his wife, seize the moment when she had opened up to him, but if Sally was right and the patient did have ovarian hyper stimulation syndrome, he needed to see her straight away. Although in the early stages the condition was fairly benign, it was still a potentially life-threatening illness.

Robina also jumped to her feet, the professional mask back on her face.

'I think you should stay here,' Niall said firmly. 'I'll let you know what's happening as soon as I can.'

When Sally and Niall left the room, Robina slumped back down in her chair. Just for a moment there she had been ready to talk to Niall, and it looked as if he had been ready to listen.

But the moment had passed, and Robina wondered whether she would find the strength to raise the subject again.

After a working lunch, where Robina and John had a look over the clips they had filmed, Robina went in search of Niall.

'I have decided to admit our lady with the suspected OHSS,' Niall told her.

'Would you mind explaining the condition for our viewers?' Robina asked. When Niall nodded, Robina signalled to John to start filming.

'Infertility treatment, although fairly benign,' Niall said thoughtfully, 'is not without its risks. We do our best to minimise these, which is why we take blood and scan our patients every couple of days and readjust their treatment protocol as appropriate.' Although his expression was serious, he looked calm and relaxed. This was his field and he knew it well. 'Sometimes the hormones we prescribe over-stimulate the ovaries and it can lead to very real complications, which if not treated can lead to the kidneys failing, and even death. It is rare, but something we take very seriously. Thankfully, we have never had a full-blown case, but on average one woman dies every year in the UK from this condition.'

'I wonder how many women know and understand the risk,' Robina said quietly.

'We do tell them—we make a point of it. If we didn't we'd be negligent,' Niall replied.

'Does it ever put anyone off?'

Niall smiled wryly. 'I think you know the answer to that. And anyway, as long as patients are monitored closely, as most are, the chance of it happening is greatly reduced.'

'But you had a potential case today,' Robina persisted. 'So it does happen.'

Niall narrowed his eyes at her. 'As I said, it is a risk and one that we manage. I admitted the patient who presented with symptoms of OHSS to the ward this morning, but more because she was anxious. I fully expect her to be discharged tomorrow.'

Robina opened her mouth to speak, but before she could say anything, Niall held up a hand.

'Whatever anyone might think, we always have the health of the mother foremost in our minds. But any pregnancy, whether through IVF or through normal intercourse, carries a risk, however careful the expectant mother or however vigilant those looking after her are. We can't always guarantee a positive outcome.'

This time he looked directly into her eyes and she knew that he meant his words for her. He lowered his voice. 'No matter how much we wish we could.' He leaned forward, his eyes locking with hers, and Robina caught her breath at the intensity in his eyes. For a few moments there was silence, then Niall stood.

'I will be doing the Strains' embryo transfer this afternoon,' he said, changing the subject. 'I understand they are one of the couples who wish to appear on your documentary.'

Hiding the fact that her emotions were all over the place, Robina rifled through her papers and found their name. In total ten couples had agreed to be part of her programme. Most of them already knew her work from television and were keen to do anything to help other couples. One or two of them had even read her *Guide to Infertility*, the book that had started her new career.

'Trevor and Christine. They are a lovely couple, I interviewed them yesterday to get their back story. I understand this is their first attempt?'

'Yes, and I'm optimistic. This time the problem, if you can

call it that, lies with Christine's partner. He has a very low sperm count, so we did a procedure called ICSI. It is where we searched for and selected motile—that is swimming—sperm from Trevor's semen sample and injected one directly into each of the eggs we retrieved from Christine. She responded well to the drug protocol we prescribed for her, and we managed to remove a good number of eggs. And because we injected the sperm directly into the egg, we managed to fertilise several embryos. You can go into the lab some time if you like to see how it's done. It involves a high level of expertise and a very steady hand—so no drinking for our embryologists the night before.' He grinned. 'Anyway, they'll be here about three for the transfer of their embryo back into the uterus. But I want to make it clear that if they change their mind about you being there, you must respect that. Even if they have given permission before.'

'Of course!' Robina replied, stung. 'Niall, you need to remember that I was a GP—I still am. I have taken the Hippocratic Oath to do no harm. And that means psychological as well as physical.'

'I'm sorry.' Niall looked contrite. 'That was uncalled for. I know you could never be accused of being unprofessional. Forgive me?' He smiled at her, and her heart flipped.

'Anyway,' Niall said, looking serious again, 'please remember if you are planning to come into Theatre you can't wear perfume or make-up. Not even deodorant. Is that clear? We don't want to risk affecting the embryos in any way.'

'Clear as crystal,' Robina replied, before turning on her heel and going in search of her team.

Later, in Theatre, Robina watched from a safe distance while the staff prepared Christine for the transfer.

The clinic hadn't stinted on equipment, Robina thought approvingly, taking in the latest high-tech anaesthetic monitor and ultrasound scanner. Niall, dressed as all the staff were, including Robina and John as well as Mr Strain, in blue scrubs, slowly and carefully replaced the embryo into Mrs Strain's uterus. The procedure didn't take long, but although Christine joked with Sally, there was an undercurrent of tension in the room. All anyone could do now was wait.

'Patients tell us the next couple of weeks are the worst time of the whole process.' Sally addressed Robina while looking at Mrs Strain. 'Up until this point it's all still possible. They see us regularly, but when they go away from here after the ET—the embryo transfer—there is nothing more they, or we, can do. Whether the embryo implants or not is in the lap of the gods. Patients tell us it's the longest wait of their lives.'

Niall half smiled at Christine. 'I wish we could make this part easier, but we can't. If you do want to speak to us—if you have any worries at all—you get on the phone. Don't worry that we'll think your question is trivial, we'd rather you asked. Okay?'

Christine nodded.

'We'll let you rest for half an hour or so, then you're free to go,' Sally said. 'We'll see you when you come back for your urine test. In the meantime, we'll all be thinking of you.'

Once again, Robina marvelled at the way that the staff genuinely seemed to care about every one of their patients. It was as if every pregnancy mattered personally to every member of staff. Niall had managed to gather the best possible team around him. No wonder he was so wrapped up in his work.

Later that evening, Robina was getting Ella ready for bed. Niall had telephoned to say he would be late as he had a paper to finish but he wanted to say goodnight to Ella. Robina couldn't help a pang of disappointment. Despite everything that had happened, she still missed him when he wasn't there and she had been looking forward to discussing the day's events with him.

They had come close to talking back in the clinic. Maybe there was still a chance they could start talking again—maybe even find a way back to each other.

She handed the phone to Ella. 'It's Daddy, he wants to speak to you.'

Robina busied herself setting the table, smiling to herself as she caught Ella's side of the conversation. 'I love you too, Daddy, and I'm sending you a big kiss down the phone.' She puckered her lips and blew down the mouthpiece. She giggled at something Niall said. 'I got your kiss, Daddy, but what about one for Mummy? She needs one too. Hold on a minute, I'll get her for you.' Ella turned to Robina. 'Here, Mummy, Daddy wants to send you a kiss goodnight.'

Robina stared at the receiver, horrified. What could she do? She couldn't very well refuse—what would Ella think? With a thudding heart, she held the phone to her ear.

'Well,' Niall said dryly, 'are you going to blow me a kiss?'

'You first, darling,' Robina replied, forcing her tone to remain light, painfully aware of Ella watching her with delight.

'This is ridiculous,' Niall replied, his voice echoing his embarrassment down the wire. 'That daughter of mine is too smart for her own good. Okay—here goes.' He made a smacking noise. 'Now your turn—and remember you've got an audience.'

Robina couldn't help smiling. Niall was right, it was ridiculous, but there was something bitter-sweet about it too. She pursed her lips, emphasising the required smacking sound, playing up to the watching Ella. 'Mmmmmwhah!'

They both laughed and for the first time in months Robina felt her sadness ease.

When she put the phone down, Ella asked, 'When will Daddy be home?'

'After you're asleep, darling,' Robina answered. 'But he'll be here when you get up in the morning. We both will, so we can have breakfast together.'

'Then after that can we go ice-skating? Please, Mummy. Sophie went with her mummy and daddy and they had so much fun.'

Robina kissed the top of her stepdaughter's curly blonde head. She was so like her father it made her heart ache. But her blonde hair must have come from her mother. The sloe-eyed Mairead. Beautiful, maternal Mairead who had been everything she wasn't.

'Sure we can, as long as Daddy doesn't have to work. I know tomorrow is Saturday, but sometimes his patients need him.'

'*I* need him,' Ella persisted. 'He's my daddy, not theirs.'

Robina hid a smile. 'But he's helping lots of people become mummies and daddies—you understand that, don't you? People who without his help would never know how wonderful it is to have a lovely little girl like you.'

'I s'pose,' Ella said, settling herself in the crook of Robina's arm. 'But I need *some* time with my daddy. They can't have him all the time. Just some of the time.'

Robina's heart ached for the little girl. Although their work made enormous demands on both of them, they had to find time to spend with Ella. They had promised her and it was about time they made good on their word. Although Mrs Tobin was great and Ella loved her to bits, it wasn't the same as having her parents around.

Robina made up her mind. The documentary would take

three months, including the follow-up of patients in nine months' time. The new season of her show wasn't due to start for a couple of months. Her last book was selling well, and she had almost finished the proofs of her latest. She would put off starting a new one until after the summer. That way she'd have more time to spend with Ella. Robina sucked in her breath. She couldn't blame Niall for everything that had gone wrong with their marriage. She had, as he had pointed out, been so immersed in her new career she hadn't given her new marriage, or Niall, the time and attention it had needed. When things had started to go wrong, had she been too quick to lay the blame at Niall's feet? One thing was for sure, she couldn't keep going the way she was with a show and book tours and still have enough time for Ella, let alone her marriage. The more she thought about it, the more she wondered why she hadn't seen it before.

'Why don't we ask Daddy whether we can do something next weekend? Just the three of us? We can do anything you like,' she suggested to Ella.

'Could we really?' Ella said, looking up at her with achingly familiar blue eyes. 'Daddy too?'

'Yes, darling,' Robina promised. 'Daddy too.'

But Robina didn't get the chance to discuss it with Niall that night. She waited up, reading a book on the sofa of her small sitting room. The room was still exactly the way Mairead had left it, all pale walls and deep rugs. Even the overfilled sofas were pale and there was a wood-burning stove for the cool evenings. The only item Robina had brought with her from her old life was an African stool. She stretched out a finger and felt the deep grooves of the intricate carving. Her father had given her the stool when she had graduated. It had belonged to his father, who had been a master wood cutter, and Robina cherished it. Every time she touched it, she thought of the village where her father had been raised in the old African traditions and could almost feel the heat of the sun and hear the undulating voices of the women as they called to each other. How she missed Africa and especially her mother and grandmother.

Sighing, she glanced around the room that had belonged to her predecessor. The walls were lined with floor-to-ceiling bookshelves. It seemed that along with a similar taste in men, she and Mairead shared the same literary taste. All her favourites were on the bookshelf, from the classics to the contemporary romances she liked to read before bed. Unfortunately, reading them only made her acutely aware of the lack of romance in her own life.

Despite her best intentions, she was unable to stop herself falling asleep and woke to find Niall covering her gently with a blanket. Still half dreaming, she smiled up at him and went straight back to sleep but not before she thought she felt his fingertips like a caress against her skin.

CHAPTER FIVE

'YOU'RE cutting it a little fine, aren't you?' Niall said the next evening, glancing at his watch.

Robina had almost forgotten about the charity dinner she had promised to attend. Although it was the last thing she felt like doing, she knew they were expected. She had been called in to work for an unexpected meeting and still hadn't managed to speak to Niall about the promise she had made to Ella.

'I can get ready in half an hour if need be. Ella will be in bed before then. Won't you, darling?'

Niall scooped his daughter into his arms and tickled her until Ella was shrieking with laughter.

Robina watched them for a few moments with an ache in her heart. 'I'll start running the bath, shall I?'

As she switched on the taps in the bathroom that had once been Mairead's, her thoughts turned, as they inevitably did, to her loveless marriage. At least loveless as far as Niall was concerned, she mused, but how did she feel? She had loved him once, loved him so much that she'd thought she'd burst with it. She'd been so happy, never suspecting for one minute how easily it would all come crashing down about her.

Hearing footsteps behind her and the deep growl of Niall's voice as he teased his daughter, Robina blinked furiously lest he see the moisture in her eyes. She couldn't bear him to know that she still cared. All she had left was her pride and she was damned if she would let him take that too.

Niall strode into the bathroom and deposited his giggling daughter gently on the bathroom floor.

'I'll leave you to it while I get changed,' he said. Robina ached, knowing that he couldn't bear to be in close proximity to her. 'I suppose I have to come?' he added. 'Couldn't you ask someone else to accompany you? I have something I'd really prefer to be doing this evening.'

'Of course I can't force you to come,' Robina said between stiff lips. 'But you know the press will have a field day if you don't. They'd like nothing better than to sense trouble between the author of *How to keep your man happy—in bed and out of it* and her husband.' How bloody ironic it all was.

It seemed as if the irony wasn't lost on Niall either. His lips twitched in a half-smile as he looked at Robina, his eyes glinting. To her mortification, she felt her face burn. Was he remembering how good it had been? Her book had been written from memory, it was true, but only because every moment of their love-making was burnt into her brain. She could remember every touch of his lips, the feel of his hands on her skin, the way they couldn't get enough of each other, and the memories tortured her. Her heart thumped as he held her gaze and something flickered in his eyes. If only he would tell her he still loved her, then sweep her into his arms and take her to his bed, perhaps they could find a way back to each other again. She knew he still wanted her as much as she wanted him. But what good was sexual attraction, however intense, without love? She shook her head slightly.

Niall gave her one last lingering look before he turned and walked away.

'Dr Zondi and Dr Ferguson, could you look this way, please?'

Cameras flashed in a maelstrom of light and noise. Robina supposed she should be used to it by now. But the speed with which her career had taken off and the media interest had taken her by surprise. She had gone from being a GP to a best-selling author and presenter of *Life In Focus* all within a few months, and her head still reeled. Never in a million years would she have imagined the life she found herself living. But for all its glamour and wealth and adulation, Robina knew she would have traded it all in a heartbeat for the life she had envisaged when she had fallen in love with Niall.

She sneaked a sideways glance at her husband. Although he hated these functions, no one except her would be able to tell. He cut a devastatingly handsome figure in his tux. Tall, dark-haired and incredibly good-looking, the media loved him. As a couple they were portrayed as Mr and Mrs Perfect. If only people knew the truth, Robina thought bitterly. They were as far away from perfect as was possible.

Niall took her elbow and steered her through the photographers and into the hall. As Robina had expected, it was filled with a veritable who's who from the TV world. Instantly they were surrounded, and Robina felt a pang as Niall moved away, leaving her to talk with the presenter of one of TV's most popular chat shows.

'Ah, Dr Zondi,' the presenter, a grey-haired distinguished-looking man in his early fifties, was saying. 'I was hoping we'd get a chance to talk. I would love it if you would do a slot on my show as one of the celebrities.'

Robina nodded distractedly, watching Niall from the corner of her eye as he was cornered by a journalist from one of the national newspapers. Niall had recently published a paper on a new treatment for infertility, which was causing quite a stir. She watched him bend his head to listen to what the journalist was saying, before he threw his head back and laughed. Whatever his feelings about events like this, he would play his part. Robina knew he would never do anything to embarrass her publicly. She felt the familiar stab of regret. Once she had made him laugh like that. Robina swallowed a sigh, before turning her attention back to the presenter, who was still speaking. She was on duty, and for the time being, at least, would forget about the mockery that was her private life.

'You want me to talk about the documentary I'm doing?' she asked.

The presenter frowned. 'Documentary? No, not really. People are interested in Dr Zondi the woman. Especially your new book. They know about the doctor, now they want to know what makes the woman tick.'

Robina shook her head. 'I don't do chat shows,' she said dismissively.

'Of course you do.' Richard Christchurch laughed. 'You have your own show every week.'

'That's different,' Robina insisted. 'That's not about me.'

'Isn't it?' Richard raised an eyebrow.

'It's not a chat show,' Robina persisted. 'It's a chance for patients to talk about their medical problems and get some answers. And for viewers to get information. They come on and talk about how illness affects their lives and what help they have found. It's not entertainment!'

'Isn't everything on TV entertainment?' Richard continued. 'But if, as you say, your programme is more of a public service, then you appearing on my show can only help get information to the public.'

Robina still wasn't sure. She didn't altogether trust Richard Christchurch as he had a reputation for taking cheap swipes at his guests. On the other hand, he was right. If she appeared on his show, it would help raise public awareness about her own show. And that was good. Wasn't it?'

'I'll need to speak to my agent,' she hedged. 'But I don't know if I'll have the time. I'm in the middle of this documentary, and my own programme returns in a couple of months. And somewhere in between I have to find time to promote my latest book—at least my agent tells me I have to.'

Richard smiled. 'Of course. It was only a thought, but I'll get my agent to speak to yours, shall I? In the meantime, perhaps you want to discuss it with your husband?'

Discuss it with Niall? Who was he kidding? Niall was the last person she'd be discussing it with. She glanced across the room to find her husband's eyes on her. He was too far away for her to read his expression, but as their eyes held, she felt her heart thump against her ribs. There had been a time when their eyes would have met across the room and she would have known exactly what he was thinking. That he wanted to leave, so he could make love to her. At one time, they couldn't get enough of each other. At one time no words had been necessary.

At dinner, she and Niall were placed at different sides of the table and she was thankful that they wouldn't have to pretend to everyone to be wrapped up in each other. Throughout the seemingly endless meal she would look up from conversations she was having with the guests on either side to find Niall's unfathomable eyes on her. Whenever he caught her eye he would smile dutifully and she would grin back as if her heart wasn't breaking.

After the main course, the band struck up and Niall got to his feet, came over to her side, and held out a hand to her.

'Shall we, darling?' he drawled. As usual he was playing the attentive husband role and if he had a sardonic look in his cool blue eyes, only Robina saw it.

Conscious of several pairs of eyes on them, she let him whirl her around the dance floor. His hand was low on her back as he guided her and she could feel his fingers on her bare skin, burning into her. The movement of the dance brought her body tight against his and she let her body melt into him, taking the opportunity to let herself believe, even for a few minutes, that they were a normal couple, still in love.

Her head only reached as far as his shoulder, and she rested her head against the rough material of his suit, breathing in the scent of soap and the faint smell of his aftershave.

'What did Richard Christchurch want?' he murmured into her ear, his breath like a caress.

'He wants me to appear on his show.' She smiled up at him, conscious that people would be watching.

'And will you?' He frowned. 'Be careful, Robina. He's a snake.'

The concern in his voice was unexpected. 'I can look after myself,' she responded lightly.

Niall's answer was to pull her closer and Robina let herself relax into his arms, enjoying the feeling of his arms around her, even if it was all for show. All too soon the music ended and they returned to their seats.

The evening was almost over when Robina heard a commotion coming from the rear of the room. Looking across, she noticed several people had jumped out of their seats and were standing about in confusion.

She glanced across at Niall. The noise had attracted his attention too.

'Someone call an ambulance.' The voice cutting across the room was shrill, panic not far away.

Wordlessly, she and Niall were on their feet moving swiftly across the room. As the crowd parted, Robina's heart missed a beat. On the floor lay a middle-aged man, his face grey and his lips tinged with blue. He didn't appear to be breathing. Immediately Niall took command of the situation. Squatting beside the stricken man, he loosened his tie and felt for a pulse.

'What happened?' he asked the woman who had cried out.

'Bill…my husband…he said he had indigestion earlier. He took something for it, but then all of a sudden he said the pain was getting worse and he would go to the bathroom. But when he stood he clutched his chest and just dropped to the floor.' The woman's teeth were chattering with shock. Niall looked at Robina.

'No pulse. We need to start CPR.'

'Call an ambulance,' Robina told one of the bystanders. 'Tell them we have a cardiac arrest.' In the same breath she dropped to Niall's side. Aware of the eyes of the room on her and the flash of cameras, she shut them out of her mind. First and foremost she was a doctor and this man needed their help. It had been some time since she had done any clinical practice and she was hugely relieved that Niall was with her. She knew that, as a practising clinician, he was required to keep his resus skills up to date.

He was pressing on the stricken man's chest, counting off the beats under his breath. She waited for him to count to thirty before she bent over the stricken man and, taking a deep breath, tipped his head back and blew twice into his mouth.

The room was deathly quiet as she and Niall worked together, completely in synch as they once had been in everything. As long as they could keep blood circulating in his system until the ambulance arrived, the man had a chance. They worked silently, until after a couple of minutes the man coughed.

'I've got a pulse,' Niall said. He looked at her and grinned. Robina's heart rate escalated further. With his help she turned Bill onto his side, into the recovery position. There was little they could do now until the ambulance arrived, but it looked as if Bill would make it.

'Is he all right?' his wife was asking frantically. 'Please tell me he's going to be okay.'

Robina stood, easing the stiffness from her legs. 'It's early days yet, but he's breathing on his own now. And that's good. The paramedics will be able to give him something when they arrive, and the sooner he gets to the hospital the better.'

'Oh, thank God. Thank you. Thank you.' The woman dropped to her knees and cradled her husband's head in her lap. She looked up at Robina, her eyes wet. 'Thank you, Dr Zondi. You've saved his life.'

Robina was embarrassed. 'It's Dr Ferguson you have to thank,' she said. But as she smiled into Niall's eyes she was dismayed to find the shutters had come back down and he looked as distant as he always did these days.

The doors swung open as the paramedics rushed into the room, carrying a portable defibrillator and medical supplies. Robina stepped back, knowing that Bill was in safe hands. She turned to look at Niall, but he had already turned away and was striding away from her. She bit down on her disappointment as the cameras continued to flash.

'Please,' she said, suddenly furious. 'Give this man and his wife some privacy, can't you? This isn't a live TV show, for goodness' sake.'

Chastised, the photographers lowered their cameras and stood about looking shamefaced.

The paramedics lifted Bill onto the stretcher and moved briskly towards the exit, Bill's wife following closely behind. As they left, the photographers picked up their cameras again and focussed on Robina, the flashes blinding her.

She had to get out of there. She whirled around, trying to remember what she had done with her coat, and then Niall was by her side, holding it out for her to slip her arms into.

'I think my wife has earned the right to some privacy, don't you?' he told the reporters. His tone was even, but Robina could hear the suppressed fury behind the words. He would hate the way the man's heart attack had turned into a circus. All because she was there, and everything she did was newsworthy. Robina had no doubt that her picture would be splashed all over the morning's newspaper. It was one thing not to have any privacy, it came with the territory after all, but quite another for photos of the unconscious man to make the news. She felt Niall's hand on her elbow and then she was being steered out of the room and into their waiting car.

Inside the safety of their limousine, Robina felt the adrenaline seep out of her body. Uncomfortably aware of the length of the hard muscles of his thigh against her leg, she shifted slightly in her seat, wanting to put some distance between them. Despite the tumult of different emotions she felt towards him, he still had the power to send her senses into overdrive. Tonight, working with him over that poor man, she had remembered why she had fallen in love with him in the first place. He was a good man, a kind man. Couldn't they try to put the past behind them and move on? Try to be friends at least? It had taken little steps to destroy their marriage—could little steps take them back?

She reached for his hand as she prepared the words in her head.

Niall brought her fingers to his lips and kissed the back of her hand, the feel of his lips sending shock waves through her body. But then, his eyes glinting in the semi-darkness, he took her hand and replaced it in her lap with a little pat, as if she were a child.

'Well done, darling,' he drawled. 'Another opportunity to get your name in the press. You must be delighted.'

She glared at him. Every time she thought she was softening towards him, he would do, or say, something that would cause her to clench her fists in fury. How was it possible to lust after your husband, even though you weren't even sure you liked him? And what kind of woman did that make her? In that respect she was just like him.

'Yes,' she hissed through clenched teeth. 'How very clever of me to arrange for that man to have a cardiac arrest. Just for another photo opportunity. God, Niall, what kind of person do you take me for?'

'A woman who would do anything to promote her career.' His voice was gentle, almost caressing. 'As we both know very well.'

Stunned, she edged even further away from him. 'At least you know now who you married—just as I know the kind of man I married.' Why had she thought even for a minute they could be friends when clearly he despised everything about her? It seemed the only way she could save her marriage was by giving up work and becoming some sort of earth mother. And there was no chance of that.

Niall closed his eyes as they sped towards home.

Why had he said that? It was grossly unfair and he knew it. But she got under his skin. When he had seen her dressed in a gown of simmering bronze that fell to her feet, her short black hair highlighting that impossibly beautiful face, the diamonds he had given her as a wedding present sparkling at the base of her long neck, she had taken his breath away.

He had needed every ounce of self-control he could muster to stop himself from picking her up and carrying her off to…to where? His bedroom? Hers? And there it was. She hadn't spent a night in his bed since the night they'd argued before the miscarriage. She had made it perfectly clear that she couldn't bear him to touch her. He had tried to be patient, hoping she just needed time. He smothered a groan, thinking back to the night he had gone into the room they had once shared, thinking—hoping—they could comfort each other. But when he had reached out for her, she had recoiled and the look of fear in her eyes had shocked him. He clenched his teeth, pushing away the bewilderment and pain of her rejection. Although he had known it would take time for her to recover from the miscarriage, that had gone deeper. He was sure of it. It was almost as if she hated him. Every day she had drawn further and further away from him, throwing herself back into her work. If he'd hoped that with time she would come round, he had been badly mistaken. All that time had done was to drive a wedge between them. A wedge the size of the Grand Canyon. And as far as he could see, there was no way across.

CHAPTER SIX

IT WAS the second week of filming and, once again, Robina was sitting in with Niall as he consulted with couples. At home, everything had carried on the same as it had before, with the two of them spending as little time together as possible, meeting only over breakfast or when Ella's school functions demanded their presence. She had spoken to him about her promise to Ella and Niall had wholeheartedly agreed that they needed to make some time for the three of them to spend together. Despite this, they still hadn't managed an outing as a family. Niall had been on call the day after the charity dinner and had spent the whole day seeing emergencies at the hospital.

The patients they were seeing today, the Davidsons, were an ordinary couple with an ordinary life. Patricia, an anxious looking woman with short brown hair, was a primary school teacher and her husband, Luke, was a farmer.

Niall introduced her as usual, although she had met the couple before, and reminded them that they could withdraw from the filming at any time. Then he leaned forward and asked them to explain why they had come to see him. Once again Robina was struck by his warm, encouraging manner with his patients. How could she have forgotten the way his eyes crinkled at the corners, the way his mouth lifted when he smiled, how sympathetic he could be?

'We've been trying for ages to have a baby,' Patricia was saying. 'We wanted to wait until my career was established first. Then one thing after another happened. My mother became very ill and I had to look after her as well as work full time, so we kept putting it off. Sadly she passed away just over a year ago, but as soon as everything settled down we started trying. But months have passed and nothing.' She glanced over at Robina. 'I saw you on the telly, talking about your book on infertility, and I went out and bought it. It made me realise we had to do something, and quickly. So that's why we're here. To see why it isn't happening.'

'I see from your notes that you are forty-three,' Niall said gently.

'That's not too old, is it?' replied Patricia anxiously. 'I mean, I don't feel old. I'm fit, I exercise regularly. I feel as good as I did in my twenties. Anyway, don't they say your forties are the new thirties?'

'Yeah, she even drags me to the gym,' Luke added. 'I don't know where she gets her energy from.' He smiled fondly at his wife. 'She'll be a great mother. We're even looking forward to the sleepless nights.'

Robina felt a pang of envy. Whatever difficulties these couples were experiencing, it was obvious they loved and supported one another.

'Unfortunately, people don't realise that a woman's fertility begins to tail off once they are thirty-five,' Niall said quietly. He passed the couple a chart illustrating his point. 'And once they get to forty, their fertility is dramatically reduced. It doesn't really matter how fit and healthy they are, although for younger women, being a reasonable weight does help.'

'What are you saying?' Luke was frowning. 'Are you telling us you can't do anything for us, that you won't treat us?'

'Not at all,' Niall said. 'But I do have the results of your fertility tests here; the semen analysis from you, Luke, and the blood test we did on you, Patricia, at your first visit.'

Patricia grabbed Luke's hand. It was clear to Robina that she was beginning to realise that she wasn't going to like whatever it was that Niall had to tell her.

'Go on,' Patricia said quietly. Robina could hear the tremor in her voice.

'Luke's tests came back normal, but I'm afraid, Patricia, that your ovarian reserve is so low as to make the possibility of you falling pregnant, even with IVF, just about zero.'

Robina could tell he was choosing his words carefully, and that he knew he was giving the couple the worst possible news.

'Just about zero?' Patricia echoed, clearly shocked. 'Are you sure?' Her voice cracked. 'No chance at all?' Her eyes shimmered.

'I'm sorry,' Niall said. 'There really is no point in going down the IVF route. It's not just the number of eggs you have left, it's the quality. In my opinion, even if we did manage to collect some eggs from you, and I think that is extremely unlikely, there is every chance that they won't fertilise. And even if they do, the chance of you miscarrying is about sixty per cent. And lastly, even if a pregnancy were to continue, there is the much increased risk of foetal abnormality. I'm sorry if all this sounds harsh, but you need to know the truth.'

Patricia started crying in earnest, deep, racking sobs as if her heart was being shattered, which it very probably was, Robina thought sadly. Luke placed an arm around his wife's shoulders. 'Is that it then?' he said. 'We have to give up? Never have a family?'

Robina ached for them. She felt a lump the size of a pebble form in her throat. She knew only too well how the couple would be feeling, especially Patricia. It was a devastating blow to their hopes and dreams. She gripped her hands together tightly, not wanting to let Niall see how much she was affected.

'I think it's only fair to be brutally honest with you, no matter how difficult it is for you to hear. But there are other options.'

Patricia looked up and Robina shied away from the naked hope in her eyes. 'But I'm warning you—what I am about to suggest is not for everyone. You would need to think about it very carefully, and before we went ahead, you would have to talk it through with a counsellor.'

'Please, tell us.' Luke spoke for his wife.

'The only way your wife could get pregnant is by using donor eggs. That's where we use the healthy eggs of another woman, fertilise them with your sperm, Luke, and then place one of the embryos back in you, Patricia.'

Patricia glanced at her husband and then back at Niall. 'But it wouldn't be my baby.'

'Not genetically, no. It would, of course, have half of Luke's genes, but, no, none of yours. The positive thing about using donor eggs is that the chances of achieving and maintaining a pregnancy are the same as if you were the donor's age. And since we don't accept donors over thirty-five, there is a greater than fifty per cent chance of you falling pregnant on your first cycle.'

'I don't know,' Patricia said slowly. 'It's all so much to take in. I never imagined for one moment that I wasn't going to be able to have children of my own. I guess I knew it wouldn't happen naturally, but I wasn't prepared to find out that it wouldn't happen at all except with another woman's eggs.'

'I don't expect you to make a decision right away,' Niall

said. 'In fact, I would actively encourage you to have a long hard think about it. As I said, it's not for everyone. But if you think it is something you might consider, I suggest you put your name on our waiting list. I'm afraid it's about a year's wait at the moment.'

'A year! As long as that?' Patricia's face fell. Then she looked curious. 'Do these women sell their eggs? Is that how it works? Maybe if we paid someone more…'

Niall shook his head. 'I'm afraid that's illegal. There is no money involved. The women either donate their eggs because they have had their families and want to help someone else achieve their dream, or they are women who donate a proportion of their eggs in order to help fund their treatment. There are very strict regulations around all of this. No clinic in the country can try and get around them without running the risk of losing its licence. The regulations are there to prevent women, who are often pretty desperate, from exploiting or being exploited.'

Robina was conscious of leaning forward in her chair. Of course she knew that couples could use donated eggs or donated sperm, she had written about it in her book after all, but that had been before…before she had known that there was every possibility she had joined their ranks. Listening to Niall talk to the couple was almost as if he was talking to her.

'There is one other option, and I am not necessarily recommending it either, but I think you have the right to know. There are other clinics, overseas, that have more donated eggs than we do in this country. Not all of these clinics are above board, but there is one which I'd be happy to refer you to, if you want. You need to think about it. Speak to the nursing staff who will be able to put you in touch with others who are going through the same thing. Most people find that it helps. Then, if you think you may want to go forward, make an appointment to chat things over with the counsellor. She'll help you decide whether it's the right thing for you.'

After answering several other questions from the shaken couple, Niall showed them out to where one of the nurses was waiting to talk to them.

By the time he returned, Robina had managed to get her trembling hands under control. How on earth was she going to manage another couple of months of this? When every patient's story left her feeling like a wrung-out rag. But over the last couple of weeks Robina had known that something was shifting inside her. Seeing the way couples were able to deal with their grief and move on with their lives—together— was planting the tiniest seed of optimism inside her. Maybe, in time, she too could come to terms with *her* loss. And if she was too scared to risk another pregnancy, or if her tubes had been damaged by the infection, there were other options. None of which she'd even considered. But then, unlike her, all these women had loving, supportive marriages. And that made all the difference.

'So you are saying that women are encouraged to donate a proportion of their eggs in order to fund their treatment?' she said, signalling to John to keep filming.

Niall sat down in his chair and stretched his long legs in front of him before regarding her steadily over steepled fingers.

'You'd prefer women not to have the opportunity?' he said quietly. 'Do you have any idea how short the supply of donor eggs is? There are so many women, like Patricia, whose only hope of having a child is through the generosity of those women who are prepared to donate their eggs.'

'I can see the point when it comes to altruistic donors…' Robina replied. 'Those women who have nothing to gain except the satisfaction of helping someone else, but these other women, the egg sharers—aren't they under impossible pressure to donate in order to fund their own treatment? Is that morally correct?'

Niall brought his brows together. 'Don't you think we've considered all that?' Underlying his calm tone was a thread of steel. 'Do you think for one moment that any of us here would force women, or even steer them, towards a decision that wasn't right for them? And as I explained to Patricia, it's not only the recipients who have to undergo counselling. The donors aren't permitted to donate unless we are absolutely convinced that they know exactly what they are letting themselves in for.'

'But,' Robina persisted, 'I can see how desperate these women are to have children. Surely you are taking advantage of that?'

Niall stood. He towered over her, his eyes glinting. He signalled to the cameraman to stop filming. 'Could you leave us for a moment, John?' He waited until John, after a nod from Robina, left the room.

'Don't make this about us, Robina,' he said. When she opened her mouth to protest he held up his hand. 'I told you that I thought this was too close to home for you, but you wouldn't listen.'

'It isn't about us,' Robina retorted. 'There *is* no us. Oh, we may be married but we both know it's in name only. We haven't been married, not truly, since…' She broke off, unable to bring herself to say the words. 'Actually, I can't even remember if I ever felt married.' Furious with herself, she tried to blink away the tears before Niall could see, but it was too late.

He crouched down by her side and touched her arm. She looked into his diamond eyes. 'Are you sure?' he said quietly.

'We were happy once. We can be happy again. If we are both prepared to try.'

Robina's skin burnt at his touch and she desperately wanted to say, Yes, let's start again, go back to where we were, before it all went so badly wrong. But she couldn't. She was no longer the woman he'd married.

She shook her head. 'I don't know, Niall. So much has happened. You know you want more children, but I don't. I won't risk it.'

'We could adopt.'

'We could. But do you think having children would sort what's wrong with our marriage? Because I don't.'

He dropped his arm and turned away, but not before she saw the flash of disappointment in his eyes. Despite herself she felt a flicker of hope. Was there a chance? Did he still care? Even after everything?

'But maybe,' she said tentatively, 'maybe we can be friends. Not just pretend like we do around Ella but really try. Maybe make a start this weekend. Like we promised Ella. Do you know how long it's been since we did something all together?'

Niall's expression was hooded. 'You know I'd do anything to make my child happy. And if having you and me spend time with her together makes her happy then naturally I'll do whatever she wants. You know that.'

And just like that the flicker of hope was snuffed out. Whatever Niall said, the reason he wanted her in his life was to be a mother to his child. And she'd do well not to forget that, even for a moment.

'Come on, Daddy,' Ella demanded. 'Robina's programme is about to start.'

Niall switched on the TV and sank into the leather sofa.

Richard Christchurch had phoned Robina the Monday after the charity dinner, explaining that a scheduled guest had been unable to appear on the show later that week due to a family crisis. The presenter had wheedled and begged a resisting Robina to step in at the last minute. When her agent had added her entreaties, Robina had eventually agreed.

Ella cuddled in beside Niall, popping her thumb into her mouth. He resisted the temptation to pull it out again. She'd get over the habit in her own good time.

They were just in time to watch Robina's entrance into the studio. She paused and smiled as the camera focussed in on her. She looks every bit the TV star, Niall thought proudly. She looked elegant in a floor-length gown that clung to her curves, a simple gold necklace highlighting the length of her neck, her height putting her at least a couple of inches above her host. For the programme she had chosen to dress in traditional African style and Niall thought she looked stunning.

As she settled into the chair the host Richard Christchurch held out for her, she appeared cool and at ease. They shared a couple of words off camera as they waited until the applause died down.

'Robina. May I call you Robina?' Richard asked. When she nodded he continued. 'For those few viewers who don't know you, could you tell us a little bit about your work?'

'I present a weekly show called *Life In Focus*,' Robina answered. 'It's a programme that covers a different medical topic every week.'

'Could you tell us how you came to present the show?'

'I am a qualified GP,' Robina answered. 'About a year ago, I had a book published—an-easy-to-read guide on in-fertility. When it came out, it was very well received and I was asked onto the show to talk about it. Shortly afterwards, the producer offered me the opportunity to present *Life In Focus*.'

'Aren't you a bit young to be offering medical advice on a range of topics?'

Robina smiled, her perfect teeth a flash of white against her deep copper skin. Niall felt something shift low in his belly. God, he loved her smile. It was one of the first things he had noticed about her. It lit up the room.

'I have a team of experts who work with me. They provide most of the answers because you're quite right—there is no way I could be an expert on all the different conditions we cover. All I do is translate the medical jargon into simple language the patients and viewers can understand. All of us have been in situations where we didn't grasp everything the doctor was telling us, partly because we didn't know the right questions to ask.'

'I have a clip from one of your programmes to show the audience.'

The snide smile on Richard's face made Niall uneasy, and he wondered if his wife knew what she could be letting herself in for. A couple of minutes of a show Robina had presented on autism came up on the screen. She was sharing a sofa with parents who had children with the illness. Opposite them on a separate sofa were the experts who were there to answer questions. It was evident as the couples spoke that Robina's empathy was genuine. As the screen faded Richard turned to her again.

'Before we talk about your future projects and your books, tell us a little about yourself. What about the woman behind the medical degree?'

'I was born in South Africa,' Robina answered with a smile. 'My mother is a journalist, and my father was Xhosa. He used to be a lawyer and a political activist. He died just over five years ago.'

'Isn't that how you started? As a journalist? What made you decide to take up medicine?'

'I was sent to Sudan to cover a refugee camp there,' she said. Niall saw something shift in his wife's eyes. 'The conditions were awful, completely unbearable. There was so little anyone could do. But there was a team of doctors and nurses and other outreach workers who were there, doing a tremendous job. I watched them work for three weeks and realised that medicine was the career for me. I wanted to do something—not just report it.'

'But yet here you are, working as a high-profile TV personality. Not exactly front line medicine, is it?'

Ouch, Niall thought. He'd suspected all along that Richard hadn't brought Robina onto the show for a cosy chat. He felt his fingers curl into fists.

'No.'

Niall sighed with relief when Robina refused to let the presenter rattle her.

'But one thing I did realise, after working as a doctor in a similar scenario when I finished my training, was that what really makes a difference is education and information. Doctors do what they can in these situations, but really it's just like sticking plaster on a wound. Without going to the source of the problem, we will never reach a long-lasting solution.'

'So tell me how all this relates to your work here in the UK.'

Richard's smile made him look like a shark. Niall would have given anything to wipe the supercilious grin off his face.

'It doesn't,' Robina admitted. 'But what I do is provide information to as many people as I can. Take my book on infertility, for example. If it helps even one person understand what the process involves, or points them in the right direction to find help, it can only be good. And as for the clip we have just seen, autistic spectrum disorder affects far more of the general population than most people realise. There was so much incorrect information given out about the MMR vaccine and its association with ASD that people stopped immunising their children, with a resultant increase in measles. The clip you have just seen is an attempt to share the challenges of living with an autistic child as well as debunking some of the myths that have sprung up around this condition.'

'Apart from making you a substantial amount of money,' Richard said snidely.

'Most of which I put into programmes that provide immunisations and clean water to the people in war-torn countries such as Sudan,' Robina replied without missing a beat.

Niall was taken aback. She had never told him that. It was hardly surprising since they barely spoke let alone discussed their individual bank accounts. He was beginning to realise that there was a lot more to his wife than he had suspected.

Her answer obviously took Richard by surprise too. For a moment the smile faltered, but then it was back. 'That's not public knowledge,' Richard said.

'No reason it should be.' Robina smiled sweetly, but Niall could see a hint of iron in her eyes. 'What I choose to do with my money is private.'

Niall was beginning to enjoy himself. 'Way to go, Robina!' he called out, only to find Ella looking at him with bafflement.

'Way to go, Mummy,' she chimed in anyway, making Niall laugh. God, he loved his daughter.

'Let's discuss your latest project,' Richard continued. 'I understand you are doing a documentary following women undergoing IVF treatment?'

'That's right. It will be airing in the autumn.'

'Don't you think it's a little invasive? After all, these women are going through a particularly difficult time in their lives.'

'I couldn't agree more. That's why only those women who wish to take part are filmed. We make it clear they can withdraw their consent at any time. But most of them want others to know what it's like to undergo treatment. A book can't really show the reality. It can be a terribly difficult and unpleasant experience for women and as my documentary will show, women are only prepared to put themselves through it because their need for a child is so overwhelming.'

'Do you think IVF is good use of scarce resources?' Once again the shark-like glint was back in Richard's eyes. 'After all, as you have so eloquently pointed out, there are so many other places where funding is needed.'

'Do you have children of your own, Richard?' There was a dangerous sparkle in Robina's eyes.

He nodded.

'When you watch my documentary, one of the things that will become clear is how much these women want children. If they can be helped, why deny them?'

'Especially when it helps make your husband richer. I understand he works in the private sector as well as the NHS. I'm sure the publicity of your film will do his business no harm. Quite the contrary, it's bound to generate quite a bit of income for him, wouldn't you say?' This time there was no mistaking the look in Richard's eyes—he had pinned his prey, now he was going to finish her off. Niall groaned aloud. He'd had a bad feeling about this appearance all along. He should have listened to his gut and tried to talk her out of it.

But it seemed once more he had underestimated his wife. She smiled. 'Yes, I can see why you might think there is a conflict of interests. But I can assure you, my husband makes no personal profit from his private work. He uses any income from fee-paying patients to subsidise those who can't afford it and who aren't eligible for treatment on the NHS. Any funding left over goes to research. I'm sure you know that he is a world leader in this area? His research has involved looking at taking ovarian tissue from teenage girls with cancer prior to treatment. This may be the only way these young women will be able to have children. Before, it was an impossibility, now there is hope. His research also involves polycystic ovary syndrome, one of the main causes of infertility but also a factor in significantly increasing morbidity in this group of women.'

Niall sat bolt upright. How did she know all this? Not about his reputation, that was why she had sought him out back when they had met, but about him not taking any profit from the business? Just as she hadn't shared her finances with him, neither had he felt the need to share his with her. She must have winkled the information out of Lucinda, he guessed. Part of her journalistic training. That would teach him to underestimate his wife.

'I should also tell you that my husband takes none of the profit from any new treatments his research generates. He believes that new discoveries in science shouldn't belong to an individual but to society as a whole.'

Could he be hearing right? Niall thought, growing more surprised by the minute. But was that pride he heard in her voice?

Applause broke out from the audience. Robina had clearly disconcerted Richard. Her response not what the presenter had expected.

'Oh? But you live an affluent lifestyle, don't you? A large house in one of the more expensive parts of Edinburgh, a couple of flash cars, holidays abroad.'

'I have explained my finances as far as I'm prepared to,' Robina replied coolly. 'I'm sure you wouldn't want me to ask you publicly about yours.' She arched an eyebrow at Richard. Once more Niall felt like cheering. Obviously she knew something about Richard that wasn't in the public domain. Once again, it seemed that she had put her investigative skills to good use.

'Returning to your documentary for a moment,' Richard continued. Although the famous smile was still fixed to his face, the strain was beginning to show. 'Do you really think that you can empathise with the women appearing in your documentary? What would you know about the pain they are going through?'

Niall caught his breath. This was different, much more dangerous. Ella who, since his outburst, had been watching quietly, eyes fixed to the screen, looked up at her father.

'What is it, Daddy? What did that man say to make you angry?'

Niall put his finger to her lips. 'Not now, darling.' He could hardly bear to watch as he saw the emotions flit across his wife's face. He saw shock, pain and confusion. It seemed, like Niall, she had realised that Richard knew about the miscarriage. The presenter was too clever to ask her outright, knowing that she would wonder how he had found out. Apart from the hospital staff involved in her care, only Robina, her mother and he knew. But clearly there had been a breach of confidentiality somewhere.

For a long moment Robina sat in silence and Niall wanted to put his hand through the TV screen and strangle Richard Christchurch. But then she sat up straight and slowly crossed one leg over another, only the tell-tale nibbling of her lower lip indicating to Niall how anxious she was.

'I can empathise,' she said slowly, 'because following a miscarriage a few months ago, which resulted in an infection, the likelihood is that I too am infertile.' Her eyes shimmered and she blinked furiously.

Niall could only guess at the strength it had taken her to say the words live on TV. Especially when she had been unable to even talk to him about it. Hadn't talked to anyone as far as he knew, except perhaps for her mother, but he didn't even know that for certain.

Richard's jaw dropped, her response apparently not what he was expecting, or hoping for.

'I am sorry,' he said insincerely. 'I had no idea.'

'It's not really something that has come up,' Robina said quietly. 'Obviously it is not a secret, but neither is it something I have spoken about in public before. But I think you would agree that I am well placed to be doing the documentary.'

She turned and looked directly into the camera, raising her chin. 'When my show returns, we will be covering miscarriage. I ask anyone who has gone through this and wishes to share their experiences on TV to get in touch with the producers of my show. But for you out there, for whom it is all still too raw, you are in my thoughts and my prayers.' She blinked rapidly once or twice. Niall knew that anyone else would have let the tears fall, letting their public know that they too were human. But not his Robina. She could never pretend in public what she could barely allow herself to feel in private, and he admired her for it. But at the same time he wondered what keeping it all inside was costing her.

After Ella was in bed, Niall poured himself a whisky, stoked the fire and waited for his wife to come home.

He looked around the small sitting room she had made her own and felt a wave of sadness wash over him.

The cosy room was still exactly how it had been when Mairead had been alive except for one item; a small, intricately carved African stool Robina had brought with her.

It hit him like a sledgehammer. He'd never really thought about it before, but what had it been like for her to live here surrounded by his first wife's belongings and her taste in furnishings? Although he liked the little room with its plain white sofas, elegant furnishings and pale walls, it wasn't Robina's taste. He knew enough about his wife to know she preferred richer, more vibrant colours, abstract paintings instead of landscapes. In fact, her taste couldn't be further from his first wife's.

Picking up his whisky, he started pacing. What a blind, stubborn fool he had been. Why hadn't he realised what it must have been like for Robina? To come to a strange country, to live in the house he had once shared with his wife, to look after her child? He had been only too glad to know that Ella had someone who loved her, but if he were honest with himself he had been resentful of the way Robina's career had got in the way of the life he had thought they had mapped out. He had treated her as if she were some kind of replacement for his first wife. Not a woman in her own right with her own needs and desires. Stupidly he had thought that their love for one another was enough. Seeing her on TV just now had removed the last vestige of self-delusion from his eyes. She was lonely and lost and he had failed her when she had needed him the most. He had refused to see how much living Mairead's life had eaten away at her confidence. They had married without really knowing each other, and again that had been his fault. Having fallen deeply in love with her, he hadn't been able to bear her living several thousands of miles away, and had persuaded her to marry him, although they had barely known each other. And she had unquestioningly uprooted herself from everything she had known and loved to live with him and his daughter in Scotland.

And she had mentioned the miscarriage. Publicly. What strength that must have taken when she couldn't even talk to him about it. Did that mean she was beginning to come to terms with it at last?

He drained his whisky. Somehow he needed to win his wife back, make her believe he loved her and only her. Make her understand that he could no more live without her than cut off his right arm. It was probably too late, he thought miserably, but he was going to try. Damn it! He was going to do more than try. Suddenly inspiration hit him. He had a plan. All it would take would be patience.

CHAPTER SEVEN

'DADDY says we're going out all together today. And I can choose.' Ella was practically hopping from foot to foot in her excitement. It was Saturday and for once neither Robina nor Niall planned to go into work.

Niall lowered his paper and looked at Robina. 'If that's all right? We did promise her.'

'I think it's a great idea,' Robina said, ruffling Ella's hair. 'We're all yours, sweetheart. Where do you fancy going?'

'I can't make up my mind. Swimming or ice-skating or the beach.'

Robina shuddered. 'I think it's a little cold for the beach. And I'm a hopeless ice-skater and not much cop in the water either.'

'How do you know you can't ice-skate?' Niall asked, cocking his eyebrow at her. 'Have you ever tried?'

'Not exactly,' Robina admitted. 'But I have two left feet, so I'm bound to be hopeless.'

'You can't be hopeless. You are good at everything,' Ella replied. 'Anyway, Daddy can't skate either. Can you, Daddy?'

'That's what you think, pumpkin.' Niall chucked his daughter under the chin. 'Just wait until you see my moves.'

'He can't even dance,' Ella said scornfully. 'My first

mummy said he always stood on her feet.' She looked glum for a moment. 'At least I think she said that. I can't really remember her any more.'

'Tell you what,' Robina interrupted hastily, hoping to distract Ella. 'There's a place I know, not too far from here, that I hear has a swimming pool with lots of slides, and an ice rink. What if I go swimming with you and Daddy takes you ice-skating, then we can all have dinner together? How does that sound?'

But to her dismay, Ella shook her head. 'You said I would have both of you—together.'

Niall rose from the table. 'So we did. And so you shall. If we have to pull Robina around the rink, so be it. Off you go then, and get your costume.'

Ella shot upstairs as if she were scared Niall would change his mind.

Niall grinned at Robina and her heart flipped. Damn the man, why did he still have the power to make her pulse race? It would be so much easier if she didn't still fancy him rotten. It had been so long since they had spent any time together and, despite the horrors of the ice-rink in store, Robina couldn't help but look forward to spending time with Niall and Ella. Perhaps this could be the start of them being a proper family?

'I'll just go and get my costume as well then,' Robina said, feeling suddenly shy under Niall's amused stare. 'I may not be able to ice skate, and not be much of a swimmer, but I can paddle with the best of them.'

The pool was busy with schoolchildren and the noise was deafening when Robina and Ella emerged from the changing rooms. Ella was wearing water-wings, but Robina warned her to stay close in case she got into difficulty. As soon as they spotted Niall, looking lean and sexy as hell in his Bermudas, Ella ran up to him, dragging Robina by the hand.

Robina was acutely aware of Niall's eyes raking her body. She felt the heat rise in her cheeks as his eyes travelled from her face down to her toes and back up to her face. He could only have looked at her for a couple of seconds, but to Robina, her body tingling under his gaze, it felt like for ever. She resisted the impulse to shield her body from his gaze. Once he had known every inch of her, and she of him. She recalled the scar he had below his left shoulder, where he had fallen from his bike as a child. She remembered tracing the grooves with her tongue, after tracing the contours of the raised skin with her fingertips. And how Niall had whipped over and grabbed her hands, pulling her down on top of him, kissing her until she was breathless. And then slowly, ever so slowly he had… She shook her head, horrified to feel languorous warmth spreading across her body. She had to stop thinking like that. She had to stop thinking of how it used to be, or she would go mad. But from the way his eyes darkened she guessed he was remembering too. Whatever their differences now, there had been a time when they hadn't been able to keep their hands off each other.

Thankfully, Ella was oblivious to the tension between her parents and was soon dragging them up several flights of steps to the slide. Robina tried to protest, the thought of being even the height of the slide frightening her, but one look at Ella's face and she knew she had to put her fears aside. This was Ella's day and Robina wanted it to be perfect.

Ella insisted that Niall go down the slide first, and then she followed, leaving Robina to go last. Telling herself she was being ridiculous to be scared and holding her nose, Robina flung herself down the slide and was soon caught up in a circular basin which spun her around in ever-decreasing circles. Taken by surprise, she let go of her nose and by the time she plunged into the bottom pool, she was gasping and spluttering. Her head popped up and then Niall was by her side, grabbing her under her arms. Instinctively, she wrapped her legs around his waist to keep her head out of the water. Niall's hands tightened around her waist and she felt her body being pressed into his. Despite her panic, she could feel the heat of his muscles through the cool water and the solid strength of his hips supporting her. Again there was that dizzying sense of the world spinning. She looked down to find Niall looking up at her, his expression unreadable. All of a sudden he released her and in her surprise she sank beneath the water again. This time he grabbed her arms and dragged her unceremoniously to the edge of the pool where Ella was waiting in fits of giggles.

'I thought you said you could swim,' Ella accused Robina, still laughing.

'I can swim,' Robina said, trying to hang onto her dignity. 'But no one told me about that bowl thing. It took me by surprise.' She was damned if she was going to admit there was *another* thing she couldn't do. Mairead probably swam in the Olympics, she thought bitterly. And then as Ella and Niall shared a grin, she had to laugh. She wagged her finger at the pair of them. 'Just you wait, you two, I'll get my own back.'

But her fear had left her, and for the next hour they swam and slid down slides and splashed each other in the wave machine. Robina couldn't remember the last time she'd had so much fun. It was the first time since she had lost the baby that she hadn't felt an overwhelming sense of loss and sadness. It was almost as if they had put the last few terrible months behind them and were the family they had been in those early, blissful weeks following their marriage. Seeing Niall laugh, Robina realised that it had been a long time, far too long, since she had seen him so relaxed and carefree. Why hadn't they tried to do something like this before? How could they both have been so stubborn? Even if their marriage was dead, was there a chance that they could be friends at least?

Ice-skating turned out to be just as embarrassing as Robina had expected. She just couldn't get the hang of gliding forward on her skates; instead she pushed herself around like a baby giraffe finding its legs for the first time, while holding onto the side. Niall and Ella, on the other hand, soon had the hang of it, and while not contestants for the next celebrity ice-skating TV programme, were making valiant attempts at getting around the rink.

Eventually they skated up to her.

'If we hold your hand, can you let go of the side?' Ella asked.

Robina could see that Niall was having difficulty controlling his amusement.

'I don't think so, darling.' Robina said. 'I will definitely fall on my bottom if I do.'

'No, you won't. Not if we hold onto you.'

Reluctantly Robina gave in and with Niall holding one hand and Ella on the other they skated off, with Robina doing her best not to wobble. Soon they had completed a circuit, but just when she thought she might be getting the hang of it, she tripped, pulling Niall and Ella down in an untidy heap beside her.

Robina hoped that with her woolly hat pulled low on her ears, no one would recognise her. The last thing she wanted was to spoil the day, or to have pictures in the press of her collapsed on the ice. Somehow she doubted her viewers would be impressed to see the normally cool and collected Dr Robina Zondi making an enormous idiot of herself.

Still grinning, Niall got to his feet and helped Robina to stand. But as he pulled her up, she lost her footing again and fell against him, knocking him to the ice with her on top of him. Ella stood by, watching, in a fit of giggles.

The world stopped as Robina felt the length of Niall's body underneath hers. Once again, the feel of him brought vivid memories back of their love-making. She looked into his eyes to find him regarding her with what? Pain? Hurt? Desire? She couldn't tell. Hastily, she scrambled to her feet.

'I think I've had enough,' she said, hoping that Niall would put her breathlessness down to her exertion. 'You two carry on for a bit while I grab us some burgers and drinks.'

Ella protested half-heartedly, but Robina could tell she was happy to have her father to herself for a little bit. They accompanied her back to the side, and she left them to it.

As she waited for them to join her, Robina thought back to her earlier resolve. She was the one who had pushed Niall away after the miscarriage and it was up to her to make the first move. On the other hand, Niall wanted more children, children she couldn't give him… She shook her head. What was the point? She kept going round in circles. She needed to speak to someone. Maybe her mother? Although she hated the thought of revealing the pathetic state of her marriage to Grace, she had to talk to someone.

Later that evening, once a happy but tired out Ella was in bed, Niall joined Robina in her sitting room. She had showered and was wrapped in her silky dressing gown, toasting her feet in front of the fire.

'It was a good day,' he said softly, coming to stand beside her. 'We should do it more often.'

'I know,' Robina said equally softly. 'Ella had so much fun.'

'Why don't we rent a cottage near Ella's grandparents for the weekend?' Niall suggested. 'Ella hasn't seen Mairead's parents since we got married and they are desperate to see her and her them.'

Robina's heart skipped a beat. Did he want to spend time with her or with Ella? And did it matter? She had promised Ella a trip, but the thought of being away with Niall was unsettling.

His eyes were on hers, and if she hadn't known better, she would think that her reply really mattered.

'There are some great easy walks, and some of the most beautiful hills in Scotland to climb. I haven't really had a chance to show you my country,' he coaxed.

'Okay,' she said finally. 'Why not? I'll ask my PA to try and find something in the area, shall I?'

'No,' he said firmly. 'I'll arrange it. I have the perfect place in mind.'

'Oh?' Robina felt a chill run down her spine. 'Somewhere you and Mairead stayed?'

'For God's sake, Robina. Of course not. I'm not that in-sensitive.' He pulled a hand through his thick dark hair then smiled sheepishly. 'Sorry. I know I deserved that. No, it's nowhere Mairead and I have ever been and you don't have to do anything except pack a bag. I'll see to everything else. In fact, I've already booked it for this weekend.'

Monday was spent watching Niall in Theatre as he collected eggs from three patients. He looked more relaxed than Robina had seen him for a long time. Gone was the distant, polite man she shared her home with. Instead, here was the man she had met twelve months before—the man she had fallen in love with.

As he worked he seemed oblivious to the camera, explain-ing to each of the patients exactly what he was doing and why.

Every now and again he would catch Robina's eye as if he wanted to be reassured that she was okay.

The last patient of the day was a young, single woman. Maisie had been an unexpected appointment so Robina hadn't had the opportunity to meet her in advance. However, as soon as the woman, a pretty redhead in her mid twenties, had heard about the filming she had been adamant she wanted to be part of it.

'I want other people in my situation to know if there is anything that can be done,' she said firmly.

Maisie was attending with her mother. At twenty-four, Maisie wasn't married, not even in a relationship, but earlier in the week she had received the devastating news that she had cervical cancer. Luckily the doctors had caught it in time, so while Maisie would need to undergo chemotherapy, as well as radiotherapy, the prognosis was very good. However, the treatment that would save her life would destroy her ovaries and any chance of her having children. Maisie was still reeling from the news that she had cancer, but she was friendly with one of the specialist nurses at the clinic who had suggested she see Niall.

'They've told me that it's likely I'll go through the menopause as a result of the treatment,' she said quietly, but Robina could see from the whiteness of her knuckles as she gripped her hands together that she was struggling to maintain her composure. 'And that it means that it is unlikely I'll be able to have children. Hearing that was almost the worst thing about finding out about the illness. The doctors reckon that with treatment I should make a full recovery, but that I should accept that children aren't for me.' Her voice cracked a little. But she took a deep breath and continued. 'I have always wanted children. Ever since I can remember. I can't bear it if I can't. Mairi said you might be able to help me.'

Niall leaned forward in his chair. His voice was gentle. 'The most important thing is to ensure that your illness is treated successfully. You do realise that?'

'Of course. I know that they wouldn't recommend I have chemo and radiotherapy unless it was necessary, but they say they won't be starting until next month.'

'When I read the referral letter from your GP, I phoned your oncologist,' Niall continued. 'I wanted to be clear what the treatment plan was before we spoke. I didn't want to get your hopes up.'

The spark of hope in Maisie's eyes cut Robina to the core. Why was life so unfair? Just when the woman in front of her thought she had everything to look forward to, her dreams were snatched away.

'When did you last have a period?' Niall asked.

When Maisie told him, Niall looked satisfied. 'The timing is good, then,' he said. 'What we can do is to stimulate your ovaries to produce eggs, then freeze them using a process called vitrification. Then later, when you are ready, we could thaw them and fertilise them with your partner's sperm. It would give you a chance at a pregnancy. Your oncologist would be happy for us to treat you as long as we act quickly. I'm afraid it doesn't give you much time to think, but it is an option.'

Tears were rolling down Maisie's cheeks and Robina felt tears prick her own eyes. She blinked rapidly. Despite the tears, hope had brightened Maisie's eyes. Robina just hoped Niall knew what he was doing. Surely he wouldn't take chances with this young woman? What use would she be to a child if she were no longer alive to care for it?

'But won't the hormones you need to give her speed up the spread of her cancer?' Maisie's mother asked anxiously.

'Because, darling, if they do, can't you see it's not worth taking the chance?'

'I wouldn't recommend this course of action if I wasn't absolutely certain that it won't affect the outcome of Maisie's treatment,' Niall said. 'The level of hormones we use in order to stimulate your own hormones is tiny compared to that which floods a pregnant woman's body. The latest research shows that the amount we would be giving you, along with the very short time span you'd be receiving the hormones, has no material effect on your cancer, but of course it's entirely up to Maisie. All I can do is tell you what is possible, along with the pros and cons—but the decision is entirely up to you.'

'Mairi said if anyone could help, it would be you.' Maisie smiled before turning to her mother and taking her hand in hers. 'Mum, I need to do this, do you understand? Can you support me? I don't want to live if it means not ever being able to have children. And my treatment won't be starting for a few weeks anyway.'

'You can always adopt, darling. Have you thought about that?'

'I could, Mum. Possibly. But who knows if it would ever happen? There's such a shortage of babies. Besides, I know this is really selfish of me, but I want a child that is mine genetically. If it is at all possible.'

'Well then, my love, it's up to you.' Maisie's mother tried a smile, but it didn't quite work. 'I'll go along with whatever you want.'

Maisie hugged her mother. 'Thanks, Mum. I don't want to go through this alone. I need you with me every step of the way.' Then the two women were in each other's arms, crying as if their hearts would break. Niall indicated with a nod of his head that they should be left in privacy.

Robina mumbled an excuse and fled for the privacy of the ladies' toilet. How could Niall do this every day and not be affected? she wondered. And what about the nursing staff? They saw the patients on a regular basis throughout their treatment, became involved, she knew they did, because they had told her it was impossible not to. But they had all said that for each sad and disappointing outcome, there would be successes, some against all odds. And they had hundreds of photographs of happy families to prove it.

She had to keep believing that. Just because life had been unbearably cruel to her, it didn't mean that these women didn't have every chance. The irony was that it was Niall who was helping them when he was patently unable to help her.

CHAPTER EIGHT

BY THE time Robina finished for the day, she was emotionally exhausted and looking forward to spending some time with Ella. After she had read her a story, she would work on her book before collapsing into bed. Sometimes she wondered if it *was* all too much, the filming and the writing. Most people would be happy with just one career and she had two. Perhaps she was tearing herself into pieces just trying to prove she could do it all? But prove it to whom? Niall, herself—or her dead father? The time off she had promised Ella was her first break from work since her marriage. Robina felt a shiver of guilt, remembering that she and Niall hadn't even taken a honeymoon because of her work schedule.

The thought of the weekend away was becoming more appealing by the minute. Even if it did mean Niall and her circling each other like two wary tigers. But since their day out with Ella the tension between them had eased. So perhaps it was what she and Niall both needed. But how would they cope? Thrust into one another's company for two whole days? Her heart rate upped a notch. Maybe they could build on the fragile truce of the day out.

Her thoughts turned to her mother. She missed her terribly.

Something was worrying her—that much was obvious to Robina from their last phone call, no matter how much her mother tried to pretend nothing was wrong. Perhaps she should go and see her? They were due to have a break from filming in a couple of weeks. She could take Ella with her—show her Africa, and introduce her to her family. Her spirits lifted. It was an appealing thought—a couple of weeks back in the country she yearned for, with her mother, would give her time to think at least.

Once Ella was tucked up in bed, Robina popped a lamb joint into the oven and left it cooking while she ran herself a bath. Perhaps Niall would be home in time to join her for dinner. If so, she could discuss her plan with him then. It would give them something to talk about and would make a change from the usual fraught mealtimes where they both struggled to find something uncontroversial to talk about.

The slamming of the door signalled Niall's arrival home and Robina felt the predictable squeezing of her heart. This was the bit where he should be calling out to her, running up the stairs to take her in his arms…then they would make love, uncaring that dinner was ruined.

Wrapping herself in her dressing gown, she went to greet him. He was shaking the rain off his coat. Robina's breath caught in her throat as she took in his damp hair. He looks tired, she thought anxiously. Tired, but devastatingly handsome. As she looked at him the thought hit her like a sledgehammer. She still loved him. Completely and hopelessly. All this talk about staying together for Ella's sake was only half-true. A life without Niall was no life at all.

'Robina! Is something wrong? Is Ella all right?'

He looked surprised to see her waiting for him. Once again her heart contracted. They had both been so stubborn.

They had been in love once; surely he couldn't have lost all feeling for her?

'Ella's fine. She's sleeping. I thought we might have dinner together,' she said, feeling a blush steal over her cheeks. 'And have a chat.'

'What about?' His voice was flat. 'Is there something about the documentary you want to discuss? Because I have to tell you, I'm tired and not really in the mood.'

'No, it's not work,' Robina retorted, disappointment making her brusque. 'I was thinking of taking a couple of weeks and going to see Mum. I wondered about taking Ella with me.'

They moved into the kitchen where delicious smells were emanating from the oven. Niall cocked an eyebrow in Robina's direction, but said nothing, instead taking his place at the table.

'Why now?' he asked. 'I thought we agreed that we both needed to spend time with Ella. Or had you forgotten?'

'I miss Mum,' Robina said as she removed the lamb from the oven. She had made dauphinoise potatoes and green beans to go with the roast. Somehow the potatoes looked more like mash and the lamb was burnt at the edges, but at least the beans were fine, if a little limp and anaemic-looking.

'I just know something's bothering her, and I'd like to find out what. Apart from my brothers, who have their own families, she's all I've got.'

Neil winced then dragged his hand through his hair.

'We're your family now, Robina,' he said quietly.

'Are you? I want to believe that, but I don't know if I can.'

'I thought that's why we were going away this weekend. So we can try to be a family again. Or have you already decided that it's not going to work?' He narrowed his eyes at her. 'Are you thinking of going back to South Africa for good, Robina? Because if you are, you'd better tell me.'

'No! Of course not!' Robina replied. 'I told you and Ella I wouldn't leave, and I have no intention of doing so. Niall, why are we going round in circles like this? All I want is some time with my mother. I thought Ella would enjoy the trip. We're still going away this weekend, aren't we? And I have every intention of making it a happy couple of days.' She pushed the lamb towards Niall. 'Would you carve?' she said.

Niall attacked the roast with the sharp knife and manfully tried to cut a slice, without much success.

'Shall I get the saw from the garden shed?' Robina suggested, and suddenly they were both laughing. Niall managed to carve enough for them to share and the earlier tension drifted away as they chatted about the documentary. Watching Niall as they talked, Robina revelled in the companionship she had missed for so long. It was a start; a small step in the right direction. Her sore heart began to ease.

It was late on Friday by the time they set off. Niall had been held up at the hospital. Although he wasn't on call, one of his patients had gone into labour and Niall had stayed to do her C-section.

'I'm sorry, Robina,' he had apologised when he'd eventually made it home. 'I promised her I'd deliver her baby and I just couldn't let her down.' He sat down at the kitchen table and rubbed a tired hand across his forehead.

'What happened?' Robina asked. There had been a time when they'd spend the evenings discussing their patients, sharing the ups and downs of their medical lives, but it had been a long time since they had done that. Robina handed Niall a coffee and waited.

'She had a stillbirth at thirty-five weeks in her last pregnancy. We don't know why. God, Robina, it still beats me that we lose babies, even now when we have all this technology at our disposal, and we don't know why.'

Robina felt the familiar sharp stab of pain.

'I would have done anything to have been able to save our baby. You do know that, don't you?' Niall said gently.

Robina closed her eyes, hearing the undercurrent of sadness in his words. 'I know, Niall. There was nothing anyone could do.' She took a deep breath, summoning her courage while trying to find the words to tell him how she felt, but before she could say anything, Ella skipped in and sidled up to her father. Niall put his arm around his daughter and pulled her close.

'Every baby we lose is a blow.' He glanced up and Robina sucked in her breath at the naked pain in his eyes.

They sat in silence for a few minutes, watching Ella, who had climbed up on a chair and was rooting around in the kitchen cupboards.

'Sabrina was naturally worried the same thing would happen in this pregnancy,' Niall continued. 'So I agreed to let her have an elective section. It was supposed to be this afternoon, but then I had to take another patient to Theatre who was an emergency. I'll tell you about that later,' he said with a quick glance at Ella, who appeared to have found what she was looking for—her favourite mug. 'Anyway, the emergency took most of the afternoon, so we couldn't do Sabrina's section until after five. But, she had a healthy baby girl and is absolutely delighted. So all's well that ends well.' He grinned at her and Robina's heart did a flip-flop. The way he cared about his patients was one of the things she loved most about him.

'Maybe we should leave tomorrow morning instead?' Robina suggested. 'Ella will be ready for bed by the time we get there.'

'No,' Ella protested. 'I want to go tonight. You promised.

And I'm all ready to go now I've got my cup.' She set her mouth in a mutinous line. She had been excited all day and Robina knew they couldn't let her down. Ella had even packed her own suitcase, although when Robina checked it she found it full of books and toys and not much else, and had had to pack another, more appropriate case for her.

'It's not too late, surely?' Niall said. 'I packed before I left for work this morning, so I'm ready.'

Robina gave in and soon they were following the winding roads that led them to the Highlands. She had never been to the north of Scotland before and she was looking forward to seeing more of her adopted country.

After a couple of hours they pulled up outside a cottage that seemed to be set in the middle of nowhere. Dark, gloomy mountains rose out of the darkness. There were no lights to be seen for miles. Where had Niall brought them? Where were the shops, the restaurants? What on earth were they going to do for the two days?

Predictably, Ella had fallen asleep and they left her in the car while they went to open up the cottage. As promised, keys had been left in the door.

The cottage was tiny and freezing. Again Robina wondered what Niall had been thinking. There was a stove on one side of the kitchen and an open fire on the other side, which obviously served as a small sitting room. Upstairs, Robina was aghast to find that there was only one bedroom.

'Where is the other bedroom?' she said to Niall. 'I imagined there would be at least two.'

Niall was looking baffled and dismayed. 'I'm sorry, Robina. Believe me, it's not what I expected. The website described it as luxurious with all mod cons.' He grimaced. 'I guess we can say they were a little economical with the truth.'

He looked so woebegone that Robina had to laugh. 'Never mind. We'll just have to make the best of it. We can all sleep together in the bed—it'll be a bit of a squash but, seeing as it's just for a couple of nights, I'm sure we'll manage.' All the same, a little part of her felt disappointed that she and Niall wouldn't be sleeping together alone. Even so, the thought of sharing a bed with Niall again, even with Ella beside them, was making her pulse race.

'Why don't you bring Ella in while I make us something hot to drink?' she said, keeping her voice steady. 'Then we'll see what can be done about the fire.'

Once Ella was tucked up in bed, Robina and Niall set about the fire. But the old-fashioned stove was nothing like either of them had ever seen before and soon they were forced to concede defeat.

'I'll have a look at it in the morning,' Niall said. 'There's not much point in persevering at the moment. Let's go to bed.'

There was nothing else for it. Robina was freezing and there was no way either of them could spend the night in the chair.

'I'll just use the bathroom, unless you want to go first?' she said. The room was suddenly alive with unbearable tension. Niall simply nodded.

Robina spent ages in the bathroom, first trying to get warm water out of the shower and when that didn't happen making do with lukewarm water at the sink. After washing as best she could, she slipped on the warm flannel pyjamas she had brought, refusing to think about the silky nightdress she had also packed in her suitcase. Eventually, realising she couldn't possibly spend any more time lurking in the bathroom, Robina abandoned the sanctuary. Niall was exhausted and would no doubt be looking forward to a good night's sleep—even if she wouldn't get a wink.

She slipped out of the bathroom, feeling ridiculously self-conscious. She hadn't felt this way since the night of their wedding—the same unsettling mixture of excitement and nerves. Niall had respected her views on sex before marriage and although it had been hard on *both* of them, the wait had made that night even more special. Not just special—sensational. Just thinking about it sent waves of heat and desire coursing through her body.

But she needn't have worried. Niall had obviously become fed up waiting for her to vacate the bathroom and had used the kitchen sink to clean his teeth before slipping into bed, with Ella curled up beside him on the far side. In the semi-darkness, Robina couldn't tell if he was asleep, but from the sound of rhythmic breathing it appeared he was.

Tentatively, trying not to disturb him, she slipped under the blankets, shivering as she felt the cool sheets on her skin. She lay there for a few seconds scared to move a muscle in case she woke Niall.

But it seemed as if she had been mistaken.

'You're cold,' Niall's deep voice said. 'Come here and let me warm you.' Robina felt his hand touch her shoulder and the shock of it was almost enough to make her leap out of bed. 'You're perfectly safe,' he said, and she could hear a hint of laughter under his words.

He rolled over and pulled her into the crook of his arm. She lay there rigidly, breathing in the familiar scent of soap from his skin. From his touch she knew he was naked—above the waist at least. Niall never wore pyjamas, and she absolutely refused to think about the lower half. She could feel the heat radiating from his body, the hard muscle of his shoulder underneath her, his fingertips just brushing her arm.

Robina was trembling but she knew it wasn't from the

cold. It felt so good to be back in his arms, deliciously warm and safe, and she wondered what would have happened if Ella hadn't been sleeping right next to them. Would she have been able to stop herself from snuggling closer and running her fingertips over the hard, once-so-familiar contours of his body? Would they have made love, then talked into the night? Would Niall have told her he still loved her? But to her dismay and chagrin, she heard his breathing deepen and realised he had fallen asleep. Suddenly she was furious. How could he? How could he just fall asleep with her in his arms? As if it meant nothing and he was completely unaffected by her? Grumpily, she rolled away from him and onto her side. It was more proof, as if she needed it, that their marriage was dead in the water.

On the other side of the bed, Niall was acutely aware of every inch of his wife's body as she lay next to him. He smiled, thinking that everything was going according to plan. Well, almost. Okay, the cottage wasn't exactly the way he had thought it would be, but he had known it only had one bed and that they would have to share it. He had already suggested to Ella's grandparents that Ella stay with them tomorrow night, giving him the opportunity to get his wife on her own. He bit back a groan. If it wasn't for Ella, he wouldn't have been able to stop himself from seducing his wife and, remembering the feel of Robina's hammering heart underneath his fingertips when he had held her close, he doubted if this time she would have pushed him away. As it was, he could do with a cold shower or a freezing walk, because there was no way he was going to be able to sleep feeling the way he did. It was driving him crazy, seeing her every day and not being able to make love to her. He couldn't stop the memory of her long legs wrapped around his, her head thrown back, her long neck arched as she lost herself in their love-making. Did she have any idea what sweet torture it was having her back in his bed but not able to touch her? Sweet God, the sooner he had his wife back—heart and soul—the better.

CHAPTER NINE

WHEN Robina woke up she was alone in the bed and the delicious scent of fresh coffee was filtering through the air. She could hear the rattle of plates and Ella's excited whispers.

She eased herself out from under the covers and was pleasantly surprised to find that the house was warm.

'Good morning,' Niall said as she stretched. 'Did you sleep well?' He grinned at her and her heart flipped. Had he any idea how much of the night she had spent tossing and turning? But he, he had slept like a baby, she fumed inwardly.

'I managed to get the fire going,' Niall said, pretending not to notice that she was glaring at him. 'Once I could see what I was doing, it was quite easy.'

'And we've been to the shops,' Ella chimed in, 'to get rolls for breakfast. I'm going to help Daddy make it, then we're going for a walk, then we're going to have lunch, then I'm going to see Gran and Grandpa.' When she stopped to draw a breath, Robina laughed and ruffled her hair.

'Then I'd better get dressed, hadn't I?' She remembered about the shower. Damn, it would have to be the sink again. But she slid a glance at Niall. His hair was still a little damp at the front. Had he braved the cold water?

He flashed her another heart-stopping grin. 'Come here,' he demanded. Tentatively, Robina stepped close to him. 'See this little switch here? You have to press that if you want the shower to work.' He patted her head as if she were no older than Ella. Little did he know that Robina had started to keep score. She'd get him back—one way or another.

After her shower, Robin dressed warmly in figure-hugging jeans and her favourite cashmere sweater, before adding a pair of thick socks. She wasn't going to take any chances with the weather, especially if Niall planned to get her up a hill.

Breakfast was a mixed affair. They had managed to overcook the eggs, but the bacon was crisply grilled, just how Robina liked it. But the best thing about it was that they were sitting around the table, laughing and joking again, just as they'd done in the early days of their marriage. Suddenly Robina felt herself relax. Maybe this weekend *could* be the start of something.

Niall and Ella insisted on washing up. Shooed out of the kitchen, Robina took her coffee outside. The view took her breath away. The cottage was in a little hollow, surrounded by mountains on either side. The sun had risen and although it was still cool, the air was clear, and Robina breathed in air purer than she had thought possible. There was just the hint of a breeze, and mingling with the scent of the smoke from the fire was the salty tang of the sea, meaning it couldn't be far away. For the first time in months Robina felt her spirit soar. Out in all this beauty how could anyone feel sad? All of a sudden she was keen to set out on the walk to discover what lay beyond the hills.

After breakfast had been cleared away, Robina packed a small rucksack with a flask of coffee, egg and cress sandwiches and an apple each. Although still cool, there was no suggestion of rain in the air, but they packed some waterproofs just in case.

Their walk took them along the side of a stream and then gradually upwards along a rough track. Ella skipped ahead, returning to show them various items of interest before running ahead again.

'Tell me about the emergency yesterday,' Robina said, curious. There was a time when every evening had been spent discussing their patients. Their love of medicine had been one of the things that had brought them together and she missed their discussions, even if at times they had been heated.

'Placenta praevia,' Niall said.

He didn't have to elaborate. Robina knew how dangerous the condition, where the placenta lay below the baby's head preventing natural birth, could be.

'We got her to theatre in time to deliver her,' he continued, 'but then she started bleeding and we couldn't stop it. We gave her several litres of blood as well as blood-clotting agents, but she continued to bleed out...' He pulled a hand through his hair. 'I thought we were going to lose her.'

'What did you do?'

'We called in the radiologists—one of the benefits of working in a big teaching hospital. They inserted balloons into her major pelvic arteries, which stopped the bleeding, and then embolised all the bleeding vessels that we couldn't see. She's in intensive care, but doing well. I phoned the hospital to check when we were at the shops. There's no signal at the cottage.'

'People don't realise that childbirth can still be risky for the mother.'

'Only very occasionally, but when things do go wrong, they can go wrong pretty quickly. Losing a mother in labour—

or even afterwards—is everyone's worst nightmare. No one ever wants that to happen. God, Robina, when I thought I was going to lose you...'

'But you didn't lose her. Or me.'

No, he thought to himself. Thank God, I didn't. At least not physically.

They finished climbing to the top of the hill in companionable silence. At the top they could see for miles in every direction.

'It's so beautiful,' Robina breathed. 'We could almost be the only people left on the planet.' Suddenly Edinburgh and all her heartache seemed a million miles away.

'According to the map, there's a small loch at the foot of this hill,' Niall said. 'Why don't we have our snack there? Then we can take a different route back to the cottage.'

Ella was racing off down the hill before they could stop her, her blonde hair flowing behind her.

'Does she remind you very much of her mother?' Robina asked.

Niall watched his daughter, looking thoughtful.

'Physically, yes. You've seen a photo of Mairead? Ella has the same colouring and her mother's nose. But Mairead was quiet, almost shy, and I guess we can say that Ella isn't. At least not now. After her mother died, she seemed to retreat inside herself, but since you've been in her life, she's almost back to the little girl she was. I have you to thank for that.'

'She's a child who is easy to love,' Robina said softly.

'I think so,' Niall agreed. 'But it couldn't have been easy for you, stepping into the role of stepmother.'

'She is your daughter, Niall. And now mine. I've never really felt like a stepmother.' Feeling that she was treading on dangerous ground, Robina changed the subject.

'Her grandparents will be looking forward to seeing her.'

'They haven't seen her since...' Niall broke off. 'More than a year now. She stayed with them when I was in Cape Town.'

They were both silent.

'I think I should stay behind when you take her to see them this afternoon. If I were in their shoes, I'd want to spend time with my granddaughter and son-in-law, alone, without the new wife making things seem awkward.'

'But you are my wife, and Ella's stepmother. You are part of the family and they'll love you. Especially when they see how much Ella adores you.'

Robina felt her heart melt a little at his words. Did he mean what he was saying?

'I still think you should go on your own. It's only for the afternoon. I'll find plenty to keep me occupied at the cottage.'

Niall looked at her searchingly. 'Please come, Robina,' he said softly. 'Ella's grandparents would like to meet the woman who means so much to her.'

Robina turned away so he wouldn't see the effect his words had on her. If only he had said that he wanted her to come for his sake.

In the end, Robina went with them. They followed the road across the mountain to the village of Applecross. As the road climbed up, sweeping around hairpin bends, Robina caught her breath. Every rise in the road brought new vistas of the mountains and valleys. It was wild and bleak but more beautiful than anything Robina could have imagined. No wonder tourists flocked to Scotland.

'This road's called the Bealach na Ba, Gaelic for the Pass of the Cattle, and is often impassable in winter,' Niall explained as they stopped at the summit to take in the views.

'There is another, longer way round that we could have taken, but it's not nearly as dramatic or as beautiful.'

'It is stunning,' Robina agreed. 'Almost as spectacular as the road around Chapman's Peak in the Cape.' She slid him a mischievous look. 'Remember?'

'I remember,' Niall said quietly, and Robina wondered if he too was thinking of the time they had spent together when they had first met. Then she had been showing him *her* country, seeing it afresh through his eyes.

'Why don't I drop you off at Ella's grandparents?' Robina suggested. 'Then you can have some time together on your own while I explore. I'll pick you up later.'

Niall nodded. 'And you'll come in?'

Robina nodded. 'This way they can meet me while they have some time on their own with you and Ella.' She paused. 'Do they know...?' She couldn't bring herself to finish the sentence.

Niall reached across and took her hand in his. 'About the baby? Yes, I told them. They were delighted when they thought Ella was going to have a brother or sister and very upset when they heard we had lost the baby.'

'Didn't they mind that you remarried?'

'No. They were happy for me. They knew Mairead and I had a very happy marriage and never doubted how much I loved their daughter. They saw how devastated I was when she died. As far as they're concerned, nothing can bring their daughter back and they know Mairead would want Ella and me to be happy.'

Every one of his words was like a knife cutting into her heart.

'Do you miss her?' she asked softly, not sure whether she wanted to know the answer.

Niall glanced at Robina, a strange expression in his eyes. 'I will always miss her,' he said. 'She was part of my life for almost as long as I can remember. If you are asking me whether I still love her, the answer is yes. But I'm not *in love* with her any more. She's dead, Robina, and I will always cherish her memory, but I married you. I couldn't have done that if I were still in love with my dead wife.' His words were clipped, almost cold. Robina wanted to ask him if he still loved *her*, but she knew she didn't dare—not as long as she didn't know what the answer would be.

Robina dropped them off outside Mairead's parents' nine-teenth-century croft house, promising to return later that afternoon. She explored the village before finding a cosy spot in the local pub to read a book. She was nervous at the thought of meeting Mairead's parents. Would they like her? Would they approve of the woman who had taken their daughter's place? In the event, she needn't have worried. When she arrived back at the croft, Mairead's mother met her at the front door and embraced her warmly.

'We have been so looking forward to meeting you,' she said. 'Ella has talked about you non-stop.' She ushered Robina into a cosy kitchen and thrust a cup of tea into her hands. 'I'm Seonag.'

Mairead's mother was plump and curly haired, with a face that looked as if it was used to smiling.

'The others are down by the shore,' Seonag continued without stopping for breath, and Robina wondered if this cheerful woman had been as nervous about meeting her as she had been of meeting them. 'They'll be back shortly, but it'll give us a wee while to get to know one another. Now, I've just finished cooking a batch of pancakes. I hope you won't say no.' She eyed Robina as if she was already planning to fatten her up.

'I'd love one,' Robina said. 'I'm not much of a baker myself. Not really very domesticated at all, I'm afraid.'

'Niall has told us how proud he is of you and your career,' Seonag said. 'You must tell me all about it. I've never met anyone who works in TV before.'

Instantly Robina felt herself relax under this woman's obvious warmth. Had Niall really said he was proud of her? She had thought he resented her career, blaming the miscarriage on her frantic work schedule. Or had that just been her displacing her own sense of guilt onto him? She didn't know what to think any more.

'I never thought for a second that I'd end up in TV,' Robina explained.

'You are very beautiful,' Seonag said. 'I can see why they asked you. And I have seen your programmes. You come across as if you really care about the people you interview.'

'I do care,' Robina replied. 'I can only guess at how much courage it takes for people to share their personal experiences. The last thing I want to do is make them feel uncomfortable.'

Seonag smiled. 'And it comes across. No wonder Niall is so proud of you.'

'Is he?' The words were out before Robina could stop herself. 'I think he wishes I were more like Mairead.'

Seonag set down her cup and sat down next to Robina, taking her hand.

'It can't be easy being the second wife,' she said sympathetically. 'But I don't think you should compare yourself to Mairead. The two of you are as different as it is possible to be. She was always a home bird, happy to make a home for herself, Niall and Ella. It was all she ever wanted.' Tears shone in Seonag's eyes. 'She would have been so grateful to you for looking after Niall and Ella. When she learned she was going to die, her greatest fear wasn't for herself but for her daughter—and Niall.' Despite her obvious grief, she smiled at Robina. 'Mairead and Niall went to school together, played together. I can't remember a time when he wasn't in and out of our house.' Seonag looked into the distance, as if she were recollecting the images of a much younger Niall getting up to all sorts of mischief. 'Mairead was desperately worried Niall would retreat into his work as a way of dealing with his grief. He's never been one to talk about how he feels, you see, and she knew that. She loved him too much to want him to be sad. And it's obvious to me that you love him and Ella very much. Mairead would be happy.'

But he doesn't love me, Robina wanted to protest. At least, he doesn't act as if he does. He thought he'd found a replacement for Mairead and he was wrong. Seonag didn't have a clue what their marriage was really like. But when the older woman looked at her searchingly Robina guessed that there wasn't much that escaped Mairead's mother.

'We were so sorry when we heard about the baby,' Seonag continued gently.

Robina swallowed the lump in her throat. The warmth and sympathy in the older woman's eyes made Robina feel she could confide in her.

'I fell pregnant as soon as we got married,' she said. 'I was so happy, even though it was sooner than we planned.' She smiled, thinking of how excited they had both been when they had realised they were going to have a baby. 'I always thought we'd have at least four children.'

Seonag reached for Robina's hand and took it in hers.

'It's a devastating loss for a couple. I know you'll never forget the baby you lost, but in time perhaps you'll try again?'

'I don't know. Maybe,' Robina hedged. 'I don't even know

if I can fall pregnant again. It's likely, even probable, that the infection after the miscarriage damaged my tubes and made me infertile.'

'Do you know that for certain?'

'No. I don't. I guess I'm too scared to find out.' Robina thought for a moment. 'But perhaps I should. At least then I'd *know* one way or another.'

The clattering of footsteps meant there was no more time to talk. Niall came into the kitchen followed a few moments later by Ella and an older man with faded blue eyes the colour of the morning sky.

'This is my husband, Calum.' Seonag introduced the older man who proceeded to pump Robina's arm enthusiastically.

'I have heard so much about you,' he said in his lilting Highland accent. 'Welcome to our home.'

Niall stood back, looking at Robina, a strange expression in his eyes.

'Mummy!' Ella flung herself into Robina's arms. 'We've had so much fun. You should have come with us. I missed you.'

The lump in Robina's throat got bigger as she caught Seonag's eye. Whatever else had gone wrong, at least Mairead's child was happy. Even if it hurt Mairead's parents to hear Ella *call her* Mummy.

'Niall,' Seonag said slowly. 'I wonder if you and Robina would let Ella stay the night with us—if she wants to, that is. It would give us a little more time with her.' It crossed Robina's mind that Seonag had an ulterior motive for wanting Ella to stay, but she quickly dismissed the notion. Of course Ella's grandparents would want to spend as much time as possible with her. She was all they had left of their beloved daughter.

'Oh, can I, Daddy? Please say yes. Grandpa says I can stay

in Mummy's old room and tomorrow morning he's going to take me out in his boat.'

'Only if the weather stays calm and she wears her life-jacket,' Calum said sternly, but there was no mistaking the twinkle in his eye.

'If you want to, pumpkin,' Niall said, ruffling his daughter's hair. 'And if that's okay with Robina?'

Robina was pleased that Niall had asked her opinion. For the first time she truly felt as if he really saw her as the mother of his child.

'Of course, if that's what you want. We can pick you up after lunch tomorrow.'

'Yippee,' Ella shouted, before turning to Robina and her father. 'You can go now.'

Niall laughed. 'I can see you want us out of the way so Gran and Grandpa can spoil you rotten. Come on, then, Robina. Let's leave our daughter to wallow in her grandparents' undivided attention.'

There it was again. He had called Ella their daughter. As if she truly had an equal share. Maybe she had misjudged him. Or had her own grief just clouded her judgement so she could no longer see straight? Whatever it was, she felt a surge of happiness—and hope.

After taking their leave, Niall asked Robina whether she'd prefer to stay in the village and have a bar supper, or go back to the cottage and have something to eat there. Robina felt unaccountably shy and awkward in his presence. She had so much to think about, but it was impossible to think rationally while he was so close.

'You fancy some seafood?' Niall asked. When Robina nodded he continued, 'There's a little shop on the way home where they sell freshly caught shellfish. Why don't we stop there and pick something up? I'll cook. I bought fresh bread and salad this morning. How does that sound?'

It sounded lovely, if a little nerve-racking. Robina couldn't remember the last time they had spent an evening in on their own together. She was aware of a nervous fluttering low in her abdomen. This was sounding very like a date.

'Sounds good to me,' she said through lips suddenly dry. Maybe this was the chance she had been waiting for. The opportunity to try and start over.

Back at the cottage, Niall insisted on making up the fire while Robina relaxed with a glass of wine. Soon delicious smells were wafting through the small cottage and Robina's stomach grumbled in anticipation. Her anxiety was increasing as she watched Niall move around the kitchen. She hadn't known he could cook but, then again, there were many things she didn't know about this man who was her husband.

Why, she thought, did he have to be so damn gorgeous? Why did he set her nerves on fire with one look from his blue eyes? And why was her stomach churning?

Niall smiled when he caught her looking at him—and he grinned even more when she blushed.

'You can set the table, if you like,' he said, pouring her another glass of wine. Robina rarely drank and her head was beginning to swirl, but whether it was from the wine or the way he was looking at her she didn't want to speculate.

Her hands were shaking as she set out plates and knives and forks. The atmosphere was heavy with something Robina couldn't put her finger on. She only knew she felt almost breathless and wanted to run away, yet at the same time there was nowhere she'd rather be and no one she wanted to be with more.

'Now sit, while I serve,' Niall said eventually.

Robina's heart was pounding so hard she was amazed that Niall couldn't hear it. And how she was going to swallow a morsel, feeling the way she did, was beyond her.

Somehow she managed a few mouthfuls. It was, as Niall had promised, delicious, but her appetite seemed to have deserted her. While they ate, Niall began telling her stories from his childhood. How he had grown up in the area and most of his afternoons had been spent running wild, either down by the shore or in the hills.

He made her laugh with tales of the various characters who had lived in the village and who had made it their business to send Niall home with a clip on his ear, if they thought he deserved one.

'It was like being brought up by several parents at once.' He smiled. 'There was no chance of getting up to no good with so many pairs of eyes watching you. Not that I ever did do anything very wrong, except perhaps drop a crab down the back of Mairead's T-shirt when she was eight.'

Some of the light went out of the evening at the mention of Mairead's name. For the last couple of hours she had allowed herself to forget. But now her anxieties came flooding back. Robina pushed them away. Wasn't it time she let herself believe Niall?

As if he could read her mind, Niall laid down his fork and came to stand behind her. He rested his hands on either side of her neck. His touch was like a bolt of electricity running through her body. She longed to rest her cheek against his hand, but still she couldn't bring herself to.

He dropped his hands to her shoulders and massaged the side of her neck. Robina felt a wave of desire that stole her remaining breath. Involuntarily, she turned her head towards him.

Then, without knowing how, she was on her feet and in his arms. Her head came to just under his chin and she leaned against him, breathing in the scent of soap and outdoors and just the hint of wood smoke.

'I would do anything to remove the sadness from your eyes,' Niall said hoarsely, tilting her face, forcing her to look at him. 'Don't you know that?'

He brought his mouth down on hers and she was clinging to him as if she was drowning. He kissed her hungrily and she responded, pulling him closer, feeling herself ache from her need for him. He dropped one hand to the small of her back, the other lightly on her hip. He groaned and then pulled her closer, tight up against him, where she could feel his need for her.

He picked her up and she wound her legs around his hips. He held her, still kissing her as he carried her towards the bed. They fell in a tangled heap and then Robina was tugging at his shirt, pulling it over his head while he eased her out of her clothes. Not a moment too soon they were lying naked. Niall's eyes darkened as he looked down at her, his eyes devouring every inch of her body.

'God,' he whispered, 'I'd forgotten just how beautiful you are.' And then unable to wait any longer, Robina swung herself on top, guiding him inside her. Her body exploded with pleasure as she felt him move, and she rocked against him, unable and unwilling to control her body. She gasped, flinging her head back as his hands sought her breast, one hand staying to flick her swollen nipple, the other dropping down her belly, searching for the place between her parted legs, touching gently at first, then alternating with hard and soft strokes, finding just the right place, applying just the right amount of pleasure, remembering her body and what drove her wild. Robina cried out as wave upon wave of pleasure ricocheted through her body and then they were moving together, lost in each other.

Later, they lay in each other's arms and were gentle with

one another. Re-exploring each other's bodies with hands and lips, reacquainting themselves with every inch of what had once been so familiar. The night passed without words until, finally exhausted, Robina fell asleep in his arms.

Niall propped himself on his elbow and gazed at the sleeping form of his wife. He drank in the sight of her, her long chocolate-coloured legs tangled in the sheets, her full mouth relaxed with a hint of the smile as if she was having happy dreams. God, he had missed her, and not just in his bed. He had missed everything about her; the glow in her eyes, the smile that always hovered around her lips, her touch, her laughter, her wit and intelligence. But now she was back where she had belonged and, God help him, that's where she would stay for the rest of their lives together.

Earlier, when they had been at Mairead's parents' house he had paused outside the kitchen to remove his boots and had overheard the last bit of her conversation with Seonag. Robina was thinking of having her tubes examined. That could only mean one thing. At last, it seemed, she was looking towards a future. A future with him and children.

'Good morning,' Niall whispered. She opened sleepy brown eyes and he ached to see the familiar wariness, before they cleared and the shadows in her eyes were replaced with a sleepy glow.

She raised a finger and gently touched his cheek.

'Hey, you,' she said softly.

He pulled her against him into the crook of his arm, revelling in the feel of her velvet skin against his.

'I've missed you,' he said, taking her hand and kissing each fingertip in turn.

'I've missed you too,' she said, a hitch in her voice.

'Let's never do this to one another again, Robina. Let's start over.' He felt the rise and fall of her breathing as she lay secure in his arms.

'I'd like that,' she said in a small voice.

He shifted slightly, kissing the top of her head, letting the fingers of one hand trail down her jaw, down her long neck to the hollow in her throat where he could feel her pulse against his fingertips.

'Maybe we could try for another baby,' he said tentatively. 'You could see one of the other doctors at the clinic and have a tubal patency test.'

He heard her take a sharp intake of breath and then suddenly she was out of his arms, pulling the sheet with her. She glared down at him, twin points of colour staining her cheeks.

'I should have guessed,' she said bitterly. 'I should have *known* that you wanted me back in your bed for a reason.' He reached out for her, but she backed away. 'You think if I fall pregnant again, I'll give up work and stay at home and become the kind of mother and wife that Mairead was.' Her voice was shaking with fury.

Niall was bewildered. What had he said wrong now? Then immediately he knew. He cursed himself under his breath. How could he have been so insensitive? They hadn't even talked about their lost baby, now here he was making the same mistake he had seen so many men make before him, suggesting that a new baby could replace the one they had lost, as if that was even a remote possibility. No wonder she was furious. He was acting like her doctor, not her husband. He had to make her understand she was wrong, apologise, make her see that he just wanted her to be happy.

But it was too late. Picking up her discarded clothes from the floor, Robina was already heading out of the room.

'Why don't you go and collect Ella?' She threw over her shoulder, 'while I pack up here. I think its time we returned home, don't you?'

'Wait, Robina,' he called after her retreating back, but it was too late. He was speaking to a door that had been slammed shut.

CHAPTER TEN

'I CAN'T keep it from you any longer,' Robina's mother Grace said over the phone. 'Your grandmother isn't well—isn't well at all. She didn't want me to tell you, but she's getting worse. I'm sorry, darling, but I don't think she's going to pull through.'

'You should have told me sooner,' Robina cried, distraught. 'I would have come to see her. Has she seen a doctor? What are they saying? Who is her doctor? I want to speak to him or her.'

'That is exactly why she didn't want you to know. She says the time is right for her to go, and more old people should just accept it when it is their time to die.'

Through her sorrow, Robina felt a bubble of laughter. Trust Umakhulu to say what she thought.

'The doctors say it's heart failure. They don't expect her to get better. All they can do is make her comfortable. I begged her to come and stay with me, so I can look after her, but she won't hear of it. She says she wants to stay beside her neighbours—the people she's known all her life. She says it is the Xhosa way.'

Niall, on his way to his study, stopped and listened.

'I'm coming home, whatever Umakhulu says. Give me a

couple of days to arrange things, Mum. I need to see her for myself. Please kiss her for me.'

Blinking away the tears, Robina replaced the receiver slowly. It had been a shock hearing about her grandmother. Right now, she would give anything to be back in Africa, with her mother. In her mother's arms she could let the pain out, find the comfort she so desperately needed.

'What is it, Robina?' Niall asked gently, his blue eyes soft with concern. 'Is everything okay?' He placed a hand on her shoulder, turning her to face him.

Unable to hide her tears, Robina bit her lip. 'It's my grandmother. She's not well. Heart failure, Mum says. I need to go and see her.'

Niall pulled her into his arms. Despite her grief, Robina breathed in the scent of him and revelled in the feeling of being in his arms. It had been too long since she had found shelter and comfort there. The night in the cottage had been all about sex and didn't count. Since they had come back from the weekend, a week ago, life had returned to the stilted conversations and strained atmosphere of previously. Niall hadn't even attempted to return to their bedroom, guessing rightly that she was still angry with him.

Niall tipped her chin, forcing her to look into his eyes.

'If you want to go, we should all go.'

'But what about work?' Robina sniffed.

Niall pulled away, dropping his hands to his sides. 'Can't you stop thinking about work—even at a time like this? For God's sake, Robina!'

'Not *my* work,' Robina retorted. 'We're due to take a break from filming the documentary for a month to give us time to follow up some of the patients at a later point in their treatment—you know that. And as for my books, they can be put

on hold. And even if they couldn't, I would go anyway.'
Robina felt crushed by his assumption, but could she really
blame him? 'I was referring to *your* work,' she continued.
'Can you take time off?'

'I'm sorry,' Niall said, looking a little shamefaced. 'Of
course you wouldn't let work stop you from going to see your
grandmother. And me? I'll find a way to take time off. It may
only be for a week, but it would mean we could all go together.
No time is particularly convenient, so this would be as good
a time as any. Mark and Elaine can hold the fort between
them. Anyway, Lucinda's been nagging me to take time off
for months now.' He paused. 'Besides, you have faced enough
on your own. Regardless of what you think, Ella and I are your
family now. Whatever the future brings, you have us. There's
no way I'm going to let you face this on your own!'

Robina felt a flutter of something she barely recognised as
hope. If he would put his work on hold, even for a short while,
so he could come with her, perhaps he still cared a little?

Just then Ella skipped into the hallway. One look at
Robina's face was enough to tell her something was up. She
stopped dead and popped a thumb into her mouth, regarding
her parents with the solemn blue eyes she had inherited from
her father.

'What's wrong?' she asked. 'Why does Mummy look so
sad?'

'It's all right, pumpkin,' Niall said, scooping his daughter
into his arms. Ella buried her face in her father's shoulder.
'Remember how you and Mummy were talking about going
on holiday? All of us together? To somewhere you hadn't been
before? Well, we are going to see her mummy. In South
Africa. How does that sound?'

Ella lifted her face from her father's neck. 'All of us?' she queried, as if she could hardly believe what her father was telling her. 'A proper holiday? All together? More than just a day?'

Robina saw the regret in Niall's eyes as he realised how much his daughter missed spending time with him.

'Yes,' he said firmly. 'The three of us together. All day, every day. How does that sound?'

'It sounds great!' Ella grinned from ear to ear, her small face lighting up. Still in her father's arms, she held out her hand to pull Robina into the embrace. As the three of them stood in each other's arms, Robina let hope take hold. Maybe it wasn't too late.

The next few days were frantic as Robina booked flights and tried to catch up with work. While she was away, her team would edit the footage they had already taken, ready for more filming on her return. Niall had arranged to be away for nearly two weeks, leaving his colleagues to pick up his workload. He would be back in time to carry out the egg collection on Maisie who had decided to go forward with treatment. Immediately after that, she'd be starting her treatment for the ovarian cancer, and Robina was impressed with the way Niall had arranged for her to be seen and treated so quickly. Maisie was still frightened, but seemed more relaxed now that she knew she would still have the chance to have children in the future and was loud in her praise for everyone, particularly Niall, for giving her the opportunity.

Eilidh's treatment was progressing well and Niall was quietly optimistic that the couple would have a positive outcome. Trevor and Christine Strain had had a positive pregnancy test and were anxiously awaiting the seven-week scan that would confirm the pregnancy was ongoing. Patricia and Luke were still thinking about using donor eggs, but had put their names down on the waiting list in the meantime.

All in all, between work and organising the trip there was no time to think, and that suited Robina just fine.

'I am so happy to meet my son-in-law and my granddaughter at last,' Grace said when after a very long flight they arrived at Robina's mother's home in Cape Town. It was almost midnight and Ella, tired out from the excitement of the trip, was asleep in her father's arms. Grace had never learned to drive and so they'd had to hire a car at the airport.

'We can talk properly tomorrow,' Grace said. 'After everyone has had a good night's sleep. I've put Ella in the room next to yours so you'll hear her if she wakes up during the night. I don't want her to get a fright if she wakes up and doesn't know where she is.'

Robina's heart thudded. Everything had happened so fast she hadn't had the time to think about sleeping arrangements. Of course her mother would have put them in the same room. The same bed. That was the norm for married couples. Catching Niall's eye, Robina could tell that he too was thinking of the last time they had shared a bed. She felt the heat rise in her cheeks. They had never discussed what had happened that night, both treading around the subject like wary cats, but she thought about it often. Too often.

They laid Ella down in the spare room, pulling a sheet over her, although the night air was humid. Then Grace showed them to the room that had been Robina's when she had been a child. Her little single bed had been replaced with a double, but apart from that her room was essentially the same, the books of her childhood neatly lined up in the bookcase, even her favourite teddy placed on the chair beside her bed. Robina swallowed a lump in her throat. The last time she had slept in this room had been the night of her father's funeral.

Her mother kissed her goodnight and then, after hesitating for a moment, kissed Niall too.

'It's good to have a man in the house again,' she said softly, before closing the door behind her.

Alone together for the first time, Robina looked at Niall. Suddenly he grinned and nodded towards the bed.

'It seems I am to have my wife in bed with me again,' he drawled, his eyes glinting. 'Unless you have a better idea?'

Robina, her heart racing, looked around the room. Apart from the armchair there was nowhere else to sleep except the bed. Why, oh, why hadn't she thought about this before?

'It's all right, Robina,' Niall said heavily, the veiled look returning to his eyes. 'I promise this time you'll be perfectly safe from me.'

'Too right,' Robina muttered, going to the cupboard, pulling out a pile of blankets and arranging them on the floor, while Niall looked on, baffled.

'That should do you,' she said when they had been arranged to her satisfaction. 'I don't think it'll be too uncomfortable.'

'You can't be serious!'

'Oh, but I am. There's no way I'm sharing a bed with you. Not after what happened the last time.' She looked him directly in the eye. 'Regardless of what you say, I don't trust you.' The truth was she didn't trust herself. She hadn't been able to stop herself thinking about that night—the feel of his hands on her skin, him re-exploring her body with his lips, his mouth growing ever more demanding... Stop it! she told herself as she felt a languorous heat spread through her body. She wanted him—had never stopped wanting him, but she wanted more, so much more than he seemed able to give— and she was damned if she'd accept anything less.

Thankfully, Niall seemed to realise she was serious and by

the time Robina emerged from the bathroom he was grumpily
punching the pillow as he attempted to make himself comfortable in his makeshift bed. He muttered to himself and Robina
didn't quite catch the words, but it sounded suspiciously like
'You…belong…bed and soon'.

The next morning Robina was awake as soon as it was light.
Slipping out of bed, she stepped over Niall's sleeping form
and padded into the kitchen, unsurprised to find her mother
already at breakfast.

'Good morning, darling,' her mother greeted her. 'Did you
sleep well?'

She could hardly tell her mother that she had lain awake
for most of the night as Niall had tossed and turned on the
floor. So she simply nodded and helped herself to orange
juice from the large fridge.

'Not having breakfast?' Her mother clicked her tongue in disapproval. 'I couldn't help noticing that you've lost weight. You're
far too skinny. Men don't like skinny women, you know. At least
African men don't. I can't say I'm too sure about Scottish ones.
And it is not good for your health. You should know that.'

'Well, seeing as I'm married to a Scotsman, I can't see it
matters what African men think.' Robina smiled. 'And you
know, Mum, I've always been skinny. I take after Dad.' The
two women were silent as they remembered Robina's father.
Both Robina and her mother believed that he had worked
himself into an early grave. But Robina wouldn't have
swapped her idealistic father for the world.

'How's Umakhulu?' Robina asked. 'I'm desperate to see
her for myself.'

'She's looking forward to seeing you too. She's failing,
Robina; you'll need to prepare yourself for that. Why don't

you and Niall go and see her this afternoon? I know Umakhulu likes the morning to herself. You can leave Ella here with me.'

'Sounds a good idea. I don't think it's a good idea for us to take Ella.'

'Good morning.' Robina swung around to find Niall standing behind her wearing jeans and a short-sleeved T-shirt. He looked surprisingly relaxed after his night's sleep, which was more than could be said for her.

Automatically Robina poured him a coffee and set it on the table. 'Ella still asleep?'

'I looked in on her and she's still dead to the world. I thought I would give her another hour.' He turned to Grace.

'You have a lovely home, Mrs Zondi.'

Grace smiled with pleasure. 'I like it. Would you like to see the garden?'

Leaving Niall to follow her mother, Robina went to get dressed.

It was hot. She'd forgotten just how hot it could get and she was unused to it. On the other hand, the warmth of the sun lifted her spirits. Here, at least, she felt as if she belonged.

Choosing a simple shift dress in bright colours that she knew her grandmother would like, Robina dressed. It was good to be home, although the irony didn't escape her. Here they were, she and Niall, back where they had met, but things couldn't be more different. She sighed. It would soon be their first wedding anniversary. They hadn't even managed to stay happy for a single year. How had she ever believed that they'd manage a lifetime?

By the time she returned to the kitchen, her husband and mother were chatting away as if they'd known each other for ever. A few moments later, a sleepy Ella padded into the kitchen, rubbing her eyes.

'So this is Ella,' Grace said, smiling at her. '*Molo. Unjani?* That's Xhosa for hello and how are you?'

Ella tried to make the clicking noise of the Xhosa language but failed miserably and soon had everyone laughing at her frustration.

'It's not easy for people who weren't brought up speaking Xhosa like I was,' Robina soothed. 'But I'll try and teach you a few words while we are here.'

'It's hot,' Ella pronounced. 'Can we go to the beach and swim?'

Robina caught Niall's eye across the top of Ella's head. He nodded.

'That's a great idea, but after lunch Daddy and I have to go and see my grandmother while you stay with my mum. Is that okay?'

Ella nodded shyly at Grace, who was holding out a large glass of freshly squeezed orange juice.

'Then tomorrow we can all go to the top of Table Mountain, in the cable car. Would you like that?'

Ella nodded excitedly. 'But can't I come with you and Daddy to see your grandmother?' she asked.

'Not this time. Maybe in a couple of days, after we see how she is.'

Ella seemed to accept that and scurried off to get ready for the beach.

'I can take her on my own, if you want to spend time with your mother,' Niall offered.

'Oh,' Grace said, 'I thought I'd come too. Robina and I can always catch up while you two are swimming.' Grace slid a glance at her daughter and Robina sighed. She knew what that look meant. Her mother knew something was wrong and was determined to find out what.

* * *

Robina decided on the beach at Noordhoek. It had miles of empty sand and she knew it was shallow enough near the shore for Ella to paddle safely. There were also plenty of places nearby to get snacks and shelter from the sun. She would save Boulders Beach with its famous penguin colony for another day.

As soon as they had made themselves comfortable on a blanket on the sand and Ella had dragged her father off for a swim, Grace turned to Robina. 'Something's not right, is it?'

'I'm not sure what you mean,' Robina said evasively. 'We're all just a bit bushed. Work's been hectic and we had a long flight, that's all.'

But Grace knew her daughter far better than that. 'You don't have to pretend with me, darling. I know you too well. Is it the miscarriage? I was so sorry I couldn't be with you, but you were so insistent that I didn't come.'

Robina felt tears well in her eyes. She should have known that she couldn't keep much from her mother.

'It's my fault I lost the baby,' she burst out. 'I was so busy with my new career I wouldn't slow down, even when Niall asked me to.' She laughed bitterly. 'It seems I got what I deserved.'

'Don't say that! Don't ever say that,' Grace admonished. 'You're a doctor, so you should know that these things happen, regardless of what we do or don't do. I very much doubt that the outcome would have been any different even if you had taken to your bed the moment you found out you were pregnant.'

'I know all that, in my head, but I just can't make myself believe it in my heart.'

'What does Niall say? Surely he has told you that you're feeling guilty for no reason?'

'We haven't really talked about it,' Robina admitted.

'What?' Robina didn't think Grace could have been more

astonished. 'You haven't talked about the baby you made together and lost? That you are both grieving for?'

Grace's words brought Robina up short. Niall hurting? In her grief, pain and guilt she hadn't stopped to think how he'd be feeling. He'd never shown any sign that losing the baby meant anything to him. But had she given him the opportunity? Hadn't she been so wrapped up in her own pain that she hadn't really given a thought to his?

'But it's not just losing the baby. Our marriage was going wrong before then.'

'Oh?' Grace raised an eyebrow.

'I knew about Mairead before we married, of course I did. Niall never denied that he loved his late wife, but he didn't tell me he still loves her.'

'In love with a dead woman?' Grace protested mildly. 'C'mon, Robina. Listen to yourself. The woman I know would never think like that. What's happened to you?'

'She was so perfect. The perfect wife, the perfect mother, the perfect homemaker. Everything I'm not.'

'Sweetie, surely you're not jealous of her?'

'Jealous.' Robina laughed sourly. 'Of course not.' But even as she said the words she wondered if there wasn't the tiniest bit of truth in them.

'He married you,' Grace continued. 'Doesn't that count for something? He doesn't strike me as the kind of man who would marry for convenience.'

'And that's where you'd be wrong.'

Grace patted her hand and then put an arm around her and hugged her close.

'Do you still love Niall?' she asked quietly.

'Yes. I do. I can't imagine a time when I would ever stop loving him,' Robina replied. 'But I don't think he loves me.'

She looked across to where Niall, his shirt removed and his jeans rolled up to just below the knee, was twirling Ella around over the waves. He was so many men, this husband of hers—the doctor, the father, the work colleague—but which part was hers? Even from a distance she could see the muscular chest and the narrow hips. She wanted him, he set her nerves alight, and he wanted her. She knew that without a shadow of doubt. But was that the same as love? She had thought so once.

'And I think you couldn't be more wrong,' Grace said, following Robina's eyes. 'Anyone seeing the way he looks at you can see he loves you very much.'

Robina's heart kicked against her ribs. *Did* he love her? Was Grace right?

'I can't bear the thought of a life without him.'

'If you can't imagine living without him, you need to do something about it,' Grace said firmly. 'I never thought you were a woman who gave up easily. Especially not on what's important. He strikes me as a good man.'

'He is, Mum. He's good and kind and decent and sexy as hell. He's everything I ever wanted—and more. But one thing we've never really done is talk. Even after all this time, I still don't know what makes him tick—or him me.'

Niall and Ella were beginning to make their way back up the beach. Robina could hear the tinkle of Ella's laughter followed by Niall's deep rumble in the still air, although she couldn't hear what they were saying.

'You two need to talk,' Grace said quickly. 'I can't believe that two people who have to talk as part of their jobs can be so bad at communicating with each other.' She grabbed Robina by the arm. 'Talk to him. You owe that to yourself, to him and to Ella.'

There was no time for anything but a nod as Niall and Ella

flopped down on the blanket. 'You should have come in with us,' Ella said. 'It was so much fun.'

'Another time.' Robina smiled. 'We have a few days yet. But it's time to get going. The sun gets very strong at this time and I don't want any of us to get sunburnt.'

'I've got loads of suncream on,' Ella protested. 'Anyway...' She reached out and touched Robina's arm. 'Can you burn? Your skin is dark already.'

Robina laughed. 'I won't burn as quickly as you, but even people with dark skin have to be careful, especially when they haven't been in the sun recently.'

'Let's get going,' Niall said. 'I don't know about everyone else, but I'm hungry again. Let's find a café and grab some lunch. What do you say?'

'I say yes. Can I have some ice cream too?'

On the way home, Robina thought about what Grace had said. Her mother was right. She *had* been so wrapped up in her own grief she hadn't stopped to think about Niall's pain. She had pushed him away when he had tried to comfort her, freezing him out. And if their marriage had been going wrong before the miscarriage, what had she done to make things better? Realisation hit her like a sledgehammer. She couldn't just blame Niall. And her jealousy of Mairead—and, yes, she had been jealous, she admitted ruefully—had stopped her from reaching out to him. But what was she going to do about it? She shifted uncomfortably in her seat. Didn't she owe him—and their marriage—another chance? She bit down on her lip. She had been such an idiot. Was Grace right? Did he still love her? Or was it too late? No, she wouldn't let it be. There was no way she was going to give up on her marriage without a fight. Where had the fighting Robina been all these months? The woman her father had made her? One thing was for sure, though, she was back to stay.

After lunch they dropped Ella and Grace off at the house and set off towards the village where Robina's grandmother lived. Outside the air temperature had risen and Robina was glad that the car they had hired had air-conditioning.

'You didn't have to come with me. You could have stayed with Ella,' Robina said.

Niall glanced across and laid his hand briefly on top of hers. She smiled and he felt his heart thump against his ribs.

'I want to come,' he said quietly. 'She made quite an impression on me when I met her. But why hasn't she moved in with your mother so Grace can keep an eye on her?'

'Umakhulu's stubborn. She's lived in the village all her life and she told Mum that she wants to die there, surrounded by her friends and neighbours.' Her voice caught and Niall wanted to hold her. Hadn't she had enough pain in the last few months?

'What about her other children?' Niall asked.

'There was only my father. Umakhulu made sure that my father would have the best she could afford, even if that meant doing without. She sent him to school and he won a scholarship to go to high school and then on to university. In those days, it was very rare for someone from my father's background to make it to university.' She sighed. 'I think that's why he was so driven. As soon as he qualified as a lawyer, he was determined to put something back—to help those in a less fortunate position.'

'Like his daughter, then.'

Robina glanced at him. 'I don't think I could ever match him. All I can do is work hard, so that had he lived he'd be proud of me.'

Apart from the day they had met, when she had told him

how much she admired her father, Robina hadn't spoken much about him. Was that why she was so driven to succeed? Was that why she had thrown herself into her job? Was the thought of failure so frightening for her? And if so, how much a failure would her miscarriage and infertility have seemed? At last, he was beginning to understand what made his wife tick.

'I also want to put something back—that's one of the reasons I donate to charity, but it never seems to be enough.' Once again her words struck home. Could it be that she felt as if she had never measured up to her father? If so, his lack of support for her career must have hurt.

'I know how blessed my life has been,' she continued, 'with the obvious exception. But who said life was fair? Who said you could have it all?'

Why shouldn't she have it all? Niall thought angrily. If anyone deserved it, it was his wife.

'I had no idea you were sending money back to Africa,' Niall said. 'Why didn't you tell me?'

'I didn't think you would mind. There was always plenty of money for us and Ella,' Robina said defensively. Why hadn't she told him? Surely she knew him well enough to know he wouldn't have stopped her.

'Of course I don't mind. I think it's a great idea. I just wish you had felt able to share it with me. You even found it easier to share your pain about the miscarriage with the public,' he replied sadly. 'I just wish it had been me.'

Robina looked out the window, knowing he was right. Why had she kept so much from Niall? He was her husband and they weren't supposed to keep secrets from each other. But he seemed so preoccupied with his own work and she with hers, there had never seemed the time to talk. And as for mentioning the miscarriage on air, in some strange way it had been easier than talking to Niall about it. She would have to find the courage to talk him about it—some time.

'Do you miss South Africa?' Niall said after a few minutes. 'You must find living in Scotland so different.' They were talking like two strangers, but at least they were talking.

'I miss Mum and Umakhulu, and the sunshine.' She smiled briefly. 'But I like where we live too. If only I could have Mum and Umakhulu, in Scotland…' She hesitated.

'Then what? Life would be perfect?'

'No.' She shook her head. 'You and I both know it's far from that.'

'It's not too late,' Niall said urgently. 'It could still be good. We could start over.'

Robina looked at him, her dark eyes glowing. 'Can people ever go back? Do you really think it's possible?'

'I think they can. If they want to badly enough,' he replied.

They drove for what seemed like miles, each occupied with their own thoughts until eventually they turned off towards the village.

Outside the little mud houses, children played and groups of men hung around talking. Women passed by with heavy buckets of water perched effortlessly on top of their heads. Washing hung in neat rows from lines strung up in back yards.

A neighbour looked up as they got out the car. Recognising Robina, she greeted her in Xhosa, her face wreathed in smiles.

Robin replied in the same language before turning to Niall and introducing him. The neighbour, Mrs Tambo, giggled and hid her face behind the brightly coloured scarf she was wearing.

'How is my grandmother?' Robina asked in Xhosa.

Mrs Tambo's smiles disappeared and she clicked her

tongue regretfully. 'Not so good. But she will be better when she sees you.'

Niall had to dip his head to avoid hitting it on the low doorway. Inside, Robina's grandmother was lying in bed in a small room separated from the living area by a screen. She struggled up onto her elbows when she saw Robina.

Robina embraced her grandmother, shocked by how much weight she had lost since the last time she had seen her. Her dark skin had the unhealthy dusky hue of oxygen deprivation. Her breath sounded laboured and a quick glance at her ankles revealed they were puffy, a sign of oedema, which in turn was a sign of heart failure. Robina's heart sank. Although she knew her grandmother wasn't well, she hadn't been prepared for just how unwell she was. She blinked rapidly. It wouldn't do to let her grandmother see how shocked and upset she was.

But her grandmother had no such reservations. She let the tears flow and in a long stream of Xhosa told Robina how happy she was to see her only grandchild before she died and that she had been hanging on to see her.

'You have brought my grandson back to see me?' She looked at Niall approvingly. '*Aiee*, but he is a man for you.' Robina thought Niall almost blushed under the old woman's frank appraisal.

'Hello,' Niall said softly. 'I am pleased to see you again.'

'And I you.' The words came out in short gasps as if she didn't have enough breath left.

Robina turned to the neighbour who had remained standing by the door.

'When was the doctor last here?' she asked in Xhosa.

She listened to the reply before translating for Niall. 'She said the doctor was here yesterday and will come again tomorrow. He has given Umakhulu pills, they sound like diuretics, but that her heart is getting weaker.'

'Makhulu.' She turned back to her grandmother. 'Please let us take you to hospital.'

But the old woman shook her head firmly. 'No. I will stay here.' She reached for Robina's hand. 'I am an old woman who has had a long and happy life. I am ready to die. I have seen you now. Please, do not argue with me.'

Robina turned to Niall in desperation. 'Niall, please tell her that she'd be better in hospital. Tell her that they can give her medicine to help her breathing and that they'll make her comfortable.'

Niall placed his hands on Robina's shoulders.

'Robina, look at me.' She forced herself to raise her head and look into his eyes. The sympathy in their diamond depths made her realise that it was hopeless, but she wasn't ready to give up yet.

'With the right medication and nursing care, she would get some more time. Tell her, Niall. Make her see.'

'She's made up her mind. This is what she wants. Do you have the right to force her to go to hospital so that you'll feel better? Because that's the only reason. You know as well as I do, as well as your grandmother does, that nothing is going to change the outcome.' Gently he pulled her into his arms, rubbing her back as if she were a child. 'I'm sorry, Robina. You have to be strong for your grandmother.'

Robina knew when she was beaten. All they could do now was help make the old lady as comfortable as possible and let nature take its course. But it was one thing knowing when a patient was ready to die, when nothing more could be done, and quite another when it was your own much-loved grandmother. Tears slipped down her cheeks and she could taste their saltiness.

'*Umntwana*, please don't be sad,' her grandmother said in Xhosa. 'Come now. Sit beside me and tell me about your life.' She patted the bed. 'I hear such wonderful things about you.'

Resigned, Robina perched on the side of the bed and, taking one of her grandmother's thin hands in hers, she spoke in Xhosa, telling her about her job, her book and the documentary she was doing at Niall's clinic.

Niall sat quietly in a chair opposite, watching. Eventually Robina's grandmother closed her eyes and fell into a deep sleep. Robina and Niall sat watching as her breathing slowed.

Suddenly there was a commotion outside and one of the neighbours came rushing in.

'Please, we need a doctor,' she said. 'Lydia's baby is in trouble, and she needs help.'

Immediately Niall and Robina were on their feet. 'Take us to her,' Robina said.

They found the labouring woman a few doors down, lying on a bed, surrounded by anxious women.

'The baby, it's not coming. She has been like this for a long time and she isn't well.'

'Why didn't she go to the hospital?' Niall asked.

'There is no money for hospitals.'

'Is this her first child? Has she had a baby before?'

'No. This is her first time.'

'Damn,' Niall muttered under his breath. 'I haven't any equipment with me.'

'There is a clinic a few blocks away. They'll have something,' Robina replied.

'I don't think we can move her.' Niall straightened up from his examination of the young mother. 'I can feel the head. Robina, go with the women and bring me whatever you can find. Gloves, endotracheal tubes, anything that you think could be useful.'

'I have latex gloves and an airway in the glove compartment of the car. I always carry that with me wherever I go, in case I come across an RTA,' Robina told him.

'I doubt we'll need the airway, not for Mum anyway, but the gloves would be handy.'

Robina fetched the gloves from the car and handed them to Niall. They'd probably be on the small side, his hands were much larger than hers, but they would have to do. Then Robina was running, followed by an excited gaggle of schoolchildren. As she ran, she prayed that she would find something at the treatment centre.

Happily there was an outpatient clinic on the go, and Robina found a nurse and explained what she needed. The nurse quickly collected some items and told Robina that she would call an ambulance and follow her as soon as she was able.

Robina, her arms laden, was off again. She was only away for ten minutes, but as soon as she arrived back she could see that the young woman's labour hadn't progressed. She handed a stethoscope to Niall.

'I know it's not as good as a Sonicaid monitor, but it was the best I could do.'

Niall leant forward and listened for the baby's heart beat.

'Too slow,' he said quietly. 'If we manage to deliver this baby, it could need resuscitating. Did you manage to find a paediatric endotracheal tube?'

'Yes, I don't know if it's the right size. But one of the nurses is calling for an ambulance. Hopefully they'll be better equipped.'

'Could you explain to Lydia what's going on? I tried while you were away, but I don't think she understood me.

Tell her that she needs to push as hard as she can with the next contraction.'

Niall's steady voice gave Robina comfort. Her heart was pounding against her ribs. It had been so long since she had done any obstetrics. There hadn't been a call for it when she had worked as a GP, most of the deliveries taking place in well-equipped hospitals. Lydia looked so young, so alone and vulnerable. She couldn't bear it if anything happened to this baby. She had lost hers and was damned if she was going to let Lydia lose hers. No other woman was going to experience the loss she had, not if she could help it.

She slid a glance at Niall. How could he be so calm? Although he had delivered hundreds of babies, it had always been with experienced staff around and the latest equipment, plus a fully equipped theatre. This was a completely different scenario, but he didn't seemed fazed in the slightest. Didn't he care? But when he looked up at her she could see the muscle twitching in his jaw and the concern in his deep blue eyes. Of course he cared. How could she ever have doubted it? Hadn't she seen him with enough patients to know that?

'The baby's not progressing down the birth canal. Normally I would do a forceps delivery, but I don't have the equipment. You are going to have to help me, Robina.'

They worked together as if they had done so for years, each knowing instinctively what the other needed. Without the right equipment, Niall had to improvise, using his hands to guide the baby down through the birth canal.

Finally, the baby slipped out and into Niall's arms. Quickly Robina took the clean towel the women had fetched and wrapped the newborn infant tightly. But she could see that the baby was floppy and hadn't taken a breath and her heart thumped painfully against her ribs. They couldn't lose the baby now. Not after everything they had been through.

She caught Niall's eyes. 'Where is that bloody ambulance?' she muttered under her breath.

'We don't have time to wait for it. We need to get this baby breathing, right now.' He took the tiny infant from Robina and laid it gently on the table the women had prepared.

'Could you pass me the endotracheal tube, Robina?' His voice was calm, giving no indication that intubating a neonate wasn't something he would have had to do as an obstetrician. At the hospital, there were always highly experienced paediatricians around to take over the care of the baby once it had been born. 'You'll need to deliver the placenta. Can you do that?'

Robina nodded as she passed across the tube that Niall would attempt to slip into the baby's airway. She had the easy job.

Please let it be all right, Robina prayed silently, before turning to the mother who was lying exhausted on the bed.

'My baby,' she said. 'Why isn't it crying?'

'You have a little girl, a daughter. But she needs help to breathe. The doctor is doing everything he can to help her. You have to stay as calm as you can. We still need to deliver the placenta.'

Robina knew that Lydia would be straining even more than she was to hear the sound of a cry, but as the seconds passed slowly, it was deathly quiet. She glanced across the room, but could see nothing except Niall's broad back. Then suddenly she heard him give a grunt of satisfaction.

'The tube's in and we have an airway, and baby seems to be pinking up with a good pulse. Tell Lydia that although the baby isn't out of danger yet, it has a good chance.'

The lump in her throat made it difficult for Robina to speak. 'Your daughter is breathing,' she whispered to Lydia in Xhosa. 'It will be a couple of days before we can be sure, but the doctor thinks she'll be all right.'

The wailing sound of the ambulance was like music to Robina's ears. The baby needed to be in Special Care, and the sooner the better. She and Niall, especially Niall, had done everything they could.

Niall carried the baby, still wrapped in a towel, across to Lydia. Despite the tube, the baby was making small movements with its little fingers. Lydia stroked her baby's cheek with a tender finger.

As Robina looked down at the baby her throat closed. If only things had been different and she too had been able to accept a baby into her arms. He or she would have been loved much. It was as if all the suppressed love she'd had inside her had built up like a dam. She realised that she had been too frightened of letting that dam burst, unsure if she'd ever recover from her grief. That was why she had pushed Niall away, instead of seeking the comfort he had offered her.

Looking into his eyes, she saw them darken and knew he too was thinking of the baby they had lost.

'I should go with them in the ambulance,' Niall said, once Lydia had been wheeled into the ambulance and her baby placed in the portable incubator.

'Of course.' Robina nodded tiredly. Now that the drama was over and she felt the adrenaline seep away, she felt wrung out and on the verge of tears. Today hadn't turned out the way she had imagined.

'I don't want to leave you,' Niall said urgently. 'Not when your grandmother...' He didn't have to finish the sentence. Not when her grandmother might die at any time. 'But the baby might relapse. Although the paramedics will look after Lydia, I still need to be there just in case.'

'I know.' She gave him a small push in the direction of the ambulance. 'Go. I'll be all right.'

But still Niall hesitated.

'Go!' Robina said more firmly. 'Right now that baby needs you.'

'I'll be back as soon as I can.' With a last long look at Robina, Niall jumped into the ambulance then, with the siren blaring, he was gone.

Robina returned to her grandmother's side. The old lady was still sleeping, but her breathing had become more laboured in the hour that Robina had been away and she knew it wouldn't be long before her grandmother passed away. She used her mobile to phone Grace, to warn her that her mother-in-law was slipping away.

Distraught, but unsurprised, her mother said she would take a taxi and bring Ella with her, and would be there as soon as she could. Robina didn't tell her that Niall had gone to the hospital and that she was alone. She knew her mother would be even more anxious if she knew, and there was no point in increasing her worry when there was nothing she could do.

She held her grandmother's hand and let the tears fall. And as she guessed, the old lady died without opening her eyes again.

CHAPTER ELEVEN

THROUGHOUT the journey to the hospital, Niall was torn in two. He knew Robina's grandmother only had hours left—if that—and he hated the thought of Robina facing it alone. Once again, he was unable to help his wife when she needed him most. Once again, he had let her down. But he had no choice. He couldn't stop his baby from dying, but he wasn't going to let anything happen to this one.

'I am going to call her Lucky,' whispered Lydia, who hadn't taken her eyes off her baby.

'It's a good name,' Niall agreed. The baby was doing well and he was pretty confident that it wouldn't need to stay in Special Care for very long. As soon as he had seen mother and baby safely into the hospital, he would go back to Robina. He prayed he wouldn't be too late.

And sure enough, by the time he had passed Lydia and Lucky across to the hospital staff and filled out the paperwork detailing his treatment, a couple of hours had passed and he still had no way of getting back to Robina.

'Where can I hire a car or find a taxi?' he asked the driver of the ambulance that had taken them to the hospital.

'Sorry, man, but there is no car-hire place open near here. You'll have to go to the airport to find one open.'

'What about a taxi?' Niall asked.

'There is a taxi rank over there.' The ambulance man pointed to a large group of people queuing across the road. 'But it takes a long time. It must first go to the other villages along the way. If you want a taxi that takes you there directly, you will have to phone, or go to the airport.'

Seething with frustration, Niall looked at his watch. All that would take time he didn't have. The thought of Robina alone was eating him up inside. He called Grace, hoping she would have a better idea, but there was no reply. Robina had probably called her to let her know about her mother-in-law and she'd be on her way to the village.

Niall swore under his breath. There *had* to be a way to get back to Robina.

'You're in a hurry?' the ambulance man asked him.

'A very big hurry,' Niall replied.

'In that case, I will take you myself. My shift has finished for the day.'

'But it's miles,' Niall protested, feeling the first stirring of hope. 'Well out of your way.'

The ambulance man shrugged. 'You helped someone you didn't know. Now I must help you back—it is the custom.' He held out his hand. 'My name is Tambo.'

Soon they were careering up the road in Tambo's rickety car at well over the speed limit. But Niall couldn't bring himself to tell him to slow down. All he cared about was getting back to Robina.

It seemed an interminable time before they pulled up outside Robina's grandmother's house. Niall thanked his rescuer effusively, offering to pay for the petrol. But Tambo only looked offended as he waved away the money. 'I told you, it is my duty. One day, maybe somebody will do something for me and the favour I did you is returned.' And with another wave of his hand he drove away in a cloud of dust.

As soon as Niall entered the room, he knew he was too late. The room was filled with keening women and Robina was sitting by the bed looking stunned.

'Is she gone?' he asked gently. When Robina nodded he strode across the room and wrapped her in his arms. 'Oh, my love,' he said. 'I'm so sorry.'

He felt her relax into his arms for a moment, but then she straightened and pulled away.

'Mum is on her way with Ella. She and I will need to stay, it is the custom, but you must take Ella home. It will only distress her to be here.'

'Ella knows about loss,' Niall reminded her gently. 'Let us stay. We're your family too, and everyone needs their family at times like this.'

Robina smiled wanly. 'I'll have my mother. Honestly, it's better if you go. I'll be all right. As Umakhulu said, she had a long and happy life. She didn't mind dying, she was ready to go.'

'Don't push me away again, Robina,' he said.

'I'm not. I…' She hesitated and Niall could tell she was only just holding it together. 'I'll need you later.' Her voice caught and, despite feeling wretched for his wife, Niall felt a surge of hope. She'd admitted she needed him. It was a start. He owed it to her to let her do things her own way. But this time he would make her talk to him. This time he wouldn't let her push him away. She had to know he loved her and wanted only her. They had to start talking—find a way back to each other somehow.

'I'll go when your mother comes. But I'll be waiting for you. Whenever you need me, I'll be there. I'm not going to let you go through this alone. Do you understand?'

She gazed up at him, her large brown eyes luminous.

'I understand.' She brought a hand to his face and gently touched his cheek. 'How's Lydia's baby?'

'She is going to be fine. We can go and see them in a day or two if you like.'

'I'd like that. One life into the world and another out. I understand that now. It's time for us to talk about our baby. Not here, but later.'

Reluctantly Niall released his wife and watched her being swallowed up by the crowd of women. Hearing the sound of a car, he went outside to find his mother-in-law and daughter emerging from a taxi.

'Could you hold on a minute?' he asked the driver.

Grace looked at him, the sound of keening drifting across the still night air.

'I'm too late,' she said softly. It wasn't a question.

'I'm so sorry. I think she was just holding on long enough to see Robina,' he said. 'I have seen it before in the dying.'

'How's my daughter?' Grace asked.

'She's okay. I think she's going to be all right. I think it's *all* going to be all right.' He could see from Grace's expression that she understood the true meaning of his words. 'She wants me to take Ella back to the house. I'd rather stay, but it's what she wants.'

'You should go. I'll be here with her,' Grace said. 'But later, when it all hits home—that's when she'll really need you.'

He watched as Grace enfolded her daughter in her arms, regretting that once again he hadn't been there when she needed him most. He swore that as long as it was in his power, his wife would never again face anything alone.

* * *

Niall woke to hear the sound of Robina tiptoeing around the room. Although she was quiet, too many years on call had made him alert to the slightest sound.

'You're back,' he said, stating the obvious.

'Only to shower and change,' Robina said. 'Then I'm going back again. I brought Mum home so she could have a rest.'

Niall propped himself on his elbow. In the dawning light trickling through the curtains, he could see the lines of fatigue and grief etched on Robina's face. He longed to reach out and pull her into his arms, but a sixth sense stopped him. He had rushed her before, and he wouldn't make the same mistake again—the stakes were too high.

Instead he eased himself out of bed and touched her lightly on the shoulder. 'I'll make you something to eat, shall I? Or would you prefer to sleep for a couple of hours?'

Robina lay down, still fully clothed, on the bed he had just vacated. 'A couple of hours' sleep, I think, then some breakfast would be lovely.'

Niall hesitated, before lying down beside her and pulling her towards him so that her head was resting on his chest. At first he felt her stiffen and then she relaxed into his arms. Although it took every ounce of his willpower not to pull her closer, he lay there simply holding her, until her breathing relaxed and she fell asleep.

He breathed in the faint smell of her perfume and revelled in the velvet feel of her skin under his fingertips. One loss had pushed them away from each other. This time he was determined that another would pull them together.

When Robina opened her eyes the sun was high in the sky, and the space next to her empty. Niall was up. She felt a pang of loss as sharp as any physical pain. Umakhulu was dead and she would miss the old lady terribly, but for the first time in many months she didn't feel alone any more. There had been something healing in the way Niall had held her, undemanding and yet—there.

Niall shoved the bedroom door open with his shoulder. He was carrying a tray with a pot of coffee and some toast and cereal. Suddenly, Robina's stomach revolted and she fled to the bathroom, only just making it in time. That was all she needed now, with so much to do—a tummy bug. But after she had been sick she felt better. When she emerged from the bathroom, Niall was waiting for her, looking anxious.

'Are you okay?' He frowned. 'Perhaps you should go back to bed for another couple of hours?'

'Please don't fuss, Niall. It's just a bug—I'll be fine. Anyway, there's so much to do.'

'Tell me what and I'll help.'

'There's not much you can do, Niall. Just keep Ella company.'

He didn't see much of Robina in the days leading up to the funeral. He and Ella spent most of the time exploring, either down on the beach or going for a drive. When Robina did return to get some rest, she was usually asleep within minutes. Then as soon as she was awake, she would be off again. He hardly saw her eat and he worried about her, but every time he tried to tempt her with something she pushed her plate away. Grace also looked tired and drawn but she was more concerned about Robina.

'I'm worried about her, Niall. She's so thin and unhappy,' Grace said.

'I'm going to take her away for a couple of days after the funeral. Would you look after Ella for us?' Over the week he had been finalising the plan he had put into action weeks ago. He hoped it would be enough to convince Robina. 'If you think Robina will agree.'

'I think that's rather up to you, don't you? Look, Niall, I don't know what went wrong between you and my daughter, but I hate to see her so unhappy. If you don't love her, let her go so she can move on with her life.'

'Is that what you think? That I don't love her?' He leaned across in his need to convince her. 'You couldn't be more wrong. I love Robina more than I have loved anyone before, or imagine I will love anyone again.' He hated discussing his personal life, it really wasn't his style, but he knew for once he needed to put his pride to one side.

'More than Mairead?' Grace raised an eyebrow at him and Niall realised where his wife had inherited the razor-sharp look that could turn men into babbling children.

'I loved Mairead. I won't pretend I didn't. But she's gone and it's Robina who matters now.'

'Then I think you'd better use the time to make her believe that,' Grace said gently. 'Because, Niall, I have to warn you, if you don't you could lose her for ever.'

All of a sudden Niall was nervous. What if he had left it too late? What if she left him after all? But that wasn't going to happen. He wouldn't let it.

'Over my dead body. In that case, she's coming away with me even if I have to throw her over my shoulder. I'm warning you, there's no way I'm going to lose her now, so you'd better get used to having me around.'

CHAPTER TWELVE

NOTHING and no one was going to keep him away from the funeral, Niall decided grimly, and then afterwards, once they were alone, they were going to talk. He planned to set off for the cottage as soon as the funeral was over. While she had been busy with the funeral arrangements he had put the finishing touches to his plans. He'd had no idea what to pack for his wife, so he'd more or less chucked everything she had brought into the suitcase. Ella was going to one of Grace's neighbour's to play while the funeral was taking place. Then she would stay with Grace until he and Robina returned from their trip.

The funeral surprised him. Instead of the sad and sombre affair he had expected, there was singing and dancing. It was more a celebration of life than a mourning of death. He forced himself to join the men as they clapped and danced—even though he felt ridiculous. This was his wife's country and her customs and he was determined to be a part of it. Robina laughed when she saw his ungainly attempts, but he was glad he had made the effort when he saw how touched she was. She looks at peace with her grandmother's death, Niall thought. Perhaps if they had marked the loss of their child, they too could have mourned properly and taken comfort in each other. He had learned more about himself and his wife in the last few weeks than he had in all the months since they had met. It was make-or-break time, and he was damned if he was going to lose his wife without a fight.

'This isn't the way back to Mum's,' Robina said as Niall turned left instead of right. 'You need to turn around, Niall.'

'We aren't going back to your mum's house. I've arranged for us to spend a couple of nights away. Alone.' His voice was determined, his face set, and Robina sensed immediately it would be useless to argue.

'We don't have to keep up appearances for Mum's sake,' she said tiredly. 'She knows things aren't good between us.'

'Nevertheless, we're going. You've been through a lot in the last few days and you need time to recharge your batteries. We'll be returning to Scotland in a few days' time, and it will be back to work for both of us. For once,' he continued sternly, 'you are going to do as you are told, and let me look after you.'

Robina knew that it could easily be the last couple of days that she and Niall would ever spend together and her chest tightened with the pain of it. She would make the most of every last hour, so that later she could store up the memories.

'Where are we going?'

'Wait and see,' Niall said.

It was one of those perfect summer days, Robina thought as they followed the coast road. Just enough breeze to keep the temperature at a bearable level and to stir up the sea enough to keep sailors and surfers happy.

As she cracked her window open a couple of inches, the

smell of fynbos mixed with the salt of the sea in a tantalising mix and memories of childhood holidays came rushing back. She had hoped to be bringing their child to the same places one day. Robina swallowed hard. She had promised herself that she wasn't going to think sad thoughts. For these couple of days, she was going to only think of happy things.

'Any news from the clinic?' she asked, wanting to keep the conversation on neutral ground. She knew Niall kept in touch.

'A few more pregnancies.' He reeled off a few names that Robina recognised. 'I never quite relax, though, until they're safely delivered.'

As he continued to follow the coast road, Robina began to suspect where they were going. And sure enough a short time later they drew up in front of the cottage that had belonged to Robina's grandparents—the place she had brought him to when they had first met.

'Let's stop here for a while,' Niall suggested.

Baffled, Robina slipped out of the car and joined him outside. The 'For Sale' sign had been removed and the cottage had recently been painted. Obviously someone had bought it. Although she knew it was inevitable that the cottage would be sold, she felt a pang of loss. It was another connection with her past life that had gone.

'I didn't realise it had been sold,' she said sadly. 'Mum never said. But I guess she's had other things on her mind.' She looked down to the beach, remembering how she had played there as a child, and the even more vivid memory of the first time she and Niall had kissed. How long ago it all seemed. 'Why did you bring me here?'

A smile spread across Niall's face and Robina once more felt a pang. That goofy smile of his always undid her.

'What's so amusing?' she asked.

'The image of you running along a beach, all long legs and flowery bikini.'

'Oh, no,' Robina groaned. 'Mum's been showing you the baby album, hasn't she?'

'So what if she has? You were a beautiful baby and an even more stunning teenager. I loved seeing those photos of you,' he continued softly. 'Part of me is jealous I missed all those years.'

Robina's heart missed a beat. Suddenly she felt inexplicably shy in his company. Deep inside she felt a blossoming happiness she hardly dared let herself trust.

Niall dug around in the pocket of his trousers. 'This is where we are spending the next couple of nights.' He looked like an excited schoolboy, Robina thought. So pleased with himself.

He opened the door and Robina gasped with surprise. The house had been painted from top to bottom, the wooden shutters repaired and the pine floors re-sanded and polished. Scattered across the floorboards were rose petals, leading towards the spare room.

Robina raised an eyebrow at Niall, who was looking a little bit like a boy who had been caught stealing apples.

'I'm not very good at this sort of thing,' he said. 'Do you like it?'

She wandered through the rooms, noting that the beds had been made up with fresh new linen.

'You rented it from the new owners?' she asked, moving towards the large picture windows that overlooked the sea. Niall came to stand behind her, resting his hands on her shoulders.

'Not exactly.' Niall shuffled his feet. 'Look, can we sit down?'

The sun was beginning to set, turning the sky a flamboyant mixture of red and gold. All at once the tension of the last few days seeped away and as it did, Robina felt her head spin. She grabbed a nearby chair as the room swam in and out of focus.

Immediately Niall was by her side. 'What is it, Robina?' Taking her arm, he steered her into the chair. 'Put your head between your legs for a moment.'

'I'm all right.' Robina waved him away. 'I think the last few days have just caught up with me.' She shivered. 'It's a bit cool now that the sun's going down.'

Before she knew what was happening, Niall picked her up in his arms. For a moment she was tempted to struggle, but she couldn't help herself from laying her head on his shoulder. It felt so good to be in his arms—to find the comfort and shelter she so desperately needed. Niall laid her on the sofa and covered her with a rug he found over the arm of the chair.

'Don't you move a muscle.' He glowered at her. 'I'll get some heat into this place and sort us out some supper.'

It was strange to have Niall looking after her. Strange, but nice.

She watched him rattling around with the fire, his mouth set in a determined line as he tried to coax a flame from the pot-bellied stove. 'Should have stayed in the Scouts a little longer than I did,' he muttered, but eventually, after several goes, the fire was lit. 'At least it's slightly easier than that last place in Scotland.' They smiled at each other, remembering. Robina was the first to look away.

The light continued to fade, the room lit only by the flickering fire. Neither made a move to switch on the lights. The sound of the sea crashing against the rocks echoed the tumult of emotions that were zinging around Robina's body. Niall pulled her into the crook of his arm and they sat in silence, listening to the sea.

'You still haven't said why you brought me here.' Robina broke the silence.

Niall sucked in a breath. 'It's my wedding present to you. A little bit of Africa that will always be yours.'

Robina felt her blood chill. What was he saying? Was this where he told her it was all over, and the house was somewhere for her to live while they dissolved their marriage?

'I can't believe it's only a year since we met,' Niall started hesitantly. 'When Mairead died, I thought I would never know happiness again. But I had to try and make everything all right, for Ella's sake.'

The ice around Robina's heart solidified. This was the part where he reminded her how important his daughter's happiness was and that nothing mattered except providing her with a secure, happy home.

'Then I met you. And from that day meaning came back into my life. I didn't expect ever to meet someone like you. I didn't expect to be happy again. Not really. But the moment I met you, I knew that life would never be the same again. At first it felt like a betrayal, but I couldn't help myself from loving you. Every minute away from you was torture. I knew those kinds of feelings couldn't be wrong. I was lucky. To be able to find love again.'

Slowly the icy tendrils around Robina's heart began to melt.

'When you agreed to marry me, I thought life couldn't get any better. But when you told me you were pregnant with our child, it did. I knew perfect happiness.'

'But...' Robina interrupted.

Niall placed a finger gently on her lips. 'Please let me finish. I haven't been very good up until now at letting you know how I feel. You know I'm hopeless when it comes to talking about emotions, but I have to make you understand.'

His eyes were like the sea; stormy, impenetrable.

'I don't really know when things started to go wrong,'

Niall admitted. 'I guess I had found more than I ever thought I'd ever have again, so I didn't pay attention to how you were feeling. I left you alone too much, I see that now. Just as I see I should never have asked you to live in the home Mairead and I shared.'

'You had your reasons,' Robina said softly. 'And remember, I agreed.' She smiled wistfully. 'But I did find it difficult to live up to Mairead.' This time it was she who stopped his words with a finger. 'She seemed so damn perfect. Beautiful home, great mother—everything I wasn't.'

A flash of pain crossed Niall's face and he pulled her closer. 'Why didn't you tell me you felt that way?' he said softly. 'I had no idea. You always seemed so confident, so secure in yourself. You have your work and not just any career either. How many women would sell their souls to have what you have?'

And she would have given it all up in a heartbeat to have Niall loving her and her baby back. 'Remember that dinner party we had, soon after we married? The one Lucinda and the others from the clinic came to?' she said.

'Vaguely.'

'Well, I don't think I'll ever forget it. You didn't know then that I don't do cooking, not least because I'm hopeless at it, but I thought I should make an effort. I wanted everyone to think I could at least match up to Mairead.'

Niall frowned. 'I remember it now. But why would you think that whether you could cook or not would matter in the slightest?'

'It seems silly now,' Robina admitted. 'But back then, I don't know, it seemed to matter. I spent hours in that damn kitchen trying to produce something edible, but one look at Lucinda's face when she tasted the first course told me all I needed to know.'

'You did go a bit overboard with the spices. It's the first time I've seen Lucinda's face go as red as a beetroot.' Niall grinned.

'Poor, brave thing tried to swallow, but the others couldn't manage it. You had to go out and get us take-aways. It was awful. I felt so embarrassed. Mairead, I'm sure, would have produced something that wouldn't have been out of place in a restaurant.'

Niall laughed then his face grew serious again. 'I'm sorry, I shouldn't laugh. But nobody minded. And, yes, Mairead was a terrific cook. But that's what she liked to do. She often talked about opening a restaurant when Ella was older.'

'*I* minded. I already felt so inadequate next to Mairead. I know it sounds silly now, but at the time all I wanted to do was hide until everyone had left.'

Niall pulled her closer. 'I had no idea you felt that way. To me—and I'm sure to everyone else—you were this confident, successful woman who had just produced a best-selling book and had appeared on TV. Mairead would have admired *you*. Did you think anyone cared at all that you couldn't cook? I certainly didn't. It was never a reason why I married you.'

'Why did you marry me, Niall?' Robina forced the words past the lump in her throat.

A silence, interrupted only by the crash of waves, stretched between them before Niall spoke.

'As I said, after Mairead died, I thought I would never fall in love again. I didn't want to. Ella was enough for me. And then, when I met you, here in South Africa, I tried to pretend that it was just an incredible physical attraction. That was all. But nevertheless I still felt so guilty. It seemed like a betrayal of my love for Mairead.' He paused, his expression dimming as he turned to her. 'I don't expect you to understand.'

'I think I do. Go on,' Robina prompted.

'Then when I went back to Scotland, I couldn't get you out of my mind. From the moment I woke up until I fell asleep, your face was there. The thought of you, your smile, everything. I couldn't settle or concentrate. Even at work. I tried to put you out of my head, but I couldn't. I knew we had to be together. It was as if I had met the other part of my soul. The missing piece of my heart. I knew I loved you and that we had to be together.'

'And I came to you.'

'Yes. You gave up everything for me. Your life here in South Africa, your family, your job, everything. I know now I should never have asked that of you.'

'I did it willingly. A life without you was no life at all.'

'And we were happy at first, weren't we?'

'But everything started to go wrong so quickly, I didn't even notice until it was too late. Until I lost the baby.' Her voice caught. 'You blamed me for the miscarriage, I could see it in your eyes, but I blamed myself even more. If I'd slowed down, if I'd listened to you, I could be holding our child right now.' This time Robina couldn't prevent tears from coursing down her cheeks.

Holding her face in the palms of his hands, Niall wiped her tears with his thumbs.

'Shh, Robina, I didn't blame you. God, how could you ever think that? As a doctor you know nothing anyone could have done would have made a blind bit of difference.' He swallowed. 'Losing the baby was like a kick in the chest, but coming so close to losing you was unimaginable hell…'

She frowned. 'Everything's a blur after the miscarriage. The last thing I remember was going into labour and then you looking down at me, almost as if you hated me.'

'Oh, my darling love.' He brushed his eyes with the back of

his hand. 'But you are right to a degree. If we are going to be honest with each other then I have to tell you this, even if I feel like a total bastard. When you got the infection and collapsed, I was terrified. When I saw you lying in ITU looking so pale, not knowing if you would live, all I could think about was Mairead. I was angry with you. Angry with God, with everyone. I thought I was about to lose the most important person in my life again and I cursed myself for falling in love with you.'

'I saw it in your eyes. It was the first thing I saw when I came round. I thought you were angry with me for losing the baby. Then I thought you had only married me because you wanted a mother for Ella. I knew then I had lost you. I turned away from you, because I couldn't bear to see the reproach in your eyes.'

'You wouldn't let me comfort you. You looked at me as if you couldn't bear the sight of me.'

'Only because every time I looked at you I was reminded of what I had lost. Not just the baby, but any future children. The infection on top of everything was the last straw. We both know that it's probably put paid to any chances of me having more children. Anyway, even if it hasn't, I don't think I could bear the thought of going through another pregnancy that might end in miscarriage. And you want more children, don't you? You made that perfectly clear that night in the cottage.'

Niall groaned. 'You wouldn't think that a man who is used to dealing with women every day could be so inept. How can I speak to them so easily, yet get it so wrong when it comes to my own wife? I thought if we had another baby it would bring us back together. It was stupid, crass and insensitive of me. I was a fool.'

'Yes, you were.' Robina hid a smile. A warm glow was spreading throughout her body. But she still wasn't convinced Niall loved her for what she was, faults and all.

'And you don't know that you can't have more children. We would need to look at your tubes before we can be sure, and even if they're damaged there is IVF, which admittedly wouldn't mean you couldn't miscarry again. But, Robina, I don't care about having more children—not unless you want to. Can't you see what I'm trying in my uniquely clumsy way to say? I want only you. You are enough for me. Just you. I wanted our baby because he was part of you. A symbol of our love for one another.'

Robina's heart was starting to sing. Did he mean what he was saying? Did he really still love her?

'But I wanted that baby,' she cried. 'Only *that* baby. I know you don't care as much as I do but, God, Niall, it hurts. It feels as if a little bit of my heart has been ripped out and is gone for good. I don't want to ever forget about my baby.'

'And neither do I,' Niall said sadly. 'And we won't. We'll find a way of remembering and acknowledging our first child. But I can only thank God that you lived. Had I lost you too…' His voice cracked and Robina could only guess how much it was taking it out of him to share his feelings with her.

'I am not a demonstrative man,' he said after a moment. 'I wish I was. But it's not the way I was brought up. We Scots are used to keeping our emotions in check. But you have to know that I love you. I can't imagine a life without you. All I want is to spend the rest of my life with you, making you happy, growing old together. I know it's maybe too much to ask after everything, but do you think you could love me again? As I know you once did?'

Robina looked up at him. His intense blue eyes were alight, but there was an uncertainty she had never seen before in the tension in his jaw. He turned to her and gripped her by the shoulders, his fingers almost digging into her flesh. 'If you can't...' His voice was hoarse. 'I'll let you go. It will kill me, but I won't keep you, not even for Ella's sake.'

'Do you promise me that you'll love me for ever?' Robina teased, suppressing a smile. 'Do you promise we will spend the rest of our lives reminding each other? Even if it goes against everything your Scottish heart rebels against?'

Niall looked her directly in the eyes. Whatever he saw there must have convinced him. Slowly his lips stretched in the wide loopy smile that made her heart somersault.

'But you have to tell me too,' he demanded. He pulled her close and dropped kisses that took Robina's breath away up and down her neck. She could feel the answering heat low in her abdomen as her heart began to sing.

'Of course I love you, you idiot. I could no more stop loving you than I could cease to breathe.' She wrapped her arms around his neck and, turning his head towards her, found his mouth. 'Now, don't you think we've wasted enough time?'

As soon as Niall and Robina retuned to Scotland they started re-decorating their home. Despite feeling cosseted and loved by Niall, Robina felt tired and drained from the trip. She suspected that she was still recovering from the loss of her grandmother, and knew that eventually time would continue to heal the wounds left by the loss of her baby as well as her beloved Umakhulu.

Too soon it was time to return to work and wrap up the documentary. She was thrilled to discover that so many of the patients they had followed had fallen pregnant, and although her heart would always ache for the loss of her child, she couldn't help but share in the joy.

On the last day of shooting, after John the cameraman had left, Niall turned to her. There was a new softness in his eyes and a tenderness in his touch.

'Remember we discussed you having your tubes scanned?' he said. 'Why don't we ask Elaine to do it now?'

Robina felt a flicker of anxiety. Was she ready to face the truth? But she and Niall in one of the long talks they'd had since reconciling had decided to consider IVF as an option. But before they headed down that road, they both agreed it made sense for Robina to know for certain how badly her Fallopian tubes had been affected by the infection following the miscarriage.

She took a deep breath. 'Well, I suppose we have to know some time, so why not?'

Niall gripped her hand. 'I'll be right here with you. But whatever the outcome, remember I love you. You and Ella are all I'll ever need. I couldn't be happier than I am now.'

Robina lay on the table, her lower half covered with a towel as she waited nervously for Elaine to start.

'First, I'm going to do a scan of your pelvic region to see if your ovaries are working normally. Then we'll do the tubal patency test. Okay?'

She smiled reassuringly at Robina.

'Why is it that all the stuff we tell our patients means nothing when we're on the receiving end? Perhaps every doctor should be forced to have regular medical examinations to keep them real?' Robina asked them both.

Niall squeezed her hand in sympathy, his eyes glued to the monitor. Suddenly Robina saw him frown and edge closer to the screen. Her heart plummeted. Whatever he was seeing there, it didn't look like good news. Cold tendrils of dread curled around her spine. She wouldn't cry. She had shed enough tears to last a lifetime. Whatever the future held, at least she and Niall had each other for comfort and strength. She could face anything, knowing that he loved her.

'Do you see what I am seeing?' Niall asked.

His voice sounds strange, Robina thought. Please let me be strong, she whispered to herself. At least knowing what they were dealing with, they could decide on the future. If children weren't on the cards, well, they would face that too.

But, incredibly, Niall was smiling, as was Elaine. It was obvious that they weren't the patient, Robina thought grumpily. She'd like to see how they would feel in her shoes. And had she really thought that Niall had turned over a new leaf? Where was his supposed sensitivity in that smile?

Now he was grinning. He picked her up in a bear hug that almost had her on the floor and crushed her to his chest.

'Oh, my love. My sweet darling girl. You know how you have being feeling lethargic and nauseous over the last few weeks?'

Robina barely had room to nod, she was being held so tightly.

'Well, that's because you are pregnant. About six weeks, by the look of it.'

Robina wriggled out of his arms. 'I'm pregnant?' she whispered, hardly able to believe what he was saying.

'Yes. Most definitely pregnant. It must have happened that night in the cottage.' Niall was still grinning from ear to ear.

Robina felt a wave of excitement wash over her. But almost immediately it was followed by an even stronger wave of fear.

'I could miscarry again,' she said softly. 'Maybe we shouldn't get too excited.'

'It's possible,' Niall agreed slowly. 'But somehow I've got the feeling that this time everything is going to work out fine.' And as Elaine left them alone, secure in each other's arms, Robina knew for certain that, whatever the future brought, she would have Niall there, right beside her.

EPILOGUE

ROBINA looked around the house, checking everything was in order. The guests would be arriving any minute to view the preview of the documentary and she wanted to take a moment to reflect. All the staff were coming, as well as Annette and Mike with their little girl and Eilidh and Jim and Trevor and Christine with their baby boys. Maisie, who had been given the all-clear, was bringing her new boyfriend, and Patricia and Luke, who were just beginning treatment with donor eggs, were planning to pop in as well.

As she looked out of the window, watching as the first snow of the winter covered the garden, Robina sighed with contentment. The house, apart from Ella's room, had been redecorated, and while she had kept much of Mairead's colour scheme in the walls and carpets, Robina had added splashes of vibrant reds and oranges in the soft furnishings. Now it truly felt like it was her home.

The last few months of her life had been the happiest she could remember. Although in the early stages of her pregnancy she had been anxious, Niall had been there to constantly reassure her, and the day Johnny had been born she could have sworn he had tears in his eyes. Now they talked about everything, both determined that they would never again leave anything unsaid. Weekends were spent as a family, but they always made time for just the two of them. They planned to holiday in their cottage in Cape Town at least once a year, so their children would come to understand and love their mother's country as much as they both did.

Robina picked up the photograph from the side table and studied the familiar features of her father. At last she understood he'd be proud of her whatever she did. Robina had decided not to return to her show until Johnny was a little older, but had started on her third book. She had more than enough to keep her busy. Niall too had cut back on work and most evenings managed to be home in time for them all to have supper together. He still had to work some weekends, but Robina knew he wouldn't be the man she loved if he didn't care about his work as much as he did.

She felt a movement behind her, and strong arms slipped around her waist, pulling her close.

'I've checked up on Johnny,' Niall whispered in her ear. 'I think he'll be asleep for a couple of hours yet and Ella's still at her friends'.'

Robina turned around to face him, smiling up into his beloved face. 'Are you suggesting what I think you are?'

Niall traced the curve of her cheek with a long finger. 'Have I told you recently that I love you?' he said, moving his finger to her chin and tilting her head, forcing her to look at him.

Robina made a show of checking her watch. 'Not for ages.' She laughed. 'Not since this morning, at any rate.' She blushed, remembering their dawn love-making, the familiar heat in her abdomen spreading through her limbs yet again. 'But feel free to tell me again.'

Niall picked her up in his arms and looked down at her, his

eyes darkening. 'I love you, my love, my heart. And when I get you upstairs, I'm going to show you just how much.'

Robina wrapped her arms around his neck and looked him directly in the eye. 'That's good, *sthandwa sama*, my darling love, because have I told *you* lately how happy I am with you and my second chance family?'

SHE'S SO OVER HIM

JOSS WOOD

I have so many people to thank—treasured friends far and wide who walked this amazing journey with me—but this one is for Vaughan. Firstly for handing me a set of wings and telling me to go and fly, and, on a far more practical level, for the hours you spent with the kids at the airport—not flying!—so that I could write.
Love you.

CHAPTER ONE

'NICE tattoo, Mad.'

The voice came from out of the blue, clear and distinguishable despite the high volume of noise in the bar. Such a luscious voice—deep, smooth, compelling. Like hot chocolate after a freezing walk in the winter rain, she thought as her heart roller-coastered inside her rib cage.

Maddie Shaw flicked a glance to her left and there he was, leaning against the bar counter, a bright blonde barnacle super-glued to his side. Hot damn, her memory wasn't playing tricks on her. It *was* Cale Grant and—oh, heaven help her—he'd moved up from very good-looking to stupid-making hot. Long and lanky had turned into long and strong. Instead of the ponytail she remembered, his naturally streaky blond hair was cropped so that the ends brushed the open collar of his shirt, and the goatee he'd sported on his stubborn chin was gone.

His eyes flicked over her and she watched, mortified, as they stopped at her chest. The tight sleeveless top with the image of a camp queen splayed across it was cut low enough to reveal the edges of her tangerine bra, way more than necessary of her cleavage, and most of the teeny-tiny red butterfly that she'd acquired in a fit of pique shortly after her last conversation with this same man.

'Cale Grant. Wow. Hi.'

And lift your eyes up, bud, she silently suggested, *or I might have to hurt you.*

Resisting the urge to tug up her bra, she met those fantastic eyes—the colour of old-fashioned blue ink. A deep blue that sometimes looked black. Or cobalt. Maddie had always loved his eyes...

She gestured to the bar. 'What can I get you?'

Cale snagged a barstool from under the bottom of a departing drinker. As his date, a mature blue-eyed blonde, arranged her very curvaceous body onto the barstool, Maddie filled another order and turned back to Cale, to find him dissecting her with that intense look she remembered so well.

'What on earth are you doing?'

Maddie looked around her in fake bewilderment. 'I don't know. Raising goats? Computer programming? Macramé?'

'I meant, Miss Smarty Pants, what are you doing behind a bar?'

Maddie lifted dark winged eyebrows. 'I know what you meant.'

'Well? Ten years ago you were doing a degree in Marketing and Communications. Had plans to do your Masters. So why this?'

Maddie sighed as Cale added one and one and got a hundred and two. She kept her answer short. 'It's a job. What can I get you to drink?'

'A glass of Chardonnay and a draught—'

'Maddie—oh, Maddie!'

Cale's words were drowned out by a yell from the back of the crowd of customers waiting to be served. The booming voice was loud and compelling enough to immediately snag her attention. Maddie laughed as her thin, gangly neighbour good-naturedly pushed his way through the bodies to sink against the bar.

'Hey, gorgeous!'

'Hey, back.' Maddie boosted herself up on the bar and leaned across the counter to kiss first one rough cheek and then the other. 'Nat, I've missed you! And here I was, desperate for someone interesting to show up.'

'I have so much to tell you. Jo'burg was fabulous... Thanks for the tip about that bakery in Melville. We're in the back booth;

join us when you have a break.' Nat planted a kiss on her mouth and tapped her nose before melting back into the crowd.

Maddie dropped back to her feet and sent Cale a bland smile, ignoring his narrowed eyes at her not so subtle jibe.

'Sorry, what did you want? A Chardonnay and a—?'

'Draught beer.' Cale sent her a feral smile. 'Still a chronic flirt, Maddie?'

Maddie shrugged and reached for a bottle of house wine. 'Well, I did learn at the seat of the master. You taught me so well.'

'I—' Cale's mouth snapped shut when his companion laid her diamond-encrusted fingers on his sleeve and leaned forward, so that he had a perfect view down the continental divide in her shirt. She whispered something in his ear before sliding off the seat and walking towards the restrooms.

Maddie uncorked the bottle of Chardonnay and glugged the contents into a sparkling glass. 'So, I see that you still do all your shopping at Blondes R Us?'

Maddie caught the quick grin he couldn't hide and wistfully remembered how he'd loved her dry sense of humour. Even if it was at his expense. 'She's…sweet. Not really my type, but sweet.'

'How can she not be your type? You always went for the tanned, stacked blondes.'

She clearly remembered the long-legged, long-haired creatures who had followed Cale, his twin, Oliver, and their sports-mad friends around, their tongues dragging on the floor.

Judging by what she'd read and heard over the years, he still seemed only to date a wide variety of the fairer section of her sex.

It was a point of pride—or idiocy—that he'd once broken the mould with her.

Maddie sent him a sly smile. 'Okay, I'll play… If she's not your type, why are you buying her a drink and allowing her to bat her eyelashes at you?'

Cale stared past her shoulder and Maddie thought she caught

a flash of embarrassment whip across his face. 'She's an…obligation I have to fulfil.'

Maddie's curiosity was piqued. He wasn't the type of man who felt obligated easily. 'Did you lose a bet? A blind date? A favour to a friend?'

Cale scowled at her. 'I haven't seen you for ten years. Can't we find something else to talk about other than my love-life?'

'Why, when your love-life helps fill the social pages every week?'

'It was three times in three months, not every week. I just wish they'd leave me alone.'

'They would if you got your pretty face off TV and out of the public eye.' Maddie leaned across the bar and condescendingly patted his hand. 'And maybe if you stuck to one woman for more than a month nobody would actually care who you are dating!' Maddie countered his annoyed glare with a wide smile.

'Are you quite done?' he demanded.

Maddie shrugged as she put a beer stein under the tap and pulled the lever, feeling her face heat as he watched her. He still had the ability to make her skin prickle…

Cale tapped his finger against the bar before taking the beer she slid across the bar. He ran a blunt finger around the rim. 'It's been a long time.'

Maddie nodded as she took an order for a margarita and a Cosmopolitan from two slick women who were happily drunk and singing along with the house band in the corner. Maddie waited until they'd moved off before flashing Cale a searching look, even as she kept serving drinks, knowing that she couldn't afford to take a break on a busy Friday night.

'What are you doing in this neck of the woods? Or have you moved to this side of the mountain?'

'I'm still in the same house. I heard about this place a while ago and thought I'd try it out. Can you stop for a minute so that we can have a non-interrupted conversation?'

A burly man shouted his order at Maddie and bumped Cale's shoulder at the same time. Cale sent him a look that caused him to step back a pace. Cale, Maddie noticed, still radiated harnessed power. It made men wary and women hot.

She brought her attention back to the conversation. 'Sorry, can't do that. This place is going to start pumping soon.'

Cale looked around in astonishment. 'It's already full!'

'This is nothing!' Maddie shouted back as a roar went up from a rowdy group of students in the corner.

When the worst of the shouting fell away, she placed her elbows on the bar and leaned closer to Cale. She couldn't ignore it any longer. She had to say something. Even if they'd had nothing more than a brief acquaintance, common decency dictated it. What words to use? What did you say to someone who'd lost his twin so horribly?

She decided to keep it simple. 'I'm so, so sorry about Oliver. He was an utterly amazing man.'

Privately Maddie had always thought that Oliver was a modern-day Icarus—a wild, impetuous free spirit who flew too close to the sun. His death hadn't surprised her; the fact that it had been due to cancer had.

Cale looked past her shoulder and she saw the muscle jump in his jaw, a heavy curtain fall in his eyes. His eyes dropped to look at her hand, clasping his thick tanned wrist. 'Thanks.'

He was warm and strong, and she could feel his steady pulse under the ridges of her fingertips.

'Hey, Maddie!'

Maddie jerked her hand away and turned to look at Dan, the other bartender. 'Yes?'

'We're running short on house wine. Can you cover me while I get more?'

Maddie thought that a supply run would be the perfect excuse to recover her shaky equilibrium and to break the intensity of the last minute. Who would have thought that Cale could, a decade later, still accelerate her hormones with one navy-eyed look? She was still obviously—and sadly—a sucker for his hard body and attractive face.

It was just chemistry, she decided hastily. A normal reaction to a very sexy man—which in itself was vastly reassuring.

She hadn't felt the tug of attraction, the prickling of feminine awareness for too long. This was good, given her lack of interest in men and sex these past three years. Hell, she was practically a nun! Well, except for no habit and the lack of devotion…

His was a good-looking face and a sexy body. That was what she was responding to. Nothing else. She'd grown out of her infatuation with sporty womanisers ten years ago.

Probably.

'I'll go. I need a bathroom break anyway,' Maddie told Dan, and turned back to the bar and lifted her hands in a gesture of apology. 'Five minutes, guys.'

Steeling herself not to look back at Cale, she stumbled through the door that led to the kitchen and hooked a left to the staff bathrooms of the Laughing Queen.

Jim, owner of the LQ, good friend and entirely too curious about her love-life, bustled up to her as she reached the Ladies'. 'Dish, dish, dish. Who *is* he?'

'You are such a girl!' Maddie mock scowled at him and drilled a finger into his chest. 'I'd like it put on record that this is what happens when I do you a favour!'

She banged through the door of the Ladies' and rolled her eyes when Jim ambled in after her. Maddie looked at her reflection in the mirror above the washroom taps and grimaced. In the heat and humidity of the bar, the hair that she'd spent an age straightening that morning had sprung back into wild corkscrew curls, and she'd sweated off every trace of makeup except for— naturally—a streak of mascara under each eye, which made her look like an astonished raccoon.

'He is smoking hot! Any chance that he's gay?' Jim demanded. His shoulders slumped at her cutting glare. 'Okay, so not gay. Who is he?'

'First lover.'

'First as in…the *first* first? Oooh…and you're looking like that?' Jim waved his hands at her and shuddered.

'Obviously I would've preferred meeting him again dressed in a fabulous black dress, killer heels and great hair! *Not* wearing my faded Levi's and this stupid tight LQ T-shirt,' Maddie retorted. 'And if you weren't short of a bartender on a Friday night I could at the very least be on the other side of the bar, sipping martinis and not serving them.'

Maddie, seeing that Jim was settling in for a gossip, thought she'd give him the high-speed version to satisfy his immediate curiosity.

'Met him when in my first year at uni. He was doing his PhD in Sports Psychology and some part-time work for the uni's sports department after hopping around the world for a couple of years. We had a very short relationship. Booted him. The end. Now, go away.'

Jim tapped her chin with his index finger. 'Mmm…if that was all that was to it, then I'm a monkey's uncle. You will give me *all* the deets later, Miss M.'

If only it had been that simple, Maddie thought as Jim left. Her relationship with Cale had been anything but. As she'd become part of Cale's group of friends—older than her, but not necessarily wiser—she'd watched and shaken her head as Cale turned over women with the speed of a spinning top. She had nodded when said women called him a heartless bastard for dumping them, and rolled her eyes when he'd charmed them into being friends again.

Then the man she'd laughed, talked and played with, who was the life and soul of any party, who thought commitment was spending six hours with a girl, had turned those gorgeous eyes on her and said that he thought it was time they 'stopped messing around and hooked up'.

His exact words. Mr *So*-Not-Romantic. It should have been a big clue…but she'd allowed him to cajole her into a relationship—handed him her virginity, for crying in a bucket!—despite knowing that he'd be an utterly horrible, comprehensively catastrophic boyfriend. She'd thought *she'd* be the one to change him.

This reminded her how, for a smart girl, she could be amazingly idiotic on occasion.

After wiping the mascara from under her eyes, she splashed water on her face and pulled a long clip from the back of her jeans. Pulling her sable-shaded hair into a rough tail, she twisted it and clipped it to the back of her head in a messy knot. There was nothing she could do about her heightened colour *or* the past, she told herself. And right now she had a job to do.

Maddie plucked up her courage, plastered a fake smile on her face and walked towards the store room.

Back in the bar, she dumped a box of wine under the bar and passed Dan two bottles, idly noticing that Cale's date had to hold the record for the longest bathroom visit. She took an order before tossing him a casual comment.

'Are you still doing triathlons?'

He had to be. Under the steel-grey buttoned-down shirt he wore she could see that his shoulders were as broad, and his forearms beneath the rolled-up sleeves were tanned and corded with muscle.

Cale nodded. 'Occasionally. I switched to adventure racing.'

'Which is?'

'Triathlons on acid. Trail running, cycling, paddling and orienteering. Climbing,' Cale replied, and looked frustrated when she had to turn away to serve a customer.

Maddie caught a glimpse of his date as she made her tottering way back to the bar, and lifted her chin to give Cale a heads-up.

'It was good seeing you, Cale,' Maddie told him.

Cale leant across the bar. 'Listen, can we meet for a drink later? To catch up? I can come back here after I drop Bernie off.'

Maddie cocked her head, considering. What would be the point? Except to show him that she'd made a marvellous life for himself without him? To let him see what he'd been missing out on? They were good, valid reasons, but she suspected that the real truth was that she wanted to see what *she'd* missed out on, to find out what *his* life was like, whether he'd missed her at all. Pride…one of these days it would get her into serious trouble.

Maddie took the money he held out for his drinks and slowly nodded. 'It'll have to be late. I won't finish until after midnight.'

'That's okay.' Cale's mobile and firm mouth briefly twisted. 'I don't sleep that much anyway. I'll see you back here, around midnight.'

Maddie nodded, felt a hand on her arm and turned to face Jim. She leaned into his tall, stodgy frame, briefly seeking support. Over the years this man and his partner had become her best friends, and had rented and eventually sold her the flat above theirs in the small block they owned across the parking lot of the Laughing Queen. As a result, and also because she hated cooking and loved their company, she'd made the LQ her second home. They were a strange little family: two gay older men and their wayward neighbour slash emotional ward.

'Why don't you take a break?'

Jim ran a hand down her arm and Maddie caught the piercing look he sent Cale.

'I'll take over for a while.'

Maddie shook her head. 'Don't look at me like that, Jimbo. All suspicious and speculative. Been there, done that, fumigated the T-shirt.'

Cale saw Bernie to the door of her flat and deftly sidestepped her blatant offer of sex disguised as coffee. At thirty-five he required a little conversation with his sex, some intellectual connection.

Back in his car parked on a side street, Cale leaned his forearms on the steering wheel and stared down the mostly empty road.

Madison Shaw—all grown-up and looking fine—was the last person he'd expected to see serving drinks from behind a popular bar in Simon's Town. Cale tapped the steering wheel with his index finger, staring into the inky night.

Oliver would get such a kick hearing that he'd met up with Maddie again... Habit had him reaching for his mobile to call his twin, and he cursed when sharp pain slashed through his chest. Two years dead and he still automatically reached out to him... Would the complete reality of his passing ever sink in?

Don't go there... Cale took a deep breath and forced his thoughts away from Oliver and back to Maddie. At eighteen she'd been mature and so smart, with a wicked sense of humour. Compared to those breathy, earnest girls who'd made no secret

of their availability, Maddie and her reticent and sarcastic attitude had been a breath of fresh air.

For months he'd listened to his instinct and common sense—
honed from twenty-five years of trying to keep Oliver under
control and out of trouble—that told himself that getting deeper
involved with Maddie, getting involved with *any* woman, was a
train wreck waiting to happen.

But at one of Oliver's legendary parties the combination of
one too many tequila shots consumed and Maddie in a very brief
pair of denim shorts lowered his IQ and he'd taken her to bed.

He'd kept her in it for eight tumultuous weeks.

Madison. Five-feet-four of pure attitude. She'd flipped his life
upside down and he still wasn't sure what it was about her that
had had him, Mr Cool, chasing his tail like a demented puppy.

Accustomed to calling the shots with women, Maddie had
turned him inside out. He'd had no idea how to handle her, no
clue how to deal with those weird sensations she'd pulled to the
surface. He had known that she expected more from him than
he could give—his time, his attention, a large chunk of his soul.
But his time had been split between his work and his studies, his
attention was always half on Oliver, trying to anticipate trouble,
and his soul had never been on offer anyway.

He'd known he'd lost her even before she'd frightened the
hell out of him with that pregnancy scare. He'd panicked and
reacted in comprehensive fear…throwing his pizza into the wall
and storming out to get hammered. Yeah, nobody had considered awarding him a prize for his maturity.

Cale rested his forehead on the steering wheel, wincing at the
memory. When he'd returned she'd waved the negative result in
his face and proceeded to strip ten layers of skin off him. Her
brutal rejection had been swift and non-negotiable and had left
little room for hope.

Petty enough to want to punish her, he'd ignored her calls.
Two weeks later, when his emotions had subsided into a dull
roar and he'd had a vague plan of action for how to talk her back
into bed, he'd found out that Maddie, as she'd said she would,
had dropped out of his life. Nowhere to be found.

He'd been young enough, arrogant enough, to shrug her off and shove any hurt away, choosing to concentrate on his PhD, his career, his racing, revelling in his single status.

Time passed, then his twin had died from cancer, and for months it had been a sheer battle just to get through the day.

He knew intellectually that he was still grieving. He knew how the process worked, the phases he had to get through. In every death there were unresolved issues, but he had a shed-load when it came to his twin's life—and death—and he wasn't nearly ready to deal with them.

Psychologist heal thyself...*yeah, right.*

What he also knew was that depression had gone but guilt, regret and responsibility were still his constant companions.

But then, for all of his life with Oliver those three stooges had never been far away. Guilt for the utter frustration he'd frequently felt towards his reckless, completely unaccountable twin. Regret when he'd been unable to keep him from doing something that had hurt either himself or someone else, and a feeling that he was always responsible for his brother. During his life and at his death.

Oliver had been more than a rebel, more than a free spirit. On more than one occasion, when he'd been comprehensively fed up, Cale had suspected that he might be a touch psychotic.

Guilt, regret and responsibility. *Grr,* indeed.

He knew how to treat his clients' hang-ups, but it was far easier for him to operate on the surface of his own life. He could meet, flirt and even have the odd sexual encounter with women. He wasn't interested in emotional entanglements. He didn't have the time or the energy...and even less inclination.

And he wasn't nearly ready to be in any conceivable way responsible for another person; he'd played that song all his life and he was sick of it.

So the thrill he'd felt at meeting Maddie again was just a flashback to those crazy feelings of his youth—a reminder of a golden time in his life when he'd thought he was so clever, that he'd had life under control. He'd had no freaking idea.

What could it hurt to share a drink with Maddie?

They'd catch up, have a laugh and walk away as friends. After all, he was older and smarter, and now he knew it was when he allowed people into his head—like brothers and lovers—that life tended to become chaotic. And God knew he'd dealt with enough chaos to last a lifetime.

The trick was keeping it all under control. And he'd earned his PhD in *that* as well as the real one on his wall.

After living with crazy Oliver it would take more than a tawny-eyed woman to upset the equilibrium of his life.

CHAPTER TWO

MADDIE rested her arms on the railing that ran the length of the restaurant and stopped the unwary or the intoxicated from falling into the harbour. The inky, oily water lapped the wooden pylons below, and Maddie tried to concentrate on the sounds and scents of summer morphing into autumn. Her tawny eyes drifted over the marina, idly noticing that a new catamaran now occupied the berth at the end. Hadn't Cale once dreamt of owning such a vessel?

Maddie removed the clip that kept her riotous hair off her neck and felt the heavy curls tumble down her back. The bar had quietened down and, since Dan was fully able to cope with the remaining patrons by himself, she'd called it a night.

Lord, she was tired. Even the short walk across the parking lot seemed a mission, and climbing the stairs to her third-floor flat seemed impossible. She knew she needed to rest, yet she knew that sleep—never easy—would be scarce tonight. Her mind, so used to shoving Cale into a box labelled 'Do Not Open, Stupid,' was skipping from memory to memory.

'Maddie.'

Maddie turned slowly and had to smile. With the sea breeze ruffling his hair and the shadows hiding his flat, hard eyes, for a moment he looked like his old devil-may-care self.

'Hi.' Maddie stepped away from the railing and nodded to the empty glass and the open bottle of wine. 'Help yourself.'

Cale picked up the bottle and dumped a healthy amount of Merlot into his glass. He lifted it in a salute and a smile pulled the corners of his mouth up. 'She won a dinner with me at a bachelor auction. Longest three hours of my life. I saw the question in your eyes.'

'Ah.' Maddie's eyes laughed at him over the rim of her own glass. 'She's very…um…sexy.'

'Very…except that I'm not sure how much of it is real or out of a silicone tube,' Cale said, placing his elbows next to hers on the railing.

She could feel the heat from his body, smell his soap, citrus and Cale-scent mixing with the brine from the sea.

Cale pointed his glass at the new catamaran and whistled. 'What a boat.'

'It's new. At the marina, I mean. It docked today.'

'It's new in every sense. Twin screws, dual engines—obviously—and its finer bows give it a nearly forty-five-foot waterline.'

If he said so, Maddie thought, not having a clue what he was talking about. 'I have no idea what that means,' she admitted when he looked expectantly at her.

Cale grinned. 'It significantly improves the upwind and overall sailing ability of the yacht.' He sipped his wine.

'Didn't you sail somewhere once?' Maddie wrinkled her nose, trying to remember.

'When I finished my Masters, I was sick of studying, so Oliver and I sailed a cat from here to Zanzibar. It was the start of two years of travelling. I've never been so physically scared or thrilled before or since—and that's saying a lot because, well, I *was* Oliver's twin.'

Mad Oliver and his many crazy escapades. 'That is saying a lot. What happened?'

'We hit a cyclone off the Mozambique channel. Crazy winds, crazy waves…'

'Crazy Oliver.'

'Yeah. He whooped and hollered his way through it. We nearly capsized a dozen times, and didn't sleep for two days straight, but it was a hell of an adrenalin rush.'

In his eyes she could see the flicker of pain edged with laughter. She knew about the devastation of loss, and instinctively knew that Cale had visited more than one level of hell since his twin's death.

'I really am sorry about Oliver.' Maddie heard her breath catch in her throat. Funny, wild, crazy, impetuous Oliver.

'Yeah. Me, too.' Cale took a healthy sip from his glass and nudged her with his shoulder.

Maddie opened her mouth but stopped when Cale briefly placed his hand on hers.

'It's been a really long day. Can we not talk about him?'

Maddie nodded and stared out at the ocean.

'Please tell me that you don't tend bar for a living.' Cale broke the silence.

'No, during the day I sell crack and turn tricks.' Maddie grinned when he sent her a look of resigned amusement. 'After we split up I worked here weekends for the rest of my time at uni. I still help my friends out if they're short of staff or if I'm bored. I don't normally work this long; usually they let me go home a lot earlier.'

'It's very late to be driving home.' Cale glanced towards the parking lot and she could see his protective streak rise to the surface.

'I don't drive. I walk.'

Cale straightened, and this time he looked genuinely horrified. 'You *what*? Are you insane? Do you know what could happen?'

Maddie laughed. 'Relax, Grandpa.' She nodded at the three-storey block of flats just across the well-lit parking lot. 'Third floor—my flat.'

Cale tugged on a long curl that lay on her shoulder. 'Stop winding me up,' he complained, without any heat.

'But it's so much fun!' Maddie topped up her glass and held out the bottle to Cale, shrugging when shook his head.

'So, apart from your less than legal pursuits, how do you pay for a flat in one of the more upmarket areas of the city?' Cale crossed his arms and rested his glass against his bicep.

Sexy arms, Maddie thought. What would he look like with

his shirt off? Images from long ago flashed in her head. A wide chest, lightly covered in crisp blond hair, strong shoulders—and did he still have that washboard stomach? Her eyes brushed over his lower mid-section and drifted across his slim hips. Oh, yes, it was still there...

Whoah, boy—chemical reaction.

Maddie hauled in her breath, shoved an agitated hand into her hair and counted to ten. Then she counted to twenty, frantically thinking that she might have to go to two thousand and sixty-two to get her heart-rate under control.

Damn him... If he ever gave up his day-job he could hire himself out as a defibrillator. Huh! That was a pretty impressive word for—she glanced at her watch—twenty to one in the morning.

'Earth to Maddie?'

Maddie was jerked out of her thoughts by Cale tugging on the curl again before allowing it to fall off his finger.

'You took quite a mental side trip. What were you thinking about?'

Your muscles under my hands...

'Cardiac arrest and defibrillators.'

Cale's eyebrows lifted in surprise and he scratched his forehead. 'I'd forgotten about your weird thought processes.'

'You always said that I had a mind like a grasshopper,' Maddie agreed. 'It drove you crazy.'

'Newsflash: everything about you drove me crazy.'

Maddie's glass stopped halfway to her mouth. She silently cursed when Cale turned his face away, leaving her with a very good view of his strong neck. What, for the love of all things bright and beautiful, did he mean by *that*? Was he joking? Being serious? Sarcastic? Unfortunately his neck and the back of his head didn't give her a clue.

Cale didn't give her a chance to respond. 'How are your parents?'

'Uh...fine.'

'And your grandfather Red? How is he?'

How could he ask her that? Why would he ask her that? He had to have heard that Red had passed on…didn't he?

Maddie bit her lip. 'You don't know?'

'That he eventually ordered that Russian mail-order bride he wanted?' Cale asked, his voice teasing.

Maddie stared at him. God, he really didn't know. The mind simply boggled.

Maddie turned around and leaned her bottom against the railing, crossed her legs at the ankles and ignored the stabbing pain in her sternum. Ten years? Sometimes it still felt like ten days.

'Red is—excuse the rhyme—dead. The day we broke up.'

'The day we… *What*?' Cale ran a hand over his shocked face and swore quietly. 'Mad, I'm sorry. What happened? Why didn't you let me know?'

Maddie walked away from him, boosted herself onto one of the wooden tables and placed her feet on the bench. 'He fell down the steps in his house and broke his neck. And I did let you know…well, I tried to. I left messages,' she stated, her voice devoid of inflection.

Cale frowned at her. 'What do you mean?'

Maddie stared at the deck. 'I found him that next morning. I called you…so many times. Asking you to help me. My mother was, as per usual, out of town, and my father hated Red. I never expected their help. But yours? Yes, I stupidly did. I didn't need or want them. I wanted you. Not my lover but my friend, who I trusted would be there for me.' Maddie's voice wavered as emotion seeped through her flat tone. 'But you kept dismissing my calls. I left messages asking you to come… There were so many questions. The paramedics and the police…the coroner. Where was I? Who was I with?'

Cale rubbed his face with his hands and swore. 'I don't believe this…'

Maddie shrugged. 'It wasn't a fun time.'

Cale closed his eyes. 'God, Madison. I thought that you were…'

'Begging you to reconsider?' Maddie's eyes flashed molten gold with anger. 'That I was so desperate for your delicious body, to have you back in my life, that I would call you twenty times and leave as many messages? How could you not think that something drastic had happened?'

'I— Yes.' Cale lifted his hands in a self-deprecating gesture. 'I'm sorry. I was stupid.'

'Yes, you were. And cruel. You let me down.'

Cale nodded. 'I can't apologise enough.'

Maddie lifted her eyebrows in surprise at his confession. She'd expected him to justify his actions, to find an excuse. She'd never expected him so easily to admit to being in the wrong.

'I made a lot of bad assumptions.'

'Yes—like you've assumed that I'm a bartender.' Maddie let out a small bitter laugh. 'On that point: I got my honours degree in Marketing and Communication. I work as an event coordinator and PR specialist.'

Cale rubbed the back of his neck and Maddie could see him mentally flipping through her statements. She glanced at the empty restaurant through to the bar, where Jim and Ali sat nursing a coffee. They both kept looking at her, openly curious about Cale.

'I can't believe it was a decade ago. It feels like yesterday.' Maddie rubbed her hands over her face. 'I was young and stupendously stupid but, by God, you were the worst boyfriend in the world.'

Cale nodded his agreement. 'I can't argue with that. I was.'

'You broke dates, rocked up late, didn't call—' Maddie was rattling on, but stopped when she registered his words.

'I spent too much time with my friends and not enough time with you,' Cale added. 'Hell, Mad, I'm just surprised that you didn't drop-kick me off a cliff sooner.'

Maddie shoved her tongue in her cheek. 'Oh, I kept you around for entertainment value. You could always make me laugh. Your excuses and explanations were legendary.'

'And here I thought you kept me around for my skill under the covers.'

'Dream on, dude.' Maddie slapped her hands on her thighs,

looked at the empty wine bottle and then towards her dark flat. 'Look, I've got to get some sleep. So, again—good to see you.'

Cale's strong fingers on her arm halted her progress. 'Maddie—'

Maddie stopped and hung her head, closing her eyes against the flickers of heat that radiated up her arm, the corresponding curl of attraction in her belly. She couldn't believe, after all this time, that he still had the power to turn her anger to lust, her disappointment to attraction. His physical effect on her was instantaneous, dangerous.

'Don't, Cale.'

Cale moved closer and, ignoring her desperate plea, pulled her into his embrace. Strong arms bound her and she found herself breast to chest, her face tucked into the hollow beneath his shoulder, his bent head blowing warm air across her cheek.

So this was what being held by him again felt like. Maddie had to admit that reality kicked memory's butt.

Maddie lifted her head to look into those fabulous eyes. Beneath the sadness and apology she caught a flicker of heat, and suddenly realised the attraction wasn't one-sided. A muscle ticked in his jaw as his eyes darkened and the flame flickered brighter. Maddie could feel his body change, felt the switch from comfort to awareness. It was in the way his hand flexed on her back and ran down her spine.

And that was all the warning he gave before lowering his mouth onto hers. The world fell away as she welcomed his manly, exciting taste, his firm lips and clever tongue, his strong hand on her back pulling her closer.

One of her hands, operating independently from her protesting brain, crept up his hard chest and curled into the thick hair at the back of his neck. The other gripped his hip above the ridge of his belt. Solid, warm, masculine. Oh, she'd missed the feel of hard male flesh, the texture of sun-kissed skin, the demand of strong hands and a firm mouth urging her to take more, to own the moment.

'I'm so, so sorry.'

He murmured the words against her neck and she heard the

sincerity in them. It was the mental equivalent of a tidal wave dousing her back to reality. *Whoah!* She was not eighteen any more, at the mercy of her hormones and emotions. He didn't get to step back into her life and pick up where they'd left off. She wouldn't let that happen again.

She hadn't raised herself to be a fool.

Stepping back abruptly, she sent him a cool look. 'Okay, so that's something that hasn't changed. You always were a dynamite kisser.'

'Um—thanks. Want to do it again?'

Maddie rolled her eyes. 'I'll survive.' Maddie held up her hand as he stepped forward. 'No, stay where you are, Slick.'

Cale reached out to touch her and abruptly pulled his hand back. *Good call,* Maddie thought, *or else I might just end up with splinters in my butt.*

Maddie shook her curls. 'We're not doing this, Cale. It's been a long time, and too much has happened for us to go back there.'

'I am sorry,' Cale said, and she could see the frustration on his face. Did he really expect that a couple of apologies would make it all better? That he could snap his fingers and have her in his arms and his bed again?

Not going to happen.

Maddie lifted her eyebrows. 'Sorry for what? Letting me down? Disappointing me? Kissing me?'

'One and two. Kissing you, it turns out, is still an absolute pleasure.' Cale raked his hand through his hair. 'So, where to now?'

What? Was he insane?

Maddie summoned up her frostiest voice. 'Nowhere! Cale, this is it. You carry on your merry way and I do the same.'

Cale snorted. 'You're not that naïve, Maddie.'

Maddie forced herself to step forward, to give him a patronising pat on the cheek. 'I was never naïve, and you don't know anything about me any more.'

'I know that something shifted in my world when I saw you behind that bar tonight.'

Maddie felt her heart stutter. She didn't like her heart stuttering—wasn't used to it behaving badly.

'And I don't generally kiss a woman like that and let her walk away.'

Ooh, there was that legendary Grant arrogance again. Her eyes and her voice cooled. 'There's always a first time for everything. Goodbye, Cale.'

'This isn't finished, Madison.'

Maddie thought that silence was the best response to his statement, because in truth she had no idea how to reply to the words that terrified and annoyed her in equal measure.

Maddie treasured Sunday—her favourite day of the week. Most Sundays she'd pull on a bikini and a wetsuit, grab her surfboard, then head for the west coast and the big rolling waves that made the area north of Cape Town a surfers' paradise.

Mid-morning, loose-limbed and hungry after skimming the waves, would find her at her favourite coffee shop in Scarborough, devouring the papers and scoffing poached eggs and hollandaise sauce, followed by croissants and strawberry jam.

And coffee—rich, aromatic, compelling. Just like the man walking across the packed room towards her table. This was more like the Cale she remembered: faded navy T-shirt, red board shorts and flip-flops.

She tipped her head and watched him as he stopped for a moment to talk to a fit-looking couple in the far corner. Dr Caleb Grant: consulting sports psychologist and life coach to several national teams, top sportsmen and women, sports writer, TV commentator and triathlon stroke adventure racer.

Unfortunately, due to that strong face and hot body, and the fact that he was rich and relentlessly single, he was also a favourite amongst the gossip columnists. One of, if not *the* most eligible bachelor in the city.

Good for him—but she wouldn't let it affect her; she made it a personal policy never to make the same mistake twice.

Cale took the seat opposite her, took a sip of the coffee from her cup and snagged a piece of croissant with the familiarity of a current lover and not a blast from her past.

'Order your own.' Maddie slapped his fingers as they headed towards her plate again.

Cale, for once, listened and ordered an espresso and two croissants.

Maddie folded her paper and tucked it into her bag. Folding her arms, she tapped her foot. Squinting at him, she reacquainted herself with the object of her fantasies of the last week…and the last ten years. In daylight, she noticed the little things now: a couple of laughter lines, some strands of grey mingled with the streaky blond hair at his temples, and the high-tech watch on his wrist that could be the price of a new car. Well, not an entire car—maybe just a set of tyres. The sunglasses were top of the range too. Striking and successful, he'd become all the *S*'s she'd known he would.

Back then he'd had sardonic, sporty and sexy nailed. She could add super-successful and sophisticated to the list.

'How did you find me?'

'Easy. I went to your flat and your neighbour…Jim?…he told me that you spend most Sunday mornings here.'

'You could've called.'

'You neglected to give me your number.' Cale whipped his BlackBerry out of his back pocket and looked at her enquiringly.

Maddie sighed, recited her number and handed over her mobile so that he could scan the barcode for her BlackBerry BBM. She'd never in a million years thought that she'd see Cale's number in her phone again.

'I can't believe I'm letting you put your number in my phone.'

'Was I that bad?'

'Terrible. Have you improved?' Maddie asked archly, openly curious.

'Probably not as much as you'd hoped.' Cale sat back as the waiter placed his coffee and croissants in front of him. 'What about you? How long did you pine for me before you twisted the next guy up into a pretzel?'

'About two seconds. Nearly as long as you spent missing me.'

'Yeah, I really wish it had happened that way,' Cale said, his eyes on his plate.

Maddie had opened her mouth to pursue the subject when her attention was distracted by the gaggle of young women who had entered the restaurant behind Cale, all wearing tops and shorts about three sizes too small for them. Maddie sourly wondered why they didn't just go out in their underwear. They weren't covering up much more.

Oh, man, she sounded just like a jealous old woman. Deciding it was a good time to take a bathroom break, she quickly excused herself. When she returned, she found one of the gaggle leaning over Cale's shoulder as she watched him scrawl his signature on a paper napkin.

Please, shoot me now, she thought as she ambled back to her seat.

She sat down and waited till the girl had gone, then whispered, 'That's nice, dear, now run along and do your homework.'

Cale choked back his laughter.

'Does that happen often?' she asked Cale, horrified.

He shrugged. 'Now and again.'

'It would drive me nuts.'

'You kind of get used to it. The trick is to remember that they don't know you. They know the TV you. They don't know that you hate going to sleep, or that you snore, or that you are allergic to peanuts.' Cale took a sip of his espresso and lifted a broad shoulder in a shrug. 'It keeps your head from getting too big.'

'It's already big,' Maddie teased, mostly because he expected her to. She played with her teaspoon and decided to risk a personal question. 'Why do you hate going to sleep?'

Cale bit the inside of his lip while he obviously debated what to say. Maddie was surprised when he gave her a real answer instead of responding frivolously.

'The spooks come and get me.'

'What?'

Cale sighed. 'I normally delay going to bed until the early hours of the morning and then I can't sleep anyway. The mind loves three a.m. The nastiest hour of the day.' Cale toyed with a piece of croissant and smiled thinly. 'Just because I'm a psychologist doesn't mean that I don't have my own demons to fight, Mad.'

Judging by the weariness that flashed in his eyes, she suspected that his demons were winning.

'I can understand that,' she replied, intrigued by this new side of Cale.

She sighed when she saw another member of the group stand up and head towards them, a small book in her hand. By the constant looks they sent Cale, and the animated discussion that followed, Maddie supposed that there was a bit of a dare raging to see who grabbed his attention. The fact that he was at least fifteen years older than they were didn't seem to faze them in the least. It was also galling to realise that they didn't think *her* much competition.

This one was a pale redhead with a breathy voice. 'Sorry to disturb, but would you mind?' She thrust the book under Cale's nose.

Maddie sent her a cool look. 'Excuse me, we're trying to have a conversation here.'

'It won't take a mo,' Strawberry Cake dismissed her.

Maddie looked at her super-flat stomach and the small medallion that hung off the ring in her belly button. She blinked and looked again. It couldn't possibly be...

The girl drifted away with another signature and Maddie widened her eyes at Cale. 'Did you see the picture on the medallion hanging off her belly button ring?'

'I was too scared of you to do more than quickly scribble my name,' Cale retorted.

'Funny man.' Maddie leaned across the table. 'It was a very small, very clear picture of a...a sexual position. Very inventive. You'd probably have to be double-jointed to do it...'

Cale mock turned in his seat. 'I need to see it... Let me call her back!'

Maddie pinched the skin on the back of his hand. Then she sighed heavily. 'My mother would applaud her upfront attitude to sex, but I think it looks tacky.'

Cale pushed his plate away. 'Speaking of...how are your parents?'

Maddie leaned back in her chair and rolled her eyes. 'Still mad as a box of crickets. My mother is working as a guest lecturer in Women's Studies at Edinburgh University. She's still got that waste of oxygen with her—Jeffrey. I think you met him.'

'Mmm.'

'My father is still a Professor of English Literature, drinking cheap red wine out of pottery bowls while listening to Verdi and bonking as many undergrads as he can. And, yes, they still think that I am a massive disappointment as a daughter and an outright academic failure.'

'And they still have the ability, when I hear that, to make me want to smack them,' Cale said grimly. 'How can they think that? You are *so* successful.'

'At planning parties? "Darling, any two-bit socialite can do that."' Maddie imitated her mother's crystal-clear diction. '"How do I explain to our friends, our colleagues, that our only child obtained a silly degree in Marketing? The shame, the horror!"' Maddie shuddered theatrically and slumped in her seat. 'I'm embarrassed to admit that I'm still looking for their love and approval.'

'It's a natural response. Habits that are formed in our childhood are the most difficult to break,' Cale told her, idly toying with her fingers.

Maddie pulled in her breath when his thumb caressed the inside of her wrist.

Cale glanced at Maddie's frustrated face, thinking he was glad he'd taken the risk to seek her company today. Her prickly attitude and fast mouth amused him. The vulnerability below her tough, business-girl exterior touched him. To throw in a body still slim, tanned and long-limbed was deeply unfair. Cale watched as she threw confused looks at him. Her amber eyes were dark with bewildered distrust, the colour of bold, old whisky.

Since leaving her the other night his mind had frequently

drifted in her direction, so he'd done what he always did when a subject engaged his curiosity: he'd looked for more information.

He'd spent the last week reaching out to his extensive network of contacts and found out that she was much respected in her field and solidly stable financially. How could her fruitbat parents not be proud of her? They were, to him, a very clear case of too much education and not enough humanity and common sense.

Cale moved in his chair, unfamiliar with the strange sensation he felt just being in her presence. He eventually identified it as excitement. *Excitement.* He rolled the word around his head. He hadn't felt it in a while.

The last two years had been a blur of grief, denial and self-recrimination, and he was still looking for himself...for the Cale he was supposed to be without the person who had shared his life before. Oliver had lived life on a knife-edge and Cale had been sent, he was convinced, to keep him from tumbling over. He had been Oliver's voice of reason, his compass, his navigation system. While Oliver had been brilliant academically, he'd had the impulse control of a two-year-old.

A two-year-old with the destructive capabilities of a nuclear bomb.

Don't think about that, Cale told himself. *Don't think about the chaos he created, the hurt he caused...* Besides, being Ol's voice of reason was what he'd done—except when Oliver had been at his most vulnerable and so sick he'd let him down. Cale swallowed, breathing deeply to keep the flickers of panic to a manageable level.

A slender hand slapping his jolted him from his thoughts. 'What?'

'You faded away on me—with your eyes on my chest.'

The flickers dissolved with one look at her startling eyes. Relieved, he grinned, probably unwisely, at her pinched face. He couldn't help it. Prickly or not, it was good just to look at her. He was bemused by how fiercely compelling he found her. The wave of attraction he'd felt back then had morphed into a tsunami of lust. No woman—not even his ex-model ex-girlfriend,

Gigi—had roused such thoughts. Candles. Silk sheets. A huge bed with her naked in it.

It had obviously been too long. It wasn't because he was remembering how addicted he'd been to Maddie, how much he'd craved her. He was over her; he'd been over her the minute he'd realised that she'd disappeared for good a decade ago.

She was a very good-looking woman and he was just a man. You didn't need to be a rocket scientist...

Maddie was staring at his mouth. Damn, he wished she wouldn't. It gave him ideas, and he needed those ideas like he needed an aneurysm. Naturally even the thought of kissing her had his blood rushing south. Superb, he thought sarcastically, how old was he? Thirty-five or fifteen?

He really had to get himself some action...this was ridiculous. 'Excuse me?'

Oh, hell. Not another one. He sighed and turned his attention from Maddie's visibly annoyed face to the blonde bunny looking down at him, with a far too adult promise in those admittedly startling blue eyes.

Maddie's breath hissed as she swiftly leaned across the table and picked up his plate and coffee cup and handed it to the girl. Not knowing what else to do, the blonde took the crockery and lifted it, puzzled.

'Thanks. Take this, too.' Maddie put some bunched-up used serviettes on the plate and waved her away. The blonde, caught off-guard, turned on her heel and dumped the dirty crockery on an empty table.

Maddie ignored Cale's wide grin, leaned back in her chair and hooked her arm over the back. 'How is *your* family? Still boringly normal?'

''Fraid so. All of us—parents, Megs, the twins—'

'*Whoah*! Back up. You have *kids*?'

Cale grinned at Maddie's shocked face. 'No, you idiot. They are Ollie's kids.'

More shock. 'Oliver had twins? He got married?'

Cale nodded. 'Briefly. The twins were a result of a brief fling and he thought he'd try to do the right thing. He lasted about three months. He tried to settled down with them…but you know Oliver.'

He didn't need to spell it out. Oliver had had the attention span of a gnat.

'Did he see the twins? Spend time with them?'

'He was a great father.'

What else could he say? Certainly not the truth—that he'd been a great father when he'd remembered them and when he didn't have something better to do. Not so great on the realities of fatherhood, like paying maintenance and attending PTA meetings.

To Oliver, the mundane tasks of life had had to be avoided at all costs. And when they couldn't be avoided, normally his twin had stepped in to sort them out.

Maddie cocked her head. 'Good for him.'

Her dry tone told him that he hadn't completely convinced her. But that wasn't his problem. He never openly criticised Oliver. *Ever.* His mixed-up contradictory feelings about his brother were his and his alone.

'Anyway, to get back to the subject, my parents are fine, thank you. We all had supper together a couple of nights ago.' Cale rested his cheek on his fist. 'They're talking about doing something in memory of Oliver. It's two years in August.'

Maddie tipped her head, immediately interested. 'Like what?'

'My mom has this idea that we should do something to raise money for charity in his name.'

He thought the whole idea was mad, but if an event and some funds helped his mom work through her grief he'd be all over it.

'Nice idea.' Maddie thought for a minute. 'Didn't you and Oliver organise an informal triathlon while you were doing your PhD?'

Cale dropped his fist. 'Yeah, we got all our racing friends together and did it for laughs.'

'So, do it for Oliver. Do it for charity.'

'It's an idea.' Cale took her hand again, his fingers sliding between hers. 'Would you help?'

'Cale...I can't. My plate is so full,' Maddie responded. 'Besides, you and I working together? Not wise.'

'Why not?'

'Because we'd either end up killing each other or end up in bed.'

'Or end up killing each other in bed, which sounds like an amazing way to go,' Cale said on an easy grin.

'Yeah...*not*. Anyway, play around with the idea and see what you come up with. I think it could work,' Maddie suggested, before standing up and pulling her bag over her shoulder, she threw him a cheeky grin and buzzed her lips across his cheek. 'Thanks for breakfast.' She flicked a glance at the young women next to them. 'If you take any of their numbers I will hunt you down and kill you. Too stupid and too young. Even for *you*, Slick.'

Maddie gently nipped his bottom lip before walking away. There was nothing wrong in her humble opinion, in leaving a man wanting more than she intended delivering. It was one of the perks of being a woman.

CHAPTER THREE

UNLIKE most people, Saturdays for Maddie were nearly always full work days and consistently crazy. They were family days: weddings, engagements, family reunions. It was her role to make sure that the emotional, sentimental stuff didn't interfere with the logistics.

Today, she treated herself to a fifteen minute soak before stepping out of her ball-and-claw tub and reaching for a towel. Moving in the small bathroom was always a challenge, but she refused to sacrifice her precious cast-iron bath for a few inches of space. Turning towards the basin, she nudged the open door with her bottom and, as per usual, the slightest movement caused the door to swing itself closed. Maddie heard the usual click— and then a loud clank as something inside the door dropped. Frowning, she pulled the handle of the door. Although the handle moved, the door remained firmly in place.

Maddie looked at the door, absolutely non-plussed. She jerked the handle again, heard the rattle of parts in the mechanism, yet the door remained resolutely, stubbornly closed. After five minutes she came to the unhappy conclusion that she was locked in her own bathroom.

Maddie cursed, softly and creatively, before reaching for her mobile.

'I love you, Mad, but not at six in the morning,' Jim grumbled when he finally answered her call. 'Especially on my weekend off.'

'It's seven, and I have a problem. I've managed to get myself stuck in my own bathroom.' Maddie explained the situation. 'I need you to come and rescue me.'

Jim cursed. 'Sweetie, I told you—we're away for the weekend. What about Kate? Nat?'

'Kate is also away, and I tried Nat. His mobile is off.'

'This is why you need a non-gay resident man in your life,' Jim told her. 'You know—someone to fix tyres, change light-bulbs, unscrew doors...'

Maddie knew what was coming.

'There could even be some other benefits on the side...'

'Supremely unhelpful, Jim,' Maddie grumbled before dis-connecting.

She glanced towards the open sash window and shivered at the gust of cool wind that swirled around her wet body. Who else could she call? Cale? She hadn't spoken to him since the coffee shop, and was currently ducking his calls because she wasn't quite sure how to handle him....

Ignoring the thought that Cale wasn't the type of man to be 'handled' at the best of times, Maddie told herself that she dealt with people on a daily basis...she was never at a loss for words. But Cale made her feel tongue-tied and gawky...awk-ward. Mostly because she was pretty sure that her attraction to him was tattooed on her forehead.

If she were a dog then she'd be constantly panting....

Maddie glanced down at her skimpy towel and realised that calling him would be dangerous. She was practically naked, and she suspected that she had a good chance of ending up flat on her back if Cale saw her like this.

She'd loved him as a teenager, had burned up the sheets with him—when they weren't fighting—but she'd never experienced this soul-jumping, crotch-squirming reaction that swept over her every time he was within a hundred-foot radius of her.

Lust. So this is what it really feels like, huh? It had to be lust. What else could it possibly be? Feeling like this, she assured her-self, was a very normal, natural reaction when you hadn't had sex for more than...roughly four hundred days times four—*one thousand, two hundred days!*

Or thereabouts.

She was allowed to feel all jumbled up.

She made a couple of calls: one to Thandi to cover for her, and a request to her mobile service provider for a list of locksmiths in her area. As she started to dial the first, her mobile rang. It was an unfamiliar landline number and she answered it cautiously.

'Maddie, it's Cale.'

She really had to save all his numbers into her phone, she decided.

When she didn't reply, Cale continued speaking. 'Hello? Maddie?'

'Cale...um—hi.'

'Are you okay? You sound funny.'

'I'm—I'm fine.' Maddie heard the note of hysteria in her words and hoped that Cale missed it.

No chance. 'What's the matter?' he demanded.

Maddie heaved in a breath. 'I'm locked in my bathroom.'

'You're what?'

'I'm trapped—I can't get out of my bathroom. There's something wrong with the door,' Maddie said, trying for cheerful but hearing misery in her voice.

'Right. Are the hinges on your side of the door?'

Maddie wondered if she'd really heard the faint thread of laughter in his steady voice. 'You'd better not be finding this funny, Cale! And the door swings out, into the dressing room. So the hinges are on that side.'

'Good. That makes it easier. I'll be there in...say, twenty minutes. But how do I get into the block?'

'Keypad. My code is 6541. And my front door is open,' Maddie replied, and put the heel of her hand into her eye socket. 'Look, Cale, if it's a hassle I'll call a locksmith—although they'll cost their weight in gold to do a call-out on a Saturday,' she added glumly. 'And I'll be so late for my functions.'

'Don't be stupid. Twenty minutes,' Cale said, before disconnecting.

Maddie placed her mobile on the windowsill, watched the walls recede a little and, feeling like an idiot, almost wept with relief.

Twenty-five minutes later, Cale parked in a visitor's parking bay and looked at the small brick block of flats encircled by a wrought-iron fence.

He hopped out of his car, re-adjusted his grip on his toolbox and walked up the front steps. As Maddie had said, the front door opened to her code and he walked up the stairs and straight through her front door. Her flat smelled like its owner: light, fresh, slightly intoxicating. She'd used the open space well, filling the living area with comfortable-looking furniture, and a floor-to-ceiling bookcase took up one wall. The room looked restful and lived in, although he wasn't sure about the red walls.

Cale turned into the passage and opened the first of three closed doors. He grinned at the mess. An unmade bed, a hot pink T-shirt over the back of a wingback chair and a violet bra on the duck-egg-blue duvet. Putting the toolbox down, he put his hands on his hips and looked around, taking in the details. Like the fact that the wall above the bed was dominated by an abstract painting in creams and browns. Cale nearly dismissed the painting, but something made him look at it again. It was a massive swirl of neutral colours, fluid, filled with emotion and...*sex*.

It looked like a cream and brown orgy.

Or it might just be an abstract cream and brown painting and he'd see sex in a tub of margarine.

Dragging his gaze away, Cale looked around the room. Deep brown curtains and an antique dressing table dominated the room, groaning under the weight of all the junk he'd come to expect from the female of the species. Necklaces and beads spilt out of copper woven baskets, perfume bottles vied for space, and lipstick tubes, scraps of paper and small change littered the rest of the wooden surface.

'Cale? That you?' Maddie called.

Cale walked into the dressing room. He presumed beyond the shut door was the bathroom. 'Yeah. How you doing in there?'

'Getting a bit cold.'

'Hang in there. Not long now.' Cale looked around her dressing room; in such an intimate space he felt surrounded by her.

'I see that you still keep the retail sector of the city in champagne and caviar,' Cale told her through the door.

'What are you on about?'

'Your immense selection of clothes. How can you possibly need so many shoes?' Cale asked as he bumped his thigh against an open drawer and glanced down. Naturally it was her lingerie drawer. Cale swallowed, unable to resist lifting a semi-transparent candy-pink thong that was hardly bigger than dental floss.

'It's a girl thing,' Maddie grumbled. 'You wouldn't understand.'

'I won't even try to,' Cale assured her.

'Stay out of my lingerie drawer,' Maddie warned him.

Cale quickly dropped the non-offending article. How could she know he was... Did she have X-ray eyes?

'Nothing would fit me,' Cale joked as he put down his toolbox and placed his hand against the door.

'Ha-ha. Can you hurry up? I'm getting really cold.'

Cale looked at the hinges on the door and sighed. The hinges were covered in paint—many layers of paint—which would make them difficult to unscrew. He tested the handle on the door, just in case, and heard the click-clack of the faulty mechanism. He thought he heard Maddie's snort of impatience and didn't blame her. Crouching again, he assembled his drill and, with plug in hand, stood up to find an electrical outlet. He disconnected the hairdryer and plugged the drill in. Placing himself between the door and the edge of the closet, he felt for the creases that indicated where the screws were and in a few minutes had them in his hand.

Grabbing hold of the wrong side of the door, he pulled it away from the frame and saw Maddie, wet-haired and shivering, a small towel barely covering her from collarbone to crotch.

With her makeup-free face and wide eyes she looked about seventeen.

'It's like a fridge in here!' Cale exclaimed as he stepped inside.

Maddie clutched the top of her towel, her hands white and her bottom lip almost blue. Being so close to her in the tiny bathroom, he could see the fine shivers trembling through her. Cale looked towards the sash window Maddie gestured to.

'Tell me about it. The cord got jammed ages ago. I'll have to get it fixed soon.'

'Why didn't you get back into the warm bath?'

'Hot water ran out.' Maddie shrugged

'Get dressed,' Cale ordered. 'You're going to get sick.'

Maddie looked towards the door that half stood, half hung in the doorway. She clenched the top of her towel tighter and stepped around him. Yanking some clothes off a hanger, and some underwear from the drawer, she moved into the bedroom.

Cale took a deep breath and looked down through the dressing room into Maddie's room. In her haste to get warm and out of his sight she'd started dressing in the far corner of the room and he could see her reflection in the dressing table mirror. Unable to pull his eyes away, he watched as she dropped her towel and gracefully pulled on a pair of low-cut panties. Her stomach was gently rounded, her legs long, her hips slim. Cale swallowed as she slid trousers up her legs and reached for a gauzy cream bra and snapped it into place, doing that weird jiggly thing woman did to make sure it fitted exactly right.

Cale swallowed a moan. Since he hadn't had any action for a while he was surprised that moaning was all he did.

As opposed to lying her on that bed...

'Cale?'

Cale blinked. She was shoving her arms into a shirt and turning to look at her reflection in the mirror. Stepping back just in time, he leaned against the open sash window.

'Yeah?'

Maddie appeared in the small area between the hanging door and the frame. 'Thanks. It was turning out to be a long, cold morning.'

Cale shrugged off her thanks and gestured to the window. He spoke brusquely. 'You need to get this fixed or else you'll freeze.'

'I keep meaning to and I don't seem to get it done.' Maddie nibbled at her bottom lip. 'I'm really sorry, I didn't mean to inconvenience you like this—and on a Saturday morning, too.'

'Maddie, it's fine. No worries.' Cale practically spat the words like bullets.

Her eyes heated and her mouth firmed. 'Then the least you can do is be gracious about helping me instead of a doing a great impression of a bear with a thorn in its paw!'

Cale closed his eyes as if seeking patience. 'Can we drop this, please? It's a stupid conversation.'

Her eyes lightened with frustration. 'But—'

'You just don't know when to shut up, do you?' Cale burst out, his breath ragged. He stood up and took two steps to reach her. He looked into her desperately pretty eyes and grimaced. 'Okay, Maddie, see if you can handle this. Pretty, feminine room. Sexy painting. Lingerie. Wet woman in towel. Wet woman getting dressed around the corner. Keep thinking about what I want to do to you in that bed. I want to do you in the worst way possible. Getting the picture yet?'

It almost amused him to see how the tips of her ears and then her cheeks blushed. 'Oh...'

'Yeah. *Oh.*'

Maddie stepped back into the dressing room and leaned against the shelves—yet he still managed to connect most of his body with hers as he slid past. On a low curse, he turned and cupped her face with his big hands.

'Maddie, look at me,' Cale commanded.

Maddie curled her hand around his strong wrist and looked up. He saw his desire reflected in her eyes, could feel her jumping pulse in the tips of her fingers.

'It would be so easy...'

'I don't do easy,' Maddie muttered.

Cale heard her words but they didn't make any sense. Why was she hedging when there was this heat between them? Didn't she understand that this was important—*all* that was important?

Cale dropped his hands to her waist. He just had to touch her, had to move closer. Just for one minute...

'I'm sorry, I just have to,' Cale said, stepping forward, his hands on her supple back.

Cale heard her groan as she welcomed him into her space, heard her breath hitch and felt her nipples pucker against his chest. 'You shouldn't be here.'

'In your arms or in your house?'

'Either. Both. This is wrong.'

'Why?'

'We're practically strangers. I don't know you any more.'

But her eyes said that she had an empty flat, that she wanted to get naked, that she needed him as much as he needed her. How exactly was he supposed to resist?

'Maddie...' He drawled out her name. 'Your mouth is saying one thing and your body another. Which do I listen to?'

Maddie shoved a trembling hand into her hair.

'What do you want me to say? That I just look at you and all I want to do is strip you naked and throw caution to the wind?' she said, her voice hoarse.

He frightens me, Maddie thought wildly, her eyes on his. *The way he makes me feel terrifies me. He just touches me and I feel complete... I feel him everywhere... Every cell in my body is yelling for him to take me... He feels like... God, he feels like home.*

That couldn't be good.

Cale took a step towards her and placed his finger on the beating pulse-point below her throat. 'Don't make me beg, Mad.'

Cale slowly undid the buttons of her shirt and pushed the fabric down her arms to reveal creamy shoulders. He let the shirt drop and she stood there in her semi-transparent bra. After watching her for a long, long minute, Cale stepped towards her and yanked her to him. His mouth slanted over hers as his hands grabbed her bottom and pulled her closer, allowing her to feel the hard erection he could no longer hide. He felt Maddie burrowing her hands under his clothing until she eventually found his skin.

Cale stepped backwards and cursed as he slammed into the doorway. He lifted his head to quickly scan his surroundings and bent his head again, kissing her as he walked her into her bedroom. His mouth nibbled her neck before he turned around, sat down on the bed and pulled her so that she sat across his thighs.

One strong arm banded around her waist, he half lifted her off him to take his car keys and his BlackBerry out of his jeans pocket and place them on the bed next to him. He yanked Maddie back onto his lap and lifted his hands to hold her face. He pushed a strand of hair that kept falling in her eyes behind her ear and traced her mouth with a callused thumb.

His eyes, when they met hers, were serious. 'Are you sure you want to do this?'

Maddie closed her eyes. 'I shouldn't, but...'

Cale's palm drifted over her back and his tongue thrust deeper to explore her mouth.

His long fingers were fiddling with the side button of her trousers when the ring of his mobile pierced her sexual fog. She looked past his shoulder and saw the display light up. The name 'Megan Adams' flashed on his screen.

She stiffened in his arms and felt the same familiar, burning jealousy she had as a teenager. Karen. Jenny. Amber. He'd been relentlessly chased and she knew that he always would be. She suspected that he often allowed himself to be caught...

'Saved from my own stupidity,' she muttered as she pulled back. Clambering off his lap, she pulled the cups of her bra back over her breasts.

Cale—smart man—let his mobile ring to voicemail. 'Maddie? What the hell?'

Maddie looked around for her shirt. 'I'm late and you need to get out of here.'

Cale grabbed the waistband of her pants and held her in place. 'I'm not going anywhere until you tell me what flicked your "off" button.'

'At least I *have* an "off" button! You don't seem to!'

More worrying was that he'd found her 'on' button so quickly. He'd liquefied her common sense in ten seconds flat.

'Oh, God! Here you go again, judging my love-life.' Cale

rolled his eyes. 'Trust me, you're making something out of nothing, Mad.'

'So you say.' Maddie shrugged in mock insouciance. 'But, just so we're clear, I am never going to be a woman who hangs around waiting for your calls!'

'Uh—I'll never expect you to be.'

Maddie, feeling his fingers warm against her stomach, walked around his knees and leaned across the bed. She grabbed his mobile and waved it in his face. 'Like *this* poor woman!'

'Who?'

Maddie didn't need to check the name. 'Megan! Megan Adams!'

Cale looked puzzled. 'Megan Adams often calls. So?'

Maddie jerked away, and the look she sent him was hot enough to burn a hole in sheet metal. 'And she's okay with you sleeping with other women?'

Cale grinned. 'She seems to be.'

Maddie knew that he was mocking her and wasn't quite sure why. It only ratcheted up her temper. Stomping away, she grabbed her shirt off the floor and pulled it on. 'You're not funny. Just go, Cale.'

'You've really got the wrong end of the stick, Maddie.'

'Cale, this is me—remember? I remember the incessant phone calls and the drooling girls with their flicky hair. I know. I was the girlfriend trying to compete for your attention with them!' Maddie yanked a comb through her still-wet curls. 'Megan's just another poor sap desperate for you to take her calls. FYI, I've grown up and I will never, ever again be Miss Desperate or Miss Stupid or Miss Waiting-in-Anticipation for you to call!'

Cale stood and picked up his mobile and keys from the bed. She caught his flinty eyes and his tight jaw. He walked into the dressing room, reappearing with his toolbox in hand. 'No, you now have the title of Miss Closed Mind and Miss Stubborn. Maybe Miss Childish, too,' he said coldly.

'Whatever,' Maddie snapped. 'And Cale?'

Cale stopped at the door, his fingers white as he clenched the frame of the door. 'What now?'

'I know that you were in my lingerie drawer! Where's my candy-pink thong? Did you take it?'

He found it where he'd dropped it—behind the bathroom door—and tossed the underwear towards her.

'I'd be happy for you to add it to your collection, but it's my favourite,' she called as he stormed out and slammed her front door so hard that the earth tilted off its axis and, Maddie was quite certain, set off an earthquake somewhere in the South Pacific.

BlackBerry Messaging: 16.15.

Cale Grant: *Just thought I'd let you know that you're the first woman I've killed in 3 months.*

Maddie: *What? Standing here watching my bride walk down the aisle. Pretty sure I'm still alive.*

Cale Grant: *Kissed, not killed! Can't get used to this new phone. Thought you should know that since you think I'm a man slut. Just clearing the air...*

Maddie: *Seriously? So, if you haven't kissed/killed anyone, then you haven't...? How long since you...you know?*

Cale Grant: *Not answering that.*

Maddie: *Curious. Can I still call you Slick?*

Cale Grant: *You're laughing, aren't you?*

Maddie: *MAO. So...are you waiting for an apology?*

Cale Grant: *Would you give me one? Anyway, just wanted to clear the air. Now going for a long, long run, followed by a cold, cold shower...unless you're offering alternative entertainment?*

Maddie: *Nope.*

Cale Grant: *Damn.*

'Maddie? Are you there?"

Maddie, perched on a ladder helping her crew drape a tent, mobile to her ear, mentally shook herself and concentrated on the low drawl. Finally putting a name to the voice, her lips curved in pleasure as she recognised a rival co-ordinator.

'Dennis King, what do you need? An ice sculptor? A Roman set? Some advice?'

Although they were officially competitors, they both recog-nised the value of maintaining a cordial, friendly relationship. Who else but another event co-ordinator would know the name of an ice sculptor at two in the morning? Who else would under-stand? From who else could you borrow a cream tent, supple-ment chair covers, or get a new source of blue roses?

'Hey, sweetie, you're good, but I doubt that even *you* can ex-press a Roman set to the Big Apple.'

'You're in New York? What are you doing there?'

'Got a job at Bower & Co.'

Maddie nearly swallowed a pin. How on earth had he landed a job with one of the most respected PR and eventing firms in the world? And why hadn't *she* heard about it?

'That's actually why I'm calling you.'

Maddie removed the pins from her mouth. 'Sorry?'

'They've got an opening for an events co-ordinator and I thought of you.'

'Me? Why?'

'Because I could use a friendly face here, we get along well and you already work the long hours that are standard over here. What do you think?'

Maddie sat down on the ladder and rubbed her eyes. 'Wow, Dennis. *Wow.* I'm not sure what to say.'

'Say you'll think about it. I've been dropping your name at every opportunity I get. In the meantime, e-mail me your CV.'

'I'll think about it. New York?'

'Manhattan, baby. Big money. Big kudos,' Dennis replied. 'E-mail me your CV. Later.'

Maddie looked down at her dead mobile and pinched the bridge of her nose. She carefully sat down and rested her head on her knees. New York City.

This was so exciting—a career move of stratospheric propor-tions. Bower & Co tendered for opening ceremonies at sporting events, Hollywood première parties and political balls. They were solidly big league...

She couldn't wait to tell...*Cale*?

Maddie huffed a breath. Why did her thoughts instinctively

veer to him? He'd just dropped back into her life, she wasn't even sleeping with him, and they'd shared no more than a couple of conversations. *You're being an idiot,* she told herself. He shouldn't even be a blip on her radar.

But he was, and he was blipping far too often for her physical and, more frightening, her emotional comfort. *You're just out of practice,* Maddie assured herself. *Allowing your imagination to run away with you. You're—eek!—sexually frustrated and easily confused.*

She didn't like being either.

Focus, Madison.

Maddie stood up and pushed her shoulders back. She'd send off her CV and see what happened.

New York, baby! *Wooo-hoo!*

CHAPTER FOUR

HE NEEDED her.

Okay, he needed to rephrase that. He needed to sleep with her. Better. He didn't need anyone. He was entirely self-sufficient and he liked it that way.

Cale leaned back in his office chair and propped his feet onto the corner of his desk, idly threading a pencil through his fingers as he waited for his next patient. He was exhausted, and the combination of insomnia and sexual frustration added an edge to his temper that he didn't need.

He wished it was just general sexual frustration... If it was that simple he could find meaningless sex. He could pick up the phone right now and call at least five women and know that at the end of the evening he'd get lucky. The thought left him with a sour taste in his mouth. It was his crappy luck that it seemed only sex with Maddie would do the trick.

Why only her and why now, God only knew—because he sure as hell hadn't the faintest clue. But hers was the body he currently craved...

He didn't mind her company either, he admitted. She had a quick mind and a smart mouth and he enjoyed talking to her—but then he always had.

Oliver had liked her—a lot—but he'd always been wary of her, Cale remembered. Maybe it was because Maddie was one of only a couple of women who'd looked past Oliver's handsome face and charming manner to try and find the core of the person beneath the façade he'd presented to the world. She hadn't succeeded. Very few people had known the real Oliver. Sometimes Cale wasn't even sure if he was one of them.

Exhausted, he kneaded the back of his neck, hoping to release some of the tension there. There was no point in looking back...you just had to live with what had happened. You couldn't change the past but you could learn from it.

But if he could he'd avoid the chaos that life loved to throw at him. Admittedly when Oliver had died seven-eighths of the chaos factor in his life had died, too, but he'd take every thing life could throw at him to have his brother back.

That wasn't going to happen so he had limited the turmoil; he'd learnt to recognise the people and situations that brought it into his life.

Emotional relationships were high on turmoil, so he avoided those. Woman in general came with a host of problems, so he never allowed any of them to stick around long enough to form any sort of emotional attachment. He worked alone—mostly— and he was paid to dive into his patients' heads. They stayed out of his. Win-win.

Cale knew that Maddie's chaos factor was sky high but he simply wanted her. And if he could keep it light and on a sexual level he could handle it. Handle her. He'd have to handle it... What was the alternative? Not seeing her and having this constant circus in his pants? No, thank you.

Cale placed his arms on his desk and scowled into his empty coffee cup. This raised a point...how was he going to get her into his bed? He could just suggest that they sleep together, but he suspected that she'd shoot him down in flames. And it felt vaguely hypocritical to do the bringing her flowers and dating thing...

With what they had cooking he just needed to get her on her own and let nature take its course...

Cale glanced down at the pile of messages next to his elbow and idly picked them up, flipping through them as he mulled over his problem.

Speaking engagement...cancellation of an appointment...

reminder of a meeting. His mother asking whether he'd had any more thoughts on doing something in memory of Oliver...

Cale stared at the pink slip as an idea started to take shape in his brain.

He could kill two birds with one stone...

'What are you working on?' Maddie asked her colleague Thandi the following morning.

'International Piano Festival.' Thandi rolled her shoulders, the powder-blue silk of her floaty top whispering over her smooth deep brown shoulders. 'Are you still neck-deep in fish?'

AKA the Tight Lines Fishing Contest. Maddie took a sip of cold coffee and managed not to grimace.

'For my sins. Harriet hates me,' Maddie replied, referring to their managing director and issuer of event assignments.

Thandi, Maddie noted, didn't bother arguing.

As Thandi sauntered out of the office on a wave and a promise to bring back something 'deeee-vine' for afternoon tea, Maddie wished she wouldn't. Unlike her colleague, she didn't have Naomi Campbell's figure, or her ability to incinerate fat. If she kept eating chocolate éclairs every day from Bruno's—the specialist bakery down the street—as Thandi did, she'd be the size of Table Mountain in a month.

Depressed, and feeling the waistband of her tan tailored pants biting into her waist, Maddie rolled her chair closer to her desk and filed a quote for white roses, making a quick note in her diary to call the suppliers and accuse them of highway robbery. They were *roses*, she'd remind them, not solid gold ingots.

A discreet beep from her laptop alerted her to an incoming e-mail. Dropping the spreadsheet she was working on, she pulled up her e-mail program and frowned at the address.

To: Madison Shaw (mshaw@mayhewwalsh.com)
From: Cale Grant (Cale@calegrant.com)
Subject: Triathlon Charity Race
Dear Ms Shaw
   In memory of my brother, Oliver Grant, I am embarking on

organising a triathlon race to raise funds for blood-related cancers. (Please see attached document.) The race will take place in August, on the Peninsula.

The one-day race comprises a four-mile surf-ski, an eighteen-mile mountain bike trail, a twenty-mile forest run and a two-mile beach run.

In your position as a promotions and events co-ordinator, I hope you can assist me with some pro bono work to help raise corporate sponsorship and publicity for the race. I'm sure a few letters and a couple of calls would do the trick.

For further information on triathlon racing, please visit my racing website: www.sportshuntracing.com

Thank you for your anticipated response.

Caleb Grant

A second e-mail followed five seconds later with a brief message.

I thought I'd try the formal approach. Did it work?

Maddie tapped her index finger on her desk, scowled at her laptop, and out of curiosity hit the link to the website Cale mentioned and leaned back in her chair as the pages filled her screen. She skimmed through the site, deliberately ignoring the articles around fitness, and skipped onto the photo gallery. And there he was, much as she remembered him, arms around the broad shoulders of his twin and another very sweaty man, laughing into the camera, navy eyes squinting in late-afternoon sun. His torso and face glowed with perspiration. His expression radiated confidence and pride at their obvious win.

Resting her head in her hand, she stared at his image as she gnawed her lip. Who could blame her at eighteen for falling for him? He'd been good looking and smart and, despite his being a player, she'd genuinely liked him…

So how was she supposed to have been sensible and said no when he'd talked her into bed? Her hormones had been on a low simmer for months and she'd been so tired of being a virgin. He'd been—was still—gorgeous, and since Mature Maddie couldn't keep her hands off him she couldn't blame her younger self for wanting to walk on the wild side.

Boy, she'd been stupid—and so insecure. How many times had he crawled back to her with another apology, another lame excuse for breaking a date or being late or forgetting to call? And she'd also lived in a state of simmering fear, constantly badgering him about the girls who openly chased him and demanding to know whether he was cheating on her.

Her eight weeks with Cale had been one big drama.

Having lived with drama her whole life—a by-product of one of history's most dysfunctional marriages—after two months she'd had enough. She'd been thinking of getting out when the thought had occurred to her that, despite having a regular monthly cycle all her life, she was a week overdue. It was a measure of the knots that Cale had tied her up in that she hadn't noticed earlier. Thinking of the implications of being pregnant had kept her awake for two nights straight.

The test, thank God and all his archangels, had been negative, and she'd kicked Cale's unsupportive and selfish backside into touch.

But when her world had fallen apart she'd wanted him. Needed him. She had never considered that he wouldn't listen to her messages, hadn't known of Red's death. Any way she looked at it, and however hard she tried to understand, he'd still let her down when she had needed him the most.

She'd moved on, but it had taken her a few more years—a couple of disastrous relationships—to realise that she wasn't relationship material. And, really, how often did she to need to be shown that it was better to avoid the drama than to keep trying—and failing? Maybe her best friend Kate's theory that she was 'romantically retarded' had some merit.

She knew that her career was where she should concentrate her energy. Work never let her down; it returned exactly what she put in. It was a very simple equation. The fewer distractions she had—especially those of an emotional nature—the harder she worked, the better she did and the further she went. Possibly as far as New York. No fuss, no drama. Drama and relationships seemed to go hand in hand, and failure always seemed to be the inevitable outcome.

Work was where she excelled. It was her refuge, her passion, her fulfilment. If there was drama—and there frequently was with crazy brides—she got to stand back from the emotion and find a solution.

As for sex? She could take it or leave it…and she did leave it. She was far from being a contender for tart of the decade and she was okay with that. Three lovers in ten years. Including His Hotness.

Except that Cale—blast him!—just had to kiss her a couple of times for her to remember how exciting sex and men could be…

A few hours in his company also made her recall that it was fun to flirt with a man, thrilling to see your lust echoed in his eyes, to be attracted and to be found attractive.

Maddie yanked at the collar of her shirt and fanned her hand in front of her face. Why did the air suddenly seem thinner, the room hotter? And why did she only seem to have this extreme reaction when she allowed herself to think about Cale Grant?

She tapped her keyboard so that Cale's picture disappeared as quickly as it had arrived. She wasn't sure what made her more agitated: his assumption that he could just waltz back into her life and plant himself back in it, or the cellular, chemical, blistering reaction they seemed to have re-ignited, which now burned a thousand degrees hotter.

Switching back to her e-mail, she furiously typed her reply.

Cale
Apart from the fact that I think working together would be a VERY bad idea, contrary to popular opinion, one doesn't just raise corporate sponsorship with a few letters and a couple of calls. I'd have to meet with marketing people and spend hours persuading them that your race would increase their brand's impact, their exposure, and would increase their market penetration.

And as a company policy we don't do pro bono work. Ever.

It would be better just to ignore his e-mail, or send him a brief, polite brush-off. She'd get Lucy to do a reply letter on an official letterhead.

But, since she wasn't going to send her reply, she would relieve some tension and rant a little.

I'm organising a myriad of other events—I haven't had sex in...well, four years!!! Four years, Cale! And you make me want it, which makes me remember, and that SUCKS! I have PMS, a headache and I am feeling nauseous from eating a slab of dark chocolate for breakfast...

And, by the way, why couldn't you have gone bald or grown love handles since I last saw you? It's not fair that you are still gorgeously sexy...actually, it's not only not fair, it's downright rude!

Maddie leaned back in her chair, stared at the blinking cursor, and pushed her fist into the area below her sternum, willing the burning sensation to ease.

Maddie sighed as she sent the e-mail to her Drafts folder. *Drat*, she'd meant to delete it, not save it....

'Problems, princess?'

Maddie glared at the colleague on her right. She didn't mind Jake calling her a princess, she just wished he'd treat her like one. While Thandi was sweet and funny, Jake was a shark in a suit who had no compunction about taking a bite out of anyone if it meant climbing an inch higher up the corporate ladder.

Thandi poked her head around the doorway. 'Mad? Harriet wants to see you. *Now*! She's doing her rabid rat impression— you know...foaming at the mouth.'

Harriet had found something small to nitpick about, Maddie thought. Nodding her thanks, she stood and picked up her notebook.

'Hey, Luce, can you do me a favour?' she called to the PA they all shared. Gesturing to her desktop computer, she deliberately ignored Jake. 'There's an e-mail from Cale Grant in my in-box, asking for some help with a project. Please send him a quick "sorry can't help" on a letterhead, but wish him luck with his project. Very brief. Very official.'

'Maddie!—Harriet! *Now*!' Thandi shouted. 'Before she fires you for the third time this week.'

'I'm going, I'm going…'

Maddie was in the bath and up to her neck in bubbles when her mobile rang. Not bothering to look at the display, she used the tip of a wet finger to press the little green phone. Her stomach lurched when she heard Cale's greeting.

'I got your e-mail,' Cale said.

Maddie leaned back in the bath, pushing water and bubbles over the side of the bath. She mentally thanked Lucy for her efficiency, and was grateful that she'd resisted the urge to remind Lucy of the task. She was working hard on trying not to micro-manage.

'How can anyone *possibly* eat a slab of chocolate for breakfast?' Cale asked casually.

Maddie tucked her mobile between her neck and her jaw and reached for her glass of wine. 'What are you talking about?'

'Ever heard about oatmeal or muesli? Even yoghurt? Eggs?'

'Did you call me at ten at night to interrogate my eating habits?' Maddie took a sip of wine, thoroughly confused.

'Good to know that you still find me sexy, though.'

The glass of wine stopped halfway to her mouth.

'And I'd recommend evening primrose oil for the PMS.'

'How do you know that I have PMS?' Maddie kept her voice very, very even as she carefully placed her wineglass on the edge of the bath.

Cale confirmed her worst fears. 'It's in this snotty half-finished e-mail I'm looking at.'

Maddie instantly felt icy cold with embarrassment. Yes, she'd written that stinking e-mail—but she hadn't sent it.

'Oh. My. God,' she muttered, her face flaming.

'Yeah. I was expecting a brush-off, but not…that.'

'Look, I—' In her attempt to explain, Maddie's words came out in a long gabble. 'I'm not sure how it happened. I mean, I wrote that e-mail but I was in a strop. I was just venting. I never intended to send it. It wasn't personal; I mean it *was* personal—to me. I was just cross and—'

'Pre-menstrual?'

Maddie scowled, beetroot-red. 'I never meant for you to see it!' she shouted.

'It came from *your* e-mail address,' Cale pointed out.

'I saved it. I meant to delete it but I got called out! I didn't *send* it! At least…I'm sure I didn't.' Maddie placed her fist on her forehead, knowing how lame she sounded. She was *so* going to kill Lucy. Maddie stared at her toes. 'Look, I was in a foul mood when I wrote that.'

'You really haven't had sex in four years?'

'Shut up!'

Cale laughed—a sound that made every nerve ending in her body quiver.

'Relax, Mad, it's not worth popping a vein over. So, it sounds like you're in the bath. Bubbles? Maybe some candles? I've got a great picture in my head.'

Maddie had had more than enough from him. 'Goodnight, Cale.'

Maddie rested her mobile against her forehead. She felt an absolute twit…could she be *more* embarrassed? But how had that e-mail got to Cale? She knew she'd saved it—since she'd lost a six-page e-mail three years ago, she saved everything—but why would Lucy have gone into her Drafts folder and sent it to Cale?

Anger built as she searched for Lucy's number, and Maddie let the phone ring as she drained the wine in her glass.

Lucy eventually answered, and Maddie brushed off her greeting, preferring to jump straight in. 'Do you remember I asked you to send a reply to Cale Grant, *politely* refusing to help him with an adventure race?'

'Wait—I'm still waking up,' Lucy protested.

Maddie heard sleep-tinged annoyance in her voice and forced herself to ignore it.

'Yes,' said Lucy.

'What exactly did you say?' Maddie demanded.

Lucy yawned. 'Nothing. I mean, I didn't send it. Jake wanted some urgent number from me, and he said he'd send your e-mail while I got the number.'

'The malicious, miserable, spiteful son of a low-down, stinking...!' Maddie roared. As she sat up she sent water over the edge of the bath, which sent her wineglass crashing to the slate floor.

Then she did what any strong, self-respecting woman did in a crisis. She burst into tears.

Cale didn't mind waking up at five for an ocean paddle or a five-mile run along the beach, but he wasn't thrilled that in order to have five minutes with Maddie he had to travel across town to catch her before she went to work. Which was early—*very* early, her coworker had told him. Before six. He smiled at the memory of the shudder in Thandi's voice. In his world six was a late start.

Cale grabbed the brown paper packet of pastries off the passenger seat of the car and stepped into the foggy autumn morning. Maddie would immediately see that he was using her passion for pastries to bribe her into helping with the race... She wasn't a fool, and she knew him well enough to know that he wouldn't give up. Cale bit his lip, remembering that Maddie had seemed to understand him better, and quicker, than most. That was where the danger lay, he reminded himself. When someone really knew you—knew your strengths and weaknesses, faults and foibles—then they knew how to play you, to manipulate you, to use you. Ultimately to leave you...

Cale shook his head, disgusted with his brief flash of self-pity. Cue the violins...

Cale frowned as he caught a movement from the beach and wondered what the jogger was doing. He'd run for thirty seconds, stop, then walk for a while before breaking into a stumbling jog. As the runner approached him out of the mist 'he' became a 'she'. Cale grinned and walked towards the path that led to the beach. Standing behind a sign board, he watched Maddie huff and puff her way up the steep path towards the road, her face beetroot-red from exertion.

Unlike him, exercise was *not* one of her strong points.

'Trying to give yourself a heart attack?' Cale asked cheerfully as Maddie rested her hands on her knees, trying to get her breath back.

Maddie just turned her head and glared up at him. *'Unngh.'*

Cale rested a hand on her back and waved the still-hot packet of Danishes in front of her nose. 'I brought you something.'

She groaned, finally finding her breath. 'Those are the reasons I am on the beach instead of in my warm bed! I've been living on them lately and my clothes feel tighter. Hence the exercise.'

Cale laughed. 'But why running? You hate running.'

'I hate all exercise. Except surfing.' Maddie stood up, ran a hand over her sweaty forehead, looked at her fingers and grimaced. 'Yuck!'

Cale felt the knobs in her spine and looked at her slim back. 'I can honestly say that you're no fatter than you were at eighteen.'

'Since I'm ten pounds heavier then than I was three months ago, *that* doesn't help.' Maddie started walking towards her building and Cale fell into step beside her. 'What are you doing here at the crack of dawn?'

'You seem to be avoiding my calls. Again.'

Maddie ducked her head and Cale watched her face flush: red on red. 'I'm really sorry about that e-mail.'

Cale grinned at the top of her head. He'd thought it was funny, but he could see that Maddie was mortified. He resisted the urge to tease her. 'Forget about it. I have.'

It was the image of her in the bath, soapy and rosy, that remained.

Cale watched as she keyed in the code to open the front door and then held it open for her to walk through. She smelt of sea air and flowers and his breath caught in his throat.

He kept his voice even, reluctant to fight so early in the morning. 'I bought the pastries. I'm hoping you'll supply the coffee. What time do you have to be at work?'

'I had a late function last night, so not until later this morning.' Maddie started climbing the stairs to her third floor flat. 'Are you going to harass me about organising that race?'

'Not until after we've had breakfast.'

Maddie stopped, turned to look at him, her big eyes serious although a smile flirted at the corners of her mouth. 'I just tortured myself for twenty minutes to work off yesterday's pastries. I don't have an eighteen-year-old's metabolism any more.'

Cale opened the door to her flat and ushered her inside. 'Then you can have a rice cake and I'll eat the pastries.'

'In your dreams,' Maddie told him as she opened her door.

You already are, Mad.

CHAPTER FIVE

MADDIE sent a quick glance around her lounge, relieved that she generally kept her place reasonably neat. Her bookcase could do with an overhaul, she thought, glancing towards the floor-to-ceiling shelves that covered the far wall of her open plan kitchen, dining and living room. In between the books were photo frames and wire sculptures, wooden bowls and a black velvet top hat.

Cale probably hated her cherry walls, cream couches and red-and-white checked armchairs. She remembered that his linen had been white, the duvet cover beige, and he'd always changed the subject when she'd suggested that he do some basic decorating to his fabulously situated house. Nothing drastic, but a lick of paint on the solidly white walls and a chair or two would have been nice. She remembered thinking that a twenty-five-year-old man should have more stuff than a ratty couch, a microwave and a very uncomfortable double bed.

Maddie moved across to the kitchen area and switched on her coffee machine. Taking two mugs from the cupboard above the machine, she watched Cale out of the corner of her eye as he investigated the contents of her bookcase.

'Who is the blonde in these frames?' he asked, idly examining her collection of photographs.

'My best friend, Kate. She's a lawyer.' Maddie sniffed at a carton of milk, pulled a face and chucked the contents down the sink. She really *had* to go grocery shopping some time in the next century. 'Milk's off. It'll have to be black.'

Cale picked up a weighty book and looked at its cover. 'I enjoyed this book.'

Maddie swallowed, remembering how much time they'd used to spend discussing books. 'Haven't read it yet. That shelf is all the books I still want to read and haven't got to.'

Cale replaced the book and moved towards her, dropping the brown bag of pastries onto the large wooden butcher's block in the centre of the kitchen area. 'Reading was your absolute passion. What happened?'

Maddie shrugged as she placed a cup under the spout and pushed the button on her automatic coffeemaker. 'Life. Work. Busy.'

'Mmm. Not healthy.' Cale opened the bag and withdrew a pastry. 'How long have you lived here?'

'For more than five years.' Maddie handed him the cup of coffee and gestured to the sugar bowl that lived on the butcher's block. From a shelf under her, she pulled out two black and white side-plates and pushed one across the table.

Cale took a sip of his black coffee and a healthy bite out of his Danish as Maddie doctored her own cup of coffee. 'Did you get your door fixed?'

Maddie sent him a guilty look. 'I'm getting to it.'

'And the window?'

'That too.'

Maddie took a pastry from the bag and took a delicate bite—which immediately made her feel guilty. Her clothes were feeling tight, and Cale was such a fitness freak that he made her feel like a lumbering hippo.

A sweaty, makeup-free hippo. Pride kept her from bolting to the bathroom to clean up, add some lip gloss and a swipe of mascara.

Cale dusted pastry flakes off his fingers and sent her a charming grin. 'Hey, look at us. We've been together for fifteen minutes and we've yet to draw blood.'

Maddie sipped her coffee and sent him an arch look over the rim of her mug. 'That's because I'm mostly still asleep.'

Cale's responsive chuckle made her smile. She'd always loved making him laugh and she'd been good at it.

'How are your preparations coming along for the race?'

Cale shoved a hand into his hair and pulled a face. 'I have no idea what I'm doing half the time.'

'Have you chosen a charity?'

Tension tightened Cale's shoulders, his jaw. 'That we have done. Sunbeam—they support hospices and also fund research.'

'What type of cancer did Oliver have?'

Cale balled the empty paper bag in his fist. 'Leukaemia.'

'That sucks.'

'He really liked you, you know.' Cale lobbed the bag towards a paper bin next to the antique desk across the room. His aim was spot on and the bag tumbled inside.

Maddie blinked furiously, tears stinging her eyes. 'He got my jokes.'

'He thought you were hysterical. Especially when you took the mickey out of me. He said that despite the fact that you were so young you could hold your own with me.'

Good old Oliver, Maddie thought. She'd liked him, but had never felt very comfortable with Cale's twin. He'd been too much…too loud, too over the top, too wild and an out-and-out rebel. Cale hadn't been a slouch in the partying and drinking department, but Oliver had tried everything once—legal and not. Sometimes more than once. The Grant twins had been a legend even long after they'd left university, but Oliver's reputation held cult status.

Maddie had frequently thought that Oliver was the balloon and Cale the one who kept him connected to the earth.

'He'd had a brush with cancer around puberty. We thought he was cured.' Cale stared at his coffee cup. 'Even when we discovered it was back, during a routine medical, he was as fit as ever. He fought it for a couple of years, had chemo, was in and out of hospital. God, I hate hospitals.'

Maddie placed her hand on his fist. 'I don't blame you.'

Cale's hand opened and he twisted her fingers in his. 'He ran out of energy to fight it and he died.'

Maddie blanched at his stark words. She knew how he felt. Knew about the curious insidious emptiness death left.

Cale looked out of her lounge windows to the grey morning beyond. 'His death was…'

Maddie held her breath and watched as he took a deep breath and stepped back from some internal cliff he was teetering on.

His eyes lightened fractionally and his shoulders dropped. 'Nothing. Sorry.' Cale sipped his coffee. 'The race. Right. Listen, you must understand that if I take something on I want to do it properly. It has be organised, efficient, and if I'm doing it for Oliver then it has to make a splash. I need some professional help and you're as professional as they come. And you knew him. That means something.'

Maddie pulled her hand away and stepped back to lean against the counter opposite him. 'Cale, even if I wanted to do this race I can't just take it on. My events are assigned to me. I can't pick and choose. This is why I'm currently organising a fishing competition. Can you imagine anyone less suitable than me to organise a fishing competition? To me, fish comes from Jim's kitchen, perfectly grilled.'

That brought a smile to Cale's face, as she'd intended.

'And you'd need an organiser to do it for free or else the fees would wipe out any money you'd raised for charity. Mayhew Walsh don't do pro-bono—ever. Furthermore, I have events stacked up for the next three months. I can't do it, even if I wanted to.'

'Why don't you want to?'

Maddie gripped the counter behind her and looked down at her black and white chequered floor. 'There's too much history between us.'

She felt his eyes on her back as she turned away and poured the remnants of her coffee down the sink.

'Saying sorry again is not going to cut it, and I know that I hurt you, but we were good friends and I think we could do something worthwhile with this race. Maybe we could find a way back? To friendship, at least?'

Maddie turned back to him and lifted her eyebrows. 'You want us to be friends?' she asked sceptically.

'Well, I'm hoping to be a friend with benefits, but I'll take what I can get.'

Maddie's pride surged at his amused and cocky expression. 'Well, don't hold your breath because that's not going to happen!'

Cale grinned at her. 'Want to bet?'

'I got over my childhood fantasies of you a long time ago, Caleb.'

'You're such a liar, *Madison*. You want me as much as I want you.'

Damn him. While she was an open book to him, he was binary code. Maddie tried to bat him off. 'You really should talk to a psychologist about these little delusions.'

Cale stood up and stalked towards her. 'You can keep protesting, sport, but soon you'll have to admit that our attraction burns bigger and brighter and bolder than ever.'

Maddie angled her chin. 'Why?'

'Because of this.'

Maddie lifted her hands to fend him off but he just grabbed them and used them to yank her towards him. Slanting his lips over hers, his mouth captured the words she was still trying to say, not giving her the chance to object again. His tongue slid into her mouth and he lost the ability to think. Blood drained from his head and he felt her body slump as he kissed every objection away. His fingers snaked up under her T-shirt and in one deft movement one hand was on her breast, the other was kneading her bottom and…he was lost. In the feel, taste, shape, smell of her. If she stopped him now he'd cry like a little girl…

Maddie whimpered in his mouth, hooked her hands around his neck and boosted herself up, her legs anchored around his waist. Cale held her easily and, still kissing her, walked her out of the kitchen, down the passage, nudged her bedroom door open with his booted foot.

Maddie felt the bed sink beneath her before Cale's welcome heaviness covered her from breast to thigh. Her clothes melted off her—everything except for a very tiny thong. Despite her

body being the focus of his hot stare, Maddie felt no embarrassment. How could she when he looked at her like that?

Cale took a deep breath and just held her gently, not moving,
staring at the tiny violet triangle between her legs.

Maddie slipped her hands from his grasp and pushed herself
to her elbows. 'Cale? Why have you stopped?'

Cale's eyes glittered when they met hers. 'Do you want me?'
he demanded, brushing his fingers against that soft silk.

Maddie arched her back, pushing into his touch. 'I shouldn't,
but you know I do.'

With a groan at her capitulation Cale moved off her and in a
series of highly economical sexy moves stripped off his clothes.

Maddie looked at him, impressed. 'That was amazing. You
took about ten seconds.'

Cale grinned at her. 'Racing. You learn to change fast.'

'God bless racing,' Maddie breathed, taking in the long muscles of his arms, his washboard stomach, the lean muscles in his
thighs. 'You have the most gorgeous body, Caleb.' She laughed
as red stained the tops of Cale's cheekbones. As he repositioned
himself over her, she grabbed his face in his hands and forced
him to look at her. 'You have heard that before, right?'

Cale shrugged. 'I haven't. Not for a long time. I'm usually
the one dishing out the compliments.'

'They must be stupid.' Maddie lifted her head and nipped
his lower lip. 'So, here we are naked, and I seriously need this.'

Cale dropped his pelvis and she sighed in pleasure.

'You do?'

'As you know, it's been a while...' Maddie pulled his hips
tighter against hers. 'So, if you don't have a condom in your
tightly closed fist, I swear I'll scream.'

Cale licked and nibbled his way into her mouth. 'Oh, you're
going to scream, Mad. I guarantee it.'

Cale, hammered after making love to Maddie twice, closed his
eyes and kissed the top of her head, nestled on his shoulder. His
hand stroked the length of her spine and her silky leg draped
across his thigh. This was, he decided, a perfect way to start the

morning. He lifted his wrist to squint at his watch and couldn't believe that it wasn't even eight yet...

Maddie squirmed in his embrace and rested her hand on his hip. Making love with her had been nothing like he'd expected. She'd explored and demanded, touched and teased. And made a lot of noise.

'I didn't scream,' Maddie murmured.

Cale smiled. 'No, but you moaned and wailed, and hissed and begged.'

'I didn't hiss!'

'Trust me, you made this little hissing sound...'

'Huh.'

'I'll just have to try harder to make you scream the next time,' Cale told her, and frowned when she stiffened. He pulled his head away and looked at her troubled face. 'Is there going to be a next time, Mad?'

He felt her body tense just before she rolled away to stare at the ceiling. He wondered what she was she going to say. His experience with women was that nothing good ever came from these post-coital conversations. Did she require some sort of assurance from him? Some sort of commitment? Right on cue, his skin crawling started. He just had to think about making a commitment and he started to itch.

'That depends.' Maddie rolled her head to look at him.

Cale's mouth dried up and he scratched a spot above his elbow. 'On what?'

Maddie sat up, yanked the sheet up over her breasts and twisted to face him. 'Look, Cale, this isn't easy for me. I don't do this often. Actually never. So this might not come out right.'

'Uh-huh.' Here it came—commitment, exclusivity... He squirmed on the sheet and silently cursed. Maybe he should just pre-empt her and tell her the truth, that he didn't do commitment *or* long-term. He blurted the words out. 'I can't do commitment or long-term.'

Maddie gasped, and he silently cursed when her lower lip trembled.

'So, does that mean you're not going to marry me?' she asked in a tiny, shattered voice.

Cale stared at her, utterly side-winded. She couldn't possibly expect him to... Could she possibly be serious? Then Cale heard the muffled snort of laughter deep in her throat and his heart started beating again.

'Witch,' he muttered, hoping that relief wasn't etched all over his face.

Maddie's laughter filled the room. 'That was classic! You are *such* a sucker!'

'Yeah, yeah.' Cale waved his hand in the air. 'Stop laughing and get to the point.'

'Well, that little statement of yours just made what I'm about to say a million times easier.'

'Well, that would be good to know if I knew what the hell you were talking about.'

Maddie, laughter still brimming in her eyes, took a deep breath and wrinkled her nose. 'Men and sex generally aren't worth the hassle. Usually I avoid both.'

Okay...not what he'd been expecting.

'I don't do relationships either,' she continued.

'Sorry?' Cale felt as if he'd fallen down a rabbit hole.

'I'm not good at them, I don't have time for them, and they don't work for me.'

Cale blinked, lifted his hand to rub his eyes and blinked again. What bull! Maddie was made for a husband, a house and a large garden filled with kids and animals. Not with him, obviously, but with someone.

This conversation was having the strangest effect on him, because now he could hear trumpets...trumpeting.

'Oh, hell. Mobile!' Maddie tumbled out of bed and, grabbing a towel off the chair, she held it to her chest and lunged for her phone on her dressing table.

'Gareth, hi! No, I've got about thirty seconds to talk to you. No, we need the small white tent.'

Cale stared at Maddie—the towel just covering her interesting bits—who seemed to have shifted into work mode.

'Black chair covers. The velvet ones. Thanks. Later.'

Maddie put her mobile back where it had been and looked at Cale.

'Sorry, where were we? Oh…I had a few relationships after you and they all went pear-shaped.' Maddie waved her hand in the air in a gesture of dismissal. 'I decided that it just wasn't worth the hassle.'

Cale linked his hands across his waist and frowned at her. 'So what do you want from me?'

Maddie tightened the towel around her chest and waved at the rumpled sheets and his bare chest. 'This…if our schedules don't collide and it works for both of us.'

Cale lifted his eyebrows. 'So, friends with benefits?'

Maddie blushed and twisted the towel between her fingers. 'Yes, well…if you think that's okay.'

Duh. It was way okay with him.

Her mobile rang again, and Cale considered tossing it out of the bedroom window to see if he could make it reach the sea.

'Mdu? Hey, hon. No, I can't get my lazy butt to the surf. I work for a living.' Maddie pulled a face as she glanced at the bed. 'Yeah, yeah. I know the surf is up, I'm looking at it and weeping. Kalk Bay on Sunday? Maybe. Later. Okay? So, nothing heavy?'

Oh, the 'nothing heavy' comment was directed at him. Cale shook his head to get his head in the game.

Maddie seemed to take his silence for assent, because she sent him a bright smile and inched her way to the bathroom. 'Good. I'm glad we had this chat—got rid of the elephant in the room. I think we're on the same page. Excellent. I'm going to grab a quick shower. There is another shower in the other bathroom if you're in a hurry.'

What chat? Cale looked towards the bathroom. He didn't recall being part of any conversation. She'd just thrown words at him… He slumped back on the pillows and stared at her ceiling.

However, if he'd written a script for what he wanted from Maddie then he couldn't have chosen a better scenario.

So why, exactly, did he feel vaguely unsatisfied?

CHAPTER SIX

THE following Monday, Maddie whistled U2's 'Beautiful Day' as she tossed her soft leather tote onto her desk. Dropping into her chair, she placed her booted feet up on her desk and folded her hands against her designer shirt. It was so good to stride into a busy office and smirk at your harassed colleagues when you had just completed a hugely successful project. Tight Lines had attracted record entry numbers and she'd doubled the sponsorship. The press coverage had been astounding. Frankly, she rocked.

Thandi, custard tart halfway to her mouth, walked past and slapped her raised hand before picking up a box from her desk and offering her a cake. Maddie sighed and took the smallest one she could find, which was about half the size of a submarine.

'Way to go, girlfriend.'

'Thanks, Thands.'

Jake just ignored her. They hadn't spoken since Maddie had lambasted him about his practical joke. She'd also put codes on her computer and threatened Lucy with disembowelment if she gave them to Jake.

'Isn't this supposed to be your day off?' Thandi asked, perching on the corner of her desk.

Maddie shrugged. 'Thought I'd get a head start on the week.'

'You're mad,' Thandi told her, drifting back to her own desk. 'And, worse, you make the rest of us look like slackers.'

Maddie scooped off some custard that threatened to escape and placed her feet on an open drawer of her desk. Between the fishing competition and crazy brides, work had been insane this last week—so much so that she'd asked Cale to give her a week before they saw each other again.

Mostly because she needed some time to work through the fact that she'd a) slept with a man without any thought about the implications thereof, b) she really wanted to do it again and c) she thought the best way to make sure it happened again was to convince him that she wanted nothing more from him but sex.

Which hadn't been a lie…exactly.

'Cale called this morning,' Thandi told her and Maddie felt grateful for the interruption to her train of thought, because she was sure that the train was about to plummet off a cliff.

She'd expected him to call today. If he was feeling a fraction as flustered—frustrated—as she was, then they were in for a hot date later. But why had he called the office and not her mobile? Strange.

'Well, well, well.'

Maddie looked across and caught her friend's smirk. 'What is that supposed to mean?'

'He's getting to you.'

'Don't be daft,' she retorted. 'He's just a guy I'm seeing occasionally. I refuse to be scared of any man.'

Thandi grinned. 'Did I say scared?'

Maddie narrowed her eyes. 'I said I wasn't scared!'

'Mmm. You have an "I want him but I don't know what the hell to do with him" look on your face.'

'Thands, with respect, you don't know what you're talking about.' Maddie resisted the urge to shift in her chair—a clear non-verbal statement of the opposite.

'And that's why you've been working like a demon on speed. Work is easy. Cale is hard.'

Maddie sighed, momentarily distracted. Since it was a lot easier to think of how Cale affected her physically than emotionally, she went with her little fantasy.

Thandi, a closet prude, waved her hands in agitation. 'Not like that! Get your mind out of the bedroom, please! *Hard* as in you don't know what to feel with him, how to handle him.

Work is your safety zone, the place you run to when real life gets complicated.'

'You're really irritating and I'm not listening to you any more.' She couldn't possibly be right.

Thandi scowled in irritation when her phone rang and Maddie sighed her relief. Thandi pointed a finger at Maddie, her hand hovering above the receiver. 'You know I'm right… Thandi speaking.'

Nuh-uh. Thandi was wrong. Work was just the strongest reason why she couldn't have a 'normal' love-life. The reality was that her career demanded enormous sacrifices. She didn't have time for a proper relationship even if she wanted one. Before now, in this age of AIDS, creeps and idiots, there hadn't been anyone who had captured her interest enough to tempt her into an affair. Unfortunately Cale epitomised temptation, and when she was around him her 'take it slow' button seemed to malfunction.

'He's got you all tied up in knots,' Thandi commented as soon as she'd disconnected her call.

Maddie banged her head against the back of the chair and closed her eyes in frustration. 'Don't you have work to do?'

'Sorting out your head is work. It's a dirty job but someone has to do it.'

'Thands, Cale and I have something going physically. I admit that. But am I supposed to blow off work for my love-life?'

'That's a rubbish excuse. Millions of woman have crazy careers and happy relationships. It's called balance, sweetie. Oh, wait—let me explain that foreign concept…'

Maddie scowled at her. 'Funny.' She took a bite of her cake. 'You're assuming we're in a relationship but we're not. Neither of us wants one.'

'He said that?'

'Very clearly. So I need to keep this as simple as I can. That way we'll both have some fun, and at the end of our run we'll walk without either of us feeling like we've given more than we received.'

In theory it was relatively simple. Sleep with him and do not let it go beyond sex. She could do this, couldn't she? Hundreds of women did it every day.

Maddie wondered how many got it right.

Conscious of the silence from the other side of the room, she looked at Thandi. Maddie rolled her eyes when she saw that Thandi was bent at the waist, doubled over with silent laughter. Tears were running down her face and she was making a strange gurgling sound...

Maddie shook her head. 'For the love of God, what is the matter with you *now*?'

Thandi lifted a trembling finger as she snorted through her mirth. 'You! You crack me up. You really think that you can control this, don't you?'

Maddie threw up her hands. 'There's nothing to control!'

A slamming door interrupted their useless—as far as Maddie was concerned—conversation, and she looked up as a pair of broad shoulders moved across the entrance to their open-plan offices and stopped. The shiny head of the owner of Mayhew Walsh, Jens Mayhew, bobbed and nodded. The person next to him Maddie recognised immediately—those shoulders, that head of sun-streaked hair. Who else would feel totally comfortable in these swish offices dressed in faded Levi's, battered trainers and a casual Zoo York T-shirt? Who else wouldn't bother to shave and yet still managed to look...hot. And stylish.

Maddie picked up her custard cake and stared at Cale, who was nodding at something Jens was saying. At the moment Cale noticed her, and sent her a wink over Jens's balding head, a great big glob of custard cream dropped and splattered down her grey shirt and landed on her black skinny jeans.

Maddie swore and Cale grinned. Placing the pastry on her desk, she took a handful of tissues from the box she kept on her credenza and frantically dabbed at her blouse while Jens and Cale walked towards her. Thandi just delicately licked her fingers and sent Cale interested looks from her Bambi eyes. Maddie threw a sour look her way.

'Maddie!' Jens bellowed, using his 'this is an important client, impress him' voice. 'This is Cale Grant.'

Maddie nodded and inspected the mess on her clothes while Jens introduced Thandi and Jake. In all honesty she wasn't surprised to see Cale at her offices; Cale wanted her to work on the race and he never gave up and never gave in.

Jens slapped Cale's back with a bonhomie that was as false as it was loud. 'We're going to organise Cale's charity race. For free.'

Maddie lifted her eyebrows at Jens. Who *was* this man and what had he done with her boss? Jens was not a philanthropist on any day of the week. Maddie caught Cale's look and saw the glint of mischief in his eyes. Whatever he was up to, he was enjoying it immensely.

Maddie thought she'd better clarify the terms of the agreement. 'We're organising the race?'

'Yes!' Jens replied jovially, but Maddie could see the panic in his eyes.

'For free?' Maddie persisted. 'You've signed a contract?'

'Madison, your lack of trust is hurtful,' Jens blustered. 'This is your project, by the way. Cale is insistent.'

Maddie looked at her desk and blew out a long breath. How was she going to manage an additional project? She turned to Thandi and widened her eyes in disbelief.

Thandi, back to being a sweetheart, picked up her panicked expression. 'I'll help. I'll take over the Whitsun wedding.'

'The Whitsun bride is neurotic and temperamental. And she trusts me,' Maddie replied, mentally juggling her schedule. She'd have the wedding off her hands in two weeks and then her schedule would be marginally lighter. 'I'm snowed under but I think I can manage it—if I get a break from the reports and quotes.'

'Consider it done,' Jens breezily agreed.

Maddie knew when to press her advantage. 'You'll clear it with Harriet?'

'Of course. So, is this settled?' Jens rubbed his hands together.

Maddie smiled at him. 'Absolutely, Jens. Cale and I'll take it from here.' She made a point of glancing at her watch. 'You probably have a full morning?'

Jens took the gap she'd created to leave. He hastily shook Cale's hand and told him that he was leaving him and his event in capable hands. He hustled out without a backward glance and they watched him leave.

When he was out of earshot Maddie turned to Cale. Opening her mouth to interrogate him, she caught a glimpse of Thandi's and Jake's very interested faces. Grabbing Cale by the hand, she led him down the passage to an empty private conference room and slammed the door behind him.

Cale wasted no time and pulled her into his arms, planting his mouth on hers. Maddie fell into his kiss for a minute, and then forced herself to step away. In order to avoid temptation she positioned herself on the other side of the conference table and placed her hands on the back of a chair.

'What on earth did you say to him?'

Cale shrugged, grinned and followed her around the table.

'C'mon, Cale, he never does things like this,' Maddie said as he loomed in front of her.

Cale used his index finger to scoop a blob of custard off a button. 'You're a mess, Maddie.'

Maddie slapped his hands away. 'Cale!'

Cale's slow grin had her stomach flipping. 'I used my connections. I know some people who would consider sending some of their business Jens's way if he allowed you to work on my race.'

Maddie narrowed her eyes, suspicious. 'Like who?'

'One or two national sports federations.'

Wow. Big accounts, Maddie thought. National accounts. Jens would think her time was worth sacrificing for a shot at those contracts.

Cale fiddled with the buttons of her shirt and slipped them open to reveal the top of a hot pink lacy bra. 'Nice. Very nice. Matching panties?'

Maddie nodded, her mouth drying at the heat in Cale's eyes.

'Tiny thong?'

Maddie swallowed. 'Very.'

Cale's hand slid over her breast and rested on her hip. 'You have an insane work schedule, Madison.'

'I know. And with the race it's just going to get worse.'

'Planning on doing anything about it?'

Maddie closed her eyes as his mouth dropped to hers, but when his lips touched the corner of her mouth her eyes flew open as his words registered. 'What do you mean?'

Cale stepped away from her and half perched on the conference table. He stretched his legs out in front of him. 'Are you going to make room for a man in your life? Specifically me?'

Maddie walked across to a table in the corner where a water dispenser stood. She jammed a plastic cup under its spout and pushed the lever. When it was full, she took a sip and waved the cup in the air. Water sloshed over the side.

'I don't know. I don't even know how I am going to manage your race, let alone an affair.'

'You have some serious time issues.' Cale folded his arms and tipped his head. 'You really surprised me, making that offer of no-strings sex.'

Maddie looked amused. 'Let's not pretend it's the first offer of uncomplicated sex you've ever received.'

'I meant *you* surprised me,' Cale replied patiently.

'Why?'

'Because I thought you had marriage and for ever and hearts tattooed on your butt. So, no desire for the white fairytale dress and the trip to church?'

Maddie vehemently shook her head. 'I'm violently allergic to weddings. I didn't grow up with a great example of marriage.' Maddie toyed with the paper cup. 'If I ever do marry, probably with a gun to my head, I will be barefoot on the beach at sunset, wearing a scarlet dress with bougainvillaea flowers in my hair.'

Maddie tossed her cup in the wastebasket and faced him. She had no idea how they'd got onto the subject of marriage…and it was time to get this conversation back on track.

'Look, since you've lobbed this grenade in my lap, I'd better get back to work. I have got so much to get through before I even look at what needs to be done for the race.'

'No, not today,' Cale told her, and took her hand and pulled her towards the door.

Maddie tried to tug her hand back. 'What are you doing?'

'We're going to lunch.'

'Did you not hear a thing I just said about my work?'

'Heard. Ignored.'

'It's nine in the morning! Don't you have heads to fix?' Maddie demanded, unable to get her hand out of his.

'Such respect for my work.' Cale pulled her down the passage and back into the open-plan office, cheerfully grinning at her colleagues who were staring open-mouthed at them. 'I've taken the day off. So should you.'

'Cale, I can't—' Maddie wailed as he picked up her bag and casually draped it over his shoulder.

Cale looked at Thandi. 'Remind her why she can take a couple of hours off without the world coming to a grinding halt.'

'Absolutely!' Thandi said on a wide grin. 'As mentioned, Mad, it *is* your scheduled day off!'

Maddie scowled at her and whispered, 'Traitor!' How long had Cale been tracking her movements through Thandi?

'Excellent, let's go!' Cale pulled her away from her desk and blew Thandi a kiss as they passed.

'Stop flirting with my colleagues!' Maddie snapped.

'Okay, then, I'll just have to flirt with you,' Cale told her as he bundled her into a lift and pulled her into his arms for a soul-shattering kiss.

Maddie ran her hands over the leather seats in his Range Rover and settled back in her seat, thinking that it was quite exciting to be kidnapped by a hot man in a nice car. By the way he'd kissed her in the lift she'd assumed that they were heading back to her flat for some mid-morning entertainment, and frowned when Cale turned in the opposite direction from both their residences.

'Where are we going?' Maddie asked, confused. 'This isn't the way to my flat. Or your house, for that matter.'

'Why would we be going to either of…? Oh!' Cale laughed at her. 'You thought…'

'I wasn't… I didn't!' Maddie stammered, blushing furiously.

'When are you going to learn that you can't lie to me?' Cale stopped at a red traffic light and dropped a hard kiss on her mouth.

'Okay.' Maddie blushed and stared out of the window. 'You kissed me…in the lift… I thought…'

Cale patted her knee. 'Mmm, it did cross my mind, but I thought we'd do something different this morning.'

'Like?' Maddie looked at him suspiciously.

'When last did you go wine-tasting?'

'I don't know! Three, four years ago? I had a client who wanted a new wine label launched…'

'That's work, not pleasure. This will be all pleasure.' Cale swung onto the motorway and joined the traffic flowing out of the city. 'I have an old friend who has just bought a wine farm in Franschoek. He needs a partner and wants to know if I want to go into the wine-making business.'

'Do you?'

Cale shrugged. 'Who knows? I'll see what his business plan looks like.'

'Oh, but he won't want me tagging along!' Maddie protested.

'He's a sucker for a pretty face, and yours is one of the prettiest around. We'll take a look at the vineyards, have a chat about the winery and then we'll have lunch. He's an amazing cook,' Cale told her. 'So relax, enjoy the ride, the scenery. And maybe later, if you're in the mood, I'll kiss you again and see where it takes us. Who knows? You might have a headache later.'

Maddie flicked her hair and sent him a naughty grin. 'Or *you* might have a headache.'

'Sweetheart, trust me, no headache is going to stop me,' Cale retorted. 'So, let's change the subject before my eyes roll back in my head and I drive off the road. The race. Where do we start?'

Maddie ducked out of the side entrance of the Sea Point office block that housed Mayhew Walsh, winced at the persistent drizzle of the first cold front to hit the Cape, dodged a kissing couple and hurried through the rain to her car. She slipped inside her vintage Jag, tossed her bag onto the passenger seat and thought it was a miserable day—perfectly suited to her mood.

Starting the car, she slapped her foot on the accelerator, left the parking lot and roared through the busy city streets, a combination of colonial and modern buildings, nosing the Jag towards the motorway running north. Years ago, as a student, she'd made this journey towards Cale's house in the cosmopolitan suburb of Bantry Bay with excitement. Today she just felt comprehensively frustrated.

Her mobile rang and Maddie touched her ear to activate her headset.

'Do I have to make an appointment to see you?' Kate demanded.

'Pretty much,' Maddie admitted. 'I've taken on Cale's pro bono project and Horrid Harriet is not impressed. So much so that's she given me another product launch to co-ordinate.'

'The woman doesn't have a warm and fuzzy bone in her body,' Kate commented. 'And your new man?'

'Interesting.'

'And...satisfying?'

'Very. So much so that I spend far too much time thinking about him,' Maddie admitted, sparing a glance at Table Mountain covered in wet grey clouds.

Kate laughed and Maddie thought about how she and Cale had hooked up only twice since that first morning. 'Our schedules have been crazy lately. The nights he was free I had a function, and vice-versa.'

'And you miss him?'

'I do.' She missed his crooked smile, the way his eyes could change from cobalt to navy, Egyptian blue and denim and back again. She could spend a lifetime counting the shades of blue. His voice...

'Oh, Mad, you have it bad.'

'It's just sex, Katie. He's good at it.' Maybe if she said it often enough she'd actually begin to believe to it. And it was all Thandi's fault. Ever since that stupid talk the other morning she couldn't shake her words from her head.

'Thandi says that I use work as a safe place to hide from what she says are my scary feelings for Cale,' she blurted. 'What do you think?''

Kate was silent for a long time. 'Is she right?'

'If I knew that, Katie, why would I be asking you?'

'So, it isn't just sex?'

Maddie sighed. 'I'm trying to convince myself that it is.'

'Ah. And have you had any scary feelings?'

'I'm feeling flickers of…something.'

'Oh. It could be gas.'

'Kate! Not particularly helpful, friend,' Maddie snapped. 'Do you have any other worthwhile advice for me?'

'Sure: please don't think about how good he is at sex while you're driving. You'll cause an accident.' Kate laughed and disconnected.

Maddie did spend far too much time thinking about Cale, and while she often thought about what they did in bed—how could she not? He was a very attentive and inventive lover—she also liked the man he'd become. He was smart and funny, and so desperate to hide that he was a bit emotionally dinged up, which made him more attractive, not less. There was nothing more irritating than a seemingly perfect man. She really liked him—in and *out* of bed.

But what neither of her spectacularly unhelpful friends realised was that even if she did have any feelings for Cale, she didn't know what she was supposed to do with them. Where was she supposed to put them? Cale didn't want them. He couldn't have made that clearer if he'd drawn her a picture. They were ships passing…

So what was the point of even entertaining the idea? And the more she thought about how he made her feel, the bigger the feelings got, and where was the one place she was too busy to think about Cale? *Work.*

So really work was the safest place for her to be. *Hah*, she should have been a psychologist…

So, in the interest of not thinking about Cale, she should turn her attention to something else. The race. Maddie sighed. Unfortunately she also had issues with the race itself. Cale had the date for the race firmly fixed in his head and she knew she wouldn't be able to change it. Three months and three weeks away—the anniversary of Oliver's death.

She still had no idea how to get a couch potato to donate money to a cancer charity just because a few supremely fit nut-cases were running up and down a mountain and cresting a couple of waves. And without Joe Public's donations the race would never realise the type of money that would make a significant difference. And she wanted to make a significant difference, for Cale's sake.

But she was severely short of time.

Her mobile rang again.

'Where are you?' Cale demanded.

'I'm getting there. Ten minutes,' Maddie shot back. 'Are they there yet?'

'No. See you soon,' Cale said before disconnecting.

Seven minutes later Maddie swung into his oak-lined drive-way and slowed down as she approached the house. Close to the house a new, smaller, double-storey cottage echoed the style of the main house.

The house... Oh, the house was just the same. Two storeys of honeyed stone, but stripped of the climbing roses that had once climbed free. A deep veranda ran around the front of the house, and the shadows held comfortable couches and colourful hammocks. Three dogs bounded up to her car and enthusiastically barked their welcome.

This side of the large property held gardens and swathes of lawn, but Maddie knew that the house was perched on the side of a cliff, with stunning views of the sea. She might feel conflicted about its owner but she adored his property.

Maddie was about to get out of the car when the front door flew open and two little boys dressed in swimming shorts hurtled down the steps, whooping at full throttle. They sent her a casual look before veering around the house towards the path to the beach. A long, cool blonde appeared in the doorway, talking to Cale, who pulled the front door shut behind them. She was tall, almost too slender, and dressed in blue cut-offs and a white T-shirt, her long hair pulled back into a ponytail. Maddie watched as Cale ended their discussion by dropping a kiss on her temple. Then he flew down the steps, pulled her passenger door open and manoeuvred his six-foot-plus frame into her car.

'Help!'

Maddie draped her arms over the steering wheel, looked at him and lifted her eyebrows.

'Shopping emergency.' Cale looked a bit panicky. 'It's my mother's birthday tomorrow and I've forgotten!'

'But the charity people!' Maddie protested. 'We have a meeting with them.'

'They postponed this morning.'

'And why didn't you tell me that?' Maddie's voice had dropped several degrees.

'We haven't had much time together lately, so no way was I going to give you an opportunity to find something else to do.' Cale managed a half-turn in his seat. 'Then Megan reminded me that it's my mom's birthday tomorrow and she won't forgive me if I forget. So, *help*!'

'So that's Megan?'

'Megan. Ollie's ex-wife. They were married for about ten seconds. The hoodlums are Ollie's boys. They live over there, in the cottage.'

Maddie winced as a bankload of pennies dropped. 'Megan? As in the phone call you received when you came to get me out of the bathroom?'

Cale nodded, not bothering to hide his irritating smirk. 'And she really *doesn't* mind who I sleep with.'

Maddie bit the inside of her lip. 'I suppose I should apologise?'

'You should, but I'm not holding my breath. You can say sorry by helping me buy a gift for a sixty-something diva who rules her family with an iron fist,' Cale said, trying to get comfortable. 'Can we take my car? This is like driving in a sardine can!'

'No, we can't,' Maddie retorted, starting the car. 'Any ideas where to find this present?

'No! That's why I'm throwing myself on your mercy. I'm the world's worst shopper.'

Maddie rolled her eyes. 'I'm doing this for your mother. Because any woman who gave birth to you deserves a fantastic present.'

'Understood.' Cale sent her his slow, sexy internal-organ-melting grin. 'And because you love shopping.'

Maddie tossed her hair before pulling out onto the road. 'Well, *duh*.'

At the waterfront mall they found his mom a present in record time—a cream cashmere jersey that Maddie assured him would instantly elevate him to favourite child status—and, because he'd been dense enough to mention that he needed some new dress shoes, he found himself in an upmarket shoe shop valiantly trying to follow the conversation between Maddie and the earnest, camp shop assistant. He knew they were speaking English because he understood the individual words, but their meaning escaped him. Edward Green…John Lobb…New & Lingwood.

When they mentioned Prada, he jumped in.

'I want a pair of shoes. A normal pair of black dress shoes.'

They both rolled their eyes and Cale gritted his teeth.

'Charcoal? Ebony? Midnight?' the shop assistant asked.

'What?' Cale blinked at this insanity. 'I want black. Plain black.'

'There are *shades* of black,' Camp Boy told him.

Since when?

Maddie patted his shoulder. He knew she was patronising him, the baggage. 'What size?'

'Ten.' Cale slumped into a purple wingback chair and looked at Maddie who, after asking the assistant to get the right size in three styles of shoe that looked, to him, exactly the same, was examining a pair of leather knee-high boots in deep chocolate.

He swallowed as an image of Maddie, dressed only in one of her tiny thongs and those boots, popped into his head. He groaned silently, watching as she slipped off a stiletto to slide a foot into that high-heeled boot. He needed her in his bed, under him...

Cale dropped his head against the back of the chair and stared out through the door of the shop at the tourists and after-work Capetonians who ambled through the shopping centre.

He was deliberately portioning out his time with Maddie, not wanting either of them to fall into the habit of meeting up after work, having something to eat, climbing into bed and thereby inadvertently establishing the patterns and expectations of a relationship.

But, by God, he only realised how much he missed her now he was in her company again—how much he wanted her now she was parading between him and the mirror in those sexy boots. How much he wanted her no matter what she was doing or wearing.

This wasn't good. Cale sat up and lightly banged the ball of his hand on his temple. When he was feeling like this, churned up and out of control, it was better to distance himself, to remind himself that he liked his space, his life. They'd finish this torture she called shopping, grab a bite to eat and then he'd find some excuse to leave her at her door. He was a smart man. He was sure he could come up with something.

His libido protested loudly at this proposed course of action, but he refused to be ruled by his little head. It was time to take back control...

Cale looked up as the assistant walked towards him, juggling six equally black shoes and sending Cale a thunderous look.

'Charcoal!' *Bang.* A pair hit the coffee table.

'Midnight!' *Bang.*

'Ebony.' *Bang.*

'I'll take the first pair that fits,' Cale growled, and pulled on the shoe closest to hand. It was supremely comfortable, so he yanked it off, pulled his trainer back on and told the assistant to charge him.

Maddie, the witch, just laughed when his heart momentarily stopped when he saw the price on his credit card slip.

'Yikes,' Cale told her, yanking her towards the door. 'Why

didn't he just ask me for a pint of blood too? And a chunk of flesh? Black dress shoes—that's all I wanted, Mad. Just normal black shoes!'

Maddie squeezed his hand as she laughed. 'Charcoal, Cale. Charcoal Prada shoes. They are an investment. You'll wear them for ever.'

'I'd better be buried in them at that price,' Cale grumbled.

Maddie's laugh washed over him. She looked around and pointed towards the food section. 'Do you feel like sushi? I feel like sushi.'

Cale winced internally. As he'd decided, it was time to take back control. 'Actually Mad, sorry. I need to get back. I need to work.'

Maddie cocked her head at him. 'Really? That's such a pity… I thought you might want an introduction to my new underwear.'

He'd called her a witch before, and she was a witch who could play dirty. Cale groaned. 'What colour?'

'Chartreuse.'

'Huh?' Cale's eyes were hot on her face. 'I need to know what colour that is.'

Maddie sent him an evil grin. 'But you have to work…'

Cale yanked her towards the exit. 'What work?'

Maddie tugged, but couldn't pull her hand out of his grip. 'I'm hungry,' she wailed.

'So am I. But not for food.'

CHAPTER SEVEN

AT NOON on Saturday Maddie squeezed her car between a Porsche and a battered Toyota and cocked her head at the party noise that drifted from Cale's house. She recognised the sound. How many times had he entertained on his deck overlooking the beach and the Atlantic Ocean seaboard? Maddie smoothed down the short skirt of her favourite sunshine-yellow dress, knowing that this bright day was summer's last shout and that the second cold front approaching meant she'd have to swap halterneck dresses for turtlenecks. She rolled her shoulders, enjoying the feeling of the warm sun on her bare back and shoulders.

Maddie walked up the stairs to the front door and wondered how many people Cale had invited to this impromptu launch of the race. Stepping inside the hallway, she let out a yelp when a strong hand grabbed her arm and whirled her into a room. Maddie caught a glimpse of a desk and computer before Cale's hard mouth dropped over hers and his clever tongue slipped past her teeth and tangled with hers. His tall, muscular frame held her against the closed door as his mouth dominated hers. Maddie felt the corresponding flash of lust scuttle through her as she angled her head up to him.

Disorientated, but incredibly excited by this unexpected sensual onslaught, Maddie gripped his shoulders as a million sensations pummelled her.

'Cale…we…party,' Maddie muttered as he kissed her jawline.

'Shh, relax. Stop thinking.'

Stop thinking, indeed, Maddie thought as she looked at her

flushed face in the mirror of the downstairs powder room twenty minutes later. She had, and she'd found herself thoroughly seduced against the study door to the sound of a party upstairs.

Madison Shaw, having hot sex before she'd even made it to the party, and no liquor had been required.

Cale was a dangerous, dangerous man.

Maddie, still disorientated after Cale's assault on her senses, used the facilities to refresh herself and to gather her composure and, when she thought she could string a coherent sentence together, walked into the formal living room. Turning, she nodded her approval. The bare walls and ugly couch had been replaced with ivory paint, bold art and masculine chocolate leather furniture. Smiling, she headed towards the entertainment area at the side of the house—and stopped and stared.

Maddie felt the urge to look around for the cameras. She was waiting for someone to yell *Cut!* It looked like an advertisement for a sparkling wine or a cold beer...a stunning setting, and beautiful people in a relaxed, not overly decorated house.

This wasn't what she remembered. What had happened to the rough wooden deck? The all-but-broken sliding door that kept jamming? Now there were floor-to-ceiling windows framing the spectacular seaview and the rotten deck-boards had been replaced with a fine wooden deck. The entertainment space ran the entire length of the formal lounge, dining room and kitchen, with the middle section covered by a high roof. On one side of the deck a bright, long infinity pool glittered in the sun, and the other side held a large Jacuzzi. In between were deep cane couches and chairs with brightly coloured cushions, an outdoor kitchen and bar.

Attractive men and woman were huddled in groups, beer and wine in hand, tucking into platters of canapés. In the old days, Maddie remembered, they'd eaten barbecued meat cooked over a smoky fire and shoved into bread rolls.

Strong fingers brushed the small of her back and Maddie instinctively knew it was Cale. How could she not, since he'd just...? She blushed. 'Hi.'

'Hi, back.' Cale dropped a kiss on the corner of her mouth

and grinned at her discomfort. 'Get that into you. You look like you could use it.'

Maddie took the icy glass of wine he offered her, took a couple of large, fortifying sips and walked towards the solid wood railing. She gestured towards the ocean. 'In all of Cape Town this is still my favourite view.'

'*You're* my favourite view....' Cale said, low in her ear.

Maddie's fist hit his muscled arm with no marked effect. 'Will you stop? God, I'm sure everyone can see exactly what we... What you... *Arrgh*!'

Cale laughed at her embarrassment.

Maddie shuffled from foot to foot and stared hard at the ocean.

'Cale, please...'

Cale took a long sip of his beer, his eyes full of mirth and a very healthy dose of male satisfaction. 'Okay, I'll behave. As for the ocean—you used to spend hours on this deck. But I admit it's pretty special. It's why I bought the house.'

'Which looks fantastic, by the way.'

Cale shrugged. 'My ex, Gigi, kept nagging me to do something. Megan did the decorating for me.'

'She's got great taste.' Maddie sipped her wine and sent him a direct look. 'Gigi the supermodel?'

'Mmm.'

'Another blonde...' Maddie flashed him a naughty smile when he rolled his eyes. 'So, how long did you keep *her* around for?'

'About eighteen months.'

Maddie gaped at him in surprise. 'Oh, wow. So it was serious?'

'Serious enough.'

'No thoughts of marrying her?'

Cale shuddered. 'No, thank you. I already had Oliver demanding my time and draining my bank account. I didn't need anyone else in my life to be responsible for.'

Maddie turned that over in her head. Why did he equate marriage with responsibility? Love with the price he had to pay to receive it?

That was a conversation for another day, so Maddie thought it wise to change the subject. 'I was too polite then, but I'm not now. How on earth did you manage to buy this property in one of the most expensive parts of the city while you were still studying?'

Cale leaned against the railing and his beer bottle dangled loosely from his fingers. 'I had help from an inheritance. My grandfather was loaded, and left all of us a handy pile of cash with the stipulation that we had to buy property. I only needed a small mortgage, and I always had a money-making scheme going on campus.'

'Like?'

'I traded coins, made some money there. Bought a piece of land with a mate, flogged it and made some more. And I was a bookie for a couple of years at uni.'

Maddie smiled. 'It's a great house. You've done a lot to it.'

'Yeah, money and furniture makes a big difference.' Cale tapped her arm with the neck of his cold beer bottle. 'What did I have back then? A couch and that disgusting bed!'

'And a sick microwave that only worked intermittently.'

'And an equally sick bank account.' Cale looked at her surprised face. 'You didn't know? Maddie, when you knew me I was so comprehensively broke that I nearly lost this house.'

'I had no idea.'

'You weren't supposed to. I was young and stupid and too proud to admit that I should never, ever have bought a house in the most upmarket suburb in the city when I had student loans, a looming PhD and no career. I worked like a demon to keep it, and myself, from going under.'

Maddie couldn't find the right response. Would he find it patronising if she told him that she was proud of him for standing up and working hard to keep what he loved? Probably. So she just kept quiet and scanned the crowd. 'Quite a get-together. Are all these people involved in the race?'

Cale lifted one shoulder. 'The word got around that I was having a party so more people arrived than I expected. Racers, officials, hangers-on.'

'So who must I make nice with?'

Cale shoved his sunglasses up onto his head and glanced around. He pointed his bottle towards a grey-haired man at the head of one group. 'That's the head of the racing federation.'

'Okay. What's his name?'

Cale told her and Maddie memorised it. 'Fine. Who else?'

'Liam Peters, one of our sponsors, is here. See if you can get him to up his sponsorship offer. But I don't see him at the moment.'

'I'll find him,' Maddie said, and changed the subject. 'How did your mother like her jersey?'

'Like you said—instant favourite child.'

'And the shoes?' Maddie asked, tongue in cheek.

'I've wrapped them in bubble wrap and put them inside a protective box.'

Maddie's mouth fell open. 'Really?'

'Get real. I tossed them in with the rest of the mess at the bottom of my cupboard.'

Cale laughed at Maddie's wince and ran his thumb down her cheek. When he cupped the side of her face with his hand her eyes inexplicably and suddenly filled with tears. Maddie ducked her head as she furiously blinked them back.

'Mad? Sweetheart?'

Maddie stepped back and folded her arms across her chest, gnawing on her bottom lip. When she felt as if she had emotions under some sort of control, she tossed her head and sent Cale a rueful shaky smile. 'Sorry.'

Cale lifted his eyebrows. 'You okay?'

'Mmm.'

'Why the tears?'

Maddie gripped the end of her nose with her finger and thumb and held it. She couldn't possibly tell him that she felt as if she were floundering, utterly swept away by the passion and need he aroused in her. She couldn't tell him that he confused and terrified her, that at this moment she felt so incredibly vulnerable.

If she wasn't very careful she had it in her to love this man. This man who had no need for love...

'I'm tired,' she said in her brightest voice. 'Working too hard. When I'm really tired I tend to cry. Sorry.'

'You're crying because you're tired?'

'It's a girl thing.' Maddie took a big sip of her wine and decided to drain the glass. If there was a moment when she needed alcohol, then this was it.

'If you say so.' Cale still sounded doubtful. 'Better now?'

Maddie nodded.

Cale lifted his empty bottle. 'Want a refill?'

Maddie looked at her empty glass and shook her head. The combination of sun, wine, Cale and her unstable emotions had gone straight to her head. 'No wine. Water, please.'

Cale stepped forward and snagged the arm of the blonde that Maddie had seen the other day. 'Hey, Megs, meet someone. Maddie, this is Megan, Oliver's ex and my best mate.'

Maddie held out her hand, ignoring the emphasis he'd placed on 'my best mate'. She'd apologized—sort of.

'Hi. I'm so sorry about Oliver.'

'Hi, Maddie.' Megan squeezed her hand as Cale excused himself to greet a new arrival. 'Thanks for helping organise this race. It means a lot to us.'

Maddie winced. 'To be honest, I got shanghaied into it.'

Megan laughed. 'I bet you did. Cale never takes no for an answer.'

She knew that. Sometimes—like earlier—he didn't even ask the question. Not that she was complaining... Maddie fanned herself with her hand, hot from the instant replay in her head.

Maddie enquired after the boys, and she and Megan fell into comfortable conversation. They were talking about Megan's interior decorating business when Cale came back, with a familiar-looking dark-haired man at his elbow.

Cale swapped Maddie's glass for the tall glass of water in his hand and gestured to the man. 'Maddie—Alex. My younger brother.'

Maddie saw the resemblance to Oliver in the slow smile and dark hair, but this brother shared Cale's deep blue eyes. If possible, he was almost better-looking than Cale, but a lot less mus-

cular. Maddie held out her hand and when they shook noticed
that there wasn't even a flicker of chemistry between them.
Mmm, it seemed she was only attracted to the blond brothers
of the Grant family.

'Maddie? The one who got away?'

'Shut up, Al,' Cale snapped.

Megan patted Maddie's shoulder. 'Watch out for Alex,
Maddie. He's still single and desperately looking for a wife.'

'I am not!' Alex protested. 'Not desperately. Just looking. I'm
a slob and a terrible cook and I need someone to look after me.'

Maddie saw the glint in his eyes and knew that he was teasing. 'Well, don't look at me, I'm not wife material. I have the do-
mestic skills of a tortoise and would drive a man mad in a week.'

'I can vouch for that,' Cale agreed.

Maddie wrinkled her nose at him. 'So, are you a racer too?'
she enquired, to change the subject.

Alex looked at her as if she'd grown two heads. 'Good Lord,
no! I'm a doctor.' He cocked a head at Cale. 'A real one, not a
play one.'

'That joke is *so* stale,' Cale whipped back.

Maddie thought she owed Cale some payback for his earlier
statement. She sent Alex a mischievous look. 'Well, you look
pretty fit to me. You look like you *should* race. I mean, how
difficult can it be?'

Alex obviously believed that any chance to needle his brother
should be taken, so he picked up her cue. 'That's what I keep
telling him! He carries on as if it's the pinnacle of sport.'

'Why don't *you* try it, Dr Nerd? I guarantee I'll need to bring
you oxygen before you get to five miles,' Cale snarled.

'You're *so* full of yourself—'

'We'll race. I'll give you a handicap. And I'll take you to the
hospital when we're done,' Cale interrupted.

Maddie grinned at their bickering. She heard the love beneath the taunting. She'd love to see that race... Maddie's eyes
widened and she danced on the spot in the excitement. 'That's
a brilliant idea!'

Alex widened his eyes at her in dismay. 'It is?'

'Absolutely! It solves one of the problems I have with this race. How do we raise funds on a race that people don't really care about? Triathlons appeal only to a few idiots—'

'Thanks,' Cale said dryly.

Maddie laid a hand on his arm. 'But people would be attracted to a race, would be *interested* in a race, if they knew the people. Celebrities! So we have celebrity teams.'

'Uh—no,' Cale said.

'Uh, *yes*. They'd make teams of four, and they'd have a handicap, and they'd raise their own sponsorship. T-shirts, entry fee, donations—all to go to charity. The public makes donations on behalf of their favourite team.'

Cale slipped his hand into Maddie's and squeezed. 'Mad, at the risk of sounding conceited, they won't cope with it. Even normal sportsmen frequently aren't fit enough.'

'So we have a baby race for them, and the triathlon racers do the big race, and we work out a system for who wins.' Maddie looked up into his doubtful face. 'It doesn't matter how you structure the race. It's something new and the public will get behind it.'

'I don't know, Mad…'

Maddie nodded her head. 'I do. This is my job. We're doing it this way.'

Cale lifted his eyebrows at her sharp tone. 'Okay, okay. Geez, when did you get to be so bossy?'

Maddie sent him an easy smile. 'Another thing I learnt from you. You know, I used to be a nice, sweet, kind girl before I hooked up with you.'

Cale grinned. 'You were never nice and you know it.'

'And why would you think that?' Maddie asked haughtily.

Cale tapped her left eyebrow. 'Your left eye twitches when you lie.'

'You are such an idiot!' Maddie ducked her head to hide her smile.

'And there it goes again. Twitch, twitch.'

* * *

Maddie, exhausted after an afternoon of PR and selling her new concept for the race, decided to retreat to Cale's study to catch her breath. Taking a pad of blank paper from his messy desk, she flopped into his chair, kicked off her sandals and placed her toes on the edge of his desk. She wanted to get her ideas down on paper while they were still fresh. Some would work, some wouldn't, but she knew she might forget one or two if she didn't jot them down.

Maddie was scribbling furiously when she heard the clink of a bottle against the doorframe. Pushing back her hair, she frowned at the russet-haired man standing by the door and waving a bottle in her direction.

'Want a drink?' he slurred.

Seeing his hot eyes on her thighs, Maddie lowered her feet and clenched her knees together. 'The party is upstairs.'

He was as tall as Cale but not as well built, with a soft mouth and those hot eyes. Maddie sighed as he walked into the room and placed two glasses on the desk. He aimed the wine bottle in the general direction of a glass and Maddie winced when red wine ran down the side of the glass onto Cale's antique desk and dripped onto the Persian rug below.

'I don't want any wine, thank you.'

He ignored her. 'You're Maddie? The race organizer?'

'Yes.'

'I'm a sponsor for the race. I own Canoe Concepts.'

Maddie had seen the offer Liam Peters had made to be a sponsor of the race and thought it laughable. She could raise more money selling raffle tickets.

'I've been watching you all afternoon and I think you're kind of cute. You know, I'm *really* loaded.'

'Great!' Maddie said brightly. 'So, can I add a couple of noughts to your sponsorship offer?'

'If you kiss me.'

Maddie tipped her head back and stared at the ceiling. This was all she needed—a drunk, lecherous, manipulative man trading sex for money. 'Yeah...*so* not going to happen.'

Liam Peters looked at her with eyes that were, while bloodshot, vastly determined. Maddie knew that he wasn't very familiar with the word *no*.

'I'd rather jump into a bath full of maggots,' Maddie muttered. Lifting her hands, she raised her voice and sent him a very small, very cold smile. 'Liam, you're drunk, and I'm getting annoyed. Go away.'

'If you sleep with me then I won't only not pull the money, I'll double it.'

Whoop-dee-do. Maddie slipped her feet into her sandals and rolled her eyes. 'Well, that's not going to happen. This conversation is over.'

Maddie pushed her shoulders back and walked around the desk. She thought she was out of trouble when she brushed past him without incident, but at the last moment he grabbed her shoulder and spun her around. Despite being as drunk as a newt, his arms banded around her. His sour breath made her want to gag. Maddie tried to push against his arms but he was stronger than she'd thought.

'Kiss me and I'll hurt you,' she warned him.

Liam only smiled and dropped his head. As his lips neared hers Maddie grasped his biceps, lifted her knee and rammed it up into his scrotum. He dropped like a stone. Damn, that had felt good. *Thank you, Jim. Good tip.*

'You bitch,' Liam rasped, curled up in a foetal position on Cale's carpet. 'You frigid, manipulative, hideous—'

Before he could finish his sentence Cale had streaked into the room and wrapped his hand around Liam's throat. Where on earth had he come from? Maddie swallowed as Liam's eyes bulged under the pressure. Cale wouldn't…would he?

'Finish that sentence and you're a dead man,' Cale growled. As Liam tried to pull his hands away from his throat Cale tightened his grip. His hands fell away.

'Cale, he's gasping…'

'Shut up, Madison.' Cale lifted Liam's head and slammed it into the carpet.

Maddie hopped from one foot to the other, thinking that much as she enjoyed Cale playing hero, she really didn't want

Liam to suffer brain damage. The jerk obviously needed all the brains he had.

'I think you should let him go,' Maddie said, placing a hand on Cale's shoulder.

'So here's what you're going to do,' Cale said, as if he and Liam were enjoying a pleasant conversation. 'I'm going to lift my hand. You take me on and I'll beat you senseless. Then you're going to get out of my house and piss off. Understand me?'

Liam nodded frantically.

'Oh, and don't even talk to Maddie again or the press will hear about this...incident.'

Liam swallowed as Cale's hand lifted. Rolling over onto all fours, he dragged air into his lungs and cautiously stood up. Taking a moment to straighten his shirt, he pushed back his hair and looked at Maddie with hot, vicious eyes. 'You just lost your sponsorship,' he rasped.

Cale bared his teeth. 'Like I give a flying—'

Maddie quickly interjected. 'Just go, Liam.'

'You've got ten seconds,' Cale said.

His voice was even and Maddie sneaked a glance at him. His body was relaxed, his hands loose at his sides. Only his eyes, light with cold rage, gave any indication to his feelings. Cale kept an eye on Liam as he walked past Maddie and left via the study door. Maddie waited for the slam of the front door before sitting and dropping her face into her hands.

Cale crouched in front of her and rested a hand on her knee. 'Are you okay? Did he hurt you?'

Maddie ignored him as her shoulders shook.

'Maddie, talk to me.'

Cale stroked her leg from knee to ankle and Maddie eventually lifted her face. When she did, she let her ringing laughter escape. Cale lifted his eyebrows as tears ran down her face.

'I'm sorry,' Maddie gulped, waving her hands in the air, 'but it was so funny! He looked like a blowfish.'

Maddie placed her hands around her own neck and blew out her cheeks in an impersonation of the gulping Liam.

Cale pinched the bridge of his nose. 'I nearly beat him to a pulp and you think it's funny? He *attacked* you.'

Maddie's laughter died immediately. 'Amusing, maybe. Cale, he didn't attack me—he tried to kiss me! And you didn't have to half-strangle him. I had him with my knee.'

'He put his hands on you!' Cale growled. 'He was about to call you a—'

'Yeah, I know, so…thanks.' Maddie laid a tentative hand on his shoulder. She started to giggle again, but tried to stop when she saw his stony face.

As Cale stood up, he briefly considered strangling Maddie as well. All he could see was Maddie struggling to get out from Liam's arms and his stomach clenched at the renewed surge of anger. If he had the choice again, he would go with his first instinct and beat the hell out of him.

And she was calmly sitting there as if this was an everyday occurrence.

As he'd long suspected, his PhD in sports psychology meant nothing when it came to understanding women.

CHAPTER EIGHT

'LET me guess—dinner at the LQ, followed by a couple of jazz clubs?'

Cale heard the feminine voice on speaker phone as he approached the door to Maddie's flat. He really needed to have a serious discussion with her about security, he thought, clutching the thick folder of papers he'd promised to drop off with her. It was after nine and, although the front door to the building was locked, why take the chance?

He stopped at the door and peered in. Maddie lay on her cream couch, long legs dangling off the arm, throwing a scruffy tennis ball up in the air and listlessly catching it again.

'Mm, I get to drive my lunatic mother and her sidekick from club to club, where they'll dance like dorks and grope each other. They have terrible timing as well. I'm snowed under, categorically exhausted, and if one more person asks one more thing of me I am going to dissolve into a puddle of tears.'

'You can always say no, Mad.'

The slightly tinny voice floated towards Cale.

'She's my mother, Katie. I only see her twice a year.'

Cale heard and was fascinated by the misery in Maddie's voice. Unashamedly eavesdropping, he propped a shoulder against the wall outside and stayed to listen.

'Sweetie, you can say no because she leaves you feeling depressed and miserable for days.'

Maddie rested the ball on her flat stomach and draped a forearm across her eyes. 'I'm such a disappointment to my parents.'

'And why would *that* be?'

Cale had yet to meet Maddie's best friend, but he identified with the irritation in her voice.

'It doesn't matter how much I earn or how hard I work…they just don't respect what I do.'

Cale closed his eyes against the sadness in her voice. He was about to step into the room and say…what could he say?…when Maddie's voice stopped his progress.

'Why can't I be the daughter they need, Katie?'

Kate was silent for a minute before responding. 'Maybe you should be asking why they can't be the *parents* you need, sweetie.'

Cale decided that he rather liked Maddie's friend Kate. As the subject under discussion changed Cale walked away quietly, went halfway down the wooden steps and ran up again to announce his arrival.

Maddie looked around at his rap on her door and gestured him inside. Cale ignored her red eyes and pink nose and waved the file in the air. 'Homework, as you demanded.'

Maddie ended her call and took the file he held out. 'It's overdue. I needed this two days ago.'

'Stop being grumpy,' Cale ordered, running a hand over her hair. He wanted to take her in his arms and kiss away that sadness. Instead he dropped his keys and mobile on the coffee table.

Maddie looked at him, looked at her bright blue door and he could see the pennies dropping.

'The boys are at the bar and Nat is on a date. I didn't buzz you, so how did you get in?'

'Memorised your code when you gave it to me the other morning.' He shrugged, not in the least ashamed. 'What can I say? I have a head for numbers. Got anything to drink? Eat? I'm starving.'

Without waiting for a reply, he headed to her kitchen and yanked open the door to the fridge. He clucked over its meagre contents.

'Geez, Madison, you have the fridge of a college student.

Wine and leftover pizza.' Cale lifted a piece of pizza, sniffed it, and took a large bite.

'There is a restaurant within walking distance if you're hungry,' Maddie pointed out, and sat down in the corner of her couch and flipped through the file he'd brought along.

He'd tossed all the papers he had on the race inside it after she'd sent him a sarcastic BBM demanding his co-operation. Potential sponsors, lists of teams, copies of letters sent to paramedics and marshals for the race. An application form to have a road temporarily closed for a couple of hours on the day. He was still only halfway down her list of things she wanted him to do.

'Close it, Mad,' Cale said from the kitchen.

Maddie looked over the back of the couch to where he was standing in the kitchen, another pizza slice in his hand. 'What?'

'It's nearly half-nine and I took a call from you at seven this morning about the race. That means you've been working on something or the other for nearly fourteen hours. It's enough.'

Maddie started to protest, but she'd obviously heard the bite in his voice. Why did she do this to herself? Work herself to a standstill? What was she trying to prove? Holding her stare, he waited until she closed the file and put it on the table.

Cale finished the slice of pizza and, bringing the beer he'd found in the fridge with him, stalked over to where she sat. Lifting her legs off the cushions, he sat next to her and draped her feet over his lap. Instinctively he started to massage the balls of her feet with his hands.

Maddie closed her eyes and he increased the pressure on her feet. If only he could wind his way up her legs… Cale looked at her blue-shadowed sunken eyes and sighed. She was exhausted and emotional. He could make a move and within ten minutes have her flat on her back, but that would be like taking candy from a baby. She didn't need sex tonight. She needed a friend. And, besides, when they did make love again he wanted her fully in the moment with him.

A brochure on the coffee table caught his eye and he leaned forward to pick it up. Bower & Co. He flipped through the glossy pages.

'I've applied for a position with them.'

Cale heard the tremble in her voice and wondered why. 'Are they opening a branch in Cape Town?'

Maddie yawned and snuggled deeper into the couch. She stared at her hands. 'The job is in New York.'

Cale felt as if he'd been hit over the head with a sledgehammer. He struggled for his professional mask, unwilling to show her how much he instinctively hated the idea of her being so far away. He wondered why because—as he kept reminding himself—what he and Maddie had—sex-tinged friendship or friendship-tinged sex—had a finite end.

That was their unspoken agreement.

'Oh. I thought you loved this city.'

'I do!' Maddie exclaimed. 'What's not to love? We have mountains and sea and spring flowers and—'

'Freezing water.'

Maddie managed a small smile.

'Then why do you want to leave, Mad? Is it the money?'

Maddie rubbed her neck. 'It's not a factor. Cale, it's an amazing opportunity!'

'I'm not saying it isn't. I'm just asking why it appeals to you?'

'It's New York!'

Cale kept rubbing her feet in silent encouragement for her to talk. When she remained silent, he tapped her foot in encouragement. 'Those are all good and solid reasons, Mad, but I know you and there's more to it than that. C'mon, Mad, you're well enough travelled to know that once you've lived somewhere long enough even the greatest city in the world can become just another grimy, lonely place. You'll be working long, long hours in a city where you know no one.'

'I know Dennis.'

'Okay, where you know one person.' Cale shook his head. 'Dig deeper, Maddie. Why do you really want to do this?'

'You're going to make me say it, aren't you?'

Cale smiled. 'I'm not going to make you say anything, Mads. I'm just prompting you to think and to examine your motives.'

'My career is the most important thing in my life.' Maddie

took his beer from the table and took a small sip. She used the gesture to mark time. 'The biggest factor is that I'd love to work at one of the greatest PR and event companies in the world in one of the greatest cities in the world... I can't deny that. I'm enough of my parents' child to aim high—even if it is in what they call an asinine field.'

Cale took the bottle from Maddie, lifted it to his lips and took a long sip. His eyes encouraged Maddie to continue. 'Go on. What else?'

'You *are* going to make me verbalise it, aren't you?'

'Yep.'

'It's not the biggest reason for me wanting the job, but...' the words tumbled out in a rush of emotion '...maybe if I take it my parents will be impressed and proud of me.'

'Good girl. But they won't.'

'Oh, thanks for that! Why not?'

'The lack is in them, Mad, not you. Never with you.' Cale shoved a hand through his hair. 'You could get a Nobel Peace Prize and your parents would say it wasn't good enough. Because while they are book smart they don't have the emotional intelligence God gave a split pea. Stop looking for their approval. You're chasing a pot of gold at the end of a non-existent rainbow.' Cale put his bottle on the table.

'So you think that I shouldn't go to New York?' Maddie bit the inside of her lip.

'I didn't say that. I understand why it's so very attractive to you. You've always aimed high, and if you didn't go you'd probably regret it. What I *am* saying is that you have got to do what is right for you. For the right reasons.'

What had she expected? That he'd fall to his knees and beg her not to go? Where were her brains? Cale had never given her any hint that he felt anything more for her than attraction and friendship. And she didn't want him to...what they had was enough.

Cale half turned towards her and pushed her hair off her forehead. 'You have violet rings under your eyes. When did you last sleep? Eat?'

Maddie shrugged and Cale shook his head at this reply.

'You are your own worst enemy. Come with me.'

It wasn't a request.

Cale wrapped a hard arm around her waist and half picked her up. Maddie resisted for about two seconds and then collapsed against him, following where he led. Cale walked her through her dressing room and pulled her into the bathroom. Depositing her on the closed toilet seat, she watched him flip open the taps of the huge bath.

Maddie pulled her elbows to her sides as Cale lifted the hem of her shirt. 'This is so not necessary.'

'Shut up and take it off,' Cale said, bending to pull her shoes off her feet.

Maddie looked down at her breasts spilling out of her peach bra. Her mouth dried as she caught the gentle heat in Cale's eyes and wished he'd take her to bed. Instead of kissing her he made her stand, unzipped her charcoal pants and pushed them over her hips, watching as they dropped to her feet.

'I'm such a saint,' he grumbled. 'Step out.'

His eyes flicked over her high-cut bikini bottoms. With another muttered oath, he undid the clasp of her bra, pulled down her panties, and tossed the items towards the laundry basket. He held her hand while she stepped into the tub and slid below the water. He grabbed the nearest bottle of bubble bath and tossed some in. She sighed and ran a wet hand through her hair, slicking it back.

'Lie there. Relax. I'll be back with some food.'

'Cale, I can't stay here. I've got four lists waiting for me on my desk. There's a pile of work I've got to get through tonight,' Maddie fretted as he headed for the door.

'Maddie, you are mentally and physically exhausted. If you don't rest you are going to collapse.'

'Cale!'

Cale grabbed the edge of the door and looked back at her. He ran a hand over his eyes, and his words, when he spoke, held no heat. 'Mad, please? Sit. Stay. Shut up.'

* * *

A half-hour later Cale walked back into the bathroom and Maddie forced her eyes open. Steam swirled around the room as Cale looked down at her with enigmatic eyes. She was too tired to protest at his obvious inspection of her body, so Maddie discarded her modesty and rubbed a soapy loofah over her arms, around her neck, over her breasts. Cale followed her movements with his eyes, and Maddie didn't need to look to gauge his reaction.

Cale smiled lazily at her, utterly distracted. 'You're a tease.'

Maddie eyed him and licked her lips as her mouth dried up. 'Come here.'

'Thanks, Maddie, I'll take a raincheck. Not because I don't want you…I always want you.'

Yanking his eyes upwards, he shook his head and in one fluid motion reached for a towel. Opening it up, he motioned for Maddie to stand up. Helping her out of the bath, he wrapped the towel around her chest and gently dropped a kiss on her lips.

'I need you,' she whispered, stepping forward and planting her hands on his chest, sweeping them down his sides and around to cup his buttocks. How much more of a hint did the man need?

'You need to sleep, Mad,' Cale said softly, and steered her to the bedroom. Tenderly, he dried her off, before pulling a clean oversized T-shirt over her head. He pulled back the covers on the bed and indicated she should climb in. Maddie swung her legs into the bed and stared up at him, not quite believing his refusal.

'I *need* you.'

Cale grinned and tucked—*tucked!*—the covers around her. 'You need a decent night's sleep more. And if I climb into bed with you, you know that we'll be up all night. I can't seem to get enough of you. So finish that smoothie. Get some goodness into you.'

She was trying to seduce him and he was prattling on about health foods?

'Well, then I'll just have to work.' Maddie pouted and pushed the covers away.

'Okay, let's say this slowly. You…need…sleep,' Cale insisted, pushing her back on the pillows before sitting on the bed next to her. 'What's really going on in that crazy head of yours, Mad?'

'I don't know what you mean.'

'You are exhausted. I could see that you'd been crying earlier... What's going on?'

Maddie flicked her thumb over the embossed feather pattern on her white throw. She felt her breath hitch in her throat and silently cursed the rising tears. She tried to will them away but they slid down her face anyway. Look how well he knew her... He knew that she was using sex as a distraction, as a way to get out of her head for a while.

'Talk to me, Maddie.'

Maddie bent her knees and wrapped her arms around them, resting her cheek on one knee while Cale played with one of her long curls. 'I'm just feeling so overwhelmed. So much has happened so quickly, and I feel like I can't make sense of any of it. Throw my mother into the mix and my stress levels go through the roof.'

Cale wiped a tear away with his thumb.

'I'm usually a decisive person, Cale. I have to be, doing what I do. I have to decide on a course of action and then I implement it.'

'Easy to do at work but not so easy to do in real life,' he commented. 'What decisions are you struggling with?'

Whether to let myself grow closer to you or whether to pull away now, before my heart gets stomped on. Whether I really, really want to go to New York or just think that I should want to. Whether I'm happy at Mayhew Walsh.

She couldn't verbalise those concerns so went with a sweeping statement. 'Everything is changing and I don't like it.' Tears dripped onto her knee.

'Change is good, Maddie, it allows you to grow. But with change comes fear...and when you're tired it can feel overwhelming.' Cale's strong fingers gripped her neck and dug into the tense cords. 'You're a mess. Feel how stressed you are.'

'If you keep doing that I'm going to keep crying.'

'I've had six-foot-five rugby players bawling on my couch.

Tears don't scare me,' Cale said softly as he moved behind her to massage her back.

Maddie moaned as his strong hands eased into her hard muscles. 'I hate crying... I feel so weak,' she admitted.

'Don't. It's good to see you letting go, that you can be vulnerable. The more I get to know you, the more I'm realising that your tough-girl image is an act you've perfected—but it's still an act. You're not half as tough as you think you are.'

'I'm very tough!' Maddie protested, but without any heat or conviction.

'Yeah, so tough. With your piggy eyes and your red nose and blotchy skin,' Cale teased.

Maddie groaned. She knew she didn't look her best, but did he have to point it out? Her tears carried on flowing.

'Good girl, let it out. No, don't think, just cry. Let go, sweetheart. You're safe. I'm here,' Cale whispered as he rubbed her shoulders.

So Maddie quietly cried while Cale's magic hands eased the tension out of her body. He only stopped to pull tissues from the box on the bedside table and shove them into her hand, and he carried on long after her waterworks and snuffles had stopped.

After many long, bone-melting minutes, Cale's hands stilled on her back and he leaned forward to look down into her face.

'Better?'

Maddie nodded, too tired—mentally and physically—to talk. She pushed herself up in the bed and placed her head on her pillow. Cale put his feet on the floor. Maddie stopped him from getting up with a hand on his arm.

'Stay. Please?' she asked through a huge yawn. 'Would you just hold me? For a while?'

Cale lay down next to her, shoved a hand under her shoulder and pulled her close. 'Sure.'

Maddie turned and placed her head on his shoulder. *Tenderness*, she thought, sliding her arm across his chest. *So this is what tenderness feels like.*

I like it, Maddie thought as her eyes closed. *I really do.*

* * *

So, Cale thought as he trudged up the beach below his house, surfboard under his arm, surfing wasn't as easy as he'd expected it to be. When he'd asked Maddie to teach him to surf he'd thought he'd pick it up in a heartbeat—he'd always had good balance, and how difficult could it really be? Way, *way* difficult, he'd discovered. He couldn't even stay balanced on his stomach in two-feet-high waves.

Cale dumped his surfboard on the sand and picked a towel out of Maddie's beach basket. Learning to surf in autumn wasn't one of his brightest ideas either; the water's temperature came up from Antarctica and the wind had a nasty bite. He turned to look out to the back line, easily picking Maddie out from the surfers, watching as she picked up a wave and flew down it. He couldn't see her face clearly, but knew that she'd have a massive grin on her face.

He wanted to share this with her—share her passion for the sea and its many moods. He'd genuinely listened and tried to keep his weight centred in the middle of the board, his chest above the middle point of the rocking piece of plank. He'd also tried very hard to ignore her hands on his waist, her hair swirling down her back, the way the black neoprene of her wetsuit moulded her perfect breasts and fabulous bottom.

Maybe if he'd concentrated more on the surfing lesson and less on the surfer he would have done a bit better. But it was difficult to grasp the technicalities of lying prone on a board when five-foot-four of sheer lusciousness had one hand on your butt and the other on your thigh. Cale winced in embarrassment. Fifteen-year-olds, he decided, had more sophistication.

Cale stripped off the top half of his wetsuit, yanked on a T-shirt and a thick hooded sweatshirt and sat in the sand, rubbing his wet head with the towel.

He hated not getting something right. While Oliver had been good at sports but brilliant academically, he'd been the opposite. He wasn't a slouch in the brains department, but sport was what he *did*… He'd never come across a sport that he couldn't master. Sport was where he channelled his aggression, and he excelled at whatever he turned his hand to.

Except surfing, obviously.

Maddie ran up the beach and dumped her surfboard next to his, a broad grin on her face.

'Hello, grumpy.'

'Stupid sport,' Cale muttered, his eyes on her torso as she pulled her wetsuit off to reveal a lime-green bikini.

'It's time to haul out my dry suit. That water is freezing!'

Cale handed her a towel and she wrapped it around her shoulders.

'There's hot coffee in the flask,' Maddie told him, squeezing the water out of her hair.

'There is a God,' Cale replied, pulling the basket to him and digging for the flask and mugs as Maddie pulled on some warm clothes.

'You did well,' Maddie said as she dropped to the sand, briefly resting her hand on his thigh.

'I'm useless! I'm obviously surfing impaired.'

Maddie took the cup he held out and took a grateful sip. 'You're just making common surfing mistakes—albeit in a foot of water,' Maddie told him. 'With surfing, all your action needs to be performed without hesitation. If it isn't, a wave will pick you up and dump you. As it did. Numerous times.'

Cale narrowed his eyes at her. 'You're enjoying this, aren't you?'

Maddie's grin was crooked. And charming. 'Hey, you're cute when there's snot running from your nose and you're doing your wet St Bernard dog impression.'

It was supremely galling to have to accept that her description was deadly accurate. Cale gave her what he hoped was a quelling stare. When her smile deepened he suspected that he'd have to work on his intimidation tactics.

'You're really hard on yourself,' Maddie said as she wrapped her hands around the cup.

'I like getting stuff right.'

'No, I think it's more than that. I've been thinking about you, and I think that you—'

'—are amazing in bed?' Cale quipped, desperate to change the subject.

Maddie bumped him with her shoulder. 'I think that you are ridiculously tough on yourself. Why?'

'I'm just a normal guy.'

Maddie snorted. 'A normal guy who wants to control everything in the known universe.'

'Just in *my* universe,' Cale muttered in his cup.

'I heard that. I think you hang onto control because Oliver was so *out* of control.'

Cale mentally reeled back and looked at her, shocked. How did she know that? How could she know that?

'Why…? What?'

Maddie drew patterns in the sand between them. 'The other day I was remembering an incident before we even hooked up. We were at that lake, you had borrowed a speedboat, and you spent the whole day trying to keep Oliver from driving it. When you eventually ran out of excuses you tried to convince your friends not to go in the boat with him. You spent the next hour watching Oliver throw that boat around the lake, waiting for a disaster to happen. I thought then that you spent a lot of days like that, because of the look on your face. It was a mixture of fear and resignation. And anger.'

He remembered that day—remembered thinking that he was responsible if Oliver flipped that boat, if anyone got hurt. Remembered feeling resentful because he'd been so tired of constantly being on alert. 'I wasn't angry at him.'

'Cale, you've been angry with Oliver in one way or another most of your life.'

'I have not!' Cale protested. 'You don't understand what I went through with my brother.'

Maddie nodded her agreement. 'You're right. I don't. So explain it to me.'

He couldn't—not without sounding intolerably disloyal. How did he explain that Oliver had been different from birth, with the biggest attitude? He hadn't slept, he'd been demanding, and he'd worn them out. Reading at four, writing at five—he'd simply been brilliant. He'd also been stubborn and proud and, *God*, so wild. Oliver had had to touch, taste, feel, see...

He'd had no off button, no sense of responsibility, and no idea of delayed gratification. Cale's life had been spent keeping him out of trouble, because he'd been the only one he'd listen to and the only one who could get him to toe the line. Reason, bribery, sometimes physical restraint. In order to protect him—from himself, mostly—he'd had to be bigger and tougher,

Bailing him out of jail at eighteen on assault charges had taken all his savings. Then drugs and gambling. The fact that he'd been too fast with his fists and had expected to be backed up when he ran into trouble.

'He was who he was. He was wild.' They were the only words Cale could eventually force past his lips. 'I had to look after him.'

'You should've let him bump his head.'

Cale's fist punched the sand. 'You're not hearing me. I was the only one he'd listen to. Sometimes.'

'*You* don't understand, Cale. Oliver could've kept himself out of trouble. He was responsible for his own actions, not you.'

'*What?*'

Maddie shrugged. 'He was an adult, but you never allowed him to grow up because you always bailed him out.'

Cale flopped onto his back and stared up at the sky. He placed his forearm over his eyes. *Ouch.* Could she be right?

'I know you don't tolerate anyone criticising your twin but... tough. Your brother was a selfish, feckless, charming jerk. He used women, he squandered his education and he had the maturity and sense of responsibility of a five-year-old.'

Cale heard the kindness in her tough tone and wondered why it was such a relief to hear his frequent thoughts about his twin so eloquently verbalised.

'He played you all your life, and because you always looked out for him why did he need to step up to the plate?' Maddie pushed his hair back from his forehead. 'You paid his bills, literally and metaphorically, and you're still paying the price.'

Maddie crawled onto him and lifted his arm off his eyes. 'Maybe you should think about changing that?'

'Mad...'

Maddie lowered her lips to his in a kiss that was as sensual as it was comforting. Her lips soothed and reassured, comforted and caressed. Her kiss suggested that he could, just for a moment, stop being brave and tough and just mourn his brother. That he was allowed to feel vulnerable and insecure and unhappy, and that she'd be there to catch him if he fell.

Then her tongue slid into his mouth and grief and sadness were vanquished in the heat of her mouth, in the way she wiggled her crotch over his, in the way her fingers tightened in his. This was life, he thought. This girl and this time and this beach and this sunset.

'Enough heavy stuff,' Maddie whispered against his lips. 'Take me to bed.'

Cale patted her bottom. 'That would mean you getting off me and us climbing those steps back to my house.'

Maddie squinted up at his house and back at him. 'Can't we just do it here?'

Cale knew that he was far gone when he actually seriously considered her playful, jokey suggestion. Then his old friend common sense reared its ugly head. 'Too cold, too many people. We might get arrested.'

Maddie bit his ear and reluctantly rolled off him. 'Oh, well, I tried.' She glanced at the ocean and was instantly on her feet. 'Grief, look at those waves! Five, six feet... Where did they come from? They're breaking perfectly...'

Cale grabbed her around the waist as she reached for her board. 'Sweetheart, the only thing you are going to ride in the near future is me.'

Maddie wiggled out of his arms, yanked her sweatshirt off and pulled the top half of her wetsuit back over her arms. She grabbed her board and jogged to the sea. 'Maybe later. If you're very, very lucky.'

Cale threw up his hands and had to smile at the cheeky grin she tossed him over her shoulder.

At the water's edge she turned and walked backwards into the waves. 'But I'm warning you—if you don't come close to giving me the same thrill as a barrel roll, I'm kicking you into touch.'

'I've never been one to resist a challenge,' Cale shouted as she paddled to the back line.

Maddie's faint laughter drifted back to the beach as Cale trudged back to their spot. With every step he could sense his mood changing, and soon he felt the familiar but less frequent feelings of guilt and despair slide over him. He couldn't argue with what Maddie had said but the outcome was still the same. Oliver was dead. It was wrong that he was having this much fun with Maddie, unfair that he was living and laughing when his bigger-than-life brother was gone. Oliver hadn't had the chance to turn his life around because he hadn't been strong enough to say no. If they hadn't gone for that paddle in the kayak, if he'd stayed in hospital, he might have lived longer. They might have had more time to find a bone marrow donor.

Cale sank to the sand and dropped his head between his knees, fighting the rising panic. He felt his throat constrict and forced himself to breathe. Why now?

Because he was happy, having fun. He had little right, actually no right, to be either.

There were good days, there were bad days, and then there were days that were marked 'From Hell—Special Delivery'. At three o'clock on a Thursday afternoon, Maddie was thinking that such a day would be nothing compared to the last six hours. She was categorically exhausted, running on fresh air and chocolate and little sleep. The race was taking far more time than she'd allocated, and she was finding she had to work long hours to compensate.

And Cale had dropped off the face of the earth.

While he'd always been emotionally unavailable, since that day on the beach a week ago he hadn't called or e-mailed her, let alone anything else. Cale, she realised, ran away when he felt emotionally threatened, and he'd obviously been hurt or upset or angry—probably all three—at her comments about Oliver. He'd been quiet the rest of the day, and when they had made it into the bedroom making love had been more perfunctory than she was used to, and she'd seen a flicker of relief on his face when she'd said she should go.

That relief and his subsequent disappearing act hurt far more than it should. Which made her feel used, sad and more than a little angry.

Why was he allowed to delve into *her* head, and make comments about her parents and her work, but she wasn't allowed to make any observations about his state of mind? She knew—God, she knew—that Cale didn't want anything more than what they had, but weren't they allowed to be friends?

Friends shared stuff, helped each other through the bad stuff, sorted out the muddle in each other's heads... Oh, wait...that was *girlfriends*.

Anyway, thinking about Cale just annoyed her. She should think about work—another contentious subject.

So far today she'd dealt with a beyond picky bride and her pickier mother and, because Thandi had hidden in the staff bathroom, soothed the irate owners of the Piano Festival because some of their performers had eaten a bad batch of sausage rolls. She had only completed two of the three reports she'd promised Harriet, still hadn't managed to track down a creative caterer to fill in for a product launch the following week, and there wasn't a yellow rose to be found in the city.

'I'm sorry, I really am,' Thandi told her again.

Maddie looked up from a report and frowned at Thandi, who was sitting at her desk, filing her nails. Fighting her temper, Maddie ignored her and scowled at her computer.

'It's just that you are so much better at conflict than I am. They would've started shouting, and I would've shouted back, then I'd have been reported to Harriet and she'd have blamed you for my lack of training—so I saved your hide, really.'

Maddie's mouth fell open at Thandi's convoluted reasoning as to why she'd had to deal with her upset clients. 'You don't actually believe the nonsense that's falling from your lips, do you?'

The corners of Thandi's mouth twitched. 'No, but you're talking to me again.'

'You are such a brat.' Maddie stood up, and in her attempt to toss a file onto her desk banged her knee on the underside.

She danced around on one foot, swearing as stars burst, clutching her knee in agony. Thandi hurried over to her and gently helped her into her chair.

The husky sound of a clearing throat caught them both off-guard, and Maddie whirled around to see Cale standing at Thandi's desk. Lifting annoyed eyebrows at Thandi, she threw up her hands in despair.

'Maddie—Cale's here,' Thandi sing-songed, straightening her back and shoving her chest out when Cale smiled down at her.

Maddie considered pulling her long braided hair out through her nose. 'What are you doing here?'

'I thought I'd attend the meeting to persuade that farmer to allow us access to his land for the race.'

'I could've handled it on my own,' Maddie told him.

Cale ignored her as he crouched in front of her and pushed her black pants up her leg to probe her knee.

'You okay? You banged your knee pretty hard.'

Maddie winced as his hands hit the point of impact.

'Madison!' Harriet's strident voice had Maddie's head snapping up and Cale turning to look at her.

Harriet, hands on her adolescent-size hips, looked down her nose at them. 'The racer. In my offices. *Again.* It seems that every time I turn around you're here. And more often than not with your hands on my employee.'

Cale stood up and folded his arms, his eyes turning lighter with irritation.

Maddie, not wanting to see blood on the floor, stood up too, winced, and tried to take control of the situation. 'How can I help you, Harriet?'

'You can tell me why I have a very irate mother of Tasmin McGee on the telephone, complaining about your lack of support, your lack of creative ideas and your unprofessional attitude.'

Maddie looked at Thandi, whose mouth had fallen open.

'Hold on a sec!' Thandi said, when Maddie refused to defend

herself. 'I was in that meeting and Maddie was brilliant. She handled those revolting, snotty woman with remarkable calm.'

'Those "snotty women" are the wife and daughter of the CEO of one of our biggest corporate clients,' Harriet said in a clipped tone. 'I'm giving the wedding to Jake to organise since *you*, Madison, can't seem to be trusted to handle *any* important projects at the moment.' She sent Cale a pointed look. 'The sooner this wretched stupid race is over, the happier I'll be.'

Maddie flew out of her chair but Cale's hand whipped out to grab her arm. Maddie felt his silent warning, dropped her head and sucked in some deep breaths in an attempt to get her temper under control. She wanted to rage and tear Harriet stick-thin limb from limb. She stepped forward. How dared she say the race was stupid and wretched?

'Breathe,' Cale said in her ear, and she did. And as oxygen filled her lungs her temper retreated.

When Maddie thought she could walk and talk without fire coming out of her ears, she reached across her desk for the pile of documents she'd need to work on at home. When she looked up Harriet had left the room to go back to her cave.

She glanced over her shoulder and caught Thandi's eye. 'We're going to a meeting with one of the landowners whose property we need to use for the race. You. So. Owe. Me.'

She handed Cale her laptop and stormed out of the communal office.

In the lift she turned to Cale and dropped the side of her head against the lift panel. With her eyes closed, she spoke, bitterness in her voice. 'I'm in a foul mood, Cale, and if you want an organiser for your race I suggest you don't speak to me for the next fifteen minutes. You've managed to do that for over a week, so I don't imagine it'll be a feat too hard for you to accomplish.'

Cale sighed at Maddie's taut face as he opened the door of his Range Rover for her. After getting in, he tucked her laptop case behind her seat and looked at her, head back, eyes closed. His eyes slid over her classy black slimline trousers and tangerine coat. She looked too interesting to be truly beautiful, with her dark winged eyebrows and wide mouth, and was normally animated, vibrant and vivacious. Now, after an unsuccessful afternoon, she looked like a leaky balloon.

During the meeting Cale had wondered if the farmer, his son and his farm manager could see the slow trickle of energy seeping from Maddie. She'd been jaunty but firm, her words carefully chosen but resolute. Maddie had been relentless in her quest to get the runners access to a hilly area on the north side of their property, and the son and the farm manager had been prepared to give Maddie whatever she wanted—permission for the race, their firstborn child, access to their bank accounts. But the old man had been a lot cannier. Since Cale had caught a glimpse of his wife as they'd entered his house, he figured that the old man had had plenty of practice dealing with a pair of stupendous brown eyes in an animated face.

He'd held firm and they'd left disappointed. Maddie was not a happy camper.

She didn't like hearing the word no.

He ignored her crackling silence on the hour-long trip back to her office to collect her car, and when he pulled into a parking space he reached over and briefly touched the back of her hand with his index finger.

'How are you doing?' he asked.

Maddie rolled her head along the headrest to look at him. The blue shadows beneath her eyes were back, and the tiny furrow between her eyebrows suggested a headache. 'Not a happy result.'

'We have an alternative; it's not a train crash.'

'I wanted that route,' Maddie muttered as she stepped out of the car and slammed her door shut.

Cale frowned and walked around the car to where she was yanking her rolled-up plans and laptop case off his back seat.

He could see the storm racing across her eyes. 'Maddie, calm down.'

'Don't tell me to calm down.' Maddie enunciated every word through gritted teeth as she stalked to her car and tossed her belongings in the boot. She slapped her hands on her waist and narrowed her eyes. 'He was just being difficult for the sake of being difficult.'

'It was way within his rights to refuse us access. He didn't want all our runners on his land with their accompanying mess.'

'I told him we'd restore it to pristine condition!'

Cale wondered if it was even worth trying to reason with her. She was in a stew and she needed to vent and he was in the splash zone. The trick was to keep his temper when she lost hers. And she was going to. She'd been brewing up a head of steam all day. Probably all week.

'So? He said no. Move on. We have signed permission to use the other route, so we take that.'

'It's not as good a route. You said so!'

'It's good enough, Madison, and sometimes we have to settle for that!'

Maddie scrubbed her hands over her face. 'I am not arguing with you any more. I am going home, ordering a very large pizza and catching up on everything I didn't get done today.'

Typical Maddie. Her answer to a pissy day was to grab her laptop and retreat into work. 'For God's sake, Madison, go take a walk, have a glass of wine, a bubble bath. Switch off for two seconds!'

Maddie tossed her hair and narrowed her eyes at his suggestions. 'Cale, you are my friend and the man that I am currently sleeping with. You are neither my father, my brother nor my husband. You do *not* get to tell me what to do!'

He'd had more than enough of being her verbal punch bag. 'Listen, you stuck up, patronising little witch. You've had a bad day and things didn't go your way. Suck it up and be an adult about it.'

'What did you just call me?'

'You heard. You're making a mountain out of a molehill.'

Maddie's eyes threw fire at him. 'How dare you? I lost a client, had to deal with Thandi's disaster, banged my knee and didn't get the farmer to allow us to use his land. Today has been an unmitigated disaster! And I haven't even touched half of what I needed to get through today.'

'So you had a bad day? People do.'

'I had a catastrophic day!'

That pushed Cale over the edge. '*Catastrophic*? You have no freaking idea of the meaning of the word! Catastrophic is the tsunami in Japan, a ferry overturning, the melting ice caps! It's cancer and death and loss and pain. It is *not* you having a tough day and someone saying no to you!'

Cale saw remorse flash in her eyes and the embarrassment behind it. He ignored her hand outstretched in apology and spun on his heel and stormed over to his car, firing it up and backing out of his parking space more by instinct than with care. The last thing he saw before he turned into the road was Maddie's miserable, pinched, cold face.

Back at his house, Cale swiftly changed into his running gear and, conscious of a headache brewing, tossed two painkillers down his throat, chasing them down with a long stream of water from the bottle he held in his hand. No woman had ever managed to push his buttons like Maddie did. What was it about her? She was deeply annoying and a relentless perfectionist. She exhausted him…

Cale lifted the bottle again and cocked his head at the sound of a car roaring up his drive. He cursed. *Maddie.* He didn't know if he had any energy left to go another round with her. He was played out.

He leaned against his granite counter and crossed his legs at the ankles, waiting for her to find him. When she burst into the room her eyes were glinting dangerously. Her temper hadn't subsided. If anything it burnt hotter and brighter.

Oh, yay.

'Don't you *ever* walk away from me when we're having an argument!' she told him in a voice sizzling with molten lava as she drilled her finger into his chest.

Cale grabbed her finger and squeezed it before flinging it away. 'Don't pull your princess act on me. I'm not your husband or your father or your brother.' Cale threw her words back at her as he rested his bottle against his forehead. 'Go away, Mad, before I do or say something I really regret.'

Maddie cocked her head and narrowed her eyes. 'Like what?' she challenged.

'I might say that you're a spoilt brat with a wicked temper. That right now I really don't like you. That I'm battling with deciding whether I want to haul you over my knee or haul you to bed. Since I don't hit women…'

'Well, I really don't like *you* either right now,' Maddie informed him as she tossed her keys on the kitchen table. 'You're judgmental and arrogant.'

She unbuttoned her coat and flung it over the nearest chair. 'You're emotionally stunted and wrapped up in the past.'

'You're high-maintenance and would try the patience of a saint,' Cale whipped back.

'Do you have an inkling of the amount of time and effort I'm putting into this race for you? A race to honour your brother—somebody I'm not even sure that you liked!'

Cale's breath caught in his throat as anger roiled and churned. 'Be careful, Madison.'

'Or what? You're not going to talk to me for another week? Guess what? I can handle it!'

'You're treading on dangerous ground.'

'Yeah, your precious emotions,' Maddie shouted. 'How dare you make love to me, kiss me on the cheek and then not call me for a week? The least you could've done was send me an e-mail or a message saying that you needed some space!'

Cale felt the red dragon of his temper snap the ropes keeping it under control. 'How dare you walk into my house with your filthy mood and think it's a safe place for you to vent?'

'Isn't it?' Maddie demanded.

'It's mine! My house, my kitchen, my life, Madison! For the first time in over thirty years I haven't had to share my life, my toys, my clothes, my house, the money I earned and, Goddammit, my time with anyone else. I'm not responsible for anyone but me and I love it!' he roared and, because it was there, he picked up an empty coffee cup and propelled it through the nearest window.

The shattering of the glass was echoed by something breaking in his heart, and it felt amazing. While a tiny voice of reason insisted that he'd regret this later, he picked up another cup and threw it against the remaining jagged glass.

'So if I don't want to call you for a week, I don't have to!'

Maddie lifted her eyebrows. 'Nice throw.'

'Don't you stand there and smirk at me!' he bellowed. 'You have no idea of the price I've paid for having this life, Madison! Oliver had to die for me to have all this!'

'What absolute rubbish,' Maddie replied calmly. 'You only had to set some boundaries with him.'

'What was I supposed to do when he lost yet another job and couldn't pay the rent? Not find him somewhere to live?'

'Maybe?'

'And when he couldn't pay maintenance for his boys? Was I supposed to let them struggle? Was I not supposed to help him when he found himself in a bar fight, six against one? Not bail him out of jail or feed him?'

'What choices did he make to land himself in those situations? Did he start the fight? Why was he in jail?'

'I can't talk to you when you're being all calm and reasonable!'

'You're not talking, you're shouting,' Maddie pointed out.

Cale considered shaking her. Why wasn't she scared of him? And where the hell had all her anger gone?

He had to get out…had to get away from her and her sympathetic eyes and her cool, sensible, rational attitude. How had an argument about her snotty temper turned into him ranting about Oliver?

Cale shoved his hands into his hair. 'I've got to get out of here. I need to run.'

Maddie bit her lip. 'Okay.'

In the doorway Cale stopped, lifting his hands to grip the wooden doorframe and dropping his head to stare at the floor.

'Will you be here when I get back?

He heard her move in his direction and hoped she wasn't going to try and hug him. His temper was still roiling beneath the surface and he wasn't ready to make nice yet.

But Maddie, being Maddie, just lightly placed her hands beneath his shoulderblades and touched her forehead to his spine.

'Do you want me to be?'

Of course he didn't want her there—but need was a different matter. He *needed* her tonight. 'Yes,' he ground out.

'Then I'll be here. Go run it off, Cale.'

CHAPTER NINE

ON THE following rainy Sunday afternoon, on one of his long leather couches in front of the fire, Cale was paying particular attention to Maddie's pink and green bra, marvelling at how something so sexy could be so incredibly soft. However, the skin below the fascinating fabric was even softer, still lightly tanned and scattered with freckles.

Her navy shirt was unbuttoned and so were her jeans, hinting at matching panties, and Cale took a long, lazy time studying every inch of her partially clothed, amazing body.

Maddie had her fingers in his hair, idly playing with the strands, half moaning as he dropped kisses on her fragrant flesh.

'Did you hear a car?' Maddie lifted her head. 'I thought I heard a car.'

'Nah. Shut up. I'm trying to concentrate here.'

Maddie lifted herself up on her elbows. 'Seriously, Cale. I heard the slam of a car door.'

Cale sighed and cocked his head. He could hear his dogs yelp in greeting and he frowned. When his heavy front door creaked open and he heard discordant female voices he leapt to his feet and looked at Maddie with wild eyes.

'Hell! Maddie, you'd better get dressed!'

Maddie sat up and swung her legs to the floor. 'What? Who?'

'Cale? Darling?'

'My mother.' Cale swore. He yanked Maddie up and started fiddling with her shirt.

'Maybe we should have called first.' Another voice, deeper and older, drifted into the room.

His grandmother. What had he done to deserve having the two bossiest women in the world interrupt his lazy Sunday afternoon?

'The day I have to ask for permission to visit any of my children, I'll know that I've failed as a mother!'

He finished the last button on Maddie's shirt and Maddie slapped his hands away. He glanced at her jeans, which still gaped open. 'Jeans! Quick!'

Maddie flashed him a grin as she lazily did up the buttons. 'Why are you panicking? Does your mother still think you're a virgin?'

Cale shoved his hands into his hair. 'I just don't want to answer her million questions. Or my gran's. She's even worse. No concept of boundaries or privacy, either of them.'

'That bad, huh?'

'Cale?'

Cale winced as his mother's demanding voice filled the hall. 'You have no idea.' He looked at Maddie again, decided she was suitably clothed, and walked over to the door to the hall and yanked it open. 'Mom, we're in here.'

'We? Who is we?'

Maddie tried to hide her nerves behind her smile. This was, after all, Cale's mother: a well-dressed, slim woman, with sharp eyes and an instinct to protect her young. Behind her, Cale's grandmother, shorter and very obviously naughtier than her daughter, smirked at Cale.

Cale did the introductions and an uncomfortable silence ensued, which was eventually broken by Cale. 'Want to tell me why you're here?'

Maddie grimaced at his sharp question and his mother sent him a hurt look. 'We were in the neighbourhood and I made a chicken casserole.' Valerie Grant lifted a perfectly manicured hand. 'It's on the hall table.'

'Thanks, Mom.' Cale sighed but his eyes remained wary. 'That was kind of you.'

Valerie held out a shopping bag to Cale. 'I thought you and—
Maddie—might want some of these scrapbooks. Megan mentioned that Maddie wants to do a write-up on Oliver, to promote
the race.'

Maddie took the bag. She pulled out a handful of photographs
and two scrapbooks. 'Thank you. These are great.'

Maddie sensed rather than saw Cale's jerky reaction as his
eyes flew to the photos. She looked down at the image on top of
the pile in her hand. It was of Oliver, sitting in a canoe, his grin
wide in his haggard face, his bald head covered with a cap. His
once strong body was skeletal and his skin was pasty.

Maddie's eyes connected with Cale's bleak gaze and she sent
him a reassuring smile.

Cale closed his eyes. 'I suppose you want some tea or something,' he muttered.

His mother stepped towards him and patted his arm. 'Such
a kind and gracious invitation.'

Embarrassment skittered across his face and Maddie saw
the brief tremor in his hand as he lifted it in apology. Maddie
wiggled her hand into his and sighed when he jerked his hand
away. Flashing her widest grin, she gestured towards the leather
couches.

'Why don't you take a seat and I'll put the kettle on? Tea or
coffee?'

'A cup of coffee would be lovely.' Valerie smiled. 'And maybe
afterwards you could tell us what progress you've made with
the race.'

Cale dropped a hand on Maddie's shoulder. 'You talk about
the race. I'll make the coffee,' he said.

Maddie saw his gaze move to the photos on the table and saw
the muscles in his neck visibly tighten. There was something
about those photographs…

Maddie, reaching for her jacket, watched the taillights of
Valerie's car disappear down the driveway through the open
front door. She pulled it on and looked in her bag for her car
keys. Cale leaned against the doorframe to the study, looking at

her through hooded eyes. He'd been in an uncertain mood since his relatives' arrival and she wondered whether it was worth pushing him to open up.

He needed to vent, she decided. Needed to get rid of that tension, that bubbling mass of emotion that churned below the surface. Instead of heading to the door, she sat on the bottom step of the stairs and looked up at him.

'Don't go home. Come to bed with me,' Cale said, his voice rough.

Maddie cocked her head in thought. She could, and he'd lose himself for a little while, but at three o'clock, when she was fast asleep in her own bed, the spooks would arrive. No, more than sex he needed an ear.

'Want to tell me why you went white when you saw that photograph of you and Oliver in the canoe?'

'Sea kayak,' Cale corrected her.

'Don't be pedantic. Why that reaction?'

She noticed his fist clenching in the pocket of his jeans. 'I don't want to talk about this, Mad.'

'Tough, we're going to. He looked pretty sick. Not long before he died?' Maddie pushed.

'About twelve hours,' Cale muttered and slid down the wall to sit with his back against it, his legs stretched in front of him. His golden Labrador, Marilyn, ambled in and slumped next to him, her head on his thigh. Cale rubbed her ears.

'Tell me what happened, Cale,' Maddie insisted.

Cale leaned his head against the wall. 'Mad, there are some things I just don't want to talk about—ever.'

Maddie wrapped her hands around one knee. 'But you need to talk about this. You need to talk to me. It's festering, Cale, get it out.'

Cale bounded to his feet, slammed the front door closed, stomped past the stairs and headed to the kitchen. Maddie waited him out and eventually he came back, a bottle of red wine and two glasses in his hand. He shoved a glass at Maddie and filled his own glass. When he'd drained half, he took the glass and the bottle and resumed his place on the floor.

'Towards the end he kept asking—begging, actually—to go for a paddle. For me to take him.' Cale eventually spoke and his voice was low and laced with pain. 'I kept saying no, that the doctors said it was a really bad idea, that he was too weak and it was too dangerous. He kept insisting, saying that it was his dying wish. That pissed me off. I wasn't prepared to accept the thought of him dying.'

Maddie placed her glass on the step next to her. 'Go on.'

'Then Megan started on me...'

'Megan was with him at the end?'

'They became really close when he was diagnosed and she started nagging me to take him. She wanted what he wanted. They ganged up on me. I knew it was a really bad idea; everything in me knew it. He was in a bad way. Going for an ocean paddle was the most illogical, unreasonable, *emotional* idea ever. But they nagged and begged and I gave in.'

Cale gulped more wine and rested the glass against his forehead.

'I waited for the next calm day. The sea was dead flat and we took him down, doctors protesting. He was loaded up with morphine. We started paddling and it was the most stunning day, pancake-flat and hot, but Ol was bitching because he said that he wanted some swell and the adrenalin of fighting the waves. I told him to shut up and kept paddling. I was mad at him for making me do it.'

'Carry on.'

'A wind came up. I swear that Oliver conjured it. I still don't know where it came from, but the swell picked up and it was crazy. Oliver was whooping like a madman in the back and I was struggling to keep us afloat. I turned us around and got us back to shore. When I hit the beach I saw that he'd collapsed, features slack and barely breathing. Thank God we had an ambulance waiting to get us back to the hospital. They stuck him on a ventilator and said that he'd slipped into a coma.'

'And he died later that night?' Maddie said, her eyes never leaving his tormented face.

'Early the next morning. Megan later told me that she thought he knew that he was at the end. He said his last goodbyes to her.'

'And that was his goodbye to you.' Maddie spoke softly, her chin in her hand. 'He wanted to share that one last paddle with you…'

Cale wouldn't look at her and Maddie bit her lip.

'What is it, Cale? Why does that day scrape at your soul? You knew he was going to die soon… I'm sorry, but you did.'

'He should've been in hospital, getting treatment, not in a kayak with me. If he had, we might have had more time with him!' Cale shouted. 'I knew that if I took him something bad would happen!'

'Something bad was always going to happen, Cale,' Maddie pointed out. 'It just happened after he'd had a really fun time rather than a miserable day in a white room with beeping machines.'

'I let emotion overrule common sense,' Cale muttered.

'Sure—and I bet your brother would have made you do it again. It was his choice, Cale. He knew the consequences and chose to go out on a high rather than on a bleep.' Maddie smiled tremulously. 'Typical Oliver.'

'You don't understand,' Cale muttered.

Maddie nodded her agreement. 'Probably not. How can I? But I do suspect that while you were trying to control the situation, trying to protect Oliver from himself, Oliver wanted a final experience that made him feel truly alive. He was his own person, Cale, and he made his choice.'

Maddie stood up, pulled her bag over her shoulder and crouched down next to Cale. She placed her hand on his cheek.

'It was a good choice, Cale. For him. Respect that choice. Respect yourself for allowing him to live his choice. Then let it go. Seriously.'

Maddie, seated on the leather couch in Cale's study, was reading on a society page that supermodel Gigi was back in town and that she'd had dinner with an old flame. The old flame, unfortunately in Maddie's opinion, happened to be the gorgeous Cale Grant.

Maddie looked at Cale, who was frowning at his computer monitor. His wire-rimmed reading glasses killed her—made her want to take a bite out of him. Amongst other things. She couldn't help feeling a little jealous at the thought of Cale and Gigi sharing an intimate supper at a new snazzy restaurant in Camps Bay, practically perched on the beach, even though he'd run Gigi's invitation by her and she'd encouraged him to accept it.

What else could she say? If she had said no then she'd have come off sounding controlling and insecure, and she needed him to know that she'd grown up, that she trusted him—and she did. It was the thought of what would happen when she left in a couple of months that bugged her. She would be living a million miles away and wouldn't have a clue who he was dating.

That thought caused her stomach to churn. Maddie closed the lid of her laptop, put it on the floor and stood up.

Cale looked up at her. 'And now?'

'I'm bored. Restless.'

Cale rested his head on the back of his chair and smiled at her. 'You've been thinking of New York.'

Look how well he knew her. She had been, but not necessarily in the way he thought. If she went to live there he would have unlimited time to date the woman he'd once proposed to. Or anyone else.

While she'd be buried neck-deep in work. For some strange reason that picture didn't appeal as much to her as it once had. Work wasn't quite the refuge it once had been. And whenever she thought of leaving Cale the knife permanently embedded in her heart turned.

'Have you heard anything?' Cale asked her.

'They are still compiling a shortlist of people they want to interview.'

'Will you have to fly out to meet them?'

Maddie stared out of the study window onto the circular drive. 'Yes. They pay half of your fare to get to the interview and refund you in full if you get the job.'

'You sure you still want to do this, Mad?'

Maddie whipped her head around. 'Of course! Why?'

Cale put his feet up onto his desk, his face grave as he looked at her. 'You're not sounding as enthusiastic as you did.'

'I'm fine.' Maddie folded her arms. 'Am I doing the right thing, Cale? By considering this?'

Cale whipped his glasses off and tossed them onto the desk. 'Knowing you, Mad, I think you'd always regret it if you didn't. You'd wonder if you were good enough, whether you could have made the grade. I could tell you that you are and you would, but you wouldn't believe me or anybody else. You have to go through the process.'

Maddie examined her nails. He had a way of seeing past her bluster to the Maddie underneath.

Cale narrowed his eyes at her huge yawn. 'Have you been sleeping?'

'Not much.' Maddie flicked a glance at her watch and sighed. She moved away from the window, picked up her computer and slid it into its case. 'I've got to get going. Horrid Harriet wants a staff meeting at half-four.'

Cale stood up and walked around the desk as she slung her tote bag over her shoulder. He looked down and pointed to her feet.

'I told myself I wouldn't ask but...' He gestured to the four bright pink ears and two grey noses that peeked out from beneath her tailored grey pants. 'Why are you wearing slippers?'

Maddie waggled her right foot so that two ears swung under the hem of her trousers. 'Cute, aren't they?'

'No. There is something quite weird about a grown woman wearing pink animals on her feet. Why?'

'Some jerk ran into the back of my heel in the supermarket with a trolley and gouged some flesh out of it. It's hell wearing heels, so I grabbed these to wear while I was here.' Maddie looked at him, frowning at his surprised face. 'What?'

'I'm still trying to get my head around the image of you in a supermarket, pushing a trolley. Do you mean you actually have food in your house? Your fridge didn't give up the ghost in shock?'

'You do know that sarcasm is the lowest form of wit, don't you?' Maddie retorted, heading for the hall.

Cale inclined his head. 'Yeah, but it's fun. Talking about fun—what time did you say you have to be back at work?'

Maddie looked at his teasing face, his hot eyes, and hurriedly walked out of his house. She'd be fired if she was late for another staff meeting. And once she and Cale got naked time seemed to disappear.

'I'm leaving. Now,' she hurriedly informed him.

'Spoilsport.'

Maddie dumped her stuff on the passenger seat and slammed the door shut. Walking around to the driver's seat, she slid behind the wheel and jammed her key into the ignition.

She threw the car into reverse and swung the car around, narrowly missing Cale's Range Rover. She sent him a jaunty smile as he shouted a warning from the veranda. She knew her car and knew how to drive it, but she enjoyed his panicked reaction.

She was a fabulous driver. Her grandfather Red had had her racing go-karts from the age of eight, and driving a stick-shift at the age of ten. But it was fun irritating Cale…and she'd bet her car that Gigi was useless. At driving and hopefully lots of other things—except looking gorgeous…

It happened in slow motion. Her mobile rang as Maddie turned the car into the road, and at the same time an ugly, monstrous grasshopper landed on her chest and dropped down her shirt. Maddie screeched as the grasshopper, caught in the hollow between her chest and her bra, wriggled frantically against her skin. Maddie slapped her hand against her chest and felt the warm splat spread…

'*Arrrgh!*' Maddie screamed, and dropped her mobile, yanking at her top with both her hands. One spiky green leg played a death song against her fuchsia bra and Maddie slammed her foot on the accelerator instead of the brake. The car, with about a million horsepower under the bonnet, hurtled forward, choosing the path of least resistance. That path ended at one of the stately old oak trees that lined Primrose Drive.

Glancing up from the grasshopper carnage on her chest,

Maddie watched as the tree came hurtling towards her. Closing her eyes, she whipped the steering wheel to her left, and the right hand corner of her beautiful, beautiful car hit the wide oak with a resounding and deafening *clunk*!

Maddie felt her head bounce off the steering wheel and snap back. Lifting a shaking hand to her forehead, she watched steam billow between her car and the tree, hissing and whooshing in the quiet afternoon air. Hearing the whining engine, she turned off the ignition and closed her eyes…

'Maddie!'

Megan's voice penetrated the fog swirling through her brain. It was warm and fuzzy, and she really didn't want to shrug it off. But insistent hands were stroking her hair back, prodding her arms and shoulders.

'Maddie! Are you hurt?'

Maybe she should open her eyes, but she suspected opening her eyes would hurt—and it did. A lot.

'Are you all right?'

'My car is toast.' And maybe she wasn't such a fabulous driver.

'As long as you are fine, the car can be fixed,' Megan said, wrenching the door open. 'Can you get out? Have you broken anything?'

'No, just bumped my head. Why are you here?'

'I was in the garden and I heard the crash.'

Maddie tried to shake her head. Tenderly she reached up and touched the lump on her forehead. She could feel it swelling under her fingers, and she felt as if she'd experienced brain surgery without anaesthetic. Gritting her head against the throbbing pain, she swung her feet out of the car and turned to follow Megan's gaze. Cale was sprinting to the car, his eyes wild.

'What the hell happened?' he yelled, coming to an abrupt stop at the car.

Man, the man could move!

Through the scarlet haze of pain Maddie noticed his mouth tighten as he saw the bump on her head, the way his eyes briefly and competently scanned her body.

'Are you okay?' Cale demanded, hands on his hips.

Stupid question. Maddie stood up, matched his stance, and slapped her hands on her waist. She glowered at him and lifted her hand to jab a finger in his chest. 'No, my vintage Jag, beautifully restored, is having a close relationship with a tree.' Tears welled. 'No, I have grasshopper guts on my chest.' Another poke to his chest and the tears slid down her face. Maddie slapped her hand to her head and yelped. 'And I don't have violet eyes or wear itty-bitty dresses!'

'What are you going on about?'

'Your last girlfriend was a supermodel and you took her to dinner!'

'Oh, good God. You said you were okay with it!'

'I am, but she's so pretty…'

'She was a neurotic, demanding drama queen who drove me insane,' Cale muttered as his face darkened. 'That much you *do* have in common!'

'Should you be discussing this? Now?' Megan asked.

Maddie teetered as dizziness rolled over her. She swayed and did not protest when Cale manhandled her to the grass and shoved her head between her knees.

Maddie tried to lift her head but Cale's strong hand on the back of her neck kept it in position. His fingers radiated warmth into her skull as tears dripped onto the grass beneath her.

She sniffed loudly. 'Let me up!'

'Another minute,' Cale soothed.

He crouched in front of her and Maddie scrubbed her eyes with the heels of her hands. She looked down at her chest and saw the mangled remains of a very dead grasshopper. Oh, *yuck.* Its eyes looked up at her, reproachful in death. Part of its body had squished, like toothpaste, over her favourite purple shirt. It was missing a leg. Maddie felt nausea rise and struggled harder against Cale's hand.

'Let me go or I'm going to vomit over your feet.' Maddie enunciated her words clearly, and eventually felt Cale's hand lift.

Standing up slowly, because she really didn't want to fall over, adding insult to injury, she carefully backed away from Cale.

Keeping her eyes focused on her car, she shrugged out of her suit jacket, then slowly lifted her shirt and slid it over her head.

'I think she cracked her head harder than we realized,' Megan said.

Standing in her bra, her grey tailored pants and her bunny slippers, Maddie stepped closer to Cale and gestured towards her chest.

'Get it off me!'

Megan wrinkled her nose in distaste. *'Eeeew!'*

Cale's mouth kicked up in amusement. 'What? Just because I'm male, I have to deal with the insects?'

'If this is not off me in ten seconds I am going to kick you,' Maddie threatened, ignoring the icy wind on her bare skin. True, he was bigger and stronger, but she had enough adrenalin kicking around her system to take on a buffalo.

Cale reached for the lower half of the grasshopper's body and gently lifted it away. He tossed the carcass over his shoulder before reaching for a wing that was partly lodged under her bra. Amber eyes met navy as his short nail scraped under the wing to lift it away. Maddie could not believe she found the act of cleaning insect guts off her skin erotic; she obviously had severe concussion.

'There's a leg under here.' Cale placed the tip of his index finger high on her right breast.

'Get it out.' Maddie shuddered and stood perfectly still as his index finger slid under the triangle to lift the material away and the fingers of his other hand dipped in to retrieve the leg. So near and yet so very far, indeed.

Cale flicked the leg away and rubbed his fingers on his jeans. 'All done. Bit of sludge on your chest. You can put your shirt on now.'

Maddie shook her head. Whipping the shirt inside out, she showed him the other half of the grasshopper smeared on the silk. 'I don't think so.'

Cale sighed and removed his bulky white Aran sweater, his long sleeved T-shirt rising to give Maddie a quick glance of his flat, hard, Matthew McConaughey six-pack.

Maddie pulled his jersey over her head and instantly felt warmer before walking over to the Jaguar and assessing the damage. The right corner was crumpled and the radiator was history. Of course any damage was not good, but this looked repairable. Sam, an old friend and expert car restorer, would be able to fix it—but not, she was positive, without a huge lecture and a lot of cash.

Maddie walked back to Cale and Megan.

'You drive like a lunatic, Madison. You nearly swiped my car,' Cale said, picking up her suit jacket and returning to her car.

'Let's get back to the house and we can sort it all out,' Megan intervened before Maddie could reply. 'I think we all need a cup of tea.'

'I think Maddie needs to retake her drivers' test,' Cale stated, lifting her briefcase and laptop bag off the car floor.

'Cale,' Megan warned, tucking her hand into Maddie's arm. 'Stop baiting her. You're not helping.'

'Oh, he is,' Maddie assured her. 'If I concentrate really, really hard on how much I want to slap him, I might not bawl like a two-year-old.'

Maddie lay in his arms on the big couch in his lounge, deeply asleep. A fire hissed and burped in the old fireplace and a glass of wine stood on the floor within easy reach. Except for the fact that Maddie had a purple bruise the size of a tennis ball on her forehead, and that she was soundly asleep, the setting would have been deeply romantic. Cale glanced at her head and winced.

He really admired her, on so many levels. Sure, he had a problem with how much she worked, but she was so good at it. Her suggestions were creative and her work ethic was impeccable. She was doing a stunning job and he should tell her so, but every time he opened his mouth to compliment her he felt as gauche as a thirteen-year-old boy, slightly in awe of the woman she'd become.

She was successful, ambitious, funny, smart and gorgeous. And some time in the near future she was leaving. He did not enjoy the thought of not having her in his life...and the notion of being single made him feel physically ill. Not that he wasn't single now—technically he was—but the idea of going back to dating various vacuous screwed-up women made him feel ill.

He would measure them against Maddie and they'd fail. He just knew it. Because none of them would be as bright, as smart, as vivacious...

Or as dazzling. He would never, ever forget how sexy she'd looked today, standing in her pink bra, her whisky-coloured eyes criss-crossed with concussion and anger.

The door opened and Alex stepped in and quietly closed the door behind him. After examining Maddie at his rooms he'd promised to check up on her after he'd finished his rounds at the hospital, and here he was.

Alex crouched on his haunches next to Cale. 'She okay?'

Cale nodded. 'She fell asleep about fifteen minutes ago.'

'She'll have a headache for a day or two.'

'You sure she doesn't need to go to the hospital?' Cale asked, his throat tightening at the thought. He was phobic about hospitals. People went there to die.

Alex shook his head. 'What she needs is sleep. This girl is running on fresh air and emotion. She told me she's been averaging around three or four hours a night for the past three months. Nobody can function on that little sleep for that long. It's been a couple of hours since the accident, so I think it's fine for her to sleep. Don't be surprised if she passes out for the balance of the day and night.'

'You sure?'

Alex laid a hand on his shoulder. 'She'll be fine, Cale. Check on her a couple of times during the night and call me if you can't wake her up.'

Alex poured some wine into Cale's empty glass and sat on the coffee table next to him. 'You two seem to be getting pretty involved.'

Cale managed a small shrug. 'Neither of us wants a serious relationship. We're just friends.'

'Sharing some hot sex?' Alex added.

Cale frowned at Alex's choice of words. That didn't sound right. 'Something like that.'

Alex saluted him with the almost empty wineglass. 'So, when you're done being friends can *I* have a crack at her?'

'Sure.' Cale smiled thinly at him. 'If you want your head ripped off and stuffed up your—'

Alex's snort of laughter interrupted Cale's threat.

'Go away, Alex.'

Alex downed the rest of the wine and stood up. 'Just let her sleep, Cale. Trust me—I'm a *real* doctor.'

Alex just laughed when Cale threw a pillow at him.

CHAPTER TEN

THE next morning Maddie, short of a car and with a nasty bruise on her forehead, had the perfect excuse to take it easy. She'd woken up in Cale's bed with a headache and feeling disorientated. She dimly recalled Cale carrying her up the stairs and helping her into one of his T-shirts at one point, and shoving pills down her throat at another. On a chair across from the massive double bed there was a pile of women's clothing. Megan's clothes, she assumed.

After a long shower she felt like a new person. Maddie headed into Cale's study, expecting him to be at his desk. But the room was empty...messy, but empty. Maddie stepped through the doorway at the end of the study into a square room with huge windows that looked onto a scruffy garden. Three leather couches dominated the room, and half of the jewel-toned cushions were on the floor. Cale's leather jacket lay across the back of one couch, and a newspaper was anchored by a blue and white plate that held biscuit crumbs and a few wrinkled grapes.

Crossing over to the window, she looked onto the rambling, semi-wild garden. In the reflection of the window she saw the wistful expression on her face and shrugged. She had always loved this house, from the moment she had stepped into it so many, many years ago. It was exactly what she had always felt a family home should be. Large, with wooden floors and big windows. Enough room for a couple of dogs and kids and a rabbit or two. Huge fireplaces and windowseats for cats or lovers to curl up on...

Maybe she had bumped her head harder than she'd thought. She had to get out before she started imagining herself sharing this house with its owner. Maddie sighed, remembering that, despite the fact that he wasn't the player he'd used to be, Cale wasn't 'settling down' material. Neither, she told herself, was she. She had a demanding career and there wasn't a place in her life for a full-time man—even if he didn't have commitment phobias of his own.

She had a life to live, goals to reach. Talking of which… She hauled out her mobile and looked up Dennis's number.

'Where are you?' she demanded, hearing the racket in the background.

'Club in the Bronx. We just finished work.'

Maddie glanced at her watch. 'At just after midnight?'

'I told you that we work crazy hours,' Dennis shouted. 'Listen, I was going to call you! You definitely made the shortlist.'

Maddie's heart plummeted in disappointment. Wait, that was wrong! She should be ecstatic. She *was* ecstatic. She would be happy if it killed her! 'That's great! What's the next step?'

'Interviews. But not for a couple of weeks. They are determined to find the right person so they aren't rushing the process,' Dennis told her. 'So—see you in New York soon, sweet cakes.'

'Soon,' Maddie echoed, and disconnected. She stared down at her mobile, her bottom lip between her teeth. Disconnected. That was a good description of how she felt at the moment. Slightly disconnected from her job and her dreams, emotionally disconnected from Cale, totally disconnected from her parents.

Maddie brushed a tear away and struggled not to let any more fall. She furiously wiped them away and straightened her shoulders. She was just headachy, tired and emotional.

It would pass, she reminded herself. Everything always did.

Cale found Maddie on the veranda and, as always, the view of the ocean sucked his breath away. Especially on mornings like this, when the air was so clear he could see for miles up the coast. Maddie lay in the free-standing hammock, the bump on her head black and blue, her eyes shut and a cup of coffee in her hand. Megan sat cross-legged on the couch, a newspaper folded on her knee and a pencil clutched in her hand.

'Seven letters—direction. Help me, Maddie, stop being so useless,' Megan demanded, peering at the crossword.

'Tangent.' Cale withdrew his hands from his pockets and lifted them in greeting.

Maddie sat up, looked at him and flopped back down again, shutting her eyes.

'Well done, Cale.' Megan pencilled in the letters. 'Want some coffee?'

'I'd love some.' Cale nodded, helping himself to a banana from the bowl of fruit on the table.

Megan went inside and he indulged in eying Maddie's reclining form. She wore tight battered jeans and a rust jersey that brought out the gold of her eyes. Her hair was pulled back from her face in a messy knot and she looked grumpy and sultry. He thought he should just pick her up and take her to bed.

Cale swallowed abruptly.

'Thanks for letting me stay here last night,' Maddie said, and he heard the self-pity in her soft voice. She had a frightened rabbit-caught-in-the-headlights-of-a-car look whenever she caught his eye.

He turned when Maddie swung off the hammock and clutched her head as her feet found the floor. Instinctively Cale grabbed her arm and helped her stand, ignoring her efforts to shrug him off.

'Stop it!' She flapped her hands at him until he backed off, then clutched her head.

'You are such a whiner, Shaw. I've had worse bumps racing.'

Immediately her spine straightened and her eyes glinted with determination. His girl had spirit, thank God.

'That just tells me you are fit. And stupid.'

She also had a smart mouth.

'At least I'm not a melodramatic drama queen.'

'Stop picking on me! I have a headache and my car is crumpled,' Maddie said in a small voice.

Cale swallowed his grin. 'Your headache will get better, the bump will go down and your car is repairable. In the meantime you can borrow mine if you need transport.'

'You're so unsympathetic! And you drive an ugly tank.'

'Sympathy isn't going to make it better.' The eyes that looked back at him were the warm colour of aged whisky and ringed by dark lashes. What made him push away a strand of hair falling over her bump and tuck it behind her ears? Why did he want to protect her, look after her, cosset her?

He was no closer to an answer than before. Cale took her hand and led her to a chair at the wooden dining table.

'Breakfast. Eat something,' Cale said roughly, gesturing to the cereal and yoghurt on the table.

Megan deposited a pot of coffee on the table. 'The monsters have had breakfast and they are itching to get to the beach, so I'm going to skip breakfast with you. Take care of yourself, Maddie, you gave us quite a fright.'

'Thanks for the loan of the clothes,' Maddie said, and rested her arms on the table and stared out at the amazing view.

She approved of eating on the veranda—eminently sensible since it caught the best of the warm morning winter sun. In front of her there was just sky and sea. The sky was a hue that could only be found on a perfect African day: a blue so vivid, so sharp, she felt she could lift her hand and push through its thickness. The sea was mirror-flat and a cerulean blue. Perfect, sunny winter days like these normally preceded a wet, wild, windy cold front, and she wondered if one was on the way.

She turned back to the table and sighed. Her wish for a greasy breakfast of bacon, eggs and fried bread remained just that, and she listlessly stirred yoghurt into her muesli and wrinkled her nose.

'Eat it—it's good for you,' Cale said, without lifting his eyes from his newspaper.

Maddie looked at him and swallowed. Showered, dressed in jeans and a fleecy navy hoodie, with two-day-old stubble and his slightly hooked nose, Cale looked simply delicious.

'But it tastes like cardboard!'

Cale took a spoonful of her muesli and sampled it. 'It's fine,

Madison. Your tastebuds are shot because your idea of a balanced diet is a chocolate bar in one hand and a bottle of red in the other.'

Unfortunately he wasn't even wrong.

Pride had her finishing her muesli, and Cale topped up their coffee cups. She dashed some sugar into her coffee, deliberately adding more just to see Cale's pained expression.

Maddie placed her chin in her hand. 'Can we talk work just for a minute?'

'It's Saturday morning—' Cale's head whipped up. 'It's *Saturday*!'

'Ye-es? So?'

'Don't you have weddings and functions and stuff?'

Maddie bent her knees and placed her heels on the seat of the chair. 'One wedding and it's a small one. I asked Thandi to handle it.'

Cale reached over to take her temperature. 'You must have hit your head harder than I thought.'

'Ha-ha. About the race... I've updated the website. It's far brighter, splashier and a lot more interesting. I've put on accommodation establishments, restaurants and places of interest, and linked the site to relevant websites.'

Maddie caught the approving glint in his eyes, decided that a flirty reaction would be dangerous, and persevered with the subject at hand.

'I've also put a facility on the site so people can donate to the fund directly via the website.'

Cale finally looked impressed, and Maddie refused to acknowledge the little glow burning somewhere in the region of her belly button.

'Entrants to the celebrity teams are flooding in—especially since I managed to convince the producers of *Tops and Trainers*—' Maddie saw Cale's confusion '—it's that new TV lifestyle programme that's grabbing attention. Everybody—except for you and me, obviously—is watching it. Anyway, they are doing a segment every week on a different celeb team, watching them train.'

'How on earth did you manage to persuade them to do that?'

'I did the executive producer's wedding. She loved it. I could ask for the moon and she'd get it for me.' Maddie grinned. 'But my big news is that I've secured a sponsor for the pre-race charity dinner, and sourced a whole lot of items to auction to raise funds for the race and the charity.'

'What?'

'Well, since I lost you one sponsor—'

'*I* lost that sponsor,' Cale corrected her.

'Whatever.' Maddie raised her hand. 'We lost Lousy Liam's money, so I thought I'd make it up to you. Tickets are already flying out the door. The main prizes up for auction are a skiing trip to Austria, five days in the Maldives and a date with Gigi. We've already covered our costs and made some money. At least as much as that rat weasel was offering in the first place.'

Cale nearly choked on his coffee. '*My* Gigi? How the hell did you manage that?'

Maddie narrowed her eyes. 'Your *ex* Gigi. I know her agent. I twisted his arm.'

Cale laughed. 'Why didn't you tell me about this?'

Maddie looked at the sea. 'I didn't know if I could pull it off, so I just worked quietly on it when you weren't looking.'

Cale rubbed the spot between his eyebrows. 'So all those extra, extra hours you spent at work were on this?'

'Some of them.' Maddie drew patterns in the tablecloth with her finger. 'It's on the eighteenth of July—a month before the actual race. Please, please, Cale, you have to be there. You'll have to be the MC—be the official face of the project. You will be there, won't you?'

Cale nodded. 'I don't think I have any commitments for that date—'

'You don't. I checked with your PA before I committed to the date,' Maddie admitted. 'You won't let me down and fall off a cliff or plough into a rock or something?'

Cale laughed. 'I'll be there, Mad. Relax. After all the work you've put in, you can kill me if I'm not.' He reached over and grabbed her hand. 'Have I said thank you? At all? For all your work and effort and time?'

'Wait until you get my bill!' Maddie said flippantly, uncomfortable with his praise. 'Just be there, *please*. I can't manage the event and be the face of it. Besides, I absolutely loathe speaking in public!'

'No worries.' Cale frowned as she touched the bump on her forehead. 'How are you feeling?'

'A tiny headache.' Maddie tapped her teaspoon against her coffee cup. 'I'm going to call a taxi and head home to do some work.'

'You can work tomorrow.' Cale stood up, placed his arms on either side of the chair and boxed her in. 'You are taking a day off. Come and spend the day with me.'

Cale indulged himself and ran a finger along her collarbone.

Maddie sighed. 'I'd love to, but—'

'Excellent.'

'I don't have any clothes, Cale.'

'We'll swing by your place so that you can change.'

'Where are we going? What do I need?' Maddie demanded.

'Stop fussing.'

Maddie stared up into his amazing eyes and thought she saw worry and warmth—for her. Like the whisper of a butterfly's kiss, his lips grazed the huge bump on her forehead.

'Scared me, Mad.'

Cale, his eyes locked on hers, dropped his head and slanted his lips over hers. They were cool, firm and...gone. Maddie, eyes closed, touched her lips with her middle finger. It could hardly be classified as a kiss, yet she felt scorched, branded—as if he'd imprinted a set of sexual tyre-tracks on her psyche.

'Let's go.'

CHAPTER ELEVEN

SHE'D needed this, Maddie reluctantly admitted. Needed to step away from her crazy schedule in the city and into the fresh air. It was a relief to switch off, to let her thoughts float by as she ambled alongside Cale up the deserted West Coast beach in a vague attempt to work off the massive lunch they'd demolished. Fresh seafood, crayfish and prawns caught that morning, cooked to perfection in that shabby beach kitchen.

The seafood was the best—*sorry, Jim*—she'd ever eaten. Anywhere.

'God, I'm stuffed,' Maddie groaned. Taking deep breaths of the chilly briny wind, she wrapped her jacket around her torso and headed for the hard sand at the water's edge.

She shrieked as the waves flicked up her calves to touch the seam of the rolled-up hem of her jeans. She hopped up and down. 'Cold, cold, *cold*!'

Cale laughed at her. 'It's the Atlantic, brainbox, in winter. It's going to be cold!'

'It's not cold. It's freezing. I can't feel my feet!'

'Maybe if you actually took them out of the water it would help.' Cale shook his head. 'Twit.'

Maddie pulled her tongue at him and eased her way slowly up the beach towards the black-and-white chequered lighthouse about a hundred metres up the beach.

Maddie glanced at Cale, who was inspecting a piece of driftwood. His stubble glinted in the sun and his lashes lay long and thick against his skin. He tipped the log over and his muscles bunched under the sleeves of his sand-coloured sweater.

She opened her mouth to speak and abruptly closed it again, not sure what she was about to say. She'd kicked and moaned about this road trip, but she'd adored the two-hour drive to the shack restaurant outside a small fishing village on his Ducati superbike. She'd snuggled up against him, listening to the duet of the bike and the wind. Her body had relaxed and then she'd been moving in sync with him, dropping into corners, instinctively following his lead and completely trusting his mastery of the incredible machine.

He handled the motorbike like he handled her in bed: with confidence, control and supreme enjoyment.

And she'd loved every second of it. Bike and bed.

And he'd charmed her at lunch, making her laugh until she cried and making her remember why she adored his company.

Maddie looked away from Cale to the circular cast-iron light-house—a reminder of how treacherous the stormy Atlantic Ocean could be. 'When I was little Red and I used to visit light-houses. I was mad about them,' she told him idly.

'I remember you telling me that. That's why I brought you up here. I thought that maybe you should have a better memory of him than the one you currently have,' Cale added with a one-shoulder shrug.

Maddie bit her lip. Just as he'd known that she'd needed sleep and company the other night, and not sex, he knew her well enough today to bring her here to think about and to remember Red. She understood that Cale was suggesting that instead of remembering him lifeless, broken and cold on the floor of his hall, she should be remembering her small hand in his spotted one, the smell of Old Spice and those bright days when they'd visited lighthouses and talked.

Her no-strings affair partner was morphing into the most important person in her life. How would she manage this? *Think about it later,* Maddie told herself as she looked up at the black-and-white panels of the iron structure in front of her.

Cale pushed the door. It creaked open and darkness loomed beyond, a bit spooky inside.

'Is the lighthouse still in operation?' Maddie asked as their eyes adjusted to the gloomy interior. A small, grimy window deeply set into the wall provided minimal light.

'I think the lens and fog horn are powered by solar panels and batteries. But I'm not sure,' Cale told her as they moved around a rickety cart holding some empty cans towards the steep spiral staircase.

Maddie touched the handrail of the elaborate iron staircase and sighed as she started the climb. 'The staircase is so beautifully crafted. Such an elaborate design.'

'The lighthouse was erected in 1906.' Cale's voice hummed over her. 'Just take it slow and watch where you place your feet. It's dark in here.'

They climbed in silence for a long time, and Maddie's thighs were burning when they eventually stepped into the light-keeper's room below the lantern area. It lived up to her imagination: dusty, creaky, spooky. A defunct generator stood in the middle of the room and a solid table in the far corner. Maddie looked out of the salt-encrusted window and the view took her breath away. Miles and miles of deserted beach…a hazy cargo ship on the horizon below a bank of low grey clouds.

Cale moved next to her and thumped his fist against the thick casement window. Eventually the window budged and opened up onto a narrow balcony that encircled the tower. Only a rail separated them from a nasty plunge to the rocks below.

Cale boosted himself up onto the balcony and held out his hand for Maddie. 'You've got to come out here, Mad. It's brilliant!'

Maddie took his hand and allowed him to pull her onto the narrow ledge. Instantly vertigo slapped her, and she closed her eyes as Cale's strong arms banded around her waist.

'You're safe. I won't let you fall!' Cale yelled above the whistling wind.

'These railings look a bit rusty!' Maddie shouted as she leaned into his chest.

Cale chuckled in her ear. 'They've lasted over a hundred years. I think they'll hold us for ten minutes.'

Maddie opened one eye and looked out to sea. Black-backed gulls swooped over an area about fifty metres offshore and Maddie could see some disturbance in the water. A shoal? Holding her hair off her face, she turned. In the far distance she could see some people leaving the restaurant to walk on the beach.

'Southern right whale over there,' Cale told her, lifting one arm to point her in the right direction. Maddie stared at the sea and was eventually rewarded with the slap of a massive tail against the water.

They watched the whale for five minutes and Maddie shivered, feeling battered by the icy breeze off the sea despite Cale's warm body against her back. Inching her way inside, she felt her heart resume beating when her feet found the floor of the keeper's room. Moving out of Cale's way, so he could hop down, she shoved her hands into her wild curls and pushed them off her face. She felt exhilarated, petrified and proud as adrenalin pounded through her system.

'That was such a rush!' Maddie hopped from one foot to the other and Cale laughed at her exuberance. 'Mind-blowingly scary but I wouldn't have missed it for the world.'

Cale pushed back an errant curl and tucked it behind her ear. 'Red would've been proud of you, sport.'

Maddie cocked her head. 'You know what? I think you might be right.'

'I'm always right,' Cale told her huskily as his hands moved up to cradle her face. The pads of his thumbs caressed her cheekbones and he stared at her mouth. Maddie licked her lips as her hands slid under his jersey to grip his T-shirt.

Maddie flattened her hands against his hips and felt the heat of his skin through the fabric. Tipping her head, she darted her tongue out of her mouth in a silent invitation. Cale's eyes heated, darkened with passion, and then he dipped his head to feast on her mouth. Lips nibbled and soothed, and his tongue tempted and promised. Unable to do anything but cling to him, she nipped his mouth, her tongue making tiny forays into his mouth. She felt Cale's hand slide under her top to unhook her bra.

'Make love with me, Mad,' he muttered hoarsely.

Maddie looked around her. 'Here? Now?'

'Here, in this chilly, dusty room at the top of a lighthouse. Now, because this moment is ours to take. Let me love you, sweetheart.'

Well, when he put it like that...

Maddie put her hand into the back pocket of Cale's jeans as they made their way back across the sand, enjoying Cale's arm around her shoulder. It was strange that, through Cale of all people, she was rediscovering something in her that she'd thought lost a long time ago. A softer part of her nature that wanted to be loved. It scared the stuffing out of her.

For years she'd ignored attraction and emotional intimacy to focus on her career. Oh, she'd socialised and dated and led men on, but it shamed her to admit that she'd enjoyed being able to flash a smile and have men rush to her bidding to earn the possibility of dinner or—dream on—a roll in the sack. Even more, she'd enjoyed being able to walk away without a backwards glance.

It was slightly ironic that the man who had caused this turn-around in her attitude towards relationships—the thought that she might like to love and be loved—was emotionally confused himself, stuck in his own vortex of guilt and regret and fear.

The whole concept was weird and distracting. Instead of being excited about this amazing work opportunity that had dropped into her lap she was wondering how she'd cope with him not being part of her life, not being able to make love to him, laugh with him. Who would pick her up and dust her off after a bad day? Monitor her eating habits? Bully her into having fun?

Suddenly what had been so clear a few months ago was as muddy as a pond. Her career, when weighed up against not having Cale in her life, didn't seem that important any more. An event was an event. It might be bigger and glitzier in NYC but the mechanics were the same.

Maddie kicked the sand, comprehensively annoyed with herself. She was muddling love and emotion with common sense, and allowing the idea of love and happily-ever-after—she wasn't stupid enough to think that she had a shot at the real thing—to become a factor in making one of the biggest decisions of her life.

She was a sensible, smart woman, not an emotional weakling.

They reached the rickety deck leading to the restaurant, where they'd left their socks and boots, and sat on a weathered step. Cale sat next to her and unrolled his socks before dusting the sand off his long feet.

'So, what's going on in that head of yours?'

Maddie bit her lip as reality came crashing in. She flipped him a look. 'I'm not sure what you mean.'

Cale's eyes cooled at her evasion. 'Don't lie to me, Maddie. As soon as reality seeped back in you started thinking.'

'Okay. I wasn't lying to you; I was just trying to gather my thoughts.' Maddie blew out her breath as she pulled her sock on. 'I spoke to Dennis this morning.'

'Who?'

'My friend who works at Bower & Co. He said that he's heard I made the shortlist.'

'Ah.' Cale yanked on his boot with a fierce scowl.

Maddie stared at her slightly blue toes. 'It's such a massive opportunity, Cale, the biggest I'm ever likely to be offered. But I'm having such fun with you.'

Cale finished pulling on his shoes, draped his forearms over his bended knees and looked out at the ocean. 'Are you expecting me to ask you to stay?'

Maddie shook her head, thinking that he didn't need to draw her a picture. She'd heard his silent *because I won't.* 'No.'

'So, when do you think it might be finalised?'

'A couple of weeks. I might have to go to New York soon for the interview, but don't worry about the race, I'll get that done before I leave for good.' Maddie dropped her temple to his shoulder. 'I have this feeling...'

'What?'

'I've been wondering what to do if they offer it to me.' Maddie wound her arms around his neck. 'And I think I'll have to say yes.'

Maddie felt his warm hand come up to cradle her head. 'Well, we both knew that this wasn't going to last for ever, and maybe it's better this way—to walk away friends,' Cale said, his voice rough.

Maddie lifted her head, completely shocked. 'You're calling it quits? Now?'

Cale's laugh was low and rough. 'No, you twit! But I do suggest that we make the best use of the time we have left. Nights, mornings—as much as possible. If I only have limited time with you then I want every minute to count. Without it becoming a melodramatic farce.'

Maddie had to giggle. Only Cale could demand more from her without even a hint of soppy.

He turned so that her head was in his neck and his blond head rested against hers. His breath was warm against her temple when he spoke. 'In case I forget to tell you, I've had the best fun with you, too.'

Maddie watched Cale roar away on his Ducati to attend a cousin's twenty-first birthday party. With her mobile tucked into her pocket, she scampered down the path in front of her flat to the deserted beach. Plopping down on the sand, she leant back against a rock, reflecting on the turns her life had taken.

She only had, at most, four or five weeks left with Cale, and the thought of not having him in her life scared her witless. Oh, the idea of living in New York was wonderfully exciting, but would it mean anything if there was no one at the end of the day to share her success with?

She needed some support, some expert advice.

Kate answered on the first ring.

'I'm on the shortlist for the job in New York, but there's Cale, and I'm deeply attracted to him and I'm scared stupid, and I don't know if I'm doing the right thing in carrying on seeing him,' Maddie gabbled. 'Or in going to the States.'

'Maddie. Say that slowly.'

Maddie repeated herself and remained silent as Kate digested her words. It wasn't often she managed to shut Kate up, Maddie mused.

'I'm not sure what to say except, well—*wow*! Any idea what he's thinking?'

Maddie shoved a hand in her hair and puffed. 'Just that he won't ask me to stay. We both knew that this wouldn't last, Katie. It was only ever supposed to be a fun, roll-in-the-sack-until-we're-sick-of-each-other deal.'

Maddie could hear the stream of wine hitting the bottom of a glass and desperately wished she were in Kate's flat. 'And it's changed for you?'

'Yeah. My head is no longer in charge of my heart.'

'You sure he won't ask you to stay?'

'Yes.'

'And you will accept the job offer?'

'Yes. I think I have to.'

'Maddie, you've managed not to get involved with anyone for years. What is it about Cale?'

Maddie dug her bare feet into the sand and wiggled them. 'He gets to me, Katie. He's a thinker, a philosopher, a protector.'

'Good grief,' Kate muttered

Maddie stared at the sun dipping behind the horizon. 'What do I do?'

'Are you in love with him?'

'No.' Maddie checked inside herself and shook her head. No, she didn't think so. Not yet. But on the other hand how would she know? Grief, she doubted she'd be able to recognise love even if it came wrapped up in a pretty box and hand-labelled.

'But you're attracted to him?'

'Oh, yes.'

'Do you like him?'

Maddie swore. 'Yes. Yes, I like him. A lot.'

'Mad, I don't know what to tell you. All I can say is take a deep breath and live in the moment. That's all you have right now. Stop anticipating what will happen. Enjoy it. Have some fun,' Kate suggested. 'It'll work out, whatever way is meant for you. Oh, and use protection.'

'Thanks. Not for the protection comment, because I'm not a complete idiot, but for the rest.'

'I am a wise soul. Love you.'

'Love you back.'

Maddie sighed, disconnecting. Shoving her mobile phone into the pocket of her shorts, she stared at the rapidly darkening sky.

If she wasn't already—and she chose to think that she wasn't—then she was on the verge of falling in love with Cale. If she allowed herself to fall over into love and then she had to leave it would hurt. If she stayed he would end the relationship at some point, probably when he realised that she felt more for him than he did for her.

Either way it would sting. Badly. Sort of the same way having your heart ripped out of your chest without anaesthetic would sting.

You're thinking with your heart, Maddie, use your head.

The choice was still hers to make, she reassured herself. She could only get hurt if she thought she couldn't live without his love. Could only feel disappointed if she let down more of her guard. If she allowed herself to fall in love she ran the risk of having her life ripped apart again.

Choice and consequences.

She could choose to not to let her feelings go any deeper, to walk away heart intact when she had to leave. She could step into this situation with her eyes wide open. There was no way she was walking away from him now—no chance that she could. But she could try to protect herself. She had to...

She could enter into an *anti*-relationship with herself.

I, Maddie Shaw, hereby give up all possibility of love, commitment or permanence with one Cale Grant. I will remember at all times that I will be leaving, and therefore will not be swept away into any romantic thoughts. In exchange for lots and lots of lovely sex, I pledge not to leave any personal items in his house, only to sleep

*every second or third night in his arms, and not to expect
anything more from said Cale Grant except for mutual
pleasure and occasional affection for as long as this might
last.*

It wasn't a bad idea, Maddie mused. It had nothing to do with
Cale and everything to do with her. She was making the right,
the conscientious, the clever decision.

Apart from which it was the only decision she could make
and keep her sanity.

Cale pulled a grey jersey over his head and watched as Maddie
carefully folded the clothes she'd worn the night before and
placed them in a neat little pile on the end of his bed.

'Just toss them into the laundry basket. My housekeeper is
due today,' he suggested casually, and sighed when Maddie
shook her head. He'd thought he was being considerate when
he cleared out a drawer and made space for her toiletries in his
bathroom cabinet, but every time she left she gathered up her
possessions like a demented squirrel and took them with her.

'Thanks, but I'll take them home,' Maddie said as she stepped
into the bathroom. When she returned, carrying her toiletry bag,
she had a big frown on her face.

'Cale, have you seen my birth control pills?'

It had been her idea to go on the pill and he was grateful. He
wanted nothing between them, and making love without latex
was ridiculously wonderful.

'In your bag?' Cale suggested, nodding to her tote bag on
the windowseat.

Cale shook his head when the large bag landed with a thunk
on the bed. What was she carrying around in there? A portable
office? Her own tent, chairs and crockery?

Cale sat on the bed next to her as she opened the long zip and
peeked inside. He whistled, quite convinced that Maddie had
the stuffed carcass of a zebra inside.

Maddie rooted around inside and bit her lip in frustration.
'I can't see them.'

'Big surprise there,' Cale said sarcastically. 'Here, let me help.'

Cale took the bag and tipped it upside down.

'Cale, you idiot!' Maddie yelled.

Stuff—there was no other way to describe it—fell onto the bed and bounced away. Cale couldn't believe that one woman could carry around so much. There was a thick swatch of fabric samples and a sewing kit. Hand lotion. Four different colour lipsticks and other assorted makeup. Chocolate. A tiny pair of scissors and a torch. Two pairs of stockings, still in their plastic. Wet wipes. A round brush and a normal brush. An empty bottle of aspirin, a folding umbrella, two pairs of sunglasses and a wallet. And a thin pack of pills.

Cale shook his head and handed Maddie her birth control pills.

'Guys just don't get it. When you're doing events you need to be prepared. For anything,' Maddie muttered, pulling a pill out of the packet and swallowing it. She scrabbled in the mess for a lip-gloss, which she immediately slicked over those pouty lips.

Cale looked away, tempted to kiss it all off again.

Maddie pointed a finger at him. 'Put it back while I look for my phone.'

Maddie moved over to the chest of drawers that served as his dressing table and Cale was distracted by her truly excellent bottom covered in soft suede pants. He swallowed when Maddie bent over her overnight bag.

'Bingo!' Maddie called, and waved her phone in his direction.

'Leave it here, Mad. All of it.' Cale waved at her clothes and her toiletry bag. 'It's stupid carrying this stuff back and forward.'

Did she think that some drawer space and leaving the occasional piece of clothing constituted a relationship? That he'd forget for one moment she'd be walking out of his life some time in the near future?

'I can't.' Maddie dropped her head, still crouched in front of her bag. 'When I have to go, I don't want to have to look for stuff I've left. I don't want to settle in… It'll make it harder to leave.'

Maddie's mobile rang, and Cale stood up and walked over to the windowseat and stared hard out to sea.

It was more than the fact that she never even left her toothbrush in the holder or her hairbrush on the credenza. Her actions reinforced the feeling that she was keeping a part of herself back from him. Intellectually he understood her need to protect herself, but he didn't like it.

He didn't like it at all.

After a lengthy run and a shower, Cale unpacked the groceries he'd bought for the weekend. Having two comprehensively undomesticated guests in his house, he knew that if he wanted food he'd have to buy it. And unpack it. And cook it.

Alex, his other transient guest—courtesy of a burst geyser flooding his home—sat at the kitchen table, his attention on the finance section of the newspaper.

'When are you going home?' Cale asked, just because he could. He loved having Alex living with him, but the brother code stated that he had to give him a hard time.

'A week or so.' Alex sipped his coffee, his eyes on the paper. 'Why? Am I cramping your style?'

'I have no style to cramp.' Cale shoved the bottles of wine he'd bought into the wine rack and cocked his head at the sound of Maddie's Jag roaring up the driveway. 'You are, however, cramping Maddie's. How is she supposed to cook naked in the kitchen with you around?'

Alex laughed. 'And that's why they call it a fantasy. Maddie doesn't cook.'

'Tell me about it,' Cale muttered. 'Trust me to be involved with a woman whose only link to domesticity is that she lives in a house.'

'Cale? I'm home!' Maddie called from the hall.

'We're in the kitchen,' Cale called back, smacking Alex on the back of the head just because he was older and he could.

'Hi, boys.' Maddie stepped through the doorway, unravelling her scarf and draping it over a kitchen chair.

Alex waved his apple in the air and Cale stepped forward to kiss her hello. 'Hi.'

Maddie briefly touched his cheek with her cold fingers. 'Hi, back. How was your day?'

Cale deepened the kiss even as he reached out to snag Alex's arm and lift him out of his chair.

'Hey! *Ow*!'

Cale broke the kiss to send Alex an evil look. 'Get out of my kitchen... Go irritate Megan.'

Alex grinned and tossed his apple core in the dustbin. 'Yeah, okay. She's a better cook than you, anyway. Later, Mad.'

Cale took some wineglasses out of the cupboard and from the corner of his eye watched Maddie unbutton her thigh-length navy coat. She looked ill at ease and irritated, and he wondered how long it would take for her to spit out whatever was bothering her. He opened a bottle of Merlot and dashed some into a glass.

'Get that into you. You look like you need it. Rough day?'

Maddie shook her head. 'Not really.' She took a sip of wine and pulled out a kitchen chair. 'Long. The race is coming along nicely. We're way ahead of schedule. The charity dinner dance is sold out and we've raised quite a bit of money already.'

'That's great, sport.' Cale sat opposite her and put his feet up on the seat Alex had been using. 'And?'

Maddie didn't meet his eyes, which was always a bad sign. 'Sorry?'

'What aren't you telling me?'

Why did she still think she could hide things from him? He could read the smallest nuances when it came to her expressions.

Maddie tapped her nails against the glass. 'I'm flying to Durban tomorrow, to attend a gala dinner being held by the PR Association. The company is up for an award for strategic and innovative use of public relations to drive coverage of a brand.'

'And why aren't Jens and Harriet going?'

'They are. Jake was supposed to go, but he's really sick so I have to go in his place.'

The thought of not seeing her for half the weekend rankled. Especially since they didn't have that much time left.

'Do you want company?' Cale asked. 'Why don't we see if we can pick up a late flight tonight and stay the weekend?'

Maddie perked up at this suggestion. 'That sounds great. Except that you'll be alone on Saturday night.'

'I'm sure I can find something to do for a couple of hours,' Cale told her. 'I'll go see a movie.'

'You sure?' Maddie asked him, hesitant. 'If we get a flight tonight maybe we can hire some boards and surf in the morning. The sea is wonderfully warm in Durban, even in winter, and maybe I'll get you to stand up.'

'Maybe.' Cale smiled. 'So, should I go online and see if I can book flights?'

'Thanks.' Maddie stared down at her wine.

Cale cleared his throat and started to speak. Maddie shook her curls, lifted her hand and refused to look at him.

'Don't push, Cale. I'm not ready to talk to you about it just yet.'

Cale stood up and walked around the table. He dropped a kiss on her head, instinctively knowing that she'd had news from the States and had put plans in place. But he'd respect her right to choose the time when she wanted to tell him what they were.

He couldn't ask her to stay and he couldn't ask her not to go. Frustrated, he walked out of the kitchen to his study, dropped into the chair behind his desk and stared, unseeing, at the bright screen of his computer monitor. He knew what Maddie wasn't ready to tell him. It was written all over her face. She was heading for that interview in New York, and soon.

Cale shoved his hands into his hair and tugged. He understood that it was a once in a lifetime opportunity for Maddie, and that logically she really had to go. He couldn't suggest a good enough reason to stay, wasn't able to offer her stability or a future.

Permanence, love, commitment. To offer her that he had to believe in all or any of them. He didn't. And he liked the lack of responsibility that being single gave him. He'd always been half of a couple, and Oliver had been more demanding than any wife or girlfriend could ever be.

Not that Maddie was demanding… She paid her own way, made her own decisions and ran her own life. He'd never have to pay off her credit card or help her in a bar fight, but when you made any sort of emotional connection, became involved with someone, you did take on some obligations.

What if she'd been badly hurt in that car accident and she'd had only him to rely on? Would he have been happy to step up to the plate and do what needed to be done for her? What if she wanted kids one day and wanted to jack in her job and stay at home? Would he be able to cope with that and not feel resentful?

He didn't know. Until he did he had no right to ask anything from her.

If only he didn't like the freedom of not being emotionally, financially or physically responsible for someone else quite so much.

So, back to Maddie and New York. What if she got the job? To Maddie it would be a wonderful excuse to throw herself into work without the distraction of a lover getting in the way. She'd cope with the workload and the lack of friends for a couple of months and then she'd fall apart—because she was inherently a warm, sociable person and she needed the interaction of people who loved her. She wouldn't have a Laughing Queen in New York—a place with people who adored her for her to run to, where she could bitch and vent and cry if she needed to. She wouldn't have a best friend who was on the other end of a mobile with a margarita to steer her in the right direction.

She wouldn't have him to make her smell the roses.

So, here he was, stuck between the devil and the deep blue sea. He couldn't ask her to stay and offer nothing in return, and he couldn't encourage her to go because he knew that wasn't right for her either.

So basically there was nothing he could do except relish the time he had with her.

His fingers flew over the keyboard as he planned a weekend that they'd always remember.

* * *

Cale joined Maddie on the veranda forty-five minutes later and, dressed only in a sweater and jeans, stood in front of her, burrowing his arms beneath her coat to keep warm.

'Chilly.'

'Freezing,' Maddie agreed, and stared out over the deck.

Although the sun had set an hour before, she could still see the sea in the dusky half-light and watched the lights of the houses up and down the coast. It was a clear night but cold, and the icy polar wind tossed her hair around her face.

'I received the e-mail at lunchtime—a formal invitation to attend an interview in Manhattan. They'll pay half of my air fare and wanted to know when I could be there.'

'Go on.'

Maddie shrugged. 'I juggled. I'm taking a week's leave and I've booked a flight the morning after the charity ball. A week will give me time to look into accommodation, orientate myself, have the interview...consider my options.'

'When will you be back?'

'The following Sunday. If I'm offered the position I'll resign immediately. Harriet won't want me around, so I'll be able to work on the race pretty much full-time.'

As soon as that was wound up she'd fly out and start a new chapter in her life.

Maddie rested her forehead on Cale's chest. How would she cope with never seeing this view again? Never standing in this exact spot drinking wine and listening to the rumble of the sea? How could she not wake up to Cale's warm arms wrapped around her, their gentle argument about whose turn it was to make coffee? Or not be woken up with a sweaty kiss after he'd been for a run on the beach?

How was she supposed to pack up and move on when this period of her life had been so intense, so life-changing?

Maddie felt warm tears roll down her face and prayed that Cale wouldn't notice. She didn't know if she had the strength not to tell him that if he asked her to stay she would. Without a moment's hesitation.

But if he didn't—and she knew he wouldn't—then she knew

that she had no choice but to go. She couldn't cope with living in the same city, knowing that she was breathing the same air, looking at the same sea, with just a mountain separating them. A mountain and the knowledge that she wanted more from him than he was prepared to give.

She hadn't broken but shattered her contract with herself... How could she start to defend herself?

I, Maddie Shaw, tried really hard to give up the possibility of love, commitment or permanence with one Cale Grant, but what I'm feeling is bigger than my common sense, my self-preservation and my intellect. My heart has overruled my head and he is the first and only man who's touched my soul.

I don't want a lot from him. I just want everything.

CHAPTER TWELVE

MADDIE tucked her hired surfboard under her arm and laughed as they hit the warm Indian Ocean. Durban in winter, she thought, lifting her face up to the hot mid-morning sun. The world's best kept secret. The sun was hot but there was no humidity, and the water was so warm that they'd both chosen to forgo wetsuits. She wore a fluorescent pink bikini top and navy boardshorts, and Cale made her mouth water dressed simply in a pair of plain black boardshorts.

Maddie stopped when the water lapped her mid-thigh and looked at the surf. Cale should be able to manage the two-foot waves, she thought. She'd give him an hour and then head for the back line, where the waves were pumping. She tasted excitement at the back of her throat… Could she have asked for a nicer day?

Cale, on his stomach, long body stretched out on his board, pulled himself past her. 'Hey, where are you going?'

'Back line!' he shouted back, a broad grin on his face.

'You're not nearly ready for the back line! Get back here!'

'I'll just hang out there and watch you until you're done,' Cale called.

Maddie shrugged, not prepared to argue. She looked at a breaking wave as she rocked over a swell. She couldn't wait… Year-round surfing was just another thing she'd have to give up if she went to the States.

Maddie pulled up alongside Cale and straddled her board, reaching out to grab his bare shoulder. She leaned forward and met his lips with hers. 'Thanks.'

'Pleasure.' Cale ran a hand down her shoulder and arm and squeezed her fingers. 'You look seriously hot in that colour.'

Maddie pushed her wet plait over her shoulder. 'I thought you would've had enough of me by now. Once last night and twice this morning.'

'We had to test that four-poster bed,' Cale told her. 'It passes muster.'

'Did we have to test the shower and the floor too?' Maddie teased.

'Absolutely. I wanted to see if the room lived up to its claim of being the most romantic room in the city. Tonight we'll test the Jacuzzi.'

'There's a deal,' Maddie told him, her eyes on the ocean. 'God, look at that swell. That's mine!'

She hopped up on the board and caught the swell at the right moment, crouching to ride down its face. Soon she was flying on its power, the warm ocean playfully splashing her face, her board skimming the water. The wave ran out of power close to the beach and she lifted her arms in jubilant pleasure as she slid off the board.

Wasn't this the best idea he'd ever had?

Maddie flung herself back on the board and turned her eyes to look for Cale, who should have been sitting on his board behind the back line. She frowned, wondering where he'd got to, and allowed her eyes to drift over the rest of the surfers. Her eyes widened in surprise. He was up and he was surfing...

He wasn't the most graceful or the most practiced, but he was up and he was flying. Maddie let out a whoop of appreciation before laughing when his board flew out from under his feet and he crashed into the white water. His head popped up and she paddled over to him.

She mock-scowled at him. 'I see I got booted as surfing instructor.'

Cale hauled himself up on his board and grinned at her. 'Did you see me? Wasn't that cool? That was *so* cool!'

Maddie lifted her hand up so that he could slap it. 'So cool! Where? What? How?'

Cale shrugged. 'I was too impatient and frustrated to wait around for you to teach me. A couple of afternoons I headed to Muizenberg and found an eighteen-year-old who's been surfing all his life to teach me. He was happy to have the money and surprisingly patient.'

'How long did it take him to get you up?' Maddie asked him.

'A lesson.' Cale flicked water at her. 'But please remember that with you I was too distracted to get up on the board.'

'Ha-ha. You're just saying that because I'm a lousy instructor.'

They hit the back line and sat up on their boards. Cale took her hand and loosely held it as they waited for another set to come in. 'No, it's because I just have to look at you and I'm imagining you naked under me.'

Maddie closed her eyes as a rush of warmth headed straight to her core. 'Cale…'

'Want to hop off your board for a moment?' Cale waggled his eyebrows.

Maddie widened her eyes. 'Cale Grant!'

'Madison Shaw!' Cale teased, then stretched out on his board and started to paddle. 'I'll be back!'

Maddie giggled. He'd distracted her and nicked a really good wave… He was riding it well too.

She'd created a monster, she decided as she picked up the next, smaller wave. She'd just have to punish him later, she decided. In a very creative and imaginative way.

Ten minutes before they were about to land in Cape Town, Cale turned to Maddie, who'd spent the best part of the flight staring out of the window. Although her hand had stayed in his for most of the flight, he knew that she was very far away—possibly already in New York.

Their spectacular weekend away was over and it was time to pay the piper.

'I had a great weekend, sport. Thanks.'

'Ditto.'

'What's wrong?'

Maddie pulled her hand from his and shoved it into her hair.

'Apart from the fact that I'm leaving my home and my country and my new man for a situation I'm not sure I even want any more?'

'I don't know what to say,' Cale admitted, fiddling with his mobile to give his hands something to do.

Maddie shrugged and turned away.

What was so damn interesting to look at at thirty thousand feet? Blue sky and clouds?

'There's not much to say. I thought I was so smart, thought I had this under control.'

Cale scowled at the back of her head. Again, how was he supposed to respond to that? 'I keep thinking that you're waiting for me to say something.'

'Like?'

'Asking you not to go.' Cale sucked in some air. 'You've got to make this decision without me, Mad. You've got to take me out of the equation and work out if this is the right move for you. I can't sway you. What we have—whatever the hell it is—shouldn't sway you.'

'Why not? Why can't...*this*...you and I, be a factor?'

'Because if you didn't go for any reason you'd always wonder whether you were good enough. And you'd regret not finding out. You have to go and do the interview at the very least.' Cale ran his hand over his face. 'As for me and my hang-ups around relationships—can I say this? You're the only person who has even come close to getting me to consider risking my heart, my sanity, my wellbeing.'

Maddie rested the side of her head against the window and toyed with her bottle of water. 'Would it be so bad? Would it be the worst thing we could do to take the risk to be together?'

'It's hurting already, Maddie, and we're not even in love with each other.' At least he presumed they weren't. He wasn't. He didn't think she was. 'Imagine if it went wrong—and history has taught us that it probably will—and we were even more emotionally involved? I don't think either of us would recover easily, if at all.' He heaved out the words. 'You've made me realise that I'm not so hung up any more about Oliver's death, but I am still dealing with…how do I say this?…with the impact his life had on mine. He drained me, Maddie.'

'And you think that I'm going to do the same?'

'Maddie.' Cale closed his eyes at the hurt in hers. 'I just can't. I can't give you…this…us… that much control.'

'So basically you're still an emotional wimp?'

He couldn't even disagree with her. 'Yes. Absolutely. I'm an absolute nerd when it comes to this stuff.'

Maddie heaved a huge sigh. 'Me too. Make me a promise?'

'I'll try.'

'If you're going to hook up with another woman—and you will—avoid the vapid, stupid ones, okay? Even if they are stacked and blonde with legs up to their necks.'

He couldn't find the energy to smile at her stab at humour. 'Okay.'

Cale felt a piercing pain in his chest at the thought of Maddie with another man, sharing anything like the sex they had. He'd nearly come to terms with the guilt he felt around Oliver's death, the flickers of panic were nothing more than a very infrequent spark these days, but he knew that he'd now have another issue to deal with at three in the morning. Actually, the idea of Maddie with someone else would probably haunt him all hours of the day.

'A nun,' he muttered under his breath. 'God, please let her become a nun.'

'What?' Maddie frowned at him.

Cale shook his head as he stood up. 'Nothing. Don't worry about it. I'm going to take a walk.' He gestured to the toilets and his unsteady walk had nothing to do with the minor turbulence.

Locked away in that tiny space, he stared at his reflection in the mirror. He wished he could blame the seafood curry he'd had for lunch for his bout of nausea, but he couldn't. He was enough of a psychologist to know that it was a physical manifestation of his mental state. He could only pray that this queasiness would subside as he became more used to the idea of not having her in his life. Of her being on the other side of the world.

Cale rubbed his hands over his face, thinking that once again

Maddie had pulled a whole bunch of emotions to the surface and he was ill equipped to handle them.

Typical. Nothing much had changed in a decade.

Maddie, dressed in a black halterneck cocktail dress and a fixed smile, checked her bracelet watch. It was two in the morning and a good number of the charity dinner guests were left, still bopping to the band. Maddie sat at a corner table on the ballroom and rested her head against the back wall. There was no point in leaving to go home. She had her bags and a change of clothing in the car and she'd go directly to the airport. In five hours she'd be in the air, and she'd take a sleeping pill and pass out for the entire flight to New York.

Jim walked past her, stopped, and came back to crouch in front of her. 'You okay, Miss M?'

Maddie touched the hand he'd put on her knee. 'No, but I will be. Maybe in a year or two.'

Jim touched her cheek with a long finger. 'I love you, gorgeous girl. Call us as soon as you know about the job. If you get it, I'm going to miss your face.'

Maddie gulped and waved her hands at him. 'Go away, Jimbo, before I sob all over that fantastic suit.'

Jim hugged her briefly, and when he was gone Maddie looked across the room to where Cale stood by the bar, water bottle in his hand, talking to a man Maddie didn't know. His bow tie hung down the front of his snowy dress shirt and his hair was ruffled. Even in the subdued lighting she could see that his face looked drawn and ever so slightly anxious. She recognised the condition because, despite her flawless makeup and bright smile, she felt the same.

Anxiety was such a small word for what she was feeling.

In a few hours she'd get on a plane and leave her heart behind.

Love, she'd realised, despite her vigilance, had snuck up on her again. As hard as she'd tried she hadn't been able to out-smart it, out-think it, out-control it. Love had decided that Cale was her *It*. Again.

Oh, he'd hurt her years ago, but for most of their time together she'd used his youthful failure at their relationship as an excuse to justify her reasons to run away from love because she didn't want to fail again. She'd never allowed herself to love—well, love Cale—without reservation. Because if the relationship failed she would have failed, just like her parents had failed.

Maddie finally admitted that she'd done everything in her power to keep Cale at arm's length, to use any excuse she could to keep him from getting closer. To stop her from falling in love with him. As if that had worked.

And now she was getting on a plane and possibly—very probably, according to Dennis—making another life for herself in another city, another country.

But what were her options? One or two.

One, she could stay in Cape Town, stay in this one-sided relationship where she loved and he didn't, and that would be a singular type of torture. Except she suspected that if she suggested not going to NYC to Cale he'd toss her on the plane himself. He was right. She needed to know whether she was good enough for New York.

Two, she could leave and work and live in the States and hope to hell that they made her work eighteen hours a day; she'd sleep the other six. That way she would have minimum time to cry.

Maddie turned at a feminine hand on her shoulder and looked into the lovely face of Gigi.

'Mind if I sit?'

Maddie shrugged and waved at the empty chairs. 'Take your pick.'

Gigi placed her evening bag on the table, sat and crossed her mile-long legs. 'It's been a wonderful night. A hugely successful night. Well done.'

'Thank you.'

'Do you want another project?'

'Pardon?' Maddie asked politely, wishing that this vision of loveliness would go away and leave her to her misery.

'It's my thirtieth birthday coming up and I thought that I'd throw a party. I'm also launching a new modelling agency, so I thought I'd do them together. Do you want to take it on?'

'Sure...' Maddie closed her eyes when she remembered. 'Except that I'm flying to the States tomorrow for a job interview, and I think, from an inside source, that I have a good chance of getting an offer.'

Gigi looked over at Cale. 'Oh. Well, if you don't get it let me know.' Gigi draped her hands over her knees and stared hard at Maddie. 'You're leaving him?'

Maddie tried for a careless laugh and knew that it came off as sounding desperate. 'He hasn't asked me to stay.'

Gigi rolled her eyes. 'Typical Cale.'

Maddie leaned forward. 'Why did you let him go?'

Gigi didn't pretend to misunderstand. 'Because he wasn't in love with me and I want it all. Like I think you do. And, really, no woman should stay with a man who still carries an old photograph of his first love in his wallet.'

Maddie stared at her wide-eyed and Gigi sent her a small smile as she stood up. Maddie was touched when she bent down and dropped a light kiss on her cheek.

'I like you, Maddie. I hope this somehow works out for you.'

'Well,' Maddie replied, flustered, 'don't hold your breath.'

CHAPTER THIRTEEN

CALE, still in his tuxedo, sat opposite Maddie at a coffee shop at the airport and listlessly stirred sugar into his polystyrene cup. It was a measure of his tiredness that he dumped white sugar into his coffee and didn't care.

Maddie had changed from her slinky black ballgown into comfortable jeans and boots, and she wore her leather jacket over a white T-shirt. She looked calm, collected and every inch the type of woman who could work in New York. Smart, capable, ambitious.

'I have your flight details. I'll pick you up Sunday week,' Cale said, to break the silence.

'Oh, Jim already offered and I accepted. Thanks, though.'

Cale frowned at her mock-jaunty tone. She wouldn't meet his eyes. 'Is this it, Maddie?'

'I think it has to be, Cale.' Maddie played with her plastic spoon. 'What's the point in carrying on? It's pretty much over between us... You won't ask me to stay and I won't ask you to ask me to stay...'

'It's not that I don't *want* you to stay...'

'Then what is it, Cale?' Maddie demanded. 'We have something wonderful and yet you're prepared to let me go!'

'You *have* to do this!'

'Why?' Maddie shouted as she gripped his wrist.

'Because if one day you regret it, you'll blame me for not taking the chance! Because it's the logical decision. Because it's your dream, your ambition.'

'I think my ambitions have changed. Aren't they allowed to?' Maddie asked. 'Cale, we are so good together, we have such fun. We're best friends and stunning lovers. Why are you so willing to toss that—me—away?'

'I don't know.'

Maddie leaned across the table. 'Talk to me, dammit! Help me understand this—you! You owe me that much!'

'Trust me, I know exactly how much I owe you.' Cale rubbed the back of his neck. 'I'm not proud of the way I feel, and admitting this to you is hellishly discomforting. I find it difficult to put into words. It's all mixed up with my relationship with Oliver, about not being in a situation I can control, about fear.'

Cale knocked his coffee cup off the table and neither of them noticed. He touched his throat, thinking that something was strangling him. Why did she have to keep pushing this? Keep digging?

Maddie just looked at him, wanting more.

He tried, fumbling for words. 'I'm used to being self-reliant. I don't know how I'd cope if I let myself depend on you and then you left. One big fight, one hurdle, one sickness, one slump.'

'You don't have much faith in me, or in life, do you?'

'You bailed on me before. When we hit a hurdle you bailed.' Cale hadn't known that he was still carrying that resentment until the words flew out of mouth.

'I was eighteen years old, recovering from a pregnancy scare, and you were a terrible boyfriend!' Maddie protested. 'You treated me abominably!'

'Because you turned me inside out! You turned my world upside down. Do you know what that does to a control freak?' Cale demanded. 'Here you were, this slip of a girl, years younger than me, who had the power to wring out my heart! You held all the power, Maddie, and that was why I acted up!' Cale scrubbed his face with his hands. 'I don't want to anyone to have that much power over me again.'

Maddie rested her head in the palm of her hands and stared at the table. 'It wasn't power, Cale, it was love. I just wanted to love you.' She lifted her head and held out her hand. 'Show me your wallet.'

Cale reached into his pocket and passed her his slim black wallet. She flipped it open and started looking through it. What on earth for?

'What's the matter? Do you need to borrow some cash? I'm a bit short of US dollars.'

Maddie ignored his stab at humour and he watched as she pushed and probed, eventually finding a slot underneath his credit cards. She pulled out a battered photograph. She didn't look at the image of her eighteen-year-old self. Instead she threw it across the table at him.

'I'm not Oliver, Cale. Loving me doesn't mean that you have to look after me. It doesn't mean that you are responsible for me. I will always live by and take responsibility for the choices I make. You are the most incredibly clever man, Cale, but so stupid when it comes to me. I need you to man up and say a couple of words—to show some trust, to take a chance. Will you?'

Cale held the photograph in his fist and felt his chest constrict. He wished he could, but he couldn't. He couldn't take this opportunity from her, and nor could he take the chance of risking being pulled inside out again.

'I didn't think you would.' Maddie looked at him with regret and pity. 'At eighteen, I loved you with all the stupidity of youth. We had a chance then to be gloriously happy and we were too young to recognise it. I think we just missed another one. I suspect that's all we get.'

Maddie stood up and pulled her big tote bag over her shoulder. 'When I get back we've got about a month to go before the race and so much to do. Maybe it's better if we don't see each in the run-up to the race and communicate via e-mail. I don't want to have to say goodbye again. It hurts too damn much.'

Maddie, brave as always, lifted her chin, and he saw the tears tracking down her face.

'Why won't you stop being scared of what can go wrong and think of what could go right?'

Cale watched, utterly miserable, as she walked away with what felt like a very large portion of his heart.

Maddie sat in the very minimalistic, very slick boardroom of Bower & Co, situated in a very swish building on Lexington Avenue, and swallowed a bored yawn. At the other end of the boardroom table three of the most senior managers—all women—flipped through her portfolio. She'd answered what seemed like a million questions earlier in the day, had been asked to return late in the afternoon and here she sat, ready to hear what decision they'd come to.

All she could think was that she hoped Cale had remembered to sign the contract with the caterers for the race, and to pick up the permit to allow the racers to use part of the public road from Scarborough to the Peninsular. The meeting for the road marshals and safety officers would happen that evening...

'Ms Shaw?'

Maddie jerked her attention back to the present and lifted her head to look at Slick, Slick and Slicker. Oh, good grief, now she'd forgotten their names! This was disastrous!

A cool redhead dressed in a black designer suit sent a polite smile her way. Her voice was low but quick. 'You've had a long day, Maddie, and we appreciate your patience.'

She hadn't been given a lot of choice.

'We are very impressed with your portfolio and we'd like to offer you the position as events co-ordinator within Bower & Co.'

Well, *duh*. Maddie tried to feel excited and couldn't. She didn't want to be here in these smart offices, a million miles from where two oceans met at the tip of a continent. The redhead stood up on icepick heels to hand her a leather folder.

'Here is your contract, your remuneration package and your scope of duties. I suggest you take the evening to read it and return the signed copy to us tomorrow.'

Maddie placed her hand on the folder. 'Thank you.'

'However, there is a small issue that is not covered by the contract.'

Of course there was, Maddie thought. She lifted her eyebrows. 'What might that be?'

The redhead—Anna Kidd! Good, she'd remembered one name—laughed.

'Don't look so worried. It's just that we have scheduled our annual conference for the weekend of August eighteenth. We feel that it is imperative for you to be there. I understand that it means you flying back for a weekend, but we'll cover your costs. It'll give you an excellent opportunity to meet the team, establish some relationships and get an idea of how we work.'

If that wasn't a sign that this job was totally not for her, Maddie didn't know what was. It couldn't have been clearer if God had reached down and smacked her around the head.

'That's a generous offer.' Maddie tapped her finger on the folder. 'Except that I am unavailable that weekend.'

Anna's eyes cooled and her thin brows lifted in surprise. 'May I ask with what?'

Maddie considered lying, considered finding a quick excuse, and decided it didn't matter if she told the truth.

'I have a function I'm organising that weekend.'

'Surely you have a colleague who could take it over?' Slick Two asked in surprise.

'It's a function that I am organising pro-bono. A triathlon race for charity.'

Anna Kidd's dismissive laugh had the hair on the back of her neck standing up. 'Surely you can explain to them that something more important has come up?'

Maddie took a deep breath and pushed her chair back. 'Except that this job offer is *not* more important. I made a commitment and I intend to see it through.'

Three perfectly lipsticked mouths fell open. 'You are prepared to risk this job for an event that you're not even getting paid to do?'

'It looks like it.' Maddie pushed the folder away, suddenly deeply certain she was doing the right thing. She sent them a dazzling smile.

Anna looked at her colleagues and then back at Maddie, utterly puzzled. 'I'm sorry, I don't understand this.'

Maddie picked up her bag. 'I can see that. I can also see that I wouldn't be happy working for a company who can't respect the fact that once I make a commitment to a project I have to honour it. Thank you for the offer, Ms Kidd, but I think I'll pass. I've got a race to organise and a home to get back to. Send Dennis my love.'

When Maddie had closed the boardroom door behind her she dropped her head and shrugged off the weight she'd been carrying around for the past couple of months.

She didn't belong here. Her life and any future happiness lay at the tip of Africa, even if her heart belonged to someone else.

It was time to go home.

Cale had had no idea that a month could be such a long time. The sun was setting on the eve of the race and Cale still thought of Maddie as being somewhere in the house, issuing orders, chasing down a detail. He kept expecting to bump into her rounding a corner, he rolled over in sleep looking for her, waited to hear her voice lifted in temper, laughter, reassurance. Oscar and Lance whined at his feet, and Marilyn's jaw rested on her paws, her eyes on the driveway. Even his damn dogs missed her. Like them, he harboured the faint hope that at any moment he would hear the roar of her car as she careered up his driveway.

Two minutes after Maddie's plane had taken off he'd suspected that he had messed up. Now, sitting on the top step of the veranda, Cale recalled their last conversation again and admitted that he'd messed up badly. He should have asked her to stay—begged and grovelled if necessary.

The past month without Maddie had taught him that life without her was the emotional equivalent of the sixteenth level of hell—that life held no guarantees, gave no refunds. You simply had to take what blessings you were given and be grateful. Maddie was a huge blessing and he'd let her go. Cale suspected that was very bad karma.

He felt movement behind him and glanced up as Megan rested

a hand on his shoulder and sat on the concrete step next to him. Wrapping his hands around the coffee mug she gave him, he smiled his thanks.

'Oliver would have loved her as a sister-in-law,' Megan said. 'He would have said that she is perfect for you. Outgoing, vivacious, independent. Fun.'

'All the things I'm not,' Cale muttered into his coffee.

Megan leaned back and twisted so that her back rested against the wall. Cale recognised her expression—the same one she used when the boys were being particularly stroppy.

'Feeling sorry for yourself?'

'Damn right. It's the night before the race and instead of working I'm sitting here thinking about a woman.'

Megan smirked as she threaded her hand through his arm. 'How the mighty have fallen.'

Cale glared at her, resting his arms on his knees. 'If you're going to be sarcastic, you can just go away.'

'*Oooh*, testy too!' Megan chuckled at his annoyed face.

They sat in silence for few minutes, listening to the sound of the high tide crashing on the rocks and Lance's gentle huffing.

Cale placed his coffee cup on the step between his feet and stared at the dark garden.

'I know she loves you. Do you love her?'

He took a sip of coffee and scowled. That was such a *girl* question! 'Hell, I suppose so! I don't know what else could be causing me to feel so miserable. I've never wanted to be loved— in love,' he added.

Megan grinned. 'Don't be stupid. Everyone does. You're just scared. A sexy, smart, funny, independent woman loves you. You should be getting on your knees and thanking God for her.'

'What if I can't persuade her not to take the job? To stay here? Or, if she does stay, what if we can't make it work?'

Cale felt Megan's shrug.

'You've done a pretty good job of making it work so far. But you weigh it up. What would be worse? Maddie or no Maddie? How's this month been for you, champ?'

'Absolutely awful. She has the power to annihilate me.'

Megan rested her head on his shoulder. 'Well, that's the flip-side—the risk. But such joy, such exquisite joy, is on the other side of the coin, Cale. I don't know what your future holds. All I can say is on one hand you risk getting your heart stomped on by a herd of angry buffalo, but on the other you risk not experiencing great happiness.' Megan stood up and slapped her hands against her thighs. 'So, I'm here to tell you, on behalf of your twin, to pull your head out of your bum and to stop being such a wuss. Take a risk and stop sulking.'

'Ollie would've phrased that far more colourfully.'

'Yeah, with a lot more swearing.' Megan smiled her loving, sad smile and patted his shoulder on her way to the door, leaving Cale to his tumultuous thoughts.

It was odd to be in a race but not racing, Cale thought as he slowly pedalled through a pine forest at the tail end of the amateur race. He squinted as a ten-year-old beetled past him. It was also odd that he was being passed by kids barely off their training wheels.

But then again he *was* cycling with the world's most cautious doctor, Alex.

'Oliver would've got such a kick out of this,' Cale said, holding the handlebars with one hand.

'Oliver always loved attention,' Alex said dryly.

So he had.

'Have you spoken to Maddie?'

'No.'

Beneath his sunglasses, Cale's eyes narrowed. Maddie had found every excuse in the book to avoid having a face to face meeting with him, and since returning from the States she seemed only comfortable with sending him impersonal e-mails.

How was he supposed to start talking her into staying in the country, staying with *him*, if she wouldn't even have a blasted conversation with him? The woman was beyond stubborn...

Unfortunately so was he, he admitted ruefully. It had taken Maddie's leaving and his empty and cold house and his empty and cold heart to make him realise how much a part of his life she was. The best part...

Love, she'd taught him, didn't mean sacrificing himself or who he was for someone else. Unlike Oliver—and how could he not have realised this sooner?—Maddie was a fully functioning adult.

She was responsible and thoughtful and had a work ethic second to none. She'd never asked him to look after her emotionally, financially or even physically... She'd only ever asked him to love her.

And, because he was a coward, he'd run screaming into the night.

He deserved the mental and emotional beating he was currently taking.

He knew she'd got the job; he'd tagged the question on at the bottom of an e-mail about refreshments for the race and she'd said that the interview had gone well. If she'd signed the contract already he'd find the best damn lawyer he could to break it...

Maybe Kate would take the case.

He had to talk Maddie out of going, but if he couldn't he'd pack his stuff and follow her there. NYC would be hell, but he'd be with Maddie, which would be heaven...

'Talking about Maddie...' Alex said as the track veered down to the left.

Cale shook his head as Alex slowed down to a crawl. How could he possibly be related to this man? He could walk faster than he was cycling, and the slope had all the steepness of a crumpet.

'What about Maddie?' Cale asked as he reached for his water bottle. 'And can you please hurry up? You're an embarrassment.'

'Bite me,' Alex retorted. 'There are tree roots sticking out of the ground.'

'Listen, ants are overtaking you. Go over the damn roots. Maddie?'

'Oh, apparently she's not going to the States.'

Cale lowered his water bottle and stared at his brother. 'What did you say?'

'She's staying here.'

'Seriously?'

'According to Gigi, apparently so.'

Cale let out a massive whoop, and with the widest grin spun his wheels to dodge around Alex as he accelerated away

'Later!'

'Oh, okay... Man, you're fast. *Cale, watch that root...!*'

Oh, hell, Cale thought as he and his mountain bike parted company. *This is going to sting.*

The race was over, the prizes were handed out and Cale was wrapping up the proceedings. Maddie looked at him standing on the podium and winced. He had a bad scrape down the right side of his face, and she knew from Megan that he had a vicious foot-long graze from midway down his right buttock to the top of his thigh. It was ironic that his was the only injury sustained by both professional and amateur racers alike, and that it had happened when he'd tumbled off his bike going down an exceptionally easy hill in the amateur race.

It made no sense. Cale could navigate the amateur route with his eyes closed.

He and Megan and the twins, and Alex and the other two of the three Grant triplets, all wearing T-shirts sporting Oliver's naughty face, had taken on roles for the race: chatting to celebs and amateur racers alike, soliciting donations from the spectators and chivvying people along. They'd been great, and had brought a personal element to the race that Maddie felt was frequently missing from a lot of charity events.

Maddie, standing offstage, allowed her tired eyes to track over the Grant family, standing in one cohesive bunch next to Cale on the stage. His family...standing together as they always did. There wasn't much she wouldn't give to be part of that clan.

Maddie tuned in to what Cale was saying.

'They say that most people know how you seem but only some people know who you *are*. Oliver absolutely knew me. One of my favourite memories is of the two of us naked, hanging upside down from a tree branch. We were six, and while I was trying to cover up Ol let everything dangle. Even then he had made the choice to live life at full throttle. I feel his presence every day of my life and I miss him constantly. His sons remind me of his humour, his spirit, his enormous capacity for adventure. His colleagues and friends remind me how much he was loved. His death reminds me that I might not always have the time to love, to live, to be happy.'

Maddie swallowed, fighting tears. She saw Megan bury her head in Alex's shoulder and gulped.

'Oliver died of leukaemia two years ago today. He was an adventurer, in heart and body, and I have to tell you he is rolling on the floor laughing at my stupid injury. He'd also be so proud of what we—all of us—from his family, the volunteers and the racers—have done today. He'd say that we kicked racing's butt.' Cale pulled a face. 'Well, probably not as diplomatically as that.'

All the racers laughed, obviously remembering Oliver's filthy language.

'We've raised a considerable amount of money for our chosen charities, and there is one person more than anyone else who made this happen. Maddie Shaw, the only love of my life, has worked tirelessly on this project, has sweated blood and tears to do this. Mads, thank you.'

Maddie had got stuck on the 'only love of my life' comment and didn't hear the rest of his speech. Then Cale, a huge bouquet in his hand, gingerly stepped off the podium and handed her the flowers.

'Why didn't you tell me you didn't take the job?' Cale demanded as he thrust the bouquet in her general direction.

'You didn't ask.' Maddie took the flowers he was waving in front of her nose.

'You still could've told me. I've been in hell!'

He'd been in hell…? Maddie couldn't believe that the first proper conversation they'd had in weeks was starting off as an argument. Why wasn't he explaining what he meant by that comment?

'I asked how the interview went!' Cale said as he grabbed her hand and pulled her away from his family and the surge of

people heading their way. He dragged her around the back of
the clubhouse that was their base for the race, and when they
were finally alone dropped her hand. 'Well?'

'I said that it went fine. And it did. They offered me the job
but I didn't take it.' Maddie squished his flowers to her chest.
'What *is* your problem?'

Cale closed his eyes. 'I'm sore and I'm…emotional. I want
a hot shower and a handful of painkillers. And you. Most of all
I just want you back.'

Maddie cocked her head and held back a smile. 'Really?'

'Yeah. Let's go home.'

Maddie shook her head, wishing she could drop everything
and take him in her arms. 'I can't just leave, Cale. My job isn't
finished. I need to organise the clean-up. Pay some suppliers.'

'Megan said she'd do it.' Cale leant his forehead against hers.
'I can't sit and I can't drive. I haven't slept properly for weeks.
Take me home, Mads. Please.'

The next morning Maddie turned over and rolled in her bed. She
stretched out a leg and cautiously felt around. Judging by the
light peeking around the edges of the dark curtains it was mid-
morning-ish and there was no male leg or male anything else in
the immediate vicinity. She knew that Cale had climbed into bed
with her at one point, briefly waking her up when he pulled her
into his arms. Maddie sighed and rolled onto her back, thinking.

After checking with Megan that she could manage the rest
of her duties for the race Maddie had bargained with Cale, saying she'd take him back to her flat—his house was chock-full
of visiting family—but only if he first visited the medical tent.
He'd turned the air blue as the medics had picked dirt and gravel
out of his skin and disinfected his grazes. Alex, outwardly there
to mock him, had also checked him over for pulled ligaments
and given him an injection for pain, warning that it might make
him woozy.

It had been past eight when Alex had helped him to his Range
Rover, where Cale had lain on the back seat and promptly passed
out. It had been an effort to wake him up, and then she had bul-

lied, cajoled and at times lugged him up the steps to her flat. She'd got him as far as her biggest couch and left him there, with a down duvet to keep him from freezing.

She'd stumbled to her room and after a brief shower tumbled into bed. Immediately she'd fallen deeply asleep. Cale wasn't the only one who hadn't slept much lately.

Now, her heart galloping, she peeked around her bedroom door and swallowed a whistle at the tsunami that had obviously hit her small kitchen. Maddie lifted her eyebrows; this was so unlike Cale's usual meticulous style of cooking.

'What on earth are you doing?' Maddie asked him, briefly resting a hand on his back.

Cale sent her a frustrated look. 'Eggs. Bacon. I thought you deserved a greasy breakfast.'

Maddie ducked behind him and lifted the lid on a saucepan. She hid her grimace from Cale. Burnt bacon rashers lay in congealed grease. In another pan oil sputtered. Surreptitiously she turned off the heat.

'Bit distracted, aren't you?' Maddie grinned at his surly face before lifting her hand to briefly touch his cheek.

'Yes, well, I've been waiting for you to wake up for…for *ever*!'

'You could have just woken me up,' Maddie said, dunking the smoking pan in the sink. She turned back to him and lifted the back of his brief running shorts, wincing at the foot long purple-black bruise and the still-bloody graze. No wonder he was wearing shorts on a grey winter's day. He wouldn't want any material near his damaged skin.

'Cale! That looks really sore.'

'It is—and it's all your fault, by the way. That's what happens when I think about you rather than about what's in front of me, like a tree root.'

'I knew that you'd somehow blame it on me,' Maddie grumbled as she dropped the fabric of his pants. 'I assumed we were very over.'

'Well, you assumed wrong,' Cale muttered as he turned away to open her fridge to stare inside. He closed it again without removing an item and leaned his shoulder against it. 'Why didn't you take the job?'

'How did you find out?'

'You told Gigi. Gigi told Alex. Alex told me as we were going down that hill and I, literally, fell off my bike.'

'Oh.'

'Well?'

'I left my heart in Africa,' Maddie simply said. 'I came home, looked at my life and made a few changes. Let's forget about breakfast and have some coffee.'

Maddie quickly put two cups under the spout of the coffee machine and hit the button. Doctoring them quickly, she handed Cale a cup, took his hand and pulled him towards the couch. Sitting down next to him, she kept his hand in hers, searching for something to say.

Cale beat her to it. 'What changes?'

Inside she was screaming. *Explain what you meant about me being the only love of your life!* She pulled her attention back to his question and told him that she'd handed Harriet her resignation.

Cale stared at his feet. 'Are you okay with that?'

'Absolutely! I think I'm starting my own business, since I already have an offer to organise a rather high-profile event.'

'Oh, well…good. What?'

Maddie started to laugh. 'Gigi's thirtieth birthday party.'

'What? *My* Gigi?'

'You are going to *have* to stop calling her that!' Maddie exclaimed. 'I met her at the charity dinner and she offered me the job. I called her when I got back and said that I was going out on my own, and she said that she'd be my first client.' Maddie placed her cup on the table and curled her legs under her. 'I must say it will be the party of the year by the time we're done.' Maddie flashed a grin. 'Actually, I quite like her.'

'I have great taste in women,' Cale dead-panned. 'Where are you going to work from?'

Maddie shrugged. 'Not sure yet.'

'Move in with me and use this place as your office,' Cale

suggested. 'Or use my study. Or I'll convert another room for you. When are you moving in?'

Maddie's eyes laughed at him. 'I'll think about it,' she teased.

'You won't!' Cale clasped her face in his hands. 'I've missed you so damn much.'

'Well, you could've fooled me,' Maddie told him. She tipped her head. 'What would you have done if I had taken the job, Cale?'

'Cried, begged, grovelled. I was planning on doing all three,' Cale told her. 'It wouldn't have been pretty. I'd have followed you there. I'm glad you didn't, Mad, you belong here. With me.'

Maddie placed her fingers on his lips. 'Are we still talking about a no-strings affair?'

Cale kissed them. 'Hell, no! Come live with me, Mad. I'll make you happy, I promise.'

'Only if you'll stop hounding me about exercising—' Maddie ran her fingers along his jaw.

'No.'

Maddie scooted forward and placed her mouth close to his. 'Not quite so many vegetables?'

'You've got to start eating like an adult at some point.' Cale's hands slid around her hips, over her bottom.

'Okay.'

Cale grinned, love and laughter—relief—in his eyes. His eyebrows lifted when Maddie scooted away. 'And now?'

Maddie returned two minutes later, holding a scarlet low-scooped dress to her chest. She twirled around. 'What do you think?'

'Nice. But why are we looking at dresses?' Cale asked, utterly confused.

Maddie grinned, tossed the dress over the nearest chair and snuggled into his side again. 'It's my red dress. I'm allergic to white weddings. You know…just in case…some day.'

Cale's coffee cup rocked dangerously in his shaky hand. He carefully put it down on the table and pulled away. 'Are you saying that you'll marry me?'

'I think so.'

'Um…why?'

'Your beautiful eyes, your Ducati, I love your house—' Maddie yelped as Cale tickled her ribs in an effort to get her to be serious. She looked into his beloved familiar face, her heart in her eyes. 'I love you. You are my soft place to fall,' she told him quietly. 'It's always been you. My first and last.'

Maddie smiled at him when he remained silent, not fazed by his lack of response, perfectly at peace. This was going to work out. She'd have her happy-ever-after.

After all, she'd worked really hard for it.

Maddie held her breath as Cale tipped his head back and stared at the ceiling. 'I don't know what to say. You take my breath away, Madison.'

'You don't have to say anything.'

Cale squinted at her. 'Isn't this fun? I've rehearsed this a hundred times. For a public speaker and a writer, I *suck* at this!'

Maddie stifled a laugh. 'Now, don't get sarcastic just because you can't express your feelings,' she teased.

Cale sent her an exasperated look. 'I *can* express my feelings! Just give me a moment. I'm waiting for my brain to restart after the red dress comment.'

Maddie grinned. She hoped she'd always be able to keep him a little off-balance. Then she took pity on him. 'It's okay, I don't need the words. But some time in the future I still expect a proposal and a socking big ring—because I *do* want it all.'

Cale pushed her hair off her forehead as a strange, tender look crossed his face. 'You need the words, Mad, more than anyone I've ever known. So here are your words.' He swallowed and they poured out in a rush. 'Love, commitment, devotion, fidelity. Utterly, irrevocably, totally. For ever.'

Maddie's chin dropped. 'Wow.'

'Is that expressive enough?'

'You really do love me?'

'Yeah, I really do. God help me, because I know you will drive me crazy.'

Maddie laughed through her tears and touched his lips with her fingers.

Cale pulled his head back to look at her, and his love and relief were easy to see in his eyes. Ten years, Maddie thought. But
he was so worth the wait.

Talking about waiting—it had been far too long since he'd
had her hands on her body...

Maddie ran her hands down his back and over his buttocks
in a silent invitation. She jumped skywards when Cale let out
a whoop of pain.

'Ow! Dammit, sport! Watch my butt!'

Maddie dropped her face into his neck and giggled. 'Oh,
Cale, I plan on watching it for a long, long time. Sixty, seventy
years...for ever.'

'I can live with that. Now, if you move your hand this way
I feel no pain...'

EPILOGUE

Six months later...

MADDIE, lounging in the corner of the couch on the veranda, watched as Cale bounded up the steps to her after his afternoon run on the beach with the dogs. Her stomach started to freefall as Cale sent her that slow, melting sexy grin while he unhooked Marilyn's leash.

After dropping a long sigh-making kiss on her mouth, he took the mug from her hands and took a healthy sip, lifting his eyebrows when he realized that he was drinking chamomile tea. 'Are you feeling all right?'

Maddie tipped her head and settled her hand on his thigh as he dropped into the seat next to her. She wrinkled her nose. 'I didn't feel like coffee. Or wine.'

'It's official. The world has stopped turning,' Cale teased. He placed the cup on the coffee table and shook his head as Marilyn flopped down on the tiles in front of them, her once golden now tinted hindquarters in the air. 'She's still pink.'

'It's fading...' Maddie protested, hiding her grin.

Cale shook his head. 'I still don't understand where the twins got the idea to put red food colouring in the pool. How would they *know* that?'

'They are smart kids,' Maddie said, choking back her laughter. One of these days she'd have to tell him that she'd helped the twins temporarily turn the water from a sparkling blue to a blood-red. And a blonde dog to pink...

Maddie kicked off her heels and placed her bare feet on the coffee table. 'Well, maybe the twins are a practice run. A test to see how we'll cope with our kids.'

'But we won't have to deal with two at once.'

'No?'

'We won't have twins,' he stated resolutely.

Maddie lifted her eyebrows. 'We won't?'

'Absolutely not! Apart from the fact that I'd need a sedative drip, twins normally skip a generation. Our kids might have twins, but not us.'

'Mmm.' Maddie scratched her chin, hiding her smile. Oh, this was going to be fun... 'I hate to point out the obvious, but Oliver and Megan had twins.'

Cale shrugged her comment away. 'A fluke, and statistically speaking the chances are minimal that we'll have any sort of multiples.' Cale patted her knee reassuringly. 'We'll have a nice quiet girl who has her mother's eyes.'

Maddie took a deep breath before speaking. 'That's really sweet, but that's not what your brother says. Or the ultrasound technician in Alex's practice.'

Cale's eyes narrowed. 'What are you talking about?'

Maddie pulled her bag towards her and removed a black-and-white photo from the side pocket. Cale, puzzled, looked at the photo and quickly back at Maddie's face.

Joy, hard and hot, flashed across his face. 'You're pregnant?' he shouted. 'Why? How? *You're pregnant*?'

'Very pregnant.' Maddie shoved a hand into her hair and gave him a shaky smile. 'As pregnant as I can possibly be.'

'Did you know? Did you suspect? Why didn't you tell me?'

'The possibility didn't even cross my mind. I skipped a period last month... I thought that was just from the stress and craziness of organising our wedding. But I've been feeling flat, and *yuck*, so I called Alex and he told me to come over. He suggested a quick pregnancy test. When that showed positive we found out that the ultrasound technician was free and she scanned me.

It all happened so quickly. I tried to call you, but you had that meeting and your mobile was off...'

Cale stared down at the photograph in his hands, a myriad of emotions moving across his face. 'Oh, Mad. When we got married I thought I couldn't be any happier, but this...a baby... with you. God, you steal my breath—every day.'

Maddie bit her lip as her eyes filled with tears. She sniffed and gestured to the photo. 'Meet your nice quiet daughter.' She leaned forward and ran a finger over the image of the three blobby kidney shapes. 'Or your nice quiet son and two hellion daughters.'

Cale's mouth fell open when he added one plus two. 'Three?'

Maddie grinned. 'Three. What did you say? Statistically speaking not much of a chance?'

Cale sat up, and Maddie saw that his knees were bouncing ever so slightly. It was amusing to see her new husband so completely unhinged.

'Oh—and Cale?'

'Mmm?'

'I love you.'

Cale looked shell shocked, so Maddie turned on the couch to face him and cupped his face in her hands. 'Breathe, darling, and listen to me. Are you breathing?'

'Barely,' Cale croaked.

'You and I, we can do anything together—even raise three kids simultaneously.'

'You don't understand! Triplets? I lived with triplets. It's craziness.'

'If your mother can raise twins and trips we can do it too.' Maddie ran her thumb over his bottom lip. 'I can move mountains with you standing next to me.'

Cale rested his forehead against hers. 'Sweetheart... Well, I knew that my life with you wouldn't be boring.'

'Tell me you're excited. I am.'

'Yes, of course I am. A baby...babies...terrified but excited.' Maddie's lips curved into a smile. 'Love me?'

'You have no idea how much.'

'Then maybe this is a good time to tell you that it was my idea to put red food colouring in the pool…'

* * * * *

THE LAST GUY SHE SHOULD CALL

JOSS WOOD

I love the idea of my characters living happily ever after, but it happens in real life too. My parents and in-laws have been married for 110 years between them. It's a huge achievement and a shining example of the commitment marriage and relationships (in whatever form they might take) require. So this book is dedicated to Frank and Rose and Mel and Elsie for showing us, and our children, how it's done.

CHAPTER ONE

Rowan Dunn sat in the hard chair on one side of the white table in an interrogation room at Sydney International Airport and reminded herself to be polite. There was no point in tangling with this little troll of an Immigration Officer; she looked as if she wanted a fight.

'Why have you come to Australia, Miss Dunn?'

As if she hadn't explained her reasons to the Immigration Officer before her—and the one before him. *Patience, Rowan.* 'I bought these netsukes in Bali…'

'These what?'

'A netsuke is a type of miniature carving that originated in the seventeenth century.' She tapped one of the fifteen ivory, wood and bone mini-sculptures that had been stripped of their protective layers of bubble wrap and now stood on the desk between them. Lord, they were beautiful: animals, figures, mythical creatures. All tiny, all perfectly carved and full of movement and character. 'These are uncommon and the owner knew they had value.'

'You bought these little carvings and yet you have no money and no means of income while you are in Australia?'

'That's because I drained my bank account and maxed out my credit cards to buy them. Some of them, I think, are rare. Seventeenth, eighteenth-century. I suspect one may be by Tamakada, circa 1775. I need to get into Sydney to get Grayson Darling, an expert on netsuke, to authenticate them and hopefully buy them from me. Then I'll have plenty of money to stay in your precious, I mean, lovely country.'

'What are they worth?'

Rowan tipped her head. 'Fifteen at an average of two thousand pounds each. So, between twenty and thirty thousand, maybe more.'

The troll's jaw dropped open. 'You've got to be...joking!' She leaned across the table and her face radiated doubt. 'I think you're spinning me a story; you look like every other free-spirited backpacker I've seen.'

Rowan, not for the first time, cursed her long, curly, wild hair and her pretty face, her battered jeans, cropped shirt and well-used backpack. 'I'm a traveller but I am also a trader. It's how I—mostly—make my living. I can show you the deed of sale for the netsuke...'

Officer troll flipped through her passport. 'What else do you sell, Miss Dunn?'

'You've gone through my rucksack with a fine-tooth comb and I've had a body search. You know that I'm clean,' Rowan said wearily. She'd been here for more than six hours—could they move on, please? *Pretty please?*

'What else do you sell, Miss Dunn?'

God! Just answer the question, Rowan, and get this over with. 'Anything I can make a profit on that's *legal*. Art, furniture, antiques. I've flipped statues in Buenos Aires, art in Belize, jewellery in Vancouver. I've worked in construction when times have been lean. Worked as a bar tender when times were leaner. But mostly I buy low and sell high.'

'Then why don't you have a slush fund? A back-up plan? Where is the profit on those deals?'

Fair question.

'A large amount is tied up in a rickety house I've just co-bought with a friend in London. We're in the process of having it renovated so that we can sell it,' Rowan admitted.

And the rest was sitting in those little statues. She knew

that at least one, maybe two, were very valuable. Her gut was screaming that the laughing Buddha statue was a quality item, that it was by a famed Japanese artist. She hadn't planned to wipe out her accounts but the shopkeeper had had a figure fixed in his head and wouldn't be budged. Since she knew that she could flip the netsukes for two or three times the amount she'd paid for them, it had seemed like a short, acceptable risk. Especially since she knew Grayson—knew that he wouldn't quibble over the price. He was the best type of collector: one with deep and heavy pockets. Pockets she couldn't help lighten unless she got into the blinking country!

'The reality is that you do not have enough money on your person to last you two days in Australia.'

'I explained that I have friends...'

The troll held up her hand. 'Your not having enough funds has made us dig a little deeper and we've found out that you overstayed the visa—by six months—on your South African passport.'

Crrr-aa-aa-p!

Rowan felt her stomach sink like concrete shoes. That had happened over eight years ago, which was why she always used her UK passport to get into Oz. She'd been into the country four times since then, but they had finally picked up on her youthful transgression.

Bye-bye to any chance of getting into Oz any time in the next three years. Hello to a very sick bank account for the foreseeable future, to doing the deal with Grayson over the phone—a situation neither of them liked—or to finding another netsuke-mad collector who would pay her well for her gems. There weren't, as she knew, many of them around.

'You are not allowed to visit Australia for the next three years and you will be on the first flight we can find back to South Africa. In a nutshell, you are being deported.'

Rowan looked up at the ceiling and blew a long stream

of air towards the ceiling. It was the only place in the world where she, actively, passionately, didn't want to go. 'Crap.'

The troll almost smiled. 'Indeed.'

Sixteen hours later Rowan cleared Immigration at OR Tambo International in Johannesburg and, after picking up her rucksack, headed for the nearest row of hard benches. Dropping her pack to the floor, she slumped down and stared at her feet.

What now?

Unlike many other cities in the world, she didn't know Johannesburg, didn't have any friends in the city. She had one hundred pounds in cash in her wallet and thirty US dollars. Practically nothing in both her savings and current accounts and her credit cards were maxed out. All thanks to that little out-of-the-way antique shop in Denpasar...

Stupid, stupid, stupid, she berated herself. What had she been thinking? She'd been thinking that she'd triple her money when she flipped them.

'Hey.'

Rowan looked up and saw a young girl, barely in her twenties, take the seat next to her.

'Do you mind if I sit here for a bit? I'm being hassled by a jerk in that group over there.'

Rowan cut a glance to a group of young men who were just drunk enough to be obnoxious. One of the pitfalls of travelling alone, she thought. How many times had she sat down next to a family or another single traveller to avoid the groping hands, the come ons and pick-up lines. 'Sure. Take a seat. Coming or going?'

'Just arrived from Sydney. I saw you on the plane; you were a couple of rows ahead of me.'

'Ah.'

'I'm catching the next flight to Durban. You?'

'Haven't the foggiest.' Rowan tried to sound cheerful

but knew that she didn't quite hit the mark. 'I was deported from Oz and I'm broke.'

Bright blue eyes sharpened in interest. 'Seriously? How broke?'

'Seriously broke.' Rowan lifted her heels up onto the seat of the bench and rested her elbows on her knees. '*C'est la vie.*' She looked at her new friend, all fresh-faced and enthusiastic. 'How long have you been travelling for?' she asked.

'Six months. I'm home for a family wedding, then I'm heading off again. You?'

'Nine years. Can I give you some advice…? What's your name?'

'Cat.'

'Cat. No matter what, always have enough money stashed away so that you have options. Always have enough cash to pay for an air ticket out of Dodge, for a couple of nights in a hostel or hotel. Trust me, being broke sucks.'

She'd always lived by that rule, but she'd been seduced by the idea of a quick return. She'd imagined that she'd be broke for a maximum of three days in Sydney and then her bank balance would be nicely inflated.

It sure hadn't worked out that way… Deported, for crying out loud! Deported and penniless! Rowan closed her eyes and wondered if she could possibly be a bigger moron.

'Can I give you a hundred pounds?' Cat asked timidly.

Rowan eyes snapped open. Her wide smile split her face and put a small sparkle back into her onyx-black eyes. 'That's really sweet of you, but no thanks, honey. I do have people I can call. I would just prefer not to.'

Look at her, Rowan thought, *all fresh and idealistic. Naïve.* If she didn't get street-wise quickly the big bad world out there would gobble her up and spit her out. Travelling in Australia was easy: same language, same culture, good transport systems and First World. Most of the world wasn't like that.

'Your folks happy with you backpacking?'

Cat raised a shoulder. 'Yeah, mostly. They have a mild moan when I call home and ask for cash, but they always come through.'

Rowan lifted dark winged eyebrows. Lucky girl. Could her circumstances be any more different from hers, when she'd left home to go on the road? Those six months between being caught in a drug raid at a club with a tiny bag of coke and catching a plane to Thailand had been sheer hell.

Two months after being tossed into jail—and she still hoped the fleas of a thousand camels were making their home in Joe's underpants for slipping the coke into the back pocket of her jeans, the rat-bastard jerk!—she'd been sentenced to four months' community service but, thanks to the fact that at the time she hadn't yet turned eighteen, her juvenile criminal record was still sealed.

Sealed from the general public, but not from her family, who hadn't reacted well. There had been shouting and desperate anger from her father, cold distance from her mother, and her elder brother had been tight-lipped with disapproval. For the rest of that year there had been weekly lectures to keep her on the straight and narrow. From proper jail she'd been placed under house arrest by her parents, and their over-the-top protectiveness had gone into hyperdrive. Her movements had been constantly monitored, and the more they'd lectured and smothered, the stronger her urge to rebel and her resolve to run had become.

She'd tried to explain the circumstances, but only her BFF Callie had realised how much it had hurt to have her story about being framed dismissed as a lie, how much it had stung to see the constant disappointment on everyone's faces. So she'd decided that she might as well be the ultimate party girl rebel—sneaking out, parties, cigarettes, crazy acting out. Anything to live up to the low expectations of her parents—especially her mother—and constantly, constantly planning her escape.

It had come the day after she'd written her final exam to finish her school career. Using cash she'd received from selling the unit trusts her grandmother had bought her every birthday since the day she was born, she'd bought a ticket to Thailand.

Everyone except Callie had been furious, and they'd all expected her to hit the other side, turn tail and run back home. That first year had been tough, lonely, and sometimes downright scary, but she'd survived and then she'd flourished.

And she really didn't want to go home with her tail tucked between her legs now, broke and recently deported.

She didn't want to lose her freedom, to step back into her family's lives, back into her parents' house, returning as the family screw-up. It didn't matter that she was asset-rich and cash-poor. She would still, in their eyes, be irresponsible and silly: no better than the confused, mixed-up child who'd left nine years before.

'So, who are you going to call?' Cat asked, breaking in on her thoughts.

'Well, I've only got two choices. My mobile's battery is dead and all my contact numbers are in my phone. I have two numbers in my head: my parents' home number and my best friend Callie's home number.'

'I vote for the best friend.'

'So would I—except that she doesn't live there any more. Her older brother does, and he doesn't like me very much.'

Cat leaned forward, curious. 'Why not?'

'Ah, well. Seb and I have always rubbed each other up the wrong way. He's conservative and studious; I'm wild and rebellious. He's mega-rich and I'm currently financially challenged—'

'What does he do?' Cat asked.

Rowan fiddled with her gold hoop earrings. 'His family have a shed-load of property in Cape Town and he oversees that. He also does something complicated with computers. He has a company that does…um…internet security? He's a nice hat… No, that doesn't sound right.'

Cat sat up suddenly. 'Do you mean a white hat? A hacker?'

Rowan cocked her finger at her. 'That's it. Apparently he's one of the best in the world.'

'Holy mackerel…that is so cool! I'm a bit of a comp geek myself.'

'So is he. He's a complete nerd and we've always clashed. He's book-smart and I'm street-smart. His and Callie's house is within spitting distance of my parents' house and I spent more time there than I did at home. I gave him such a hard time.'

Cat looked intrigued. 'Why?'

'Probably because I could never get a reaction out of him. He'd just look at me, shake his head, tell me I was a brat and flip me off. The more I misbehaved, the more he ignored me.' Rowan wound a black curl around her index finger.

'Sounds to me like you were craving his attention.'

'Honey, I craved *everyone's* attention,' Rowan replied.

This was one of the things she loved most about travelling, she thought. Random conversations with strangers who didn't know her from Adam.

'Anyway, I could bore you to death, recounting all the arguments I had with Seb.' Rowan smiled. 'So let this be a lesson to you, Cat. Remember, always have a stash of cash. Do as I say and not as I do.'

'Good luck,' Cat called as she walked towards the bank of public phones against the far wall.

Rowan lifted her hand in acknowledgement. She sure as hell was going to need it.

* * *

Seb Hollis shot up in bed and punched the comforter and the sheets away, unable to bare the constricting fabric against his heated skin. He was conscious of the remnants of a bad dream floating around the periphery of his memory, and as much as he tried to pretend otherwise it wasn't the cool air colliding with the sweat on his chest and spine that made him shiver. The blame for that could be laid squarely at the door of this now familiar nocturnal visitor. He'd been dreaming the same dream for six days... He was being choked, restrained, hog-tied...yanked up to the altar and forced into marriage.

Balls, was his first thought, closely followed by, *Thank God it was only a dream.*

Draping one forearm across his bended knees, Seb ran a hand behind his neck. He was sweating like a geyser and his mouth was as dry as the Kalahari Desert. Cursing, he fumbled for the glass of water on the bedside table, grimacing at the handprint his sweat made on the deep black comforter.

Habit had him turning his head, expecting to see his lover's head on the other pillow. Relief pumped through him when he remembered that Jenna had left for a year-long contract in Dubai and that he was officially single again. He didn't have to explain the nightmare, see her hurt face when he wouldn't talk about the soaked sheets or his pumping breath. Like most women, and despite her corporate career, Jenna had a need to nurture.

He'd never been nurtured and he had no need to be fussed over. It wasn't who he was, what he needed.

Besides, discussing his dreams—emotions, thoughts, desires—would be amusing in the same way an electric shock to his gonads would be nice. Not going to happen. *Ever.*

Intimacy hadn't been part of the deal with Jenna.

Intimacy would never be part of the deal with anyone.

Seb swung his legs off the side of the large bed, reached for the pair of running shorts on the chair next to the bed and yanked them on. He walked over to the French doors that opened onto the balcony. Pushing them open, he sucked in the briny air of the late summer, early autumn air. Tinges of the new morning peeked through the trees that bordered the side and back edges of his property: Awelfor.

He could live anywhere in the world, but he loved living a stone's throw from Cape Town, loved living at the tip of the continent in a place nestled between the mountains and the sea. In the distance, behind those great rolling waves that characterised this part of the west coast, the massive green-grey icy Atlantic lay: sulky, turbulent, volatile. Or maybe he was just projecting his crappy mood on the still sleepy sea.

Jenna. Was *she* what his crazy dreams were about? Was he dreaming about commitment because he'd been so relieved to wave her goodbye? To get out of a relationship that he'd known was going nowhere but she had hoped was? He'd told her, as often and as nicely as he could, that he wouldn't commit, but he knew that she'd hoped he'd change his mind, really hoped that he'd ask her to stay in the country.

It hadn't seemed to matter that they'd agreed to a no-strings affair, that she'd said she understood when he'd explained that he didn't do love and commitment.

Women. *Sheez.* Sometimes they just heard what they wanted to hear.

Seb cocked his head when the early-morning silence was shattered by the distinctive deep-throated roar of a Jag turning into the driveway to Awelfor. *Here we go again,* he thought. The engine was cut, a car door slammed and within minutes he saw his father walking the path to the cottage that stood to the left of the main house.

It was small consolation that he wasn't the only Hollis

man with woman troubles. At least his were only in his head. *Single again,* he reminded himself. Bonus.

'Another one bites the dust?' he called, and his father snapped his head up.

Patch Hollis dropped his leather bag to the path and slapped his hands on his hips.

'When am I going to learn?'

'Beats me.' Seb rested his forearms on the balcony rail. 'What's the problem with this one?'

'She wants a baby,' Patch said, miserable. 'I'm sixty years old; why would I want a child now?'

'She's twenty-eight, dude. Of course she's going to want a kid. Have you told her you've had a vasectomy?'

Patch gestured to the bag. 'Hence the reason I'm back in the cottage. She went bat-crap ballistic.'

'Uh…why do you always leave? It's your house and you're not married.' Seb narrowed his eyes as a horrible thought occurred to him. 'You didn't slink off and marry her, did you?'

Patch didn't meet his eyes. 'No, but it was close.'

Seb rubbed his hand over his hair, which he kept short to keep the curls under control, and muttered an expletive.

'Don't swear at me. You had your own little gold-digger you nearly married,' Patch shot back, and Seb acknowledged the hit.

He'd been blindsided when he'd raised the issue of marriage contracts and his fiancée Bronwyn wouldn't consider signing a pre-nup. Like most things he did, he'd approached the problem of the marriage contracts intellectually, rationally. *He* had the company and the house and the cash, and pretty much everything of monetary value, so *he'd* be the one to hand over half of everything if they divorced.

Bronwyn had not seen his point of view. If he *loved* her, she'd screamed, he'd share everything with her. He *had* loved Bronwyn—sorta…kinda—but not enough to risk sharing his company with her or paying her out for half the value of the house that had been in his family for four generations in the event of a divorce.

They'd both dug their heels in and the break-up had been bruising.

It had taken him a couple of years, many hours with a whisky bottle and a shattered heart until he'd—mostly—worked it all out. He believed in thinking through problems—including personal failures—in order to come to a better understanding of the cause and effect.

It was highly probable that he'd fallen for Bronwyn because she was, on the surface, similar in behaviour and personality to his mother. A hippy child who flitted from job to job, town to town. A supposed free spirit whom he'd wanted—no, *needed* to tame. Since his mother had left some time around his twelfth birthday to go backpacking round the world, and had yet to come home, he'd given up hope that he'd ever get her love or approval, that she'd return and stay put. He'd thought that if he could get Bronwyn to settle down, to commit to him, then maybe it would fill the hole his mother had left.

Yeah, right.

But he'd learnt a couple of lessons from his FUBAR engagement. Unlike his jobs—internet security expert and overseeing the Hollis Property Group—he couldn't analyse, measure or categorise relationships and emotions, and he sure didn't understand women. As a result he now preferred to conduct his relationships at an emotional distance. An at-a-distance relationship—sex and little conversation—held no risk of confusion and pain and didn't demand much from him. He'd forged his emotional armour when his mum had left so very long ago and strengthened it after his experience with Bronwyn. He liked it that way. There was no chance of his heart being tossed into a liquidiser.

His father, Peter Pan that he was, just kept it simple:

blonde, long-legged and big boobs. Mattress skills were a prerequisite; intelligence wasn't.

'So, can I move back in until she moves out?' Patch asked.

'Dad, Awelfor is a Hollis house; legally it's still yours. But I should warn you that Yasmeen is on holiday; she's been gone for nearly a week and I've already eaten the good stuff she left.'

Patch looked wounded. 'So no blueberry muffins for breakfast?'

'Best you're going to get is coffee. No laundry or bed-making service either,' Seb replied.

Patch looked bereft and Seb knew that it had nothing to do with his level of comfort and everything to do with the absence of their elderly family confidant, their moral compass and their staunchest supporter. Yasmeen was more than their housekeeper, she *was* Awelfor.

'Yas being gone sucks.' Patch yawned. 'I'm going back to bed, Miranda has a voice like a foghorn and I was up all night being blasted by it.'

Seb turned his head at the sound of his ringing landline. 'Crazy morning. Father rocking up at the crack of dawn, phone ringing before six…and all I want is a cup of coffee.'

Patch grinned up at him. 'I just want my house back.'

Seb returned his smile. 'Then kick her whiny ass out of yours.'

Patch shuddered. 'I'll just move in here until she calms down.'

His father, Seb thought as he turned away to walk back into the house, was totally allergic to confrontation.

'Seb, it's Rowan…Rowan Dunn.'

He'd recognised her voice the moment he'd heard her speak his name, but because his synapses had stopped fir-

ing he'd lost the ability to formulate any words. *Rowan?
What the...?*

'Seb? Sorry, did I wake you?'

'Rowan, this is a surprise.' And by surprise I mean...
wow.

'I'm in Johannesburg—at the airport.'

Since this was Rowan, he passed curious and went
straight to resigned. 'What's happened?'

He would have had to be intellectually challenged to
miss the bite in the words that followed.

'Why do you automatically assume the worst?'

'Because something major must have happened to bring
you back to the country you hate, where the family you've
hardly interacted with in years lives and for you to call *me*,
who you once described as a boil on the ass of humanity.'

He waited through the tense silence.

'I'm temporarily broke and homeless. And I've just been
deported from Oz,' she finally—very reluctantly—admitted.

And there it was.

'Are you in trouble?' He kept his voice neutral and hoped
that she was now adult enough to realise that it was a fair
question. For a long time before she'd left trouble had been
Rowan's middle name. Heck, her first name.

'No, I'm good. They just picked up that I overstayed
on my visa years and years ago and they kicked me out.'

Compared to some of the things she'd done, this was
a minor infringement. Seb walked to his walk-in closet,
took a pair of jeans from a hanger and yanked them on.
He placed his fist on his forehead and stared down at the
old wood flooring.

'Seb, are you there?'

'Yep.'

'Do you know where my parents are? I did try them but
they aren't answering their phone.'

'They went to London and rented out the house while they were gone to some visiting researchers from Beijing. They are due back in...' Seb tried to remember. 'Two—three—weeks' time.'

'You've got to be kidding me! My parents went overseas and the world didn't stop turning? How is that possible?'

'That surprised me, too,' Seb admitted.

'And is Callie still on that buying trip?'

'Yep.'

Another long silence. 'In that case...tag—you're it. I need a favour.'

From him? He looked at his watch and was surprised to find that it was still ticking. Why hadn't time stood still? He'd presumed it would—along with nuns being found ice skating in hell—since Rowan was asking for *his* help.

'I thought you'd rather drip hot wax in your eye than ever ask me for anything again.'

'Can you blame me? You could've just bailed me out of jail, jerk-face.'

And...hello, there it was: the tone of voice that had irritated him throughout his youth and into his twenties. Cool, mocking...nails-on-a-chalkboard irritating.

'Your parents didn't want me to—they were trying to teach you a lesson. And might I point out that calling me names is not a good way to induce me to do anything for you, Rowan?'

Seb heard her mutter a swear word and he grinned. Oh, he did like having her at his mercy.

'What do you want, Brat?'

Brat—his childhood name for her. Callie, so blonde, had called her Black Beauty, or BB for short, on account of her jet-black hair and eyes teamed with creamy white skin. She'd been a knockout, looks-wise, since the day she'd been born. Pity she had the personality of a rabid honey badger.

Brat suited her a lot better, and had the added bonus of annoying the hell out of her.

'When is Callie due back?'

He knew why she was asking: she'd rather eat nails than accept help from *him*. Since his sister travelled extensively as a buyer for a fashion store, her being in the country was not always guaranteed. 'End of the month.'

Another curse.

'And Peter—your brother—is still in Bahrain,' Seb added, his tone super pointed as he reached for a shirt and pulled it off its hanger.

'I know that. I'm not completely estranged from my family!' Rowan rose to take the bait. 'But I didn't know that my folks were planning a trip. They never go anywhere.'

'They made the decision to go quite quickly.' Seb walked back into his bedroom and stared at the black and white sketches of desert scenes above his rumpled bed. 'So, now that you definitely know that I'm all you've got, do you want to tell me what the problem is?'

She sucked in a deep breath. 'I need to get back to London and I was wondering whether you'd loan…'

When pigs flew!

'No. I'm not lending you money.'

'Then buy me a ticket…'

'Ah, let me think about that for a sec? Mmm…no, I won't buy you a ticket to London either.'

'You are such a sadistic jerk.'

'But I *will* pay for a ticket for you to get your bony butt back home to Cape Town.'

Frustration cracked over the line as he listened to the background noise of the airport. 'Seb, I can't.'

Hello? Rowan sounding contrite and beaten…? He'd thought he'd never live to see the day. He didn't attempt to snap the top button of his jeans; it required too much processing power. Rowan was home and calling him. And sounding reasonable. Good God.

He knew it wouldn't last—knew that within ten minutes of being in each other's company they'd want to kill each other. They were oil and water, sun and snow, fire and ice.

Seb instinctively looked towards the window and saw his calm, ordered, structured life mischievously flipping him off before waving goodbye and belting out of the window.

Free spirits...why was he plagued with them?

'Make a decision, B.'

She ignored his shortening of the name he'd called her growing up. A sure sign that she was running out of energy to argue.

'My mobile is dead, I have about a hundred pounds to my name and I don't know anyone in Johannesburg. Guess I'm going to get my butt on a plane ho...to Cape Town.'

'Good. Hang on a sec.' Seb walked over to the laptop that stood on a desk in the corner of his room and tapped the keyboard, pulling up flights. He scanned the screen.

'First flight I can get you on comes in at six tonight. Your ticket will be at the SAA counter. I'll meet you in the airport bar,' Seb told her.

'Seb?'

'Yeah?'

'That last fight we had about Bronwyn...'

It took him a moment to work out what she was talking about, to remember her stupid, childish gesture from nearly a decade ago.

'The one where you presumed to tell me how and what to do with my life?'

'Well, I *was* going to apologise—'

'That would be a first.'

'But you can shove it! And you, as you well know, have told *me* what to do my entire life! I might have voiced some comments about your girlfriend, but I didn't leave a mate to rot in jail,' Rowan countered, her voice heating again.

'We were never mates, and it was a weekend—not a lifetime! And you bloody well deserved it.'

'It was still mean and...'

Seb rolled his eyes and made a noise that he hoped sounded like a bad connection. 'Sorry, you're breaking up...'

'We're on a landline, you dipstick!' Rowan shouted above the noise he was making.

Smart girl, he thought as he slammed the handset back into its cradle. She'd always been smart, he remembered. And feisty.

It seemed that calling her Brat was still appropriate. Some things simply never changed.

CHAPTER TWO

SIX HOURS LATER and it was another airport, another set of officials, another city and she was beyond exhausted. Sweaty, grumpy and... Damn it. Rowan pushed her fist into her sternum. She was nervous.

Scared spitless.

It could be worse, she told herself as she slid onto a stool in the busy bar, her luggage at her feet. She could be standing at Arrivals flicking over faces and looking for her parents. She could easily admit that Seb was the lesser of two evils—that she'd been relieved when her parents hadn't answered her call, that she wasn't remotely sure of their reaction to her coming home.

Apart from the occasional grumble about her lack of education they'd never expressed any wish for her to return to the family fold. They might—and she stressed *might*—be vaguely excited to see her again, but within a day they'd look at her with exasperation, deeply puzzled by the choices she'd made and the lifestyle she'd chosen.

'So different from her sibling,' her mother would mutter. *'Always flying too close to the sun. Our changeling child, our rebel, always trying to break out and away.'*

Maybe if they hadn't wrapped her in cotton wool and smothered her in a blanket of protectiveness she'd be more...normal, Rowan thought. A little more open to putting down roots, to having relationships that lasted longer than a season, furniture that she owned rather than temporarily used.

She'd caused them a lot of grief, she admitted. She'd been a colicky baby, a hell-on-wheels toddler, and then she'd contracted meningitis at four and been in ICU for two weeks, fighting for her life. After the meningitis her family had been so scared for her, so terrified that something bad would happen to her—again—that they hadn't let her experience life at all. All three of them—parents and her much older brother—had hovered over her: her own phalanx of attack helicopters, constantly scanning the environment for trouble.

The weird thing was that while she'd always felt protected she hadn't always felt cherished. Would her life have taken a different turn if she had felt treasured, loved, not on the outside looking in?

It hadn't helped that she'd been a fiery personality born into a family of quiet, brilliant, introverts. Two professors—one in music, the other in theoretical science—and her brother had a PhD in electrical engineering. She'd skipped university in order to go travelling—an unforgivable sin in the Dunn household.

The over-protectiveness had been tedious at ten, irritating at fourteen, frustrating at sixteen. At seventeen it had become intolerable, and by the time she was nearly eighteen she'd been kicking and screaming against the silken threads of parental paranoia that had kept her prisoner.

After spending that weekend in jail she'd realised that to save herself and her relationship with her family she had to run far away as fast as she could. She couldn't be the tame, studious, quiet daughter they needed her to be, and they couldn't accept her strong-willed adventurous spirit.

Running away had, strangely enough, saved her relationship with her parents. Through e-mail, social media and rare, quick phone calls they'd managed to find a bal-

ance that worked for them. They could pretend that she
wasn't gallivanting around the world, and she could pretend that they supported her quest to do more, see more,
experience more.

They all lied to themselves, but it was easier that way.

Now she was back, and they couldn't lie and she couldn't
pretend. They had to see each other as they now were—not
the way they wished they could be. It was going to suck
like rotten lemons.

Rowan hauled in a deep breath… She had two, maybe
three weeks to wrap her head around seeing her parents, to
gird herself against their inevitable disappointment. Two
weeks to find a place to stay and a job that would keep her
in cereal and coffee and earn her enough money to tide her
over until she sold her netsukes.

She just had to get past Seb—whom she'd never been
able to talk her away around, through or over. He'd never
responded to her charm, had seen through her lies, and had
never trusted her for a second.

He'd always been far too smart for his own good.

The image of Seb as she'd last seen him popped into her
head. Navy eyes the colour of deep denim, really tall, curly
blond hair that he grew long and pulled back into a bushy
tail with a leather thong, and that ultra-stupid soul patch.

Yet he'd still turned female heads. Something about
him had always caught their attention. It was not only his
good looks—and, while she wished otherwise, she had to
admit that even at his most geeky he *was* a good-looking
SOB—he had that I-prefer-my-own-company vibe that had
woman salivating.

Live next door to him and see how you like him then,
Rowan had always wanted to yell. *He's bossy and rude, patronising and supercilious, and frequently makes me want
to poke him with a stick.*

Rowan draped her leg over her knee and turned her head

at deep-throated male laughter. Behind her a group of guys stood in a rough circle and she caught the eye of the best-looking of the bunch, who radiated confidence.

Mmm. Cute.

'Hey,' Good-looking said, in full flirt mode. 'New in town?'

I'm tired, sweaty, grumpy and I suspect that I may be way too old for you.

'Sort of.'

Good-looking looked from her to the waiter standing next to him. 'Can I buy you a drink? What would you like?'

A hundred pounds would be useful, Rowan thought. *Two hundred would be better...*

'Thanks. A glass of white wine? Anything dry,' she responded. Why not? If he wanted to buy her a drink, she could live with it. Besides, she badly needed the restorative powers of fermented grape juice.

He turned, placed the order with the waiter, and when Rowan looked again she saw that he wasn't quite so young, not quite so cocky. Tall, dark and handsome. And, since she was bored waiting for Seb, she might as well have a quick flirt. Nothing picked a girl up and out of the doldrums quicker than a little conversation with a man with appreciation in his eyes.

She thought flirting was a fine way to pass the time...

Rowan pushed a hand through her hair and looked at the luggage at their feet. 'Sports tour? Hmm, let me guess... rugby?' Rowan pointed to the bags on the floor with their identical logos. 'Under twenty-one rugby sevens tournament?'

'Ah... They are under twenty-one...I'm not.'

Rowan smiled slowly. 'Me neither. I'm Rowan.'

She was about to put her hand out for him to shake when a voice spoke from behind her.

'Isn't it about time you used your powers for good instead of evil?'

Rowan closed her eyes as the words, words not fit to speak aloud, jumped into her head. Knowing that she couldn't keep her eyes shut for ever, she took a deep breath and slowly turned around.

He was leaning against the stone pillar directly behind her, those dark blue eyes cool. His lower jaw was covered in golden stubble and his mouth was knife-blade-thin.

That hadn't changed.

A lot else had. She squinted... Tall, blond, built. Broad shoulders, slim hips and long, long legs. He was a big slab of muscled male flesh. When his mouth pulled up ever so slightly at the corners she felt a slow, seductive throb deep in her womb... Oh, dear. Was that lust? It couldn't be lust. That was crazy. It had just been a long trip, and she hadn't eaten much, and she was feeling a little light-headed... It was life catching up with her.

Mr Good-looking was quickly forgotten as she looked at Seb. She'd known a lot of good-looking men, and some devastatingly handsome men, but pure lust had never affected her before... Was that why her blood was chasing her heart around her body? Where had the saliva in her mouth disappeared to? And—oh, dear—why was her heart now between her legs and pulsing madly?

Rowan pushed a long curl out of her eyes and, unable to meet his eyes just yet, stared at his broad chest. Her gaze travelled down his faded jeans to his expensive trainers. Pathetic creature to get hot and flustered over someone she'd never even liked.

Hoo, boy. Was that a hint of ink she saw on the bicep of his right arm under his T-shirt? No way! Conservative Seb? Geeky Seb?

Except that geeky Seb had been replaced by hunky Seb, who made her think of cool sheets and hot male skin under her hands… This Seb made her think of passion-filled nights and naughty afternoon sex. Of lust, heat and attraction.

Thoughts at the speed of light dashed through her head as she looked for an explanation for her extreme reaction. She was obviously orgasm-deprived, she decided. She hadn't had sex for….oh, way too long. Right! If that was the problem—and she was sure it was—there was, she re-membered, a very discreet little shop close to home that could take care of it.

Except that she was broke… Rowan scowled at her shoes. Broke and horny…what a miserable combination. Yet it was the only explanation that made a smidgeon of sense.

Seb stopped in front of her and jammed his hands into the pockets of very nicely fitting jeans.

'Brat.'

His voice rumbled over her, prickling her skin.

Yep, there was the snotty devil she remembered. Under that luscious masculine body that looked and—oh, my—smelled so good. It was in those deep eyes, in the vibration of his voice. The shallow dimple in his right cheek. The grown-up version of the studious, serious boy who had ei-ther tolerated, tormented or loathed her at different stages of her life. Always irritating.

'I have a name, Seb.'

He had the audacity to grin at her. 'Yeah, but you know I prefer mine.' He looked over at Mr Good-looking and his smile was shark-sharp. 'Lucky escape for you, bro'. She's trouble written in six-foot neon.'

As rugby-boy turned away with a disappointed sigh, inside his head Seb placed his hands on his thighs and pulled in deep, cleansing, calming breaths of pure oxygen. He felt as if his heart wanted to bungee-jump from his chest without a cord. His stomach and spleen were going along for the ride.

Well, wasn't *this* a kick in the head?

This was *Rowan*? What had happened to the skinny kid with a silver ring through her brow and a stud in her nose? The clothes that she had called 'boho chic' but which had looked as if she'd been shopping in Tramp's Alley? Skirts that had been little more than strips of cloth around her hips, knee-high combat boots, Goth make-up...

Now leather boots peeked out from under the hem of nicely fitting blue jeans. She wore a plain white button-down shirt with the bottom buttons open to show a broad leather belt, and a funky leather and blue bead necklace lay between the wilted collar of the shirt. Her hair was still the blue-black of a starling's wing, tumbling in natural curls down her back, and her eyes, black as the deepest African night, were faintly shadowed in blue. Her face was free of make-up and those incredible eyes—framed by dark lashes and brows—brimmed with an emotion he couldn't immediately identify.

Resignation? Trepidation and fear? Then she tossed her head and he saw pride flash in her eyes.

And there was the Rowan he remembered. He dismissed the feeling that his life was about to be impacted by this tiny dark-haired sprite with amazing eyes and a wide, mobile mouth that begged to be kissed.

He'd said goodbye to a kid, but this Rowan was all woman. A woman, if she were anyone but Rowan, he would be thinking about getting into bed. Immediately. As in grabbing her hand, finding the closest room and throwing her onto the bed, chair, floor...whatever was closer.

His inner cave man was thumping his chest. *Look here, honey! I'm a sex god!* He felt embarrassed on his own behalf. *Get a grip, dude!*

He hoped his face was devoid of all expression, but in his mind Seb tipped his head back and directed a stream of silent curses at the universe. *When I asked what else could go wrong, I meant it as a figure of speech—not as a challenge to hit me with your best shot.*

Rowan broke the uncomfortable silence. 'So…it's been a long time. You look…good.'

'You too.'

Good? Try sensational!

'Where did you fly in from?' he asked. Politeness? Good grief, they'd never been civil and he wondered how long it would last.

'Sydney. Nightmare flight, I had a screaming baby behind me and an ADD toddler in front of me. And the man in the seat next to me sniffed the entire time.'

'Two words. Business class.'

Rowan grimaced. 'One word. Broke.'

She shoved a hand into her hair, lifted and pushed a couple of loose curls off her face.

'Would you consider changing your mind about loaning me the money to get back to London?'

Rowan threw her demand into the silence between them.

Thirty seconds from polite to miffed. It had to be a record.

'Well? Will you?'

Sure—after I've sorted out climate change and negotiated world peace. 'Not a chance.'

Rowan tapped an irritated finger on the table and tried to stare him down. Seb folded his arms and kept his face blank.

Eventually her shoulders dropped in defeat. 'My mobile battery is dead, I have less than two hundred pounds to my name, my best friend is out of the country, my parents are away and their house is occupied. I'm in your hands.'

In his hands? He wished… Their eyes met and sexual attraction arced between them. Hot, hard… *Man!* Where was this coming from?

Pink stained Rowan's cheekbones. 'I mean, I'm at your mercy...'

That sounded even better.

'What is the matter with me?'

Or at least that was what he thought he heard her say, but since she was muttering to the floor he couldn't be sure.

What was cranking their sexual buzzers to a howl? *Dial it down, dude; time to start acting as an adult.* He dashed the rest of what was left in the tiny bottle of wine into her glass and tossed it back.

Think with your big head. It didn't matter that she looked hot, or that he wanted to taste that very sexy mouth, this was Rowan. AKA trouble.

Seb put his hands into the back pockets of his jeans. 'You ready to go?'

'Where to? Where am I sleeping tonight?'

'Awelfor.'

Awelfor... It meant sea breeze in Welsh, and was one of the few small holdings situated between the seaside villages of Scarborough and Misty Cliffs, practically on the doorstep of Table Mountain National Park. Her second home, Rowan thought.

The house had originally been an old school building, added to over the generations. The oldest part was made from timber and redbrick, and she could still feel the cool warmth of the Oregon pine floors beneath her bare feet. Nearly every room had a fireplace and a view of the Atlantic, with its huge rolling waves and its white beaches peppered by black-backed gulls.

She'd been raised next door, in the house that had been built by a Hollis forefather for—rumour had it—a favourite mistress. It had been sold off in the forties to her grandfather and separated from the Hollis house by a huge oak and a high, thick Eugenia hedge.

She knew Awelfor as well as she knew her own home:

which floorboard creaked if you stood on it the middle of
the night, that the drainpipe that ran past Callie's window
was strong enough to hold their combined weight, that Yasmeen the housekeeper hid her cigarettes in the flour canis-
ter at the back of the pantry. For most of her life she'd had
two homes and then she'd had none; now she bounced from
bed to bed in different accommodation establishments,
depending on her cash flow. Once or twice she'd slept on
beaches and on benches in railway stations, she remembered, even standing up.

Dots appeared behind her eyes.

Tired...so tired.

Rowan blinked furiously as the dots grew bigger and
brighter and her vision started to blur. She reached out
in Seb's direction and cool and firm fingers clasped her
clammy hand.

'What's the matter?' Seb demanded as she abruptly sat
down again. .

'Dizzy,' Rowan muttered as she shoved her head between her knees. 'Stood up too fast.'

Rowan opened her eyes and the floor rose and fell, so
she closed them again.

'Easy, Ro.'

Seb bent down in front of her and held up three fingers.
'How many?'

'Six thousand and fifty-two.'

Seb narrowed his eyes and Rowan gnawed the inside of
her lip, ignored the squirming sensation down below and
tried to act like a mature adult.

'Sorry, I'm fine. Tired. I haven't really eaten properly.
Shouldn't have had that wine.' Rowan rubbed her eyes. 'It's
just been a horrible couple of days.'

Seb let go of the hand he'd been holding and stood up,
looking away from those slim thighs in old jeans, that
mad hair and those deep, deep eyes. She had always been

gorgeous—hadn't all his friends told him that?—but for the first time in his life he saw her as something other than his sister's friend.

That felt uncomfortable and...weird.

His eyes dropped lower. Full breasts under that white cotton shirt, long fingers that were made to stroke a man's skin, long legs that could wrap around a man's hips...

This was *Rowan*, he reminded himself harshly. She was not somebody he should find attractive. He'd known her for far too long and far too well. Seb frowned, irritated that he couldn't break their eye contact. Her eyes had the impact of a fist slamming into his stomach. Those eyes— the marvellous deep dark of midnight—had amused, irritated and enthralled him. When he'd first met her he'd been a young, typical boy, and babies were deeply uncool but her eyes had captivated him. He remembered thinking they were the only redeeming feature of a demanding, squawking sprat.

Her face was thinner, her bottom rounder and her hair longer—halfway down her back. He imagined winding those curls around his fingers as he slipped inside her... Seb shook his head. They shared far too many memories, he reminded himself, a whole handful of which were bad, and they didn't like each other much.

Have you totally lost your mind?

'Let's get you home and we can argue later, when you're back to full strength.' Seb bent down and easily lifted her rucksack with one hand, picking up her large leather tote with the other. 'You okay to walk?'

Rowan stood up and pulled her bag over her shoulder. 'Sure.'

Seb briefly closed his eyes. It was a struggle not to drop her bags and bring her mouth to his.

'What's the problem now?' Rowan demanded, her tone pure acid.

He stared at the ceiling before dropping rueful eyes back to her face. 'I keep thinking that it would've been easier if you'd just stayed away.'

'Loan me the cash and I'm out of here,' she pleaded.

'I could…'

Rowan held her breath, but then Seb's eyes turned determined and the muscle in his jaw tightened. 'No. Not this time, Ro. You don't get to run.'

CHAPTER THREE

ROWAN SAT IN the passenger seat of Seb's Audi Quattro SUV as he sped down the motorway towards Cape Town. Although it was a little before eight in the evening, the sun was only just starting to drop in the sky and the motorway was buzzing with taxi drivers weaving between cars with inches to spare and shooting out the other side with toothy grins and mobiles slapped against ears.

Cape Town traffic was murder, no matter what the time of day. It came from having a freaking big mountain in the middle of the city, Seb thought. He glanced at his watch; they'd been travelling for fifteen minutes and neither of them had initiated conversation. They had another half-hour until they reached Awelfor and the silence was oppressive.

Seb braked and cursed as the traffic slowed and then came to a dead stop. Just what he needed. A traffic jam and more time in the car *not* speaking to each other. At the best of times he wasn't good at small talk, and it seemed stupid, and superfluous to try to discuss the weather or books, movies and music with Rowan.

And on that point, since it was the first time that Rowan had been in the same time zone as her parents for nearly a decade, he felt he owed it to them to keep her in the country until they got a chance to see her, hold her. Like him, they didn't wear their hearts on their sleeves, but he knew that they had to miss her, had to want her to come back. He could sympathise. He knew what it felt like, waiting for a loved one to come home.

He had never been able to understand why she didn't value her family more, why she rebelled so much. She had parents who took their jobs seriously; he and Callie had a runaway fickle mother and...Patch. As charming and entertaining as Patch was, he was more friend than father.

Rowan's parents, Heidi and Stan, had always been a solid adult presence right next door. Conservative, sure, but reliable. Intelligent, serious, responsible. On a totally different wavelength from their crazy daughter. Then again, it sounded as if Rowan operated on a completely different wavelength to most people, and he had enough curiosity to wonder what made her tick.

Since this traffic was going nowhere they had time to kill and nothing else to talk about, so he would take the opportunity to satisfy his nosiness.

He and Ro had never danced around each other, so he jumped straight in.

'I want to know why you're broke. I know that you consider yourself a free spirit, too cool to gather material possessions, but surely a woman your age should have more to her name than a hundred pounds?'

She'd known this was coming—had been bracing herself for the lecture. Because Cape Town was synonymous, in her mind, with being preached to.

Rowan pursed her lips as she looked straight ahead. Seb hadn't lost his ability to cut straight through the waffle to what he thought was important. Lord, she was too tired to tangle with that overly smart brain of his. Too weirded out by the fact that he made her ovaries want to dance the tango. What to say without sounding like a complete idiot?

Keep it simple, stupid.

'I was doing a deal and I was supposed to get paid for delivering the...the order when I got into Oz.'

'What were you peddling, Rowan?'

Seb's eyes turned to dark ice and his face hardened when she didn't answer. Of course he couldn't take that statement at face value. He needed more and naturally he assumed the worst. She knew what he was thinking...

Here we go again, Rowan thought, *back where I started.* As the memories rolled back her palms started to sweat and she felt her breath hitch. Even after so many years Seb still instinctively assumed the worst-case scenario. As her parents would... And they wondered why she hadn't wanted to come home.

'It wasn't anything illegal, Seb!'

'I never said it was.'

'I'm not an idiot or a criminal! And, while I might be unconventional, I'm not stupid. I do not traffic, carry or use drugs.' Rowan raised her voice in an effort to get him to understand.

'Calm down, Ro. For the record, back then I never believed you should have been arrested,' Seb stated, and his words finally sank in.

Rowan frowned at him as his words tumbled around her brain. 'You didn't? Why not?'

'Because while you were spoilt and vain and shallow—and you made some very bad decisions—you were never stupid.'

She couldn't argue with that—and why did it feel so good that Seb believed she was better than the way she was portrayed? Just another thing that didn't make any sense today.

But she knew that Seb's opinion was one that her parents wouldn't share.

'But, Rowan, this lifestyle of yours is crazy. You're an adult. You should not be getting kicked out of countries. You should have more than a backpack to your name. Most women your age have established a career, are considering marriage and babies...'

Shoot me now, Rowan thought. *Or shove a hot stick in my eye.* This was why she hadn't wanted to come home, why she didn't want to face the judgment of her family, friends and whatever Seb was. They'd always seen what they wanted to see and, like Seb, wouldn't question the assumption that she was terminally broke and irreversibly irresponsible.

Rowan's eyes sparked like lightning through a midnight sky. 'What a stupid thing to say! You don't know anything about me!'

'And whose fault is that? You were the one who ran out of here like your head was on fire!'

'I didn't run!' Okay, that lie sounded hollow even to her.

'Within days of writing your finals you were on a plane out of the country. You didn't discuss your plans with anybody. That's running—fast and hard.' Seb's finger tapped the steering wheel as the car rolled forward. 'What really happened that night?'

Rowan lifted her chin. 'I don't know what you mean.' He couldn't know, could he? Callie might have told him... No, she'd sworn that she wouldn't, and Callie would never, ever break her word. Seb had to be talking about her life in general and not that night she'd got arrested in particular.

That stupid, crazy, change-her-life evening, when she'd fallen from heaven to hell in a few short hours.

'Sure you do.' Seb scanned the road ahead, saw that the traffic wasn't moving and sighed. 'Something in you changed that night you were arrested... You were rebellious before, but you were never spiteful or malicious or super-sarcastic.'

Her attitude had been that of a rabid dog. In the space of one night she'd gone from being wildly in love and indescribably happy to being heartbroken, disparaged and disbelieved. That night *had* changed her life. After all, not everybody could say that they'd lost their virginity, got dumped and framed by their lover, then arrested all in the same night. And her weekend in jail had been a nightmare of epic proportions.

Was it any wonder that she equated love with the bars of a jail?

'You were never that hard before, Rowan.' Seb quietly interrupted her thoughts. 'Those last six months you fought constantly with your parents, with me, with the world.'

Rowan clenched her jaw together. Every night she'd cried herself to sleep, sick, heartsore, humiliated, and every day she'd got up to fight—literally—another day.

'Maybe I was crying because my parents, my sibling and everyone close to me left me to spend the weekend in jail when they could've bailed me out any time during the day on Friday. The party was on a Thursday night.'

'Your parents wanted to teach you a lesson,' Seb replied, his voice steady.

Rowan stared at the electronic boards above his head. 'Yeah, well, I learnt it. I learnt that I can only rely on myself, trust myself.'

When she dared to look at him again she saw that his eyes were now glinting with suppressed sympathy. Then amusement crept across his face. 'Yet here you are relying on me.'

'Well, all good things have to come to an end,' Rowan snapped back.

She was so done with being interrogated, and it had been a long time since she'd taken this amount of crap from anyone.

'So...' She smiled sweetly. 'Hooked up with any gold-diggers lately?'

Annoyance replaced sympathy in the blink of an eye. 'Sending me those sunglasses when you heard that we'd split was a very unnecessary gesture,' he said through gritted teeth.

'I know, but I thought you might need them since you finally saw the light. It took you long enough.'

'Very droll.' Seb's hands tightened on the steering wheel.

'Still annoyed that flighty, fey Rowan pegged your ex's true characteristics and you didn't?' Rowan mocked, happy to shift the focus of their conversation to him.

'Remind me again as to why I didn't leave you to beg in Jo'burg?'

'You wanted to torture me. So, are we done biting each other?'

'For now.'

As the traffic began to move Rowan watched Seb weave his way through the slower-moving vehicles to speed down the fast lane.

'Has the traffic got worse?' she asked when Seb slammed on his brakes and ducked around a truck. Her hand shot out and slammed against the dashboard. The last vestiges of colour drained from her face. 'Sebastian! Dammit, you lunatic!'

Seb flipped her a glance and then returned his attention to the road, his right hand loosely draped over the steering wheel. 'What's the problem?'

'The problem is that you missed the bumper of that car by inches!' Rowan retorted, dropping her hand. 'The traffic hasn't got worse—your driving has!'

Seb grinned. 'Don't you think it's a bit early in our relationship to start nagging?'

'Bite me.'

Seb flipped the indicator up and made a production of checking his side and rearview mirrors. He gestured to a sedan in front of him. 'Okay, brace yourself. I'm going to overtake now. Here we go.'

Rowan sighed and rolled her eyes. 'You are such a moron.'

Seb ducked around another sedan, and flew across two lanes of traffic to take the exit. Rowan leaned back in her seat, closed her eyes and thought it was ironic that she'd crossed seven lanes of motorbikes in Beijing, a solid stream of tuk-tuks in Bangalore and horrific traffic in Mexico to die in a luxury car in her home country at the hands of a crazy person.

Rowan sat up and looked around as they drove into a more upscale neighbourhood and she recognised where she was. 'Nearly ho... there.'

'Yep, nearly *home*. And, despite your inability to say the word, this *is* still your home, Ro.'

'It hasn't been my home for a third of my life,' Rowan corrected, thinking that she had a twitchy heart, a spirit that was restless, a need to keep moving. Coming back to Cape Town broke made her feel panicky, scared, not in charge of her own destiny. She felt panic well up in her throat and her vocal cords tighten.

Seb's broad hand squeezing her knee had her sucking in air. When she felt she had enough to breathe she looked at his hand and raised her eyebrows. Then she pulled her eyebrows closer together when she clocked the gleam in his eyes, the obvious glint of masculine appreciation.

'You've grown up well, Brat.'

Bemused by the sexual heat simmering between them, she tried to take refuge in being prosaic. 'I haven't grown at all. I'm the same size I was at eighteen—and don't call me Brat. And take your hand off my knee.'

The corners of his eyes crinkled. 'It worked to take your mind off whatever you were panicking about. You always did prefer being angry to being scared.'

Seb snorted a laugh when she picked up his hand and dropped it back onto the gearstick.

'Have you developed any other serious delusions while I've been away?'

'At eighteen...' Seb carried on talking in that lazy voice that lifted the hair on her arms '...you wore ugly make-up, awful clothes and you were off the scale off-limits.'

Rowan, because she didn't even want to attempt to work out what he meant by that comment, bared her teeth at him. 'I'm still off-limits.'

Seb ignored that comment. 'Is that why you are still single at twenty-eight...nine... What? How old *are* you?'

'Old enough to say that my relationship status has nothing to do with you.'

'*Relationship status?* What are you? A promo person for Facebook?' Seb grimaced. 'You're either married, involved, gay or single. Pick one.'

Rowan snorted her indignation. 'Gay? For your information, I like what men have. I just frequently don't like what it is attached to!'

'So—single, then?'

'I'd forgotten what an enormous pain in the ass you could be, but it's all coming back.' Rowan turned and tucked herself into the corner between the door and seat. At least sparring with Seb was keeping her awake. 'And you? Any more close calls with Satan's Skanks?'

She hoped the subject of his ex-fiancée would be enough of a mood-killer to get him off the subject of her non-existent love-life.

'You really didn't like her.' Seb twisted his lips. 'Was it a general dislike or something more specific?'

There wouldn't be any harm in telling him now, Rowan thought. 'She was seriously mean to Callie. I mean, off the scale malicious.'

Seb's eyes narrowed. 'I thought they got along well.'

'That's what she wanted you to think. She was a nasty

piece of work,' Rowan said, staring at the bank of dials on the dashboard. 'I really didn't like her.'

'I would never have guessed,' Seb said dryly.

'My "money-grabbing" comment didn't clue you in?'

'It was a bit restrained.' Seb's tone was equally sarcastic. 'Your efforts to sabotage our engagement party were a bit subtle too.'

'What did I do?' she demanded, thinking that attack was the best form of defence. 'And why would I do it since I was looking forward to you being miserable for the rest of your life?'

Seb slid her an ironic glance. 'Apart from spiking the punch with rum? And turning the pool that violent green that totally clashed with the puke-orange colour scheme? And placing a condom on every side plate? Anything I've missed?'

Rowan dropped her head back on the headrest. 'You knew about that?'

'I had a good idea it was you.' Seb's lips twitched. 'Okay, hit me. What else did you do?'

'Nothing,' Rowan replied, far too quickly.

'Come on, 'fess up.'

Well, he couldn't kill her now. She didn't think…

'I put itching powder in your bed.'

Rowan felt as if she wanted to dance to the sound of Seb's laughter. Despite her now overwhelming fatigue, she noticed the scar bisecting his eyebrow, the length of his blond eyelashes. Man, she wanted to link her arms around him, curl up against him and drift off.

'Ro, I knew about that too.'

He spoke softly and Rowan felt both warm and chilled, her nerve-endings on fire.

'Luckily we had a fight after the party and I chose to sleep in the spare room…she itched for days.'

'Good.' Rowan grinned and fought an enormous yawn. 'You had really bad taste in women, Seb.'

'She wasn't so bad. And if I didn't know any better I'd say you sound like a jealous shrew.'

'You really should give up whatever you're smoking.'

Rowan lifted her nose. As if she'd be jealous of that waste of a womb. Seb might be a thorn in her side but he was *her* thorn in the side—and Callie's, obviously. Nobody else was allowed to treat him badly. Especially not some lazy, stupid... Oh, dear God, the old oak tree was still on the corner of their road.

And there, through the trees, she could see the redbrick corner of Awelfor.

'No, don't panic. Just breathe. It's only a house, Ro.'

His house. And next door was her old home. And a life she didn't want to go back to—a life she'd outgrown a long time ago.

Seb turned into his driveway and parked in front of a new rectangular automated gate. While he waited for the gate to slide open he looked at Rowan, his blue eyes serious. 'Stay the three weeks, spend some time with your parents, and then I'll loan you the money to fly anywhere in the world.'

'Why?'

'Because I think it's long overdue.'

Rowan shook her head, suspicious. 'How much time, exactly, must I spend with them?'

Seb looked frustrated. 'I don't know! Make an effort to see them—have dinner with them—talk to them and we'll have a deal.'

It was too good an offer to pass up. It wasn't ideal but it was a solid plan of action. If she got some money together before that she'd go sooner... No, she couldn't do that. She was here. She had to see them. To leave without saying hello would be cruel, and she wasn't by nature cruel. Three weeks. What was twenty-one days in the scheme of things?

Twenty days too long in this city, her sarcastic twin said from her shoulder.

'I'll pay you back.'

Seb grinned. 'Yeah, you will. Yasmeen is on holiday and we're short of a housekeeper. You can start tomorrow: shopping, cleaning, laundry, cooking. You know what Yas does.'

'Are you mad? I'm not going to housekeep for you!' Rowan protested.

It wasn't that she couldn't—she'd worked as a maid before—but she wasn't going to pick up after Seb and his 'we'.

'We're? You said *we're* short of a housekeeper? Who else lives here?' Rowan demanded. If he had a live in lover/partner/girlfriend then she'd just go and sleep on the beach.

Seb steered the car up to his elegant house. 'Patch has hit a hiccup with his current girlfriend and has moved back into the second floor of the cottage.'

Oh, thank goodness. She didn't know if she could cope with Seb and any 'significant other'.

'So, housekeeping in exchange for your bed and food?'

'S'pose,' Rowan reluctantly agreed, thinking that she was jumping from the frying pan into... Well, the third level of the hot place.

After lugging Rowan's luggage up to Callie's old bedroom Seb finally made it to his office—the bottom floor of the two-bedroomed cottage Patch had moved into—temporarily he hoped! His workaholic staff worked flexible hours, so he was accustomed to seeing them at work at odd times, and Carl, his assistant/admin manager, like his hackers, was still around.

Seb listened to Carl's update and accompanied him into what they called the 'War Room'. The huge room was windowless, and a massive plasma TV attached to the far wall was tuned to MTV at a volume level that made his ears bleed. He picked up the TV remote that stood in its cradle on the wall and muted the volume. Two male heads and one female head shot up and looked in his direction.

His hackers needed junk food, tons of coffee and music. Deprive them of one of the three and he had their immediate attention. Seb walked into the centre of the room and rapidly scanned the long row of screens where computer code rolled in an unending stream. He read it as easily as he did English, and nodded when he didn't immediately pick up any problems.

'Anything I should know about?' he asked, folding his arms.

He listened while they updated him on their individual projects—testing the security of a government agency, a bank and a massive online bookseller—adding his input when he felt he needed to but mostly just listening while they ran their ideas past him. There was a reason why he'd hired all three and paid them a king's ransom: they were ethical, super-smart and the best in the field.

Nearly, but not quite, as good as him.

Seb wrapped up the meeting, left the room and headed for his office, which was diametrically opposite to the War Room. There were computers—five of them—with a processing power that could run most Developing World countries—but his office had lots of natural light, a TV tuned to ESPN, an *en-suite* bathroom and a door directly linked to the gym. Although he nagged and threatened, his staff members rarely used the up-to-date equipment.

Seb tossed his car keys and mobile onto his desk, hooked his chair with his foot and pulled it over to his favourite computer. Having Rowan return with her battered backpack and her world-weary attitude made him think of his mother and had him wondering where she was laying her head these days. He checked on her once or twice a year—

with his skills he could find out exactly where she was, how much money she had and pretty much what she was up to. He'd first tracked her down when he was sixteen and he'd found her passport and identity number on a supposedly coded list—ha-ha!—on his father's computer.

His fingers flew across the screen as he pulled up the program he'd written specifically to let him track her. Within minutes he found out that she'd drifted from Peru to Brazil and then moved around a bit within that country. She was currently in Salvador and running seriously low on funds.

He experienced the usual wave of resentment and anger, wondered if he was a hundred types of a fool—after all, what had she ever done for him?—and then transferred a thousand untraceable dollars into her account. It was less than petty cash to him, and if he didn't do it he'd lie awake at night, wondering what she'd have to do to dig herself out of that hole. She was, after all, his mother.

Rowan was in pretty much the same position, he thought, and he wondered how she'd come to the same point. He looked at his screen speculatively and thought that with a couple of clicks he could find out exactly what had happened to bring her home. He had everything he needed: her passport number, her bank details. He could, by inputting a line of code into that program, see her travel movements and everything she'd ever purchased with a credit or debit card.

It was that easy.

He'd done it before—not for five years at least, but once or twice a year before that, when her parents hadn't heard from her for a while and her father had asked him to take a peek. He'd skim over the information, not particularly interested, and report back that she was in London or Perth and reassure them that she seemed to have enough money to cover her costs. There were big deposits and big withdrawals, but there was always a savings account with excess funds. He wondered why she hadn't had one this time…

Seb dropped his hands to his lap and fought temptation. He could, but he didn't—as curious as he was, he didn't have the right to invade her privacy. She wasn't the child they had all worried about anymore, she'd grown up.

She was now the knockout she'd promised to be. Eyes the colour of night, wild hair, creamy, creamy skin and a body that was all woman. He felt his zipper straining and leaned back in his chair, spun around and stared out of the window to the pool area beyond his floor-to-ceiling windows. He wanted her. And, equally and as intensely, he didn't want to want her. She was everything he avoided in the opposite sex: complicated, gregarious, communicative…free-spirited and forthright.

Why hadn't he just loaned her the money and sent her on her way? Then he wouldn't be sitting here—being totally unproductive—with an urge to see if she slept naked.

He was such a moron.

'Gray, I'm really sorry…'

Seb propped his shoulder against the doorframe to his newly refurbished kitchen, with its sleek cupboards, black granite and black and white checked floor. Yasmeen had designed the kitchen and, since this was where she ruled from, he'd been happy to write out the rather hefty cheque. It was filled with light, modern appliances and Yasmeen's precious ferns and African Violets. If he let those die his life would be over.

He grinned. It was just another job he could add to Rowan's growing list of housekeeping duties.

'Grayson…take a breath. There's a monkey, a tiger with cubs, a squid, a seal and a horse. Those are the highlights. And a Hotei.'

What on earth was she up to? Seb wondered as he stepped into the kitchen and headed for the coffee machine.

'I'm pretty sure the Hotei is rare. It has that…class, a mastery that just can't be ignored.'

Rowan nodded when he lifted a cup towards her, asking whether she wanted coffee.

'Now that my mobile is charged again I'm about to e-mail you some photographs. Take a look and see what you think… Yes, I know that you won't buy anything without looking at it…'

Rowan murmured a couple of soothing phrases into the mobile before disconnecting the call. She quickly e-mailed Grayson the photographs she'd promised and placed her mobile onto the kitchen table.

'I *know* that you can't buy them without seeing them. I've only been dealing with you for ten years. Jerk.'

Seb handed her a cup of coffee which Rowan reached for with the enthusiasm of a true coffee addict.

'Thanks. You need a master's degree to operate your machine.'

Seb leaned against his counter and thought that Rowan looked a great deal better than she had when he'd picked her up. That was what a solid night's sleep did for you, Seb thought. She still had faint blue shadows under her eyes, but there was at least some colour in her cheeks. He'd checked on her a couple of times and discovered that she didn't—unfortunately—sleep naked, that she had a slight piggy snore and that she slept on her stomach.

'Are you trying to sell a zoo?' Seb said, his eyes on her long legs. She wore a simple pair of denim shorts and another button-down cotton shirt and had pulled her clean hair into a fat plait. She wore no make-up except for a slick of gloss on her lips.

She took his breath right away.

'Of sorts. I picked up some stuff in Bali which I hoped to flog when I got to Oz.'

And he'd thought that *he* was tight-lipped and uncommunicative. It made him want to shake her...or kiss her. 'You know I *could* just avoid pulling your teeth for information and find out for myself.'

'How?'

He wiggled his hands. 'Magic computer fingers.'

'Corny. And, like most men, I think you exaggerate your computer skills.' Her expression was a mixture of pity and disbelief, as if he was a child telling tall stories.

'Sweetheart, I hacked into the FBI's website and left them an Easter egg when I was sixteen—'

'A what?'

'An Easter egg. It's a surprise in a program that a hacker leaves...a signature or a message or a picture. It's non-malicious. Anyway, if I wanted to I could tell you what you had for breakfast six years ago, so finding out what you bought in Bali would be child's play.'

Rowan's look threatened to cut him off at the knees. 'If I find out that you've done that—ever—I will make it my personal mission to make your life on earth resemble the hottest part of hell.'

Seb knew that that she'd certainly try. And he'd watch her try for a while and then he'd get bored and haul her off to bed... Actually, that didn't sound like a bad plan at all. Entertainment in and out of the bedroom. Win-win.

'*Have* you ever done that?'

'Cyber checked up on you?' Seb slid his innocent expression into place—the one he'd been practising since he was fourteen and had discovered code and that he could speak it. And have some fun with it. 'Why would you think that?'

'Because I don't trust you further than I can throw you. Have you?'

Of course he had. She'd been nineteen, on her own in

countries where she couldn't speak or read the language. Her parents had been beside themselves with worry—actually, her father had. Her brother Peter had been concerned. Callie a little less so. Himself? Not so much… He'd always known that Rowan was stronger, smarter than they gave her credit for. He'd known that she'd be fine but he'd used his skills to check up on her so that the family and friends she'd left behind could sleep at night.

'Have you?'

He was saved from answering that question by her chirping mobile, which rattled and vibrated on the dining room table as if it was possessed. Rowan narrowed her eyes at him—a non-verbal threat that he wasn't off the hook—and frowned when she looked down at the tiny screen.

'Grayson…again?'

Rowan yanked the mobile up to her ear as her heart bounded up her throat. There was no reason for Grayson to be returning her call so soon unless she'd found the netsuke of the century or there was a huge problem.

It turned out to be both. Rowan listened to his garbled words and tried to make sense of what he was saying. 'Are you saying that my netsukes might have been stolen? From a West End art gallery a year ago?'

Rowan rested her forehead on her hand and tried to force the panic far away enough so that she could listen to Grayson.

'A seal, a stag antler, a tiger with cubs and a squid were stolen from the King and Cross Gallery. There's been a lot of interest in netsuke lately, and consequently a lot of theft. They are also easy to transport, being not much bigger than the size of a golfball.'

'If they were stolen, how did they end up in a hole-in-the-wall shop in Bali? They were covered in dust, forgotten. Nobody had looked at them for years.'

'I can't take a chance that these might be stolen. Didn't you get any provenance?'

'Gray, the guy said they were pawned. The owner never came back to pick them up and that was six years ago.' Rowan rubbed her neck. 'They are *not* stolen.'

Grayson was silent for a minute. 'Well, if these are genuine eighteenth-century netsuke and aren't the same objects that were stolen then I think you've got a heck of a find on your hands.'

'So, it's either really good or really bad news?'

'Essentially. Can you prove how you paid for them?' Grayson demanded.

Rowan's eyes flicked to Seb's face. He was listening to her side of the conversation with avid interest.

'Yeah. Every cent. I drained my bank accounts to pay for them.'

'That's good. Of course you might take a financial hit if they *are* stolen, but if you can prove you paid for them then it shows you didn't have criminal intent.'

'Yay me. And they *aren't* stolen.' Rowan closed her eyes at the thought of waving goodbye to twelve thousand pounds. She rested her forehead on the dining room table and tried not to hyperventilate.

'Of course if they are not stolen, then I think you've hit a massive pay-day,' Grayson added.

Rowan heard Seb move from his chair and thought that he was finally giving her some privacy. Instead she felt his hand warm and big on her neck, gently stroking the tense cords.

She wished she could just lean back and soak up his strength, ask him to help her sort this out. But she couldn't. She never asked for help...mostly because there had never been anyone around she could ask.

Besides, he'd just think that she was stupid and

irresponsible... And because she liked his hands on her skin a little too much she swatted them away.

'Do you have any documentation or photographs of what was stolen from that gallery so that I can compare them myself?' Rowan asked Grayson.

'No, that's not my problem—it's yours. I just know that it was those four subjects.'

And Japanese artists never did the same subjects. Damn Grayson! He was getting all paranoid and crazy without even knowing if the netsukes looked the same. Stupid man. Grayson was rich, but he wasn't bright.

'You need to do some research. Try to identify the pieces. Then we'll talk again,' Grayson said as Seb dropped his hand and walked away to refill his coffee cup.

'You know you want them.'

'And I'll buy them—after you tell me that they are definitely not stolen.'

'They are definitely not stolen.'

'Smarty pants,' Grayson said, before disconnecting.

Aarrrrgh. It wasn't as if she was a total amateur, Rowan thought on an internal eye-roll. She stared out of the window and tried to push her way through her panic to think the problem through.

'I can smell your brains burning,' Seb said, taking his seat again and pushing another cup of coffee in her direction. 'Sip and spill.'

Rowan instinctively shook her head. 'Don't worry about it. I'll figure something out.' She pushed against the table to haul herself to her feet. This wasn't Seb's problem, she thought. It was hers, solely.

Rowan looked down in surprise when Seb's hand snagged her wrist and tugged her back to her seat. 'Sit down, drink your coffee and tell me what's happened.'

'Seb...I can deal with it. It's fine.'

Seb shoved a frustrated hand through his hair. 'That's

the problem, Rowan. You don't need to deal with it on your own. Why won't you let me help you?'

'I don't need your help! This is minor, Seb. I *needed* your help nine years ago. I needed lots of help then! Since then I've learnt to rely on myself.'

Seb flicked his thumbnail against his bottom lip. 'Something happened that night—something more than any of us realised.'

Rowan shook her head. 'What is your obsession with that damned party? It was at a club, I got caught with a baggie, I did community service for it... End of story.'

'Really? I suspect you took the rap for that slick character you were so in love with. Jason... Jack...' Seb clicked his fingers in frustration.

'Joe Clark.'

He frowned. 'The same Joe Clark who runs that sports betting company? The one that's just been listed on the Stock Exchange?'

'I presume so. His father owned a couple of betting shops, so it must be the same family.'

'You haven't kept in touch with him?'

Revulsion passed across Rowan's face, accompanied by a visible shudder. Oh, yeah, there was a story here.

Rowan cocked her head. 'What's with the twenty questions? I feel like I'm back in the interrogation room at Sydney.'

'You're tough. You can handle it.' Seb looked over the rim of his coffee cup. Her remote, distant façade was back in place and it annoyed him. She wasn't cool and remote. She never had been. Loud, vivacious, spontaneous... He'd used to be able to read every emotion on her face.

'Are you in trouble—again?' If she was there was no way that he'd just sit back and watch her go through hell a second time. 'Tell me.'

Rowan recognised that determined look on his face and

realised that he wasn't going to be shrugged off. And she felt…relieved. Glad to have an excuse to tell him, to tell somebody.

Another part of her wanted to show him—tell him that she *wasn't* the ditsy, silly, crazy child who bounced from job to job, wafting her way through the world. Well, she did waft, but she worked as well. Being an art 'picker' took determination, time and a good eye. And hours and hours of studying jewellery, art, sculpture.

Maybe he could respect that—respect her?

Was it so wrong to want a little affirmation, a little admiration from a super-smart man? From anybody?

'Criminal trouble? No. Financial trouble? Oh, yeah. And to make you understand I have to show you something,' Rowan said, and walked out of the room to fetch her baby sculptures.

CHAPTER FOUR

'I LOVE THIS one,' Seb said, holding the chubby, joyful figurine of a Buddha in the palm of his hand. 'Simply stunning.'

'It's a Hotei, also called a Laughing Buddha, symbolising contentment and abundance and luck.' Rowan's finger drifted over the Buddha's cheek. 'I love him too. I think he's the prize of the collection.'

After Seb had spent at least fifteen minutes looking at the tiny ivory netsukes, pointing out details that she hadn't noticed, Rowan rewrapped the carvings and put them back into their box. Closing the lid, she wrapped her hands around her coffee cup. She wondered where to start. At the beginning, she supposed...

'After six months in Thailand I left and headed for Hong Kong, I had a job teaching English and was barely scraping by. One day, after I'd just been paid, I was on my way to buy groceries, and there was a little shop I passed every day, full of...curiosities, I suppose. Mostly junk, to be honest. I had some time and I went in. I was browsing through a box of costume jewellery and I found a brooch. I knew right away that it was special. The craftsmanship was superb. The owners thought it was paste but I knew it wasn't. Don't ask me how. I just did.'

Seb leaned his arms on the table, listening intently.

'I went straight to the Causeway District and found an antique shop.'

Seb's mouth kicked up in a smile. 'Don't tell me... It was solid gold and studded with diamonds.'

'Better. It was Fabergé and worth a freaking fortune. I was lucky. The owner paid me a fair price. He could've ripped me off. I didn't know what it was. The profit on that funded my travels for the next eighteen months, but I was hooked on the chase. I started studying antiques, jewellery, art. I realised I had an eye for spotting quality and, while I never found another Fabergé brooch, I *did* find Lalique glassware, Meissen pottery, minor works of art. I made some money.'

Well, that explained the deposits and withdrawals. Smart girl, Seb thought. Smart *and* gorgeous. A very dangerous combination.

'Most of my capital is tied up in a house I co-bought in London which I am planning on...'

'Flipping?'

Rowan tipped her mouth up. 'It's what I do.'

'So, coming back to these...'

Rowan told him what Grayson had said and waited through his resultant thoughtful silence. 'So, basically, you need to know whether these are previously undiscovered, undocumented netsuke or whether they've been stolen?'

'They aren't stolen. I'm pretty sure of that. But no one is going to buy them at the price I want without further information.' Rowan rested her chin on her fist. 'And obviously it also means that I'm going to be broke for a lot longer than I anticipated.'

Seb waved her money troubles away. Easy for him to do, Rowan thought.

'So, what's the next step?' he asked.

'Research. Lots of it. I don't know nearly enough about netsuke.'

'But you know that they are quality pieces? Do you need my computer skills?'

'I don't think so… I just need to trawl through databases of documented netsuke and see if I can find any of them.'

'Well, if you need to get into places that you can't get into…'

'Is that what you do? Poke around in places?'

Seb shrugged. 'At a very basic level.'

'What exactly are you paid so much money to do?'

Seb tapped his finger against his coffee cup. 'I guess you can call me a consultant. Companies hire me to evaluate their computer systems for vulnerabilities. So I go in there, try to hack their system—and pretty much always do. Then I point out where they have problems. Sometimes I fix the problems for them; sometimes they get their people to do it. Either way I get paid.'

'Huh. So you use your powers for good and not evil?' Rowan threw his words back at him.

'Yeah.'

'And you'd be willing to…poke around for me? Isn't that illegal?'

'Slightly unethical, maybe.' Seb's eyes were determined when they met hers. 'Look, I'm not going to use the information for personal gain, and if it helps you out of a jam then so much the better.'

Rowan nodded her understanding, thought for a minute, then said, 'Let me do some research. If I need your help, I'll ask.'

'Promise?' Seb shrugged at her gimlet stare. 'It's just that you don't have a great track record when it comes to asking for help, Brat.'

'Promise. Can I borrow a computer?'

'Sure. There's a couple you can use in my office, or there's a few you can use in my bedroom.' Seb deliberately wiggled his eyebrows suggestively and Rowan, as expected, rolled her eyes. Yep, time to bust her chops, he thought, and to banish the tension he saw in her eyes.

'I am not going anywhere near your bedroom, Hollis.'

Seb leaned back in his chair. 'Why? Scared you won't be able to keep your hands off me?'

'What? Are you mad? You're like my…my…er…'

'Don't say brother,' Seb ground out. 'That would be too creepy for words.'

'No…geez! *Eeuuuw!*' Rowan shuddered as she banged her cup onto the table. 'No talk of bedrooms!'

Seb liked the colour in her face and the snap in her eyes so he thought he'd wind her up some more. 'Okay, can we talk about what happens in bedrooms, then?'

'We could *never* have sex!'

'Uh, yes…actually we could. You see, my Part A would slot into your Plot B—'

Rowan's look was meant to freeze. 'Stop being facetious! It's a crazy idea! Yes, I think you've got some heat happening, but it would be a really stupid thing to do. We don't even like each other.'

Seb stood up and ran a hand over her head. Then he placed one hand on the back of her chair and bent down so that his face was next to hers. She just folded her arms and lifted a perfectly arched, perfectly arrogant eyebrow. *Man,* that look made him hot.

'Are you trying to intimidate me? It didn't work when I was ten—what makes you think it'll work now?'

'I was just wondering whether you taste as good as you smell.'

'You'll never find out.' Rowan pushed him away, stood up and put some distance between them. She placed her fists on her hips and tipped her head. 'Back to business. So, if I ask you for help what is it going to cost me?'

'What?'

'Your computer skills? I'm already paying for my food and bed by being the housekeeper…'

Seb looked at the stack of dishes in the sink. 'Not that you've done any housekeeping yet.'

'Give me a break. I'll get to it! So, what's the price?'

'We'll work something out,' Seb said, deliberately vague.

'And that statement scares the hell out of me,' Rowan retorted. 'As per usual you've managed to drive me crazy, so I need to leave. I'm going to do some shopping, since there isn't anything to eat in this house!'

'Want me to come with you?'

'I've been shopping on my own for a long time now. I think I can manage.'

Rowan made her tone even and unemotional, but Seb smiled at the twin strips of colour on her cheekbones. Her chest was flushed and her nipples were puckered against her shirt. Her mind and mouth might be protesting at the thought of them sleeping together but her body wouldn't object. He could reach for her right now and he knew that she wouldn't take much persuading...

Except that he wanted her to want this—him—with both her body and mind. He didn't want her to have regrets, to think that she was coerced. That would be giving that smart mouth of hers too much ammunition to chew his ass off.

Rowan wasn't known for playing fair.

'Money.' Rowan held out her hand and bent her fingers backwards and forwards. When he just looked at her, she sighed. 'I can't go shopping without money, Einstein, and I don't have any.'

Right. Try to keep up, Hollis! Seb reached into his back pocket, pulled out his wallet and handed over a wad of bills. He had no idea how much was in there and it didn't matter. Money was easy. She could blow every cent he had and he would just put his shoulder to the wheel and make some more.

People—it was people who baffled him, he thought as Rowan tucked the cash into the pocket of her jeans.

'Keys?' she asked.

'To what?'

'Your car. Or were you expecting me carry the groceries back in the basket on the front of a bicycle?'

'There is no way I'm letting you drive my precious car.' Seb walked over to a row of hooks by the door and lifted off a set of keys. 'Here's a remote to the gate and garage and the keys to Yas's runaround. Use that.'

'I can't use Yasmeen's car!'

'It's my car, and Yas uses it to do errands so that she doesn't risk getting her own dinged.' Seb tossed her the set of keys and Rowan snatched them out of the air.

Their glances clashed and electricity buzzed between them again. Except that this time—dammit—it wasn't all sexual, wasn't only a caveman impulse to score with a pretty girl. Rowan wasn't just a pretty face and a spectacular bod; she'd be easier to resist if she were.

She had a brain behind those amazing eyes, a sharp sense of business and a talent to spot art. Being physically attracted to her was enough of a hassle. To be mentally drawn to her as well was asking for trouble.

Yet he was having to fight to keep from taking those couple of steps to her, pulling her against him and making her his.

Seb placed his fists on his hips and blew out a long, frustrated breath. He needed to think this through, to rationalise this attraction he felt to her. Needed to try to find out where these crazy impulses to get her naked were coming from. He believed in being rational, in analysing that which he didn't understand.

And he didn't understand what was happening with him where Rowan was concerned. He needed to get a handle on these unpredictable and swamping impulses he had whenever she was in the same room.

Like the impulse to strip her naked and bend her over the back of that chair...

Oh, man. He was in a world of trouble here...

'Okay, well, I'll be back later.' Rowan flashed him an uncertain look and belted out through the kitchen door.

Seb gripped the back of a chair with both hands and dropped his head. What was wrong with him? He never went nuts over a woman—never, ever felt out of control. Sex was important and, like all men, he liked it—no, he loved it—but he had always been able to walk away. Always.

Until now. Until Rowan.

And she hadn't even been back in his life for twenty-four hours. She had already tipped his world upside down and Seb shuddered when he thought of the chaos she could create in the immediate future.

He was still so annoying, Rowan thought as she went into the empty, cavernous hall of the supermarket and walked over to the fresh fruit section.

'My Part A would slot into your Plot B—'

Seb's words rattled around her brain. A stupid phrase that had lust whirling in her downstairs regions, that made her feel light-headed—oh, dear, that made her sound like a heroine from a historical romance, but it was the perfect word—and created an impulse to reach up and yank that sardonic mouth to hers.

She'd never felt the impulse to yank—*yank?*—any man's mouth to hers, and that it was Seb's that she now had the urge to taste went against all the laws of the universe.

She could not believe that she—cool, competent and street-smart—was acting like a horny teenager, about to collapse in a panting, wet, drippy, drooling heap at his feet.

It was humiliating. Really!

Rowan pushed a tendril of hair out of her eyes and blew

air into her cheeks as her mobile chirped. Pulling it from the front pocket of her shorts, she did an excited wiggle when she saw the name in the display window.

'Ro? Honey?' The gravelly voice of her best friend boomed across the miles.

'Why aren't you in Cape Town, where I need you?' Rowan demanded. 'The one time I get back and you're not here, Callie!'

'Sorry, darling. I got delayed... He's six-two and has soulful green eyes. And I need to see a designer in LA who can only see me next week. Or maybe the week after.'

'Naff excuse,' Rowan muttered.

'So, how and why are you back home?'

'It's a long story.'

Rowan gave her a brief synopsis of her last couple of days. After thinking about and then refusing Callie's offer of a loan, she sighed into the mobile.

'Something else is wrong,' Callie stated. 'Come on—spit it out.'

'I don't know what you're talking about.'

'In the last fifteen minutes I think you said Seb's name once. Normally you would've insulted him at least ten times by now. What's going on?'

And that was the problem with knowing someone for all your life. You couldn't sneak stuff past them. 'I don't know if you want to know.'

'I always want to know. Spill.'

'I think I suddenly have the screaming hots for my best friend's brother.'

When Callie stopped roaring with laughter Rowan put the mobile back to her ear.

'Holy fishcakes,' Callie said. 'Sweetheart, when you muck it up, you do it properly.'

Rowan frowned at Callie's uncharacteristically mild expletives. 'Holy *fishcakes*? *Muck* it up?'

'My temporary fling nearly had heart failure when I dropped the F-bomb yesterday; he's a bit conservative. I'm cleaning up my potty mouth.'

Rowan laughed and winced at the same time. That would last as long as the fling did: until Callie got on the plane to come home.

'Anyway, tell me about wanting to do my brother.'

Rowan grimaced. *Do* her brother? *Eeew.* Knowing that Callie wasn't going to drop the subject without getting something out of her, she thought about what to say. 'I've never had this reaction to anyone—ever! I just want to take a bite out of him.'

While she wasn't a nun, she'd had some sex over the years. Sporadic, erratic, infrequent, but it had been sex. Two one-night stands, a few season-long relationships, and once a relationship that had lasted a year.

'It's about time you ran into someone who set you on fire. The fact that it's Seb just makes we want to wet my pants with laughter.'

'Glad you find it amusing. I don't. I don't know how to deal with it,' Rowan muttered, leaning her hip against a display stand of orange sweet potatoes. Instead of discussing Seb further, she chose to shove her head in the sand. 'So, tell me about your fling.'

'Hot, conservative, sweet. And you're changing the subject because you don't want to deal with your sexy side!'

'Bye, Cal, love you.'

'Avoiding the issue isn't going to change it—'

'Miss you. Hurry home, okay? I need you!' Rowan interrupted, before disconnecting.

Rowan rolled her shoulders in frustration, thinking about her 'sexy side'. Sex had always just been nice and pleasant. Uncomplicated. It gave her a little buzz. But she could probably live without it if she had to. Just as she could live without having a permanent man in her life, being in a permanent place. She had never given her heart away—couldn't, because she still hadn't learnt not to look at a man and wonder if he she could trust him. She didn't need sex and she definitely didn't need love.

She'd managed without it all these years and probably wouldn't know what to do with it if she found it. And if she occasionally yearned for it then it meant that she was human, didn't it?

She wouldn't mind some respect, though.

She'd loved Joe. Had been passionately, deeply, mind-blazingly in love with him. The type of love you could only experience when you were eighteen and everything was black and white. Somewhere in the part of her that was all woman—mysterious and wise—she'd known that Joe would be the guy who would change her destiny, would alter her mindset, would change her in ways that she'd never believed possible.

She'd never considered that her love for him would spin her life in such a different direction…

Rowan was pulled back from her memories by a store announcement and found herself staring at piles of fruit, multi-coloured vegetables, the perfection of the display.

Apples as red as the poisonous fruit in *Snow White*, atomic orange carrots, purple eggplant. Six different types of lettuce, herbs, sweet potatoes…and no people. At nine in the morning the supermarket was all but deserted.

She looked down and saw the aisles, shelves packed full of consumer goods. Where were the shouts of the vendors in Tamil? The smell of lemongrass and hot oil? So much abundance, so much choice, no people. So much artificial colour, piped music that hurt her ears…no people. Where was everybody? How could there be so much choice and no one to choose?

She wanted to be back in the markets in Hanoi, standing in a queue to touch a statue of Buddha in Phuket, on a crowded train on her way to Goa.

She didn't want to be back here, in the city that held so many bad memories for her. She didn't want to deal with Seb, who set her blood on fire, made her feel things that were hot and uncomfortable. She didn't want to deal with her parents, revisit her past.

She wanted to be back on crowded streets, on the Inca trails in Peru, in an Outback logging town in the Yukon. She wanted to be on her own, having transient relationships with people who expected little or nothing from her.

She wanted her freedom, she thought as she left the supermarket empty-handed. Her independence, solitude.

Money in the bank.

Money... *Dammit,* Rowan thought as she turned around and walked back into the shop. She'd made a deal with the devil and part of that deal required her to shop for food.

Ugh.

After she'd spent a healthy amount of Seb's money Rowan drove towards the coast and onto the main road that led to the beach in the area. Behind her sunglasses her eyes widened with surprise as she took in the changes that had occurred since she'd left. Her favourite beach was still there—of course it was—but the buildings on the other side of the road had been converted into upscale boutiques and gift shops, restaurants and a coffee shop-slash-restaurant-slash-neighbourhood bar.

Rowan headed straight for the restaurant/bar and slid into a tiny table by the window. She ordered an espresso and a slice of cheesecake and silently told herself that she'd add it to the mental tab she owed Seb.

It was such a stunning day. She could see Table Mountain, blue, green and purple, a natural symbol of this incredibly beautiful city. The sea was flat, aqua and green, and the sun glinted off the white sand.

Rowan looked up at the waitress and pointed to the 'Help Wanted' sign on the door. 'I see you need another waitress?'

'A bartender, actually.'

Even better, Rowan thought. She loathed waitressing. 'Tips good?'

'Very. You interested? If you are, I can call the manager over.'

Rowan nodded and within fifteen minutes had agreed to tend bar on Friday night as a trial. If that worked out she could have three night shifts a week. Rowan agreed with alacrity… She'd do anything to add cash to her depleted coffers so she could leave this city as soon as possible.

A stream of feminine cursing distracted Rowan from her appreciation of the scenery and she turned to see a fifty-something fashion plate slip into a chair at the table next to her. She was fantastically turned out, with styled curly hair, large breasts and long legs in skinny jeans. She wore Audrey Hepburn glasses and a very sulky expression.

Rowan felt like a garden gnome next to her.

Rowan took a bite of cheesecake and sighed as the flavours burst onto her tongue. The lady gestured a waiter forward and pushed her sunglasses up into her hair. Fine lines surrounded her light green eyes and Rowan revised the estimate of her age upwards. Maybe closer to sixty, but looking good. She pointed to Rowan's cup and cheesecake.

'I think she wants the same,' Rowan told the confused waitress, and smiled when the blonde lifted her thumb.

'What do you mean you've made a mistake?' she shouted into her cell, in a French-accented voice. *'L'imbécile!* I booked the Farmyard on the fourth, and I don't care if you double-booked with the President himself. Unbook it!'

Rowan rested her chin in the palm of her hand and didn't

pretend that she wasn't listening. She was fascinated. What was the Farmyard? A brothel? A nightclub? A restaurant?

'How am I going to explain to my seven-year-old grandson that he can't have his party there? Are *you* going to explain?'

Or a children's party venue.

After swearing very comprehensively, in both English and French, at the Farmyard's representative, she snapped her mobile closed and rested her head on her folded arms.

Rowan felt her sympathy stirring and leaned over and touched her on the arm. 'Hey.'

She might not be able to make emotional connections to places or things but she'd never had a problem talking to anyone, making casual connections that could last a minute, an hour, a day…

The blonde head lifted, the sunglasses slid down the pert nose and Rowan noticed tears in the dark eyes. 'What's the matter? Can I help?'

The woman shoved her glasses up her nose and sniffed. 'Only if you can provide a venue for twenty-five kids in ten days' time, complete with horses and a mini-quadbike track and paintball shooting. And an army tank cake.'

'Pardon?'

'I booked this exclusive children's party venue for next Saturday and they double-booked it. I'm going to have to cancel the party and I am going to break my grand-baby's heart. I'm Annie, by the way.'

'Rowan,' Rowan replied as her mind started to whirl. She knew of a place that had horses, a paddock suitable to make a mini-quadbike track, and haybales to make up a mock battle field for paintball-shooting. 'What's your budget?'

The Jane Fonda look-alike frowned at her and named a figure.

Rowan swallowed and wasn't sure if she'd heard her

properly. Who paid that sort of money for a kid's party? Were these people nuts? He was seven and not the Sultan of Brunei's kid!

Rowan stood up, picked up her plate and moved to the blonde's table. 'My name is Rowan, but my friends call me Ro…let's chat.'

When Seb was twenty-two, Patch had told him that he was handing over the family's property portfolio to Seb to manage and that he was going to open up a company in Simon's Town, doing sea-kayaking tours.

Seb hadn't believed him, but within six months he'd had the added responsibility of managing various warehouses, office blocks and houses around Cape Town, Patch had moved out of Awelfor and into a house in Simon's Town and had started leading tourist tours showing off Signal Hill, Lions Head and Table Mountain from a sea perspective.

The company had taken off, and he'd opened a branch in Hermanus, but most days he still went out on the water and led a tour. For Seb, Patch's Kayak Tours was just across the peninsula, and he often found himself driving to Simon's Town, running along the promenade and joining his dad for an early-evening paddle.

Today it had been easy, paddling in the shelter of the harbour, and he'd soon pulled ahead of the group in the open sea, wanting to feel the strain in his arms and his shoulders. Skirting a navy striker ship waiting to dock, he headed south towards the world-famous Boulders Beach as he kept an eye out for whales. He flew past the huge rocks at Boulders, laughing at the penguin colony that stood on the beach contemplating hunting for food, and after a half-hour turned back and caught up with the sluggish tour.

Seb laughed again as two endangered Black Oyster Catchers pecked at Patch's hat and with a pithy insult drew abreast with him. He cursed when his mobile jangled in its waterproof jacket. He put it to his ear and ignored Patch's hiss of displeasure.

'No mobiles on the water, Sebastian!' Patch said loudly.

Recognising the number at Awelfor, Seb ignored Patch and quickly answered it. 'Rowan, what's wrong?'

'Nothing. Well—um—I need to ask you a favour.'

Rowan's voice sounded hesitant and his face cleared. Oh, this should be good. Another favour? She was racking them up!

'What is it?'

'May I hold a function here on Saturday?'

'I thought you were broke! Do you have money to entertain?'

'It's not entertaining...exactly. I need a place to host a birthday party for some kids and I kind of suggested Awelfor.'

Seb thought that she had to be joking. 'You kind of *what*?'

'This lady will pay me a grotesque amount of money to organise a kid's birthday party and I need a place to make a track for mini-quads and to set up a paintball course.'

Seb dropped his hand, looked at his phone and shook his head. 'Are you nuts? I don't want kids all over my property!'

'You won't even be here! I saw that notice on the fridge for a trail run you're doing on Saturday!' Rowan protested.

'Rowan, you've been in the country two days and you've already managed to meet someone who can give you a job. How is that possible? And how do you know she's not a con?'

'Oh, maybe because she'll pay me sixty per cent of the fee up front,' Rowan whipped back. 'Yes or no, Seb? If it's no I need to go to Plan B.'

'Do you have a Plan B?' Seb asked, curious. Patch leaned over to yank his mobile out of his hand and he jerked away.

'No, but I will have to find one if you say no. Please don't say no.'

'Why do I suspect that you've already told her that you can host the party at Awelfor?'

'Because I have,' Rowan said in a small voice. 'Sorry. But I'll make another plan if you *really* mean no.'

He wasn't even surprised or, come to think of it, that upset. If anyone else took such liberties with his house and his property he'd have a fit of incredible proportions, but Rowan had been such a part of Awelfor for so long that it wasn't that much of an intrusion or an imposition. Weird, but true.

'Okay, knock yourself out. However, when you agree to house a shedload of monkeys, or a circus comprising of Eastern European acrobats, run it by me first, okay? Got to go.' Seb disconnected and shoved his mobile away before Patch could yank it away. He'd lost two mobiles to Patch's strict rule about 'disturbing the peace'.

'I'm going to ban you from joining my tours,' Patch complained.

'Sorry,' Seb replied, and picked up his paddle again and pulled it through the water.

They rowed for a while in companionable silence until Patch spoke again.

'So, what's Ro done this time?' Patch asked.

Seb explained and Patch laughed.

'Life certainly has been less...colourful without her presence.'

'But a great deal more sensible.'

'Sensible...*pshaw*! I had coffee with her this afternoon. It's lovely to have her home,' Patch said. 'I've always loved that girl.'

Seb sent him a measuring look. 'I know you did when she was a kid, but...'

Patch pointed out a seal to his group, exchanged some banter with them and turned back to Seb. 'But?'

'Doesn't she remind you of...Mum?'

Patch was silent for a minute and then shook his head. 'The only commonality between the two is that they both like to travel. No, Seb. Ro is nothing like Laura. Ro would never leave her kids—leave the people she loved and never make contact again.'

'She did for a couple of months,' Seb pointed out.

Why was he pushing this? What did he hope his father would say? *Yes, she's exactly like Laura and that he should run as if his tail was on his fire*? Would that make his big brain override his little one and cancel out all the X-rated visions he was having about her?

Patch's slow, measured words pulled him back into the conversation.

'Everyone seems to have forgotten that Ro sent Callie regular e-mails, asking her to tell Stan and Heidi and us that she was fine. She was a little lost and she was trying to find herself. When she had enough distance from her parents she made contact again. Ro didn't have it easy at home, Sebastian.'

'They loved her, Dad,' Seb protested.

'As much as they could. But she needed so much more. She wouldn't have run if she'd felt loved. They didn't understand her, and sometimes I think that's worse. Don't get me wrong—I like Stan and Heidi—but I think Peter fulfilled all their requirements for a child. Studious, quiet, introverted, brilliant and unemotional. Having to deal with an emotional hurricane like Rowan rocked their world.'

'Maybe. And she *is* an emotional hurricane.' And, because he could really talk to his dad, he cursed and muttered. 'And she's freakin' *hot*.'

Patch pursed his lips but his eyes danced with mischief. 'I might date younger women, but I'd never look at my second daughter and think she's hot. But I can see why my healthy son would think so. He might notice that she's grown up very well and has a killer bod.'

Seb twisted his lips. 'And I have a killer hard-on for her.'

Patch let out a low, rumbling laugh. 'Oh, geez, this is not going to end well. Especially since your modus is to bag her, tag her, and send her on her way when you're done with her. Isn't that the way you roll?'

Crude, but true.

'And if you hurt her I'll kick your ass,' Patch added.

Seb rolled his head around in an effort to relieve the knots he'd discovered in his shoulders and neck since Rowan had moved into his life. 'We have a history. My sister is her best friend. Her parents are important to me. I don't particularly like her; she's everything I'd run from in any other woman. Unconventional, free-spirited, slightly eccentric. And I forget all that every time I look at her. All I want to do is—'

'Don't say it.' Patch held up his hand and grimaced. 'Like Callie, I prefer to think of her as untouched and unsullied.'

'Hypocrite.' Seb laughed and then turned contemplative. 'I've never had such a strong reaction to any woman—ever. So why her and why now?'

'It's fate bitch-slapping you. It likes to do that.'

'Sucker-punching, more like it.' Seb picked up his oar and dipped it into the sea. He glanced over to Patch as they easily covered the gap between them and the group. 'No pithy words of advice?'

'From me? The king of bad decisions pertaining to women? Nah! I'm just going to sit back and enjoy watching you making a fool of yourself over this girl.'

'That's not going to happen. My brain is still firmly in charge of my junk,' Seb lied through his teeth.

Patrick's deep laugh rippled across the sea. 'Yeah, you keep telling yourself that, my boy!'

'Thanks for your help,' Seb said dryly. 'I'm going to head back. Which bed are you sleeping in tonight?'

'The cottage, since crazy Miranda changed the locks on my house.' Patch shrugged. 'I'm really going to have to do something about her soon.'

'You think?' Seb did a quick turn, slapped Patch's hand and started to paddle away. His dad's soft words had him looking back.

'Is she okay? Your mum? I know that you…check up on her now and again.'

Seb blew out his breath. 'As far as I can tell, Dad.'

'Where?'

'South America.'

Patch suddenly looked every one of his sixty-plus years. 'Ro's not like Laura, Seb. She's kinder, smarter, less self-involved.' Patch dipped his paddle into the water and launched a stream of water into Seb's face. 'Go on—get out of here.'

CHAPTER FIVE

WHEN HE WALKED into his kitchen forty minutes later—sweat-slicked and puffing—and saw Rowan bending over the kitchen sink, eating a juicy peach, he knew that Patch was right about his brain not being in control.

In fact it pretty much dissolved as he watched her from outside the door. Juice dripped down her chin and down her toned, tanned arms. She'd pulled her hair up into a messy knot and wore a lumo-purple bikini, the bottom half of which was covered by a thin multi-coloured wrap. Thanks to the afternoon sun pouring into the kitchen he could see the outline of her legs beneath the wrap, the shape of her hips, the rounded perfection of her butt. Sunlight on her back illuminated her spine, the soft skin between her jaw and neck, the slope of her thin shoulders.

Unaware that he stood there, she groaned as she bit into the peach again and more juice dripped.

He didn't—couldn't—think. His feet moved of their own accord, his hand whipped out to grab her hips and spin her around, and his mouth slammed onto hers. Peach juice, warm and sweet, thundered over his tongue, quickly followed by the taste of Rowan, as sweet and a hundred times spicier. He thought he heard—felt?—her squeak of surprise, but he didn't care; all he needed was to taste her, to feel her breasts flattened against his chest, her pelvis lifting into his to ride his erection.

Seb hooked his hand around her thigh and yanked her leg upwards, mentally cursed when her thigh encountered the barrier of her wrap. Without leaving her mouth—how could he?—he dropped his hands and fumbled at the loose knot at her hips. He needed to feel her, taste her, consume her... This was madness and fiercely unstoppable.

Unable to undo the knot, he pushed his thumbs between the fabric and her hips and shimmied it down so that it fell into a rainbow at her feet. Plastering his hands on her back, on her butt, he yanked her even closer until he doubted they could slip a piece of paper between them.

And, miracle of miracles, she was as into the kiss as he was. Little nips here. A long slide of her tongue there. Small hands were exploring his bare chest, down his ribcage, over his obliques and around to his back. She linked her arms around his neck and he was dimly aware that she still held the half-eaten peach in her hand, the juice from which was dripping down his back.

She could lick it off... She could lick anywhere she wanted to. Hopefully the thought would occur to her...

It was like being caught up in a hot, sexy, whippy storm, Rowan thought. One moment she'd had a peach in her hands and mouth, the next moment they were filled with a hard, sweaty, sexy man.

With the peach still in her hand she made a sticky path of juice across his shoulder, down his pec and over a flat nipple, lightly covered in blond hair. Dropping her head, she watched a bead of juice hit that nubby surface and shot her tongue out and licked it up, sighing as she tasted the saltiness of his skin, felt his muscles contract under her tongue.

'What's good for the goose...' Seb muttered, pulling the half-eaten fruit from her hand.

Rowan's eyes clouded over as he pulled the triangle of fabric covering her right breast away and touched her with the tips of his fingers, tanned against her much lighter skin. Her eyes watched his intense concentration as he played with her breast, running the wet peach over her distended nipple, alternating with subtle brushes of his thumb.

'To hell with this.'

Seb tossed the peach onto the floor, wrapped one strong arm around her bottom and, with the other arm, lifted her onto the dining room table, yanking the chair out of his way. Rowan barely noticed that the chair had toppled over and clattered to the floor because Seb's warm tongue was curled around her nipple and his other hand was burrowing into the back of her bikini pants, tracing erotic patterns on her butt.

He claimed her mouth again in a kiss that flew past heated and went straight to molten. Her legs, operating independently, hooked themselves around his waist and she scooted closer to him to feel that hard ridge against her mound.

Nothing else was important but to feel Seb, taste him, know him.

Seb pulled his mouth away and his hands, still on her breast and her butt, stilled. 'Point of no return, Ro. Yes or no?'

Like she had a choice, Ro thought, dazed. There was only one answer and her body was screaming it. 'Yes. Now.'

'Here?' Seb demanded.

She couldn't wait—had no patience to climb the stairs to a bedroom, to spare the couple of minutes that would take. 'Here. Now. Please.'

Seb muttered a curse and tried to step away. Rowan slapped a hand against the back of his neck and dragged him into a kiss that caused their feet to curl.

Seb yanked his mouth away and held up his hands. 'Ro, one sec…condom.'

Rowan bounced on the dining room table, her body one

long electrical current. 'If you have to go upstairs for one I'm coming with you,' she told him, deadly serious.

'There's a deal.' Seb picked up his wallet from the counter near the door and cards and cash were scattered over the floor. 'There should be one in here. Bingo.'

He held it up in his fingers as he stood between her legs again. 'You going to do the honours or must I?'

Rowan smiled slow and deep as she pulled the little packet from his fingers. 'Oh, I think I will. Why don't you make yourself useful and get me naked?'

Seb nipped the corner of her mouth as she pushed his running shorts over his erection, down his hips. 'That's a hell of an offer, Brat.'

Rowan sighed as her fingers whispered the latex over him, encircling all that masculine strength in her fist. 'I'm a hell of a girl, Hollis. Now, why don't we slide your Part A into my Plot B and see if we fit?'

The luminous hands on the bedside clock informed Rowan that it was past midnight as she rolled over onto her stomach to watch Seb walk into his *en-suite* bathroom. She'd been in Seb's arms, in his bed, for more than six hours. Six hours of intense, bone-dissolving, earth-spinning pleasure. She was one gooey, sexy mess and she wanted nothing more than to roll over and drift off to sleep.

Instead, she forced herself to sit up, then stand... Ooh, wobbly legs. The nearest garment was one of Seb's T-shirts and she pulled it over her head, unable to stop herself from sniffing the collar for that special combination of soap and cologne that she couldn't get enough of.

Just as she couldn't get enough of his kisses, of the feel of his hard muscles under her hands, the way she felt... *complete* when he slid inside her.

In between their lovemaking they'd dozed, before one

of them reached out for another kiss, another stroke, and they fell into passion again...

It was time to face reality. She didn't want to, but she had to.

She didn't know how to do this. She didn't do this... Well, she had—but not enough to feel comfortable waking up naked in his bed, with his room looking as if a hurricane had hit it after them rolling around like maniacs and bouncing off the furniture. She didn't want to stay but she couldn't just leave.

She really, really needed to polish up on her one-night stand etiquette.

And a one-night stand was all it was—all it could ever be. She had to be sensible about this... This was sex. Nothing more. They had acted on impulse, had used each other's bodies for brief, intense pleasure. It wasn't anything more—could never be anything more...

Rowan placed the balls of her hands into her eyes and pushed. It was okay, she told herself. She was allowed to have sex with a single man. The world hadn't stopped spinning. Wasn't free choice high on her list of values? She hadn't agreed to anything more than one night, to a casual hook-up, a night of pleasure.

It didn't change anything... In a couple of weeks her parents would be back. She'd say hello and how are you doing, make nice, and then she'd borrow that money from Seb and fly away. Because that was what she did best: she flew, caught trains, ox-carts, buses... That was how she lived her life. She didn't stay in one place, in one house, couldn't imagine a steady life with one man.

Staying still, coming face to face and heart to heart with a man terrified her. Mostly because she'd been disappointing people all her life and she'd have to love a man very much to stay still. The thought of losing her freedom—so hard earned—caused a cold, hard ball of something *icky* to form in her stomach.

She should leave, go back to her own room…take some time to regain her equilibrium.

'God, you look like someone shot your favourite dog,' Seb said from the doorway of the *en-suite* bathroom.

Rowan's eyes shot up and met his. Earlier they'd been warm with desire, laughter. Now they were cool and flat, and his expression was guarded and remote. Ah, so she wasn't the only one in the room having second—or third—thoughts.

Good to know.

'Ah… I was just…' Rowan placed her hands on her hips and looked around.

'Leaving?'

Since she was clear across the room and two feet from the door, what was the point in lying? 'Yeah…'

Was it her imagination or did she see his face harden? It was hard to tell in the dim light spilling from the bathroom.

'No cuddling required? After-dinner pillow-talk?'

Oh, that was sarcastic, and it blew any of her few remaining warm and fuzzies away. The problem was that there was a part of her that would have loved a cuddle, a gentle hand down her back, listening to his heartbeat under her ear, drifting off to the sound of him breathing next to her…

Because she felt weak and vulnerable—girly—she gave herself a mental slap and straightened her spine.

'Do you need pillow-talk and cuddling?' Rowan demanded, equally facetious.

'Of course I don't,' Seb ground out, walking naked back into the room.

There was no point in feeling embarrassed, Rowan realised, since she'd explored most, if not all of that luscious body. He had a swimmer's build, broad shoulders, slim hips, muscular thighs.

Rowan felt she should say something to dissipate the heavy, soggy blanket of emotional tension in the room. 'Look, Seb, you don't need to get all weirded out by this... I'm not going to get all hearts and flowers over you.'

'Oh, goody.'

Sarcastic again. He did it so well. 'For someone who is anti-commitment, and who doesn't do emotional connections, I would've thought that me leaving and getting out of your face would be the perfect scenario for you.'

'Yep, you'd think,' Seb said, in that bland voice that made her itch to smack him.

Rowan threw up her hands. 'How can we be so great in bed but so pathetically useless at actual talking?'

'Beats me.'

'You're ticked because your big brain is running at warp speed, trying to rationalise this, trying to intellectualise what just happened. You're frustrated because you don't understand how you can have mind-blowing sex with a woman you're not sure you like and who has driven you nuts your entire life.'

'I am not doing anything of the sort!' Seb retorted.

But Rowan caught the flicker of guilt in his eyes. Of course he was. She sighed. It was what Seb did. When something caught him off guard he put his extraordinary intellect to work and tried to figure it out on a cerebral level. Hadn't she watched him do exactly that growing up? She and Callie would wail and whine when things went wrong. Seb and her brother Peter would ignore the emotion and look for the cause and effect.

Men are from Mars, indeed...

'Your brain is going to explode. Attraction and lust can't be measured, analysed, categorised. It just *is*—like some things just are,' Rowan said softly. 'It was just sex, Seb, not quantum physics.'

'Yeah, whatever.'

Seb made a production out of yawning, pulled back the covers on his bed and flicked her a quick glance before climbing into bed.

'I'm going to sleep. Night.'

Rowan narrowed her eyes at him as he punched the pillows before rolling over and snuggling down. No *Thanks for a fun time*? No *See you in the morning*? He couldn't be more clinical about it if he left a couple of notes on the dresser table...

No—*no!*—that wasn't fair.

Be honest, here, Dunn. You were the one who set the tone for the way this ended... You were heading out of the door when he returned to the room. You were running scared and saying that you didn't need the mushy stuff...

And you don't.

You don't need anything but to research your netsuke, gather some cash, say a brief hello to your folks and hightail it back to...where? London? Canada? South America?

You need to be free, on the road, responsible to no one but yourself.

Rowan sent Seb one more look—was that snoring she heard? Really?—and half banged, half slammed his bedroom door closed.

Tangling with him had been fun physically, but mentally—huh! A toxic spill...

His brain, when blood finally reached it, was red-lining, Seb decided as the door banged shut behind Rowan and his eyes flew open. He was doing exactly what she'd said: intellectualising, categorising, analysing. He didn't understand what had happened earlier—that tsunami of want and need and pure animal instinct. He was a rational and stable guy. He didn't get caught up in the moment or swept away by passion.

He needed to understand why it had happened tonight

with Ro. He had to understand. Because if he could comprehend it then he would regain control of the situation. It was his modus operandi—the way he approached and dealt with life, with his problems. When his mum had left he'd expected her home within a month, then three, then six. The only way for him to deal with the slow-dawning reality that he and Callie had been essentially abandoned by the person who was supposed to love them most had been to rationalise it, to find a plausible—though mostly improbable—explanation.

She was ill and couldn't come home. She'd been kidnapped by Colombian drug lords and/or an alien space ship. She was an international spy.

He'd think it through, dissect the problem, and in that way he could subdue the bubbling, unpredictable mess emotions generated.

He didn't cope well with unpredictable and messy emotions.

And Rowan was five-foot-four of unpredictable and messy.

And why on earth did he feel ticked because Rowan didn't want to spend the rest of the night in his bed? Didn't want to be held? Her reaction should have him slipping off to sleep guilt-free, with a satisfied body and a huge smile on his face. Instead he was lying here like a freaking moron wanting...*what?* He cursed. Was he actually considering wading into messy and unpredictable?

Was that what had sent his brain into hyper-drive?

It couldn't possibly be, he decided. *You don't do emotional and you don't do connections, Butt-face.* And, really, if he decided that was something he suddenly wanted— through alien possession or a punch to his head—why would he choose a world-wanderer who couldn't stay in one place for more than a heartbeat? Choose a connection with someone who, when the thrill of those first couple of weeks wore off and the excitement of great sex started to fade away, would be on the first plane...

Oh, wait...he was going to lend her the money to do that anyway!

Seb stood up and walked back into the bathroom, gripped the edge of the counter. It shouldn't be this way, he thought. He should be glad that she'd walked out through that door and left him alone—instead of feeling as if he wanted to go to her, pull her back to his bed, fall asleep and wake her up by making love to her again. Again...why was he wondering whether they could connect on some sort of intellectual level as well as they did in the sack?

It didn't matter... Bottom line, he shouldn't be thinking about her this way. She'd been a good way to spend the night—an exceptional way to spend the night.

His junk twitched and pulsed at the memory of her... under him, over him...her hair brushing his chest, her warmth enclosing him like a warm, wet perfect glove...

Oh, hell, now he was never going to get to sleep with those thoughts rattling around in his head.

Seb walked back into his room and saw the shadows of his computers sitting in the far corner of his room.

Okay, well...he might as well give his big brain some work to do.

The following evening Seb stood just outside his front door and watched as Rowan, standing in front of the antique mirror in the hallway, tugged at the short white T-shirt that showed an inch of her waist above black low-slung jeans. Good grief, she looked hot!

They hadn't seen each other since their awkward goodbye last night and, thanks to having to jump on the super-early flight to Durban this morning, he hadn't had a moment to touch base with her.

He'd thought that the meeting in Durban would be a

morning affair, but he'd run into some serious challenges—
his clients had been more paranoid than normal and had
required a lot of reassurance that their precious information was safe in his hands—and the entire day had been a
nightmare, with suits peering over his shoulder, checking
and rechecking his progress.

Blerch.

And Rowan hadn't reached out to make contact. Then
again, neither had he… Should he have? He didn't have
the faintest clue—mostly because women always chased
him. It was what they did. They normally followed up with
a BBM, an SMS, a hello-how-are-you-doing e-mail. But
Rowan? Nothing.

He was equally intrigued and annoyed…and didn't *that*
make him sound like an egotistical jerk? He'd thought about
calling to check up on her but he hadn't been sure what
to say.

He hadn't slept much and he rubbed his eyes with his
thumbs. Why was he still so wigged out about the way the
evening had panned out? Maybe it was because Rowan
had blown every perception he'd had about women and
sex out of the window.

He'd thought that most women needed some kind of
emotional connection to have sex—that they needed to talk
before and after. Rowan hadn't required before-sex cajoling
or after-sex reassurance and she'd approached the whole
experience like a guy would. Like he did.

It was a blessing in disguise that she hadn't needed him
to talk, because thanks to that damned peach and the see-
through wrap his tongue wouldn't have been able to form
the words.

She was keeping him at an emotional distance, they'd
had sex and practically no conversation—which he normally considered the ideal relationship—and it bugged the
crap out of him.

Could he say hypocritical and bastard and then put them together in a sentence?

Rowan jumped as he stepped into the hall. Dropping his laptop and briefcase onto the old yellow wood table, he pulled off his wire-rimmed glasses, tossed them down and raised his eyebrows at Rowan. 'Going somewhere?'

To keep from tugging her shirt down, Rowan shoved her hands into the pockets of her jeans and rocked on her heels. 'Hi. You're...back.'

'It is Friday night,' Seb pointed out. And it was his house.

'I thought you might have plans—like a date,' Rowan said to his back as he disappeared down the passage.

He was back in under a minute, a bottle of beer in his hand. A date? He'd slept with her last night and she had him already trawling for another woman?

He didn't know whether to be ticked or flattered that she thought him to be such a player. Seb thought for a moment; nah, he was definitely POed.

'My plans? Nothing more strenuous than a burger, a beer and an early night. It's the Fish and Fern tomorrow.'

Rowan wrinkled her nose. 'The what?'

Seb gave her a long look before emptying his pockets, placing his mobile, keys and a thin wallet on the table. 'The triathlon race. The one on the fridge. Swimming, running, biking?'

'Oh, right. What time do you think you'll be home?'

Seb shrugged. 'Eight-ish, I suppose. There's a barbecue after the prize-giving and I'll probably stay for that. Problem?'

'No.'

Rowan tugged the shirt down but it sprang up her tummy with all the obstinacy of stretched cotton. He clocked her tousled but elaborate hairdo, the subtle make-up, the bangles at her wrist and the beaded earrings. She looked as if *she* was going on a date… Was that why she'd asked him whether he had plans? Because she did?

Hell, no. That wasn't happening.

'So, what are *you* up to tonight? That's one heck of an outfit, by the way.'

Rowan responded to the thinly disguised annoyance in his tone by raising her chin. 'What's wrong with my outfit?'

'Tight low-rise jeans, short top, fixed hair. Wherever you're going, you are going to get hit on all night.' The beer was not doing the trick of relaxing him; Rowan changing and staying at home would.

'Don't be ridiculous.'

'I'm a guy and I know exactly what *I'd* read into your outfit.'

'Guys would read sex into a nun's habit.'

He noticed that she still hadn't told him where she was going. What was the big deal? His temper, on a low simmer all day, started to heat. He shrugged out of his jacket and threw it over the newel post of the staircase. He yanked his pale green dress shirt out of his black pants and sat on the bottom stair to pull off his shoes.

Seb rested his elbows on the stair above, took a long sip of his beer and picked up a shovel to dig his own grave. 'So, where are you going? And who are you going with?'

'I'm going to a bar.'

'A bar?'

'You make it sound as if I am about to do a deal with the local meth supplier! I feel like I've been catapulted back to my teenage years with my over-protective parents. I'm not sixteen any more, Seb. What is your problem?' Rowan demanded when he just looked past her in stony silence. 'Why are you acting like this?'

Fair question.

'I didn't expect to come home to…' Seb rubbed his temple '…this.'

'*This?*' Rowan felt the bubbles of her temper rise to the surface and pop. '"This" being jeans and a tee?'

'"This" being you dressed up and looking hot.'

'I did my hair and put on some make-up...this is pretty normal!'

'Nothing about you is normal!' Seb sprang up, his eyes tired and sparking. 'Do you know how sexy you look? You'll have every male tongue dropping to the floor in that bar. You were mine last night and the thought of you going out and being someone else's is making me want to punch something.'

As soon as the words left his mouth and their meaning sank in Seb knew that he'd made a crucial mistake—that he'd been a total tool. Her eyes shimmered with hurt and she bit her lip to keep it from wobbling. He *never* spoke without thinking, but those words had just bubbled up, over and out...

Seb swore at himself and ran an agitated hand through his hair.

'Excuse me?'

Oh, crap. She'd kicked 'hurt' into the back seat and now she was seriously ticked. Wonderful. And could he blame her?

Seb twisted his lips and thought he'd attempt to explain. 'Okay, look, that came out wrong...'

'You think I am so easy that I could jump from your bed to someone else's?' Rowan laughed and the sound didn't hold a teaspoonful of mirth. She held up a hand. 'No, don't answer that, because I'm very close to smacking you silly! What a joke!'

If it was, he failed to see it.

Rowan shook her head, snapped a set of car keys off the hall table and picked up the bag that she'd hung on the coat stand. She walked towards the door.

Seb was thinking of how to keep her in the room when

she turned around abruptly and looked at him with blazing eyes. 'No, I'm not going to do this again.'

'Do what?'

'Leave you to your assumptions. I think that's a mistake I keep making over and over with you and my family. I allow you to jump to these crazy assumptions about me because…because of habit, maybe. Pride, maybe. But this—you thinking that I treat sex casually just because we had a great time in the sack—I can't let this ride. The reason we had great sex is because we obviously—who knows why?—have amazing chemistry. Why we have this chemistry when I think you have the personality and charm of a horse's ass is a mystery for another day.'

'I—'

'My turn.' Rowan cut him off with a sharp wave of her hand. 'As for my sexual history—do you know how hard it is, as a female travelling on her own, to get laid?'

She looked as if she was waiting for a response so Seb thought it was safe to say: 'Uh…no?'

Rowan looked momentarily triumphant. 'Hah! Of course you don't. You just assume that it's what we travellers do.' Her chest rose and fell with temper. 'Every man I meet— all the time—is a stranger. I don't know him. I'm not given the time to know him. I can think he's cute, but psychos come cute as well. Now, say I decide to take a chance… I have to get into a room with him—because, you know, I like a bit of privacy with my sex. That means I put myself in danger every time. And do you want to know how many times I've done that?'

Seb, now feeling like a first-prize fool, shrugged.

'None, Seb. I've *never* done it. I've had a couple of relationships over the years with guys I've known for a long time. I don't do hook-ups. It's a dangerous and stupid thing to do when you don't have any friends or family to rescue you if something goes horribly wrong.'

Seb scrubbed his face with his hands, feeling equally relieved and foolish.

'And, just so that I'm very clear about this, *we* rocked it because you have a heck of a bod and you are a good kisser and I haven't had any for a while.'

Okay, how deep was that hole he'd dug for himself and when could he throw himself into it?

But Rowan wasn't quite finished; she still had another layer of skin to strip off him. 'And I'm not going *to* a bar, you moron. I've got a job *tending* bar so that I can make some cash to pay you back and get out of your stupid, judgmental face!'

With that last verbal slap—which he so deserved—Rowan turned on her heel and walked out of his house.

CHAPTER SIX

ROWAN, EXHAUSTED AND smelling of beer and bar, walked back into the hall of Awelfor shortly after twelve-thirty and sighed when she saw Seb standing in the doorway to the small TV lounge, dressed in casual track pants and a loose-fitting T-shirt.

She was still feeling raw, hurt and angry that Seb—smart, smart Seb, who apparently had the emotional intelligence of an amoeba—had assumed that she was back-packing baggage with the morals of an alley cat. She was exhausted from not sleeping much last night, from career-ing around Cape Town today picking up all the equipment she needed—haybales, paint guns, food—for the party the next day, and she was depressed that she hadn't had a sec-ond to research the netsuke and that she'd been reduced to serving beers and martinis again. Dammit, she was twenty-eight years old—not nineteen.

'I don't want to fight, Seb.' Rowan dropped her bag to the floor and rubbed the back of her neck. 'If you're going to take any more shots at me, can I ask that you do it in the morning? I'm wiped out.'

'Come in here for a moment.'

Rowan cursed silently as he walked away without waiting for her response. *Let's just get this over with,* she thought, following him into the messy room. A large screen, big boys' TV dominated one wall and dark chocolate leather couches, long and wide enough to accommodate his large frame, were placed in an L-shape in front of the screen. A wooden coffee table held a large laptop and a bottle of red wine and two glasses.

Seb lifted the bottle and filled a glass, topping up his own half-full glass after he did so. He handed her the glass and nodded to the couch. Rowan, figuring that it was easier just to take the glass and sit down rather than argue with him, dropped to the couch and sighed as the pressure eased off her feet. She had forgotten how hard bartending was on the feet.

Seb sat down on the coffee table in front of her, his knees brushing hers. He held his wine glass between his knees and stared at the brown and cream carpet beneath him.

'I owe you the biggest apology.'

Okay, she knew she was tired, but was she really hearing Seb correctly? He was apologising? Seriously?

'Saying what I did earlier was…unkind and ugly and… Sorry. I really didn't mean it. It was a stupid off-the-cuff comment that slipped out because I was annoyed and tired and not thinking.'

'Now, there's a first—you not thinking,' Rowan teased, and Seb's face was transformed by a relieved smile.

Seb dropped a casual hand onto her knee. 'Friends?'

'Can we possibly be?' Rowan asked him, cocking her head and looking into those dark blue eyes.

Seb tugged on his bottom lip, placed his glass on the table next to his powerful thigh and put his elbows on his knees. 'Your verbal slap about making assumptions also hit home. Although I never believed those drugs were yours, I *did* think that you were reckless and rebellious and irresponsible as a kid.'

'I *was* reckless and rebellious and irresponsible as a kid,' Rowan pointed out.

'But I carried on assuming that. I didn't think that you

had changed, that you'd grown up. There's so much that I—we—all of us—don't know about you. I don't know you and I wonder if I ever did.'

Rowan felt her throat tighten. Finally. Finally someone from her past was looking at her differently, trying to see her and not the person they wanted her to be. Rowan put her fist to her lips and nibbled at the skin on her index finger. And, in fairness, how much did she know about *him*? About any of them? Surface stuff. Social media stuff. And how much of that was the truth?

She had to have some preconceived ideas about him and her family that weren't based in reality either.

'So, how about we try to get to know the grown-up versions of ourselves?' Seb suggested.

There was nothing she wanted more. Acceptance and understanding. While she craved her freedom, she also wanted the freedom to be herself in this place where she'd always felt she could never be that.

Rowan dropped her hand and picked up her glass with a shaky hand. 'I'd like that, but...'

'But?'

'But what about the other thing? The last night thing?'

'Sex?' Seb lifted his glass, drained half its contents and tapped his finger against the crystal. 'Let's not make this any more complicated than it has to be. What if we just put that onto the back burner for now and try to be friends?'

Rowan's smile was wide and true. 'Okay, let's try that.'

'Good.' Seb placed his hands on the table behind him and leaned back. 'And, as your friend, I'm going to ask you something.'

Rowan groaned theatrically. 'Oh, no.'

'Why haven't you been home? Why haven't you popped your head through the fence, looked at your house, walked through the gardens? Said hello to the dogs?'

'New dogs. They don't know me.'

'Hedging, Ro.'

'The house is occupied, Seb. I can't just go wandering through.'

'Hedging. I told the occupiers that you were home and not to worry if they saw you hovering around. They were cool about it. So, again, hedging...'

She was, and she didn't know what to say. She'd been avoiding going home because that way she could avoid thinking about her parents, about what she'd say to them when she saw them again, what they would say to her. And the truth was seeing the house made her remember how unhappy—no, not unhappy, just how excluded she'd felt from her family. Her parents and brother had been so close, sharing the same interests, the same quest for knowledge and mental improvement.

It made her feel eighteen again and all at sea.

'Were you so miserable at home, Ro?'

'Miserable? No.' Rowan looked around. 'But I always felt so much more at home here in Awelfor. Here I could dance and sing and laugh loudly...home was so quiet.'

Seb smiled. 'And you were the most lively child we knew.'

'I suppose I should take a look at the house... I can't avoid it for ever.' Rowan brushed her hair back. 'I don't know what I'm going to say to my parents, Seb. Should I apologise for living my own life? For not coming back for so long?'

'Did you want to?'

Rowan shook her head. 'No, I wasn't ready to come home. Didn't feel strong enough.'

'Then don't apologise, Ro.' Seb leaned forward and rested his elbows on his knees. 'I've been listening to your folks—mostly your dad—moaning about your travelling for years, but tonight for the first time I looked at it from another angle. Your parents are wealthy enough to travel and you've always returned to London. They could've met you there, or anywhere else, quite a few times during the last decade.'

'I've thought about that often,' Rowan admitted in a whisper. 'Why didn't they do that?'

'Because they didn't want you there; they wanted you here. Because it would have given you their tacit approval of your travelling, for choosing your own way of life, if they did that.' Seb grimaced. 'I like your parents, Ro. They were good to me growing up. But I could engage them on an intellectual level. As Patch said, you were always way too emotional for them.'

'Patch said that? I love that man.'

'I do too. He's been the best dad—apart from his habit of dating too-young, too-stupid-to-live gold-diggers.'

Rowan laughed, loosely linked one arm around Seb's neck and placed her cheek to his. 'I like this—talking to you. I think it's the first proper conversation we've had.'

'And I'm pretty sure that it's snowing in hell.' Seb ran his hand down Rowan's back before pulling away. 'You need to go home, Ro. Take a look. Confront those demons. They aren't as big as you think. And you need to go to bed— because if you don't I'm going to become very unfriendly and kiss you stupid.'

Rowan pulled her head back and her eyes were smoky with passion. 'I was thinking exactly the same thing.' She stood up and scooted around his legs. 'Sleep well, Seb.'

'You too, Brat.'

Rowan handed out the last goodie bag, ruffled the last head and placed her hands on her hips as she watched the last expensive car—this one was a Bentley—cruise away.

Thank God, thank God, thank God! Rowan felt almost dizzy with relief. Hauling the envelope out of her back pocket, she took out the cash and nearly did a happy dance in the middle of the driveway. Annie's son and daughter-in-law, although taken aback by their very muddy, very happy boy, had instantly recognised by his jabbering, excited conversation that his party had been a huge success. His father, his neck pulled forward by the rope-thick gold chain around his neck, had added a bonus of five hundred to the highway robbery price Annie had already paid her.

Three other mummies, obviously in awe of Seb's property, had asked for her business card. Not having one, she'd hastily scribbled her contact details on a serviette.

Professional, she was not.

But the cake had been perfect, and the mini-quadbikes and paintball shooting had been fun. She'd had her own gun and was supposed to be treated like Switzerland—but all that meant was that the rug-rats had had a common enemy and had shot at her whenever the opportunity arose. She had a bright purple paint mark on her neck and her T-shirt, jeans and legs were multi-coloured blotches.

Looking towards the paddock, she noticed that the hay-bales and used car tyres that had formed the track for the mini-quadbikes, as well as Seb's white fence poles, were splattered as well. Nothing that a hosepipe or a good thunderstorm couldn't fix… Rowan looked up at the sky and cursed the lack of clouds. She was exhausted already, and she had the kitchen to clean up. She didn't feel like hosing down the poles as well.

Crab-fishing in the stream at the bottom of the property had been another highlight of the day. It had been a bit of a problem finding enough branches to make adequate poles, and she had sacrificed a nice piece of fillet steak she'd found in the fridge to use as bait, but they had pulled up a lot of the unwelcome creatures that populated the small stream.

None of the kids had got hurt, lost or even cried. They'd had enough sugar to put them on a high for days, had a whole lot of fun, and if their parents had to throw away their mud-and paint-stained designer clothes Rowan was pretty sure they could afford to buy more. She had some cash in her pocket and she felt a sense of accomplishment that was different from buying and selling.

It was being around innocence, having fun doing the simple things she'd done with Callie, feeding off the kids' joyous energy. She'd run, skipped, hopped, climbed and crawled, and she'd frequently thought that she couldn't believe she was getting paid to have this much fun.

Kids. Not having had much to do with them, she would never have believed that she would enjoy them so much.

Rowan grimaced as she sank onto the bottom of the four steps that led to the wide veranda. She rubbed her lower back—she'd tumbled backwards off a stack of hay-bales and was now paying the price—and rested her aching head against the stone wall. She'd had minimal sleep over the past few days—sleeping with Seb and bartending had both translated into very late nights—and she'd been up with the sparrows this morning to get everything done before the kids arrived.

She shouldn't have stopped, shouldn't have sat down. Now that she knew how tired she was she didn't think she could find the energy to get up, never mind clear up the mess that the kids had made and the disaster area that was the kitchen. She'd just sit here for a minute with her eyes closed and try to recharge her batteries...

When Seb shook her awake the sun was dipping behind the mountains and she felt slightly chilly. She yawned as she glanced up at him, still dressed in his exercise gear, although he'd pulled on a hooded sweatshirt. Seb held out his hand and pulled her to her feet.

'I've made tea,' he said, leading her by the hand to the kitchen.

'You hate tea,' Rowan said on a smothered yawn.

'Not for me, for you.' Seb pulled out a chair from the table and shoved her into it.

As her eyes focused Rowan noticed that, instead of looking as if a nuclear bomb had exploded in it, the kitchen was tidy, all the surfaces were clean, the chip and sweet packets were packed away and the remains of the cake were in a big plastic container.

'You cleaned up.' Rowan took the cup he held out and wrapped her hands around it. 'You shouldn't have. I was going to.'

'Anyone who could fall asleep against a stone pillar for an hour was not up to cleaning up.' Seb held a cup of coffee in one hand, his fingers curled around the mug.

Rowan wished, passionately, that they were curled around something attached to her.

'So, that was your function?'

'Mmm. My stupid way to make some money.'

'If it's legal, there is no stupid way to make money,' Seb responded. 'Was it worth it?'

Rowan nodded. 'Yes, it was. Do you mind your property being invaded by a horde of kids? They didn't come into the house, by the way, except to use the downstairs bathroom.'

'No, of course I don't mind,' Seb said, and shook his head at her puzzled look. When he spoke again, he sounded frustrated. 'Ro, you could fill this place with a hundred kids and I wouldn't mind. I *do* mind you working so hard that you fall asleep with your head on the wall as soon as you sit down. You coming home is supposed to give you some space to sort your life out, but you're bartending and arranging kids' parties and you're exhausted. You don't need to do this...'

'I need to earn some money, Seb. Quickly. I hate being...'

Seb waited through her silence, then added his own words. 'Beholden? In my debt? That's such crap, Ro. You're sleeping in a bed that isn't being used, you don't eat enough to feed a mouse, and you are housekeeping...'

Rowan looked around at the neat kitchen. 'I pack the dishwasher and I throw a load of laundry into the machine...it's hardly housekeeping.'

'True; any chance of you actually mopping anything?'

'Maybe.' Rowan blew a tendril of hair away from her mouth and stared down into her strong tea. 'Worse than feeling in your debt is feeling that I'm trapped. That I'm in this city, this place, this house, and I can't leave. It makes me feel...panicky.'

Seb pulled out a chair and sat down opposite her, wincing as he did so. 'Why? Why is being here so difficult for you?'

'Because I am so free out there, and when I am free I'm happy. Being here just makes me remember how controlling and protective my folks were, and...'

'They were trying to protect you, Rowan. From yourself, mostly.'

Rowan sighed. 'You always defend them...' She held up her hand to hold off his hot reply. 'I don't want to argue with you, Seb. I know that you think that they were good parents because yours—'

'Mine weren't. Well, Patch was okay. My mother was a train wreck.'

'Patch gave you freedom to move, to explore. I was never allowed beyond the walls of our two houses.'

'They—'

Rowan interrupted him. 'My point is that whether the ties that bind are silk scarves or barbed wire you still can't move, and I've always had the need to be unconstrained, unfettered...free.' Rowan sipped her tea. 'That makes me jittery, but coming home broke just makes me mad. I wanted to show them that I am successful, together...responsible. Not in their way but in *my* way. Now they are going to hear that I'm broke and homeless, they'll roll their eyes and launch into one of their what-did-we-do-wrong? speeches.' Sadness swept across her face. 'Do you think I could've been adopted and they never told me?'

'Considering the fact that you look exactly like your mum, I'd say the chances are slim,' Seb said, his tone bone-dry.

'It's just that I couldn't be more different to them if I tried.'

Seb stroked a hand over her head. 'Different isn't bad, Ro, it's just different. I'd like to believe that they'd like to be part of your life but have no idea how to achieve that—especially since you hop around the world like a schizoid bunny.'

Rowan glared at him.

'Have you ever thought about how scary your life must be to them? To them, going to London was a massive challenge: the crowds, the congestion, the unfamiliarity of a new city. You do that all the time. They would be terrified to live your type of life. They are not as brave as you, Ro.'

She'd never thought about her parents from that angle and she realised that Seb was right. Her parents thought that going to their timeshare unit up the coast was a mammoth undertaking, so going to London would be equivalent to going to the moon. Doing what she did would be, to them, inconceivable.

She understood that. But why couldn't *they* understand that while they needed to stay in their cocoon she needed to be free.

'Why did they go? I haven't even asked.'

'Your dad was asked to present a paper at some conference and Peter was going to meet them in the UK.' Seb wriggled in his chair, winced again, and Rowan frowned.

'What have you done to yourself?' she demanded.

'Tumbled down a hill on the trail run.' Seb took a sip

of his coffee and stood up. Taking a bread knife from the drawer, he lifted the lid off the container holding the cake and cut two healthy slices. Putting them onto the lid of the container, he carried it back to the table and slid the lid between them. Sitting again, he snapped off a square and shoved it into his mouth. 'Yasmeen's chocolate cake. God, that tastes good. Who made it?'

'How do you know I didn't make it, using her recipe?' Rowan asked indignantly.

'Because I've tasted enough of your disastrous cakes to last me a lifetime. I don't think you ever made one that tasted like…well, like cake.'

'You're right. I didn't make it. I found a lovely lady who makes cakes, gave her a copy of Yas's recipe—'

'If she finds out, you'll hang,' Seb told her.

'Are you going to rat me out?' Rowan asked indignantly.

Seb smiled. 'She'll find out. She always does. None of us have ever been able to sneak anything past her.'

'I'll be out of the country by then,' Rowan replied, relieved.

'You poor, naïve, deluded child. You think that matters? If I could harness her powers I could rule the world.'

'I'll change my name and she won't find me. Anyway, if I do more parties I'll use this woman again.'

'More parties? You want to do it again?'

'Strangely, I enjoyed it.' Rowan lowered her cup. 'And it's really good money, Seb. Two of today's mummies said that they'd call me because they have parties they need to arrange. If they want them done in the next two weeks or so I'll do it.' Rowan forced herself to meet his eyes. 'Will you let me have them here?'

Seb stared down at the cake in his hand for the longest time. 'I'd like to say no, but I know that won't stop you. You'll just find another venue. So I'll say yes—with certain conditions attached.'

Rowan bit the inside of her lip and waited for his words.

'Do the parties, Ro, but with help. There is no way that you can keep an eye on thirty kids by yourself. And that blonde who was hanging around was as much help as a corkscrew in a bottle-free desert. I mean proper help. Someone who can lift chairs and move tables and carry stuff, run after the kids if necessary,' Seb said, his tone serious. 'No help, no party. Deal?'

'But where would I find someone to help?' Rowan demanded.

'There are lots of kids in the area looking for casual work,' Seb replied, breaking off another piece of cake. 'Or me.'

Rowan hooted with laughter. '*You'd* help?'

'If you needed me. It wouldn't be my first choice on how to spend my time, but if you needed my help I'd give it.'

And he would—of course he would. 'Okay, thanks. *If* I get another party and *if* I need help I'll ask for it.'

'Good.' Seb's face softened as he handed her a piece of cake. 'Eat.'

Rowan placed it on her saucer and shook her head. 'Yank down your track pants.'

'I thought we discussed this? We were going to be friends…'

'Stop being a jerk and let me see your injury,' Rowan stated patiently. 'Anyway, I've seen all you have, so it's a bit late for modesty.'

'Why?'

'Because you're in pain and I want to see what is causing it.'

'And congratulate it?' Seb grumbled.

'Of course. I live to see you hurting!' Rowan replied, her voice chock-full of sarcasm. 'Seb, you know how stubborn I can be, and I'm going to nag you until I get to see it.'

She *was* stubborn and she *would* nag.

Seb tipped his head back in frustration, thinking about the foot-and-a-half-long graze that ran from his buttock to his knee. His elbow also displayed the results of connecting with the ground at speed. After fifteen years of doing trail runs and triathlons he should know better than to hurtle down a mountainous track with his mind somewhere else—like in bed with Rowan.

It also burned that he'd been lying fourth at the time, feeling strong, with a good chance of catching the front runners. If he had seen that loose gravel right in front of his nose he would have finished the race—except that he'd broken the front joint on his bike as he'd tipped head over heels and had to retire. He hated not finishing a race almost as much as he hated not doing well.

He made the mistake of looking at Rowan, who was watching him...and waiting. For the love of God...

He pushed his track pants over his hips, stepped out of them and pulled up the back of his running shorts. He knew it looked bad when Rowan said nothing for a long time.

'It needs to be cleaned, and you can't reach to do it properly. Where's the first aid kit?'

Seb shook his head. 'If you think I'm going to let you come within a mile of me with a bottle of peroxide, you're mad.'

'First aid kit?'

'Ro, you're a better baker than you are a nurse!'

Rowan just folded her arms and tapped her foot and waited. Then she waited some more. Stubborn, obstinate and wilful; she gave a deeper meaning to those three words.

Giving in, with very bad grace, he stomped to the cupboard and lifted the first aid box from the top shelf. Banging it onto the kitchen table, he scowled at Rowan. 'Try not to kill me, Nurse Ratched.'

Rowan pulled her tongue at him before ordering him to

lie with his chest on the table and his legs stretched out. Doing as he was told, he felt like an idiot.

When nothing happened, Seb turned around to see her inspecting his leg. 'What's the problem?'

'Small pieces of stone and gravel are imbedded in the skin,' Rowan replied as she reached for the tweezers, the cotton wool and the peroxide bottle.

Seb gritted his teeth as she picked out pieces of stone and gravel. Taking a peroxide-wet cotton ball, she dabbed it over the spot and Seb swore viciously.

Rowan used the tweezers and dabbed again. Seb repeated the words.

He kept up his litany of swear words as Rowan tweezed the bigger pieces out.

A little while later he heard Rowan's stomach rumbling. 'So, any ideas about supper? I'm starving,' she said.

'Steak, potatoes and a green salad? Bloody hell, Ro!' Seb shouted, clenching every muscle in his body in pain as she worked on the area directly behind his knee.

Rowan stopped, glanced towards the fridge and pulled a face. 'Is that fillet steak?'

'Yes. Can you get a move on, please?' Seb demanded through a red haze of pain.

Rowan peered at the graze, and when she dropped the tweezers Seb realised that she was finally satisfied that he was stone-and dirt-free.

'Problem. I used your fillet steak to bait the hooks for crab-fishing.'

Seb turned his head and glared at her.

'Sorry,' Rowan responded, dousing another cotton ball in peroxide and swabbing it across his elbow this time.

Seb flew up, ripped the ball from her hand and launched it in the direction of the dustbin. 'You're having a bit too much fun at my expense, Rowan.'

Rowan met his hot eyes and clearly saw the mixture

of desire, frustration and amusement bubbling there. She licked her lips and risked lifting her hand to touch his cheek. 'Not fun, exactly. Maybe a tiny little bit of revenge for all those times you were so mean to me growing up.'

'You deserved everything I ever gave you,' Seb muttered, his gaze on her luscious mouth, wishing he could bend his head and cover it with his. He still wanted her... didn't think he'd ever stop wanting her.

Rowan, surprisingly, made the first move. Standing on her tiptoes, she brushed her lips against his, her tongue darting out to lick his bottom lip. His mouth softened as his hands gripped her upper arms. He started to pull her forward, to deepen the kiss...

Dammit! He couldn't do this—couldn't start something neither of them could finish. Seb placed his hands on her waist, lifted her up and away—as far away from him as possible—and dumped her, bottom first, on the kitchen table. He reached past her to pick up his mobile, which he slapped into her hand.

'What's this for?' she asked, puzzled and annoyed.

'Pizza. Order it. You can pay, since you fed my steak to the crabs. And no girly stuff like capers and asparagus!'

The past week of living with Rowan had been like living within a twister, Seb decided as he strolled into the kitchen. He'd had a tough day at work and his kitchen held Patch, an attractive blonde around Patch's age and Rowan, and they were all stuffing brightly coloured bags with sweets.

'Seb, do you know where I can hire a boat?' Rowan demanded.

'Hello to you too,' Seb said pointedly, and looked at Annie, his face quizzical.

'Seb, this is Annie—my friend. She hired me to organise the party last weekend. Annie, this is Seb, Patch's son,' Rowan gabbled, grabbing a handful of sour worms.

'Hi, Annie. Speaking of that party, the paddock poles still have paint splotches on them,' Seb pointed out.

'I'll get to it. Now, do you know where I can hire a boat?'

'A Hobie? A catamaran? An ocean liner?' Seb asked as he shook hands with Annie. He took the beer Rowan pulled from the fridge for him and twisted off the top.

Rowan wrinkled her nose. 'Something that can accommodate ten teenage girls for a sunset cruise around the harbour.'

Seb, who thought he had a reasonably fast mind, was battling to keep up. 'What are you talking about, Brat?'

Rowan sent him a try-to-keep-up look. 'I had an enquiry about a boat party: food, drink, sunset cruise. I need a boat.'

Seb took a long sip of his beer and rested the neck between his eyes. 'Was she always this exhausting?' he asked Patch.

'Pretty much. Rowan has always only had two speeds: fast and super-fast,' Patch replied, sliding a look at Annie.

Annie smiled slowly, dropped her eyes and lifted them again in a look that was all seduction. Oh, wow, Patch was flirting with a woman his own age. *His own age!*

Seb felt like looking out of the window to see if a pig was flying past. He leaned against the far counter and crossed his legs at the ankles. 'And these bags are for another party you're organising?'

'Yep, for tomorrow.' Rowan flashed him a grin. 'Not here, though. The mummy wanted it at her house, but she didn't want to take the time out from her business to organise the details. So she's paying me an insane amount to set out snacks, organise a magician and a Slip and Slide and to make party bags.' Rowan looked at her watch. 'And Patch and Annie are helping me because I need to get to the bar later.'

As he'd said—a twister. He'd barely seen her this past week. She'd dashed in and out of the house like a woman possessed. He'd tried to get her to stop for a glass of wine, a meal, a conversation. She'd brushed him off, saying that she didn't have time to do anything, and it had annoyed the crap out of him. He'd never been put in the position of running after someone, waiting for someone to give him a minute of their time, and it wasn't fun. Was this how his previous girlfriends felt? Was this a touch of karma?

Karma? Jeez, he sounded like a hippy girl... *Get a grip, dude! You're just freakin' miserable and, frankly, ticked off because you're horny.*

He switched gears fast. 'And your netsukes? Have you done any research yet?'

Rowan pulled a face. 'Not really. I've been so busy...'

'You have a shedload of money tied up in those statues and you're messing around with children's parties?'

Rowan's shoulders stiffened as she sent him a cool look. 'I thought that if I could earn some money I could get back to London and take them to the experts there. That would save me the hassle of trawling the net.'

The reluctance in her voice as she said 'trawling the net' had him shaking his head. 'You don't know where to start, do you?'

Rowan wouldn't meet his eyes. 'Not really.'

'And you couldn't ask me for help? Ro, what do I do for a living?'

Annie's and Patch's eyes played ping-pong as they bounced off their faces.

'It's just that you are busy...'

'That's an asinine excuse! You just didn't want to ask for help—again! I thought we'd talked about your stupid independent streak?'

Rowan launched a sweet at his chest. 'Don't you dare call me stupid!'

Seb snatched the sweet out of the air. 'I never said you were stupid. I said you had a stupid independent streak!'

Patch sighed and looked at Annie. 'I feel like I've been transported back to their childhood. This could go on for a while, so what do you say to leaving them to argue and coming to have a glass of wine at my place?'

And that reminded him… When was his father going to move out of the cottage and back into his own house? Seb opened his mouth to ask, then snapped it closed again. Finish one argument first.

He waited for Patch and Annie to leave—Patch's hand was very low on Annie's back…definitely something happening there—and then banged his bottle down on the counter. He looked at Rowan, who was still packing bags, and rubbed his hands across his face. It annoyed the pants off him that she was living in his house and yet he hardly saw her, that she was so damn close—across the hall from him—yet might as well be in China in terms of being available. He wanted to spend time with her, get to know her, but she was never in the bloody building!

And that felt strange—very bizarre. He'd never actively wanted to seek out a woman's company before, had never wanted to deepen the connection between him and his lovers.

Yet here he was, wanting to spend time with a woman he wasn't sleeping with. It didn't make any sense.

Look at her, Seb thought. Sexiness on steroids. She wore her hair up in a high ponytail and a tank top revealed the curves of the tops of her breasts. It skimmed her long, slim torso and ended an inch above the waistband of her white cotton shorts. Endless slim legs ended in bare feet tipped with fire-red nails. Rowan turned away, bent over to pick up a sweet that had fallen to the floor, and he saw the thin string of the top of her thong, a little red heart on the cross of the white T.

His saliva disappeared as his eyes slid over the rounded

curve of her ass, the knobs of her spine under that thin shirt. The band of her bra, the slim column of her neck.

He took two steps to reach her, and his arm banded around her waist as he hauled her back against him, his hand low on her stomach, pushing her into his throbbing erection.

Rowan spun round and her hips slammed into his. Her eyes were on his mouth as her hands went up to his neck and she mashed her chest against his. Then her mouth slammed against his and she yanked him into a kiss that set his blood on fire.

Rowan was poised for a moment on the edge of that precipice and then she tumbled into kissing Seb. She'd been thinking of this, dreaming about being in his arms again, all week—a mess of sexual frustration—and she'd kept herself super-busy to keep her mind off jumping him again. But now, as his hand grabbed her butt and yanked her up and into him, she could indulge in her need to rediscover those strong muscles, the heat of his skin, his talented hands, his sexy mouth.

Rowan yanked at his shirt and pulled it up his chest, her lips kissing the skin it revealed. Seb pulled the shirt over his head with one hand and Rowan placed her lips on the edge of the fabulous geometric tattoo that covered his shoulder and his bicep.

'I love this,' she murmured against his inked skin. 'So hot, so sexy.'

'I love the way you smell,' Seb replied, his words blowing warm air against her neck. 'Of sunshine and flowers.'

The tip of Rowan's tongue swirled against his collarbone. 'I thought we weren't going to do this…that we were going to get to know each other.'

'I know that you are a brat and that you kiss like a dream,' Seb replied, his hand curling around her breast and his thumb swiping her nipple. 'So I'm good, knowledge-wise, for now.'

Rowan's breath caught in her throat. 'And I know that nobody spikes my temper like you do and that you make my blood boil when you touch me like that. That's all I need to know right now.'

'Bed?' Seb demanded, clasping her face in his hands.

Rowan licked her lips. 'Bed, couch, floor. Take your pick.'

Seb grinned. 'I really like the way you think.'

CHAPTER SEVEN

'ONE OF THESE days we are going to have a post-coital conversation,' Seb muttered as Rowan bounded from his bed and headed into his *en-suite* bathroom.

She grinned as she shoved her hand into the shower and flipped on the taps to boiling. She popped her head around the doorway and smiled again. Seb lay face down on the bed, his head turned in her direction. 'Poor baby, are you feeling neglected?' she teased. 'Do you need me to act like your girlfriend?'

His eyes narrowed. 'I've never needed my actual girlfriends to act like my girlfriend so…no. You're exhausting. You never stay still for a second.'

He was right. She didn't. Staying still gave her too much time to think about things she'd rather not think about—needs that had gone unrecognised for far too long. Like affection and friendship, a sense of belonging, a house to come home to. Since they were too high a price to pay for losing her freedom she pushed them away and refused to think about them.

'One of these days I'm going to tie you to this bed with silk scarves and keep you here.'

Rowan flushed at the thought of being at his mercy, being under his control. Instead of making her feel panicky she felt excitement and…lust. Excitement? Good grief.

But she'd ignore the silk scarves portion of that sentence for a minute...

'Does that mean that you want us to carry on sleeping together?' Rowan demanded, ignoring the pounding shower.

'Since I spend so much time thinking about sleeping with you I might as well just have sex with you.'

'Ooh, don't stop. I just love it when you say such sexy, sweet things,' Rowan drawled.

Seb winced, turned over, and pushed himself up on his elbows. 'Sorry, that sounded churlish.'

Rowan folded her arms against the towel she'd wrapped around her torso. 'Churlish is the least of it.'

Seb rubbed his hand over his head and scowled. 'Dammit, Ro...this situation is going to bite me—us—in the butt, yet I can't stop wanting you. Sleep with you...don't sleep with you. Either way my ass is on the line to get chomped. I look at you and my control flies out of the window.'

Seb had looked as if he was passing a kidney stone as he'd said that, Rowan thought on an internal hiccupped laugh. Still, he was trying to express himself and she appreciated the effort, even if it was clumsy and ass-related. And, really, didn't she feel exactly the same way? She was leaving soon, and had no intention of letting Seb get under her skin, yet here she was, newborn-naked in his room, wishing he'd get out of bed and join her in the shower. And if they did this—continued to sleep together—they had to be very careful about what they were jumping into.

'If we're going to do this then we need to be very sure of what we are doing.' Rowan repeated her thought. 'I'll lay my cards on the table... I like you, and I love sleeping with you, but I *am* going to leave.'

Seb nodded, his gorgeous eyes holding hers. 'I *love* sleeping with you, I like you, and I don't want you to stay.'

Why did that sting? Rowan asked herself. It shouldn't—

couldn't. He was saying what she wanted him to say! Stupid, stupid girl...

'But...'

Rowan tipped her head at his hard tone, his intractable face.

'While we *are* sleeping together we're together. There's only me and you. No one else. No colouring outside the lines.'

She could live with that—wouldn't actually accept anything else. Rowan pushed her shoulders back and tossed her hair. 'Just so you know, I won't act like your girlfriend.'

'Good. I won't act like yours...boyfriend, that is.' Seb pulled a face. 'That's such a juvenile term. How come the word boyfriend sounds so much worse than girlfriend?'

'It's a moot point, since we're not either,' Rowan said firmly as Seb swung his legs off the bed, stood up and walked over to her, all long, lean, masculine grace.

'What time will you be home from your shift at the bar?' he asked, running a possessive hand down her arm.

'My shift ends at twelve. So around half past twelve,' Rowan replied as he put his hands on her hips and backed her into the steaming shower.

He bent his head to her breast and tongued her nipple.

'That sounded remarkably like a question a boyfriend would ask, Hollis,' Rowan said, streaking her hands over his broad shoulders.

Seb picked up his head and sent her a wicked look that had her toes curling.

'Nope, just trying to work out how much time I have to buy some more condoms.' A foil packet appeared as if by magic between his thumb and finger. 'This is the last one. Shower sex?'

Rowan sighed. She was definitely going to have to buy herself a toy when she left... Then she'd be able to drift back to memories of what Seb was doing to her. And why did that thought make her feel instinctively sad?

'Ro?' Seb lifted his head and his hand stilled on her breast. 'You okay to go again?'

She needed to make as many memories as she could. 'Yes, please.'

It was past three in the morning when Rowan parked her car—Yas's car—in the carport next to the three-car garage. Seb's hog sat in one spot, Patch's Jag in the other and his SUV in the last space. Poor little car, Rowan thought, left out in the cold. She glanced up at the house and saw that the light was off in Seb's room. Rowan considered slipping quietly into bed with him, snuggling down for the night, with his back warm against her chest, her legs tucked in behind his knees. And if he woke up so much the better…

No! Rowan shook her head. That would be a girlfriendy thing to do, and she wasn't going to act like that. She and Seb were having sex, for a defined period, then she was leaving and he was staying. Getting cosy was a sure way to get her heart involved, and that would be a disaster of magnificent proportions! Leaving would be so much harder than it needed to be, and settling back into her transient life would take more effort than normal.

Was that why she'd accepted the offer from a couple of the pub's regulars to accompany them into the city and listen to a blues band in a late-night café? Because it was an impulsive decision? Because it was something that she'd do if she was on her own…accept a random invitation from strangers to try something different?

She sometimes felt that she was too comfortable in Seb's house—in his bed, his arms.

She couldn't afford to get too attached to him, to his house or this city, Rowan told herself as she climbed out of the car and headed towards the front door. She had a little over a ten days left here; her parents were due back at the end of next week and she'd spend the weekend with them. Hopefully, if she could land the boat party gig, she'd have enough money to feed and house herself when she got back to London.

Of course if she actually did some work researching those netsukes she could be out of here sooner. She knew Grayson wanted them, and she suspected that, judging by his increasingly frequent e-mails on the subject, and as long as she could prove that they weren't stolen, he might buy them unseen. At the very least she'd recover the cash she'd laid out and then she could go anywhere she wanted to…

She should start with researching the Laughing Buddha—the miniature she'd spotted first in the shop, instantly recognising that it was the stand-out piece of the collection—so why wasn't she carving out some time to research the wretched thing? Sure, it would take a bite out of her money-collecting time, but she wasn't a total numpty on the computer, as she'd made herself out to be to Seb.

Did she want to keep it? Or could it be—dammit—because she was feeling slightly sentimental? A tad grateful to that tiny little object that it had been the catalyst to her coming home?

Home. There—she'd said it. And it was time she acknowledged that, no matter what had transpired before, this *was* home. This house,—*not* the house next door… *This* was home.

Whoomph!

Rowan let out a high-pitched squeal and cannoned into a hard shape as she pushed open the door to Awelfor. Familiar arms grabbed her before she toppled over and her heart steadied as she realised that she'd run into Seb.

'You scared my breath out of me!' She wheezed as she placed a hand on her chest. 'Jeez, Seb!'

Seb flicked on the hall light and Rowan blinked at the

brightness. When the black dots receded she turned to Seb, and her smile faded when she saw that he was dressed in jeans and an old T-shirt and held his car keys in his hands.

'Where are you going at three in morning?' she asked, puzzled.

'To bloody look for you!'

Rowan took a step back as his roar washed over her. Then she saw his wild eyes, his dishevelled hair and his inside-out T-shirt. He was in a complete tizzy and it was fairly obvious that *she* was the cause of it.

'You said that you would be home around half-twelve!' Seb paced the hallway, tension bunching every muscle in his body. 'At twelve-forty-five I was worried. At one-fifteen I was concerned enough to call you on your mobile and I've been calling every ten minutes since then. Why don't you bloody well answer your phone?'

Rowan pulled the mobile out of her bag and checked the display. *Oh, yeah...* She'd missed more than a couple of calls...like fifteen.... 'I'd put my mobile on silent...I didn't think to change it back.'

'And doesn't that just explain a whole lot?' Seb shouted. 'You don't *think*, Rowan. Where on earth have you been?'

Crap. She hadn't seen Seb this mad since she'd chirped him about his ex-fiancée. And he'd passed that level of anger five minutes ago. 'I went to a late-night blues café in Simon's Town.'

'You *what*?'

Rowan thought that she saw the chandelier tremble. 'Whoa, hold on a sec! I thought you'd be sleeping—'

'Like I could *sleep* until I knew you were home safely!'

'Seb, the pub is five minutes away.'

'And I expected you home fifteen minutes or so after the pub closed. And I know it closed at one because I called there too!' Seb shoved his hands into his hair. 'I've been imagining you stabbed or raped or driven off the road—'

'Oh, come on, Seb! You're overreacting!' Rowan retorted. When his eyes lightened she knew that she'd made an tactical error. His anger had just deepened and his eyes had gone cold.

'You know, I *get* that you have this free-spirit, answer-to-no-one gig going on, and I know you well enough to choose my battles with you,' Seb said, his voice colder than an Arctic breeze. 'So I'm prepared to let the little things go… But when you roll in at three in the morning, after saying that you'll be home a lot earlier, I get to yell at you!'

'I'm not a child, and you're not allowed to place restrictions on me!' Rowan snapped, going on the defensive because she suspected that she'd crossed a rather big line.

'You keep telling me that you're not a child, but you're acting like one. A responsible, thoughtful grown-up would've picked up the phone and called me, told me not to worry.'

Seb rubbed the back of his neck with his hand. His anger had faded and she could see disappointment and resignation on his face. She could fight anger. The other two were like acid on her soul.

'Rowan, you're free to come and go as you please. I can't and won't ask you to be something you are not. But I do expect you to think, occasionally, about other people. I was worried. I had a right to be. If not as your lover, then as a man who has known you all your life.' Seb twisted his lips. 'And if you can't see that then you are even more screwed up than any of us thought.'

Seb's words hovered in the air as he walked up the stairs and a minute later she heard his bedroom door close. Rowan sank to the third step of the staircase and dropped her head to her knees. He was right and she couldn't run away from it. She had been selfish and thoughtless and she didn't like being either.

Why couldn't people understand—and why couldn't she explain?—that restrictions felt like chains to her? That rules felt like the bars of that long-ago jail cell and that she couldn't trust anyone not to change the rules on her to suit their needs better?

She knew that he had a point—a really valid point. She knew she should apologise, ask for forgiveness for being thoughtless, but the words were stuck in her throat. Why did she feel that if she apologised she would also be apologising for her lifestyle? For being impulsive, freedom-seeking, for being who she was?

She was at fault and she knew that she should admit it—just go up those steps and say sorry. Wake him up if she had to... But saying *I'm sorry* had become incredibly difficult for her. Maybe it was because she hadn't had anybody in her life for so long to say sorry to—or was it because she'd apologised constantly as a child and a teenager for her high spirits and impulsive behaviour? Back then her apology had always been followed by more lectures, more disappointment, more opportunities to throw her indiscretions back in her face.

By seventeen she'd stopped saying sorry—mostly because nobody had heard her any more. They certainly hadn't believed she was remorseful, and no one except for Callie—God, she loved that woman—had ever attempted to understand why she felt the need to push the barriers, to taste, touch, experience life.

Geez, she sounded like a whiny, childish...victim. *Damn*, she sounded like a *victim*? Did she subconsciously see herself that way? As a casualty of her parents' narrow-minded world view, Joe's deception?

Maybe she did.

And she didn't like it.

So, she could sit on these stairs and think about how misunderstood she was, justify why she should brush this incident under the carpet, but then she'd feel guilty and dreadful—especially since it was pure pride standing in the way of her saying sorry.

Seb would probably give her another lecture on thoughtlessness and selfishness, but she was a big girl. She'd take it, say goodnight and go back to her own room. She could do this—she *had* to do this! If only to prove to him that she had grown up...

Rowan dragged herself up the stairs, hesitated outside Seb's door. When she saw the sliver of light under the door she gently knocked. She heard his 'Come in' and when she entered saw that he was in bed, a computer on his knees. His face was blank when he looked at her.

Rowan put her hands behind her back and gripped the doorframe behind her. 'Sorry. That was selfish and thoughtless of me.'

Seb's face remained inscrutable while he closed his computer and placed it on the bedside table. Rowan shifted from foot to foot while she waited for him to say something.

'Okay. Come here.'

Rowan stepped closer to the bed and wondered what else was coming. When he just looked at her, a small smile on his face, she frowned. 'That's it? No more lectures?'

Seb smiled slightly as he pulled the covers back and shifted across the bed. 'Nope. Hop in.'

Rowan plucked at her T-shirt and shook her head. 'Seb, I can't. I smell of beer and booze. I'm exhausted. I'm going to take a shower and head back to my room.'

'Take a shower and head back here,' Seb said.

His face and voice were calm. Steady. God, she loved his steady.

His bed...it was tempting. So tempting. But so...*girl-friendy.* 'I—I shouldn't.'

'You really should. Come on, Ro, the world won't stop

if you simply sleep in the same bed as me. Besides, I never got to buy those condoms, so you're safe from me…tonight.'

Those eyes were dreamy again. That hard body was relaxed, his face sleepy. He was as tired as she was and she knew that it would now take a cattle prod to get her to go back to her room. 'Okay, I'll just take a quick shower.'

'Mmm, okay. Hurry up,' Seb murmured, his head on the pillow and his eyes closed.

Rowan kept his sleepy face in her mind as she rushed through the shower and brushing her teeth. When she came back into the room, dressed in the T-shirt Seb had been wearing earlier, he was fast asleep. She slid under the covers next to him and felt his arm slide around her waist. She snapped the light off and Seb snuggled closer. She felt his lips in her hair.

'You scared me, Ro. Don't do it again, okay?' he whispered.

'I'll try not to,' Rowan whispered back into the darkness. And she *would* try—but she couldn't guarantee it.

Five days later it was early morning and Rowan sat in the cushioned area of Seb's bay window. She stared over the hedge to the windows of her old bedroom, with Seb's gentle breathing the soundtrack to her thoughts.

She still hadn't gone home—still hadn't managed to slip through the gate and walk around her mum's prize rose garden, or sit on the bench outside, where her father had always used to read the Sunday papers in the winter sun.

They were due home in less than a week and she still hadn't wrapped her head around how she was going to approach them, deal with them. Should she e-mail them and tell them that she was home and staying with Seb? Should she just wait and rock up on their doorstep? How would they react? What would they say, feel, want from her?

Would they be able to see her as a grown woman who

made her own decisions and lived with the consequences thereof? Would she receive any respect from them for doing that? Any understanding? She no longer required them to be supportive of her, of her lifestyle, but she didn't want to listen to them nag her about settling down, studying further, about her clothes and her hair and her inability to make good choices...

Seb rolled over in his sleep and Rowan watched him for a moment. How would her parents react when they found out about her and Seb? Because find out they would. They weren't completely oblivious to everything around them, and she and Seb gave off enough heat to generate a nuclear reaction. They wouldn't understand the concept of a short-term, mutually satisfying sexual relationship. They'd been childhood sweethearts and hadn't, as far as she knew—and she probably didn't, because her parents were about as talk-ative as clams—dated anyone else.

They'd probably worry more about Seb than they would about her. Seb was a part of their lives, a constant presence, while she was their erratic and eccentric wayward daughter.

'Ro? You okay?' Seb asked from his massive double bed, leaning back on his elbows, his hair rumpled from sleep.

Gorgeous man, Rowan thought.

'Mmm, just wrapping my head around visiting the old house.'

'You still haven't been over?'

Rowan shrugged. 'I really should. It's funny—funny ironic, not ha-ha—that I can walk into a slum in Bombay or a yurt in Mongolia but I haven't managed to screw up the courage to go home. Every time I think about going over I feel like I'm eighteen again. Lost, alone, scared. I don't like feeling like that, Seb.'

'Understandable. Want me to go with you?' Seb asked, sitting up and crossing his legs. 'And then if you feel like you're eighteen you can tell me and I'll kiss you, or touch you, and remind you that you're all woman.'

'Generous of you.' How did he always manage to make her smile when she was feeling blue? Rowan bundled her hair up, held it on top of her head for thirty seconds before allowing it to fall again.

'Okay, we'll go over later. Tell me about your travelling.'

Rowan turned to face him, her back to the window. 'That's a pretty broad subject. Narrow it down…'

Seb thought for a moment. 'Tell me what you love about travelling.'

'The colour, the wonderful local people, their tolerance; the differences that are wonderful, the similarities that are universal. Buildings, bazaars, street food.'

'And what do you most hate about it?'

'Practically? Dirty kitchens and cheap hostel dorm rooms. The constant partying all around. The same questions all the time. "Where do you come from?" "How much of the world have you seen?" "How long have you been travelling for?" "Where to next?" Boring conversations, over and over and over again…' Rowan hesitated.

'Tell me, Ro.'

Rowan gestured to the bed. 'This…'

'This?' Seb looked puzzled. He looked at the bed and then turned his gaze back to hers. 'What?'

'One of the worst things about travelling is relationships: finding them, keeping them, losing them. I have said goodbye far too many times, Seb. Far more than any person should. Ever. I can go for weeks without meeting another traveller, depending on where I'm staying, because I don't want to…don't want to get to know them and then have to wave them off.'

'Are we talking about friendships or lovers?'

'Either. Both,' Rowan said. 'Saying goodbye always hurts.'

And it will hurt so much more when I have to say good-bye to you, Rowan thought, holding his intense gaze. She knew from talking to other backpackers and from her couple of failed relationships that a relationship limited by time, like hers and Seb's, was always more passionate than a normal, run-of-the-mill romance in the real world. They both knew that it had to end some time soon, so they had to make every moment count.

It wasn't real. Or maybe it was too real. It just wasn't built to last.

It would end with another goodbye. And she already knew that it would be absolutely the hardest goodbye she'd ever have to say.

Seb ran his hand through his very short hair and then over his stubbled jaw. He looked as if he wanted to say something, pursue the subject, but then she saw him retreat. Was he running from the emotion in her voice? From the sentimentality of her words? She knew that he'd never been good at dealing with raw emotion. He preferred to find a rational explanation behind every decision or action. She envied him that ability to be so clear-thinking, so sensible.

She couldn't be like that… She felt everything. Twice.

'Oh, hey…I've been meaning to ask you. Do you want to come with me to a cocktail party tomorrow night? It would be nice to go with someone.'

Rowan blinked at the change of subject, thought for a moment, and then said, 'I'd love to, but I don't have anything that could even vaguely pass as a cocktail dress.' She held up her hand to stop Seb from talking. 'And, no, you are *not* going to buy me a dress and shoes for one evening! What a waste! So, sorry—no can do.'

'Oh, come on, Ro. It's just money.' Seb rolled out of bed and walked over to her, his sleeping shorts riding low on his hips. He bent down, brushed his lips across hers and pulled her to her feet.

'It's money I would have to pay you back. I'm already in debt to you for the airfare from Jo'burg to here, for the airfare when I leave—though maybe I might be able to pay for some of that...'

'Then get your ass onto a computer and do something about your netsukes,' Seb complained, his hands loose on her hips. He looked down at her, assessing her. 'I have a feeling that you don't want to sell them.'

Rowan wrinkled her nose, thought about denying it and shrugged. 'I really don't want to sell the Laughing Buddha. But I have to sell the others. I can't afford a twelve-thousand-pound indulgence—especially when I owe you money.'

Seb rested his forehead against hers. 'I can understand why you want to keep it. It's stunning. As for owing me money...it's not important.'

Rowan stroked the side of his neck. 'It's important to me. I can't take your money, Seb.'

'You could give lessons in stubborn to mules, Brat,' Seb muttered.

'I know...' Rowan dug her fingers into the light smattering of his chest hair. 'Listen, are those massive chests still up in the attic?'

'As far as I know.' Seb sat back, looking puzzled at her change of subject. 'Why?'

'Callie and I used to play dress-up with your grandmother's dresses. If I remember right she was quite a socialite in her day.'

Seb—smart guy—immediately made the connection.

'Ro, you cannot possibly wear a sixty, seventy-year-old dress! Fish moths! Dust!'

'Dry cleaners! And Yas banished fish moths a hundred years ago. Haven't you ever heard of vintage dresses? I think there were shoes up there too.'

'You're nuts.'

Rowan raised an eyebrow. 'Do you want me to go with you or not?'

'Oh, okay. We'll take a look. If we don't find anything, then I'll buy you a dress and no arguments—okay?'

'Maybe.'

Seb kissed her nose. 'So, plan of action for the day... Sex, breakfast, a quick visit to the War Room for me, a tour of your old place for both of us and then up to the attic. Then sex again. And then sex later.'

'And maybe sex for pudding,' Rowan said dryly.

Seb laughed. 'You catch on quick.'

Limited time, maximum pleasure, Rowan thought as he swept her into a kiss that had her toes curling. And, yeah, saying goodbye to him was going to sting.

CHAPTER EIGHT

SEB, NOT FINDING Rowan in any of the rooms downstairs, jogged up the stairs to the main floor. Instead of turning left, as he usually did, he took the second flight set of stairs, passing the closed doors to the smaller rooms that hadn't been used since his grandparents' day—such a waste of space—and heading for the narrow stairs that led up to the attic.

He wondered when last he'd been up here. Fifteen, twenty years? Callie and Rowan had used to play up here all the time when he'd been glued to his computer.

Some things never changed, he thought sourly. He'd planned to spend most of this day with Ro, but his staff had run into sophisticated firewalls on a site they needed to crack—today—and it had taken all their combined strategy skills to climb over, under and around them. As a result he'd spent most of the day in the War Room and hadn't seen Ro since breakfast.

He wondered if she'd gone next door, but doubted it.

Seb poked his head into the attic and looked around. Instead of being dark and poky the attic was filled with natural light, courtesy of the skylights in the roof. The usual detritus filled the space directly in front of him—boxes that were labelled 'Christmas decorations', old computers, a set of water skis, and a pile of life jackets lay on top of more stacked cardboard boxes.

He really needed to toss some of this rubbish out.

'Ro?'

'To your left, Seb,' Rowan called.

Seb turned and followed her voice, walking around a wooden partition, and blinked in surprise. Thick, old-fashioned oak chests spilled garments over the rough blankets Rowan had placed on the floor, and in the centre of the clothes-spill Rowan stood in front of an antique full-length mirror framed in oak, dressed in a sleek black gown and three-inch heels. Even with her hair in a messy ponytail and a make-up-free face she looked stunning.

'What do you think?'

'That's a hell of a dress. Did you spray paint it on?'

'Ha-ha. Your gran was slightly skinnier than I am.'

His grandmother... He'd never known her, but he'd like to know how anyone could have so many clothes. He stepped over a pile of coats and looked down at the garments closest to his feet. Jeans, a thigh-length leather jacket, a velvet trenchcoat, a white linen suit.

'These are too modern to be my grandmother's clothes.'

'I think they're your mum's—what she left behind. There are a couple of nice dresses... Do you mind?'

Seb felt his throat clench and forced himself to shrug carelessly. 'Knock yourself out. She left them here, didn't she?'

Rowan looked at him with sympathetic eyes and he hoped that she wouldn't say anything. He didn't discuss his mother—ever. The longest discussion he'd had about her had been with his father a week or so ago.

Rowan ran her hands over her hips and turned back to the mirror. 'What do you think of this dress?'

Seb looked at her properly, felt the saliva disappearing from his mouth and swallowed several times. Hot, hot, *hot*. He couldn't find the words...

'Uh...' he grunted as his brain shut down.

Rowan looked at her reflection and tipped her head.
'You're right. I never liked this shade of black.'

How could she possibly take his silence to mean that he
didn't like the dress? Was she mad? It was figure-hugging,
cleavage-revealing, backless and strapless.

It sent every blood corpuscle heading south.

Seb smacked the ball of his hand against his temple to
reboot his speech function. 'I love the dress, And black is
black...isn't it?'

Rowan sent him a pitying look. The kind women re-
served for those moments when they thought men had
the understanding of a two-year-old. 'Of course there are
shades of black. Obsidian, peppercorn, domino, raven,
ebony...'

Seb felt as if he'd fallen into an alternative universe.
'Peppercorn is a shade of black?'

'There are many shades of red—fire engine, cherry,
scarlet—why can't there be shades of black?'

'I have no idea what you're talking about. And I really
don't care.' *All I want to do is get you out of that dress.* To
distract himself from that thought, he looked around again.
'Good God, look at these clothes! I never knew there was
so much still up here.'

Rowan's eyes were shining with pleasure. 'They're fabulous. I've seen six cocktail dresses I want to try on.'

'I like that one you have on,' Seb said gruffly. 'Wear
that.'

Rowan shook her head. 'This is a ballgown—too much
for a cocktail party. I just couldn't resist trying it on.'

'Aren't they out of fashion?' Seb asked, toeing a froth
of purple silk.

'Designer dresses like these are never out of fashion.'
Rowan disappeared behind a screen in the corner. 'And it
seems like your gran's taste ran to classic, timeless outfits.'

Good for Gran, Seb thought as he walked to the centre

of the room and sat on the dusty floor, crossing his legs at the ankles.

'What do you think?'

Seb glanced up and swallowed his tongue. The dress was red, a shocking slap to the senses, low-cut, and with what seemed like a million tassels falling to just under her backside. 'It's red. And short.'

'It's raspberry, and I'm decent underneath.'

Rowan twirled, the tassels whirled, and Seb saw the high-cut shorts underneath in the same shade.

'It's a heart attack dress,' Seb said. 'A bit too much for a corporate do.'

Rowan looked at herself in the mirror. 'Mmm, maybe you're right.'

Seb removed his smartphone from the back pocket of his jeans and checked his e-mails while Rowan changed again. Why she had to disappear each time to change was a puzzle for another day. He'd seen—and tasted—every inch of her, quite a few times.

'Ready for the next one?' Rowan asked cheerfully.

Seb grinned. 'Hit me.'

Seb leaned back on his elbow and almost choked at the puffball that sashayed across the wooden floor. It was orange, it was ruffled, and it was hideous. He searched for something to say and decided that no words could describe the awfulness of the dress.

'That bad, huh?' Rowan arched an eyebrow, turned to look in the mirror and laughed. 'Oh, *yuk*! I look like orange icing.'

Seb laughed. 'I think the proper shade is cosmic carrot. Take it off, please, and we'll burn it!'

'Not a bad idea,' Rowan agreed.

Seb watched as the gown got thrown out towards the chest and imagined her next to naked behind that screen. It took all his will-power to stay where he was, and the front of his jeans was growing tighter by the second.

The next three dresses were all black, sexy and sophisticated. Seb used the orange monstrosity for a pillow and spread out on the floor, lazy in the diffused sunlight that drifted through the skylights. He could think of worse ways to spend a lazy late afternoon than watching a sexy woman model slinky dresses for him.

'This is it,' Rowan declared. 'If this one isn't suitable, then I give up. I want a glass of wine.'

'Let's see it.'

Seb turned his head and his heart bumped in his chest. He slowly sat up and looked at Rowan, who was looking at herself in the mirror. The dress was a colour somewhere between blue and silver, low-cut, and a concoction of lace and fine ruffles. He could see glimpses of her fine skin through the lace and his saliva disappeared.

He remembered that dress—remembered his mother wearing it to a party some time shortly before she'd left for good. She'd grabbed him as she walked out through the door, pulling his reluctant twelve-year-old self into a hug that he'd professed to hate and secretly adored.

Mostly because her hugs had been so rare and infrequent. Laura had not been affectionate or spontaneous, and gestures like those were imprinted on his memory. She'd smelled of vanilla and she'd worn her blonde hair piled up onto her head.

Two weeks after wearing that dress out she'd been gone. For ever.

'I love this...love the lace...' Rowan bubbled, turning in front of the mirror.

When he didn't respond, she turned to look at him. She crouched down in front of him, her cool hands on his face.

'Seb? What's wrong?'

Seb tried to shake off his sadness. The hurt that he normally kept so deeply buried was frying his soul. He attempted a smile but knew that it didn't come close.

'Please, please talk to me,' Rowan begged.

Seb reached out and touched the fabric that draped her knees. 'This was my mum's.'

'Oh, sweetie. I'm sorry.' Rowan rested her head on his. 'I'll take it off, find something else to wear.'

'Actually, it's a happy memory. I remember her wearing it just before she left. She hugged me, called me her computer geek, said something about…' He tried to recall her exact words but they were lost in time. 'Um, how someone like her had managed to produce someone as bright as me. Or something like that.'

'I remember her vaguely.'

'So does Callie. You were—what?—seven when she left?'

'I was seven. Cal was six.' Rowan pulled the dress above her knees and sat down on the blanket next to Seb.

'I still feel crap that Callie didn't have a mother growing up.'

'Neither did you, Seb. Cal didn't feel the effects of her leaving as much as you did, sweetie. She had Yas…we both had Yas. My mother was so involved in Peter's life and his studies and her music that she didn't have much energy or time left over for me. So when we needed a hug, comfort, or to talk to someone we turned to each other or to Yas. Grumpy, spinsterish, with a tongue that can slice metal. It's strange without her here in Awelfor.'

Seb ran his hand down her calf, knowing that she was trying to lighten his mood. 'If she was here you wouldn't be sleeping in my bed.'

Rowan laughed and quoted one of Yasmeen's favourite expressions. '"You want the milk, buy the cow!"'

Seb grinned, and then his smile faded as he looked at the dress again. He was silent for a long time before stating quietly, 'She's in Brazil, in Salvador. Low on funds. She was in the hospital a couple of months ago with a burst appendix.'

Why had he told her that? Why did he want her to know? This wasn't like him, Seb thought, regretting the words that he'd let fly out of his mouth. He didn't have this type of conversation with the women he was sleeping with—didn't have this type of conversation at all.

What was it about Rowan that made him want to open up to her? To let her see behind the steel-plated armour he'd so carefully constructed? Was it because he'd always known her? Because she was Callie's friend and now his too? Was it those deep black sympathetic eyes that held understanding but no pity?

'When did you find out where she is?'

'I've always known where she is,' Seb said, his voice harsh.

'How?'

Seb lifted his eyebrows at her. 'What do I do for a living, Ro?'

'Oh,' Rowan whispered, connecting the dots.

Seb rubbed the material between his fingers again. 'I found her when I was about sixteen. She was in Prague. I managed to get hold of an e-mail address and I sent her a couple of letters…angry, vicious letters…demanding to know why she'd left and then, in the next breath, begging that she come home.'

'Did she ever reply?'

Seb shook his head. 'She changed her e-mail address and I lost track of her for a while. I'd tell myself that I didn't give a damn and wouldn't look for her. Then something would happen and I'd start again. But I never sent her another e-mail. I just need to know…you know…that she's alive. And okay. Not in trouble…'

'But you send her money.'

Seb's eyes flew up to meet hers and Rowan shook her head at him.

'You do send her money. Oh, Seb, you...'

'Sucker? Chump? Idiot?'

Rowan placed her fingers over his lips. 'You're putting words into my mouth. I was going to say you shouldn't.'

He felt his cheeks flush. 'She's often broke. What can I do? It's just money. I don't know why everyone gets all heated up about it. Money is easy...'

Rowan nodded her head. It was. Of course it was. To him. Money was black and white, no shades of grey, clearly defined. It held no emotion, no grudge, didn't waver or prevaricate. He understood money. People, with all their flaws and craziness and ups and downs, flummoxed him.

'What am I supposed to do, Ro? Not send her cash? Let her suffer because we suffered?' he demanded.

Rowan saw the decades of pain buried deep and bit back her protective response—the one that made her want to snap, *Yeah! You should let her climb out of the hole she's dug herself into!* Instead she bit her tongue and knew that he needed to talk to her, to someone, about his mum. Even tough guys, seemingly unemotional guys, needed to unload occasionally.

Rowan suspected that Seb was long overdue.

'How many times have you sent money?' she asked in her most neutral voice.

'A couple of times a year for the past few years,' Seb admitted reluctantly. 'Before that she seemed to be okay for funds.'

'And, if I know you, you probably sent a lump sum every time?'

'It was always an anonymous deposit. There is no way she can trace who it came from.'

Rowan sucked in her cheeks and gazed at the floor, literally swallowing the angry words at the back of her throat.

His mother was many things, but she wasn't stupid, and she had to at the very least suspect that it was Seb. How many people would she have met and had a big enough impact on for them to make anonymous, generous ongoing deposits into her bank account? Who else would it be other than her computer genius son? And she'd never sent him an e-mail to say thank you, to acknowledge him...

Oooh, that was rough.

Rowan looked down at her hands, vibrating with tension. Good grief, families were complicated. Parent-child relationships could be crazy. The ways to mess up your children were infinite, she decided.

Seb still held the hem of her dress—his mum's dress—between his fingers and Rowan looked at his bent head, at the masculine planes of his face, the tiny tick of tension in that single dimple in his cheek. Her tough guy, smart guy, good guy. So strong, so alpha, so damn attractive in his complexity. She'd known him for ever but she felt that she could spend another lifetime discovering all the nuances of his personality; he was that layered, that interesting.

That intriguing.

Ugh, pull up those reins, cowgirl. Your horse is bolting away from you... You're not going to get sappy and sentimental. You can't afford to, and you know this!

Rowan stood up, grabbed the edges of the hem of the dress and pulled it up and over her head. Seb gaped as she stood in front of him in just a brief pair of white panties and silver heels. No bra.

His eyes clouded over and Rowan smiled a tiny smile of feminine satisfaction. So sue her. She could make this hot guy salivate, and as a bonus banish the sadness from his eyes.

She looked at the dress in her hand. 'I love this dress... but I understand if you don't want me to wear it.'

Seb bit the inside of his lip. 'I want to say yes but… Maybe some day. Just…'

'Not today.' Rowan nodded her understanding. She looked at the pile of discarded dresses on the floor. 'Okay, black it is, then. Which one?'

Seb pulled a face. 'Ugh. Come on, Ro, let me take you shopping. One dress, one pair of shoes… Consider it as nine years' worth of Christmas and birthday presents I never got to buy.'

He needs to do this, Rowan realised. *He needs to spoil me—wants to do something for me that is outside of the crazy little deals we've struck to work around my pride and independence.* Could she allow him to do that, or would her stiff neck and habitual self-reliance spoil it for him?

It was hard. She couldn't lie. But seeing the pleasure on his face when she finally nodded her agreement was worth the risk.

He scooted up, dropped a kiss on her nose and grabbed her hand. 'Okay, let's go. Now.'

'Good grief, Hollis, I'm still half naked!' Rowan protested. 'Pass me my clothes, Einstein.'

Seb picked up her pink T-shirt from the floor next to his foot and Rowan saw that he did it with great reluctance. His eyes were firmly on her breasts.

She grabbed his chin and forced him to look in her eyes. 'Get your head out of bed, Seb. We're going shopping. For a dress. And shoes. Cocktail dresses and shoes are expensive, by the way.'

Seb grinned. 'I'm pretty sure my credit card can stand it.'

Rowan let him go, stepped away and picked up her shorts. She pulled them up, zipped, and placed her hands on her hips. 'Seb?'

'Yeah?'

'Your mum's failings are hers, not yours. You didn't do

or say anything that made her leave. That was on her and not on you.'

Seb pulled her close and buried his face in her hair. Just stood with her in his arms. She didn't know where those words had come from. She just knew, soul-deep, that he'd needed to hear them.

Just as she knew that all she had to do right then was hold him.

And when he pulled away to let go she pretended that the moment *hadn't* been charged with all those pesky emotions he tried so damn hard to ignore.

She did it because quite simply he needed her to.

'I need an ice cream,' Seb whined theatrically, and Rowan rolled her eyes at him.

What a lightweight, she thought. They'd only done one level of the mall and there were three more to go. She still hadn't found a dress that was both within the budget she'd set in her head—she didn't care how flexible Seb's credit card was; she was *not* going to pay a fortune for a dress she'd only wear once!—and nice enough to wear.

'Or a beer. Actually, I definitely need a beer,' Seb added as she pulled him into a tiny boutique that looked interesting.

'This was your idea,' Rowan told him, unsympathetic, and headed for a rail of dresses at the back of the shop.

Black, black, red... She pulled a coral chiffon cocktail dress off a hanger and held it up to look at it. Oh, it was pretty, she admitted as she held it against her and looked in the full-length mirror against the wall. It was sleeveless with a dropped waist and a multi-tiered skirt that fell to mid-thigh.

Take me home, it whispered urgently.

'That's the one,' Seb stated, jamming his hands into the

pockets of his shorts while Rowan looked for a price tag. 'Go try it on.'

No tag, Rowan thought, and knew that it would cost a bomb. She had an eye for picking out quality. She sighed. In clothes and in *objets d'art*.

Rowan shook her head and replaced the hanger on the rail. 'We'll look for something else.'

Seb tugged it off the rail and thrust it at her. 'Try it on.'

'It's the perfect colour for you,' the shop assistant stated, and Rowan narrowed her eyes at her.

'Stop being stubborn and try the bloody thing on.' Seb pushed her towards the discreet dressing room. He turned to the shop assistant. 'Shoes?'

'Silver diamante sandals. I have the perfect pair. Size seven?'

'Of course you do,' Rowan muttered as she stepped into the dressing room. She raised her voice so that it could be heard above the partition. 'Size six.'

Rowan slipped her clothes off, carefully undid the discreet zip and slid the dress over her head. *Yeah, this is the dress,* she thought; it was a pity she couldn't have it.

'Does it fit?' Seb demanded.

'Yes. Beautifully. It's a fairytale dress.'

And she was living in a fairytale at the moment. She had the run of a gorgeous house she'd always loved and was sleeping with a super-hot, sometimes not-so-charming prince.

She was loving every second of it.

But it wasn't real life, Rowan reminded herself. She—no, they were *both* enthralled by their sexual chemistry, and it was colouring how they saw each other. When the dust settled, they'd start to argue, and then they'd start to fight, and soon—as per usual—they wouldn't be able to stand each other.

Because the best predictor of future behaviour was past

behaviour, and neither of them had a very good track record at playing nice for extended periods.

Then why did she feel so settled, living in Seb's house, living with Seb? Was a part of her yearning for the stability of living in one place with one man? At twenty-eight was her biological clock starting to tick? Was it just being in Seb's home, waking up in Seb's arms, that had her wanting to believe that she could be happy with the picket fence and the two point four kids and the Labrador and…?

You're being ridiculous, she told herself. *The grass always looks greener on the other side.* She knew this—heck, she knew this well.

Before coming home she had never had a serious thought about settling down, about relationships and children and suburbia. Okay, that was a lie—of course she had—but only little, non-serious thoughts. Even *she* knew she was capable of being seduced by the idea of *what-if,* of thinking that a wonderful experience could translate into a wonderful life in that place. Hadn't she gone through something similar in Bali, where she'd thought she'd buy a little house and stay for ever? And when she'd first seen the Teton mountain range, and that gorgeous little cake shop that had been for sale in the Cotswolds? She'd imagined herself living and working in all those places, but the urge to move on had always come—as it would here as well.

'Rowan? You lost in there?'

Seb's voice pulled her out of her reverie.

'Coming.' Rowan pulled on her clothes, stepped out of the room and handed the assistant the dress. 'Thanks, but we'll keep looking.'

The assistant looked at Seb, eyebrows raised, as she slipped the dress into an expensive cover.

'I've already paid for it. Shoes too.' Seb took the covered dress, slung it over his shoulder and grabbed the bag holding her shoes. 'Can we please get a beer now?'

'You paid for it?' Rowan asked in a icy voice. 'What on earth…?'

'You said it fitted beautifully, it's your colour, and I could see that you love it,' Seb replied, puzzled. 'I'm not seeing the problem here.'

'The problem is that it costs a fortune!' Rowan grabbed the bag and peered inside at the shoe box. 'And the shoes are *designer*!'

'Geez, you're boring when you rattle on and on about money.' Seb yawned. 'You agreed that I could buy you a dress and shoes. I've bought you a dress and shoes. Can we move on to the next subject for the love of God? Please?'

Rowan sent him a dirty look, turned on her heel and stomped out of the shop. Outplayed and outmanoeuvred, she thought, and she didn't like it.

Yes, he was on-fire hot, and he was really good company, but she had to remember that Seb could be sneaky sharp when he wanted to be.

'Beer… Food…' Seb breathed in her ear, before grabbing her hand, tugging her around and pushing her in the opposite direction. 'The food court is this way.'

CHAPTER NINE

SEB SNAGGED AN outside table belonging to a funky-looking bistro, draped Rowan's dress on the third chair and grinned at her sulky face. She still wasn't happy about the dress... No, she loved the dress, but she didn't like the idea of him buying it for her.

She took independence to stupid heights, he thought. So the dress was expensive? So were his computers and the technology he loved to spend money on.

His last computer had cost him three times what he'd paid for the dress...

'Stop sulking and order a drink,' he told her, and grinned as her pert nose lifted in the air. He smiled up at the red-headed waitress, placed their orders and leaned back in his chair.

'Thank you for the dress,' she said primly, politeness on a knife-edge. 'And the shoes.'

'I can't wait to get you out of it,' he said, just to rattle her cage.

'Your chances of doing so are diminishing rapidly,' Rowan retorted, but her lips twitched with humour. 'Do you really like the dress or did you just want to stop shopping?'

'Both,' Seb admitted, funeral-director-mournful. 'The things you make me do, Brat.'

'Talking of that...' Rowan gestured to the huge electronic advertising board to the left of them. 'I saw a sign advertising an antiques fair and night market in Scarborough tonight. We could go take a look when we're finished eating.'

'Yeah...no. I'd rather eat jellyfish. Besides, I have a houseful of antiques and you're broke.' Seb took the beer the waitress had placed on the table and drained half the glass in one swallow.

'Thanks for reminding me,' Rowan grumbled. 'And I'm not broke. I'm financially constrained. Asset-rich and cash-poor. We don't have to buy—we could just look.'

Seb mimed putting a gun to his head and pulling the trigger and Rowan laughed.

They sat and sipped their drinks in a comfortable silence before Seb asked, 'By the way, what happened to the boat party you were organising?'

'Ah, the sixteen-year-old birthday girl changed her mind. Now she wants to go to a Justin Bieber concert instead.'

Seb shuddered.

'I'm getting party enquiries all the time, but I don't want to take on anything I can't deliver in the next week or so. You said that my parents should be home on Sunday—four days from now—and I have to be in London by the following weekend to meet Grayson, so there's no point in trying to get too involved. Pity, because it's good money.'

'So you'll be gone in a week or so?' Seb asked in a very even voice that hid all the emotion in his voice.

'That's the plan,' Rowan said lightly as her heart contracted violently. A week? Was that all they had? Where had the last two weeks gone? She wanted them back, dammit.

'God...' Seb muttered into his drink.

It would be another goodbye and the hardest one that she'd ever have to say. Harder even than that first one, when she'd run away to find herself, to find out what made sense to her. When had he become so important? So hard to leave?

'Did you go next door this afternoon?' Seb asked, changing the subject.

Rowan nodded.

'And...?'

She shrugged. 'It's just a house. They haven't changed much.'

'Your parents don't do change.'

'But I do, and maybe now I can look at them differently.' Rowan took a sip of wine and looked thoughtful. 'I did a great deal of thinking this afternoon, so maybe it was a good thing that you got tied up at work.'

'I want to hear about it, but maybe we should order first.' Seb beckoned the waitress over, asked for two gourmet burgers and another round of drinks. When the waitress had left, he gestured to Rowan with his glass. 'Talk.'

'How come you just expect me to spill my guts but you don't?'

'Because you're the emotional one and I'm not,' Seb replied.

Except that she was beginning to realise that Seb was far more emotional than anyone knew. He just had years of hiding it.

'I'm starting to think that Fate had a hand in me coming home—that it's telling me that I need to pull my head out of the sand and start dealing with all those old hurts and grievances. If I hadn't bought those netsukes, run out of cash and been flagged by Oz immigration I wouldn't be here.'

'Having amazing sex with your arch enemy?' Seb interjected.

'Having amazing sex with my old friend,' Rowan corrected, and saw the flare of appreciation, of attraction... fondness?...in his eyes. *No emotion, my ass.*

'I need to see my parents, deal with my issues around my mother, reconcile with them—her. Mostly her.' Rowan sighed. 'Maybe I'm finally starting to understand that we are very different people. I wasn't the daughter she needed and she didn't understand what I needed—especially that night I got arrested—but...but my childhood is over. I need to find a new "normal" with them.'

Seb folded his arms and placed them on the table. He linked his fingers in hers and stared down at their hands. 'I never understood why you ran. You were always a fighter. You always came out of the corner ready to fight.'

Rowan nibbled her lip. 'I got knocked down one too many times, resulting in emotional concussion.'

'That's a new one... Who knocked you down?'

'My parents—my mum especially. Peter, Joe Clark...'

'Your dipstick ex? What did he do...exactly? Apart from frame you?'

'When did you realise he had?'

'I think I've probably always known. What else did he do?'

Rowan blew out her breath and held his eye. It was time she told him—time she told someone the whole truth of that evening.

'I fell in love with him. He was kind and sweet and said all the right things to get me into bed. I kept him waiting because...you know...he was my first, and I wanted to make sure he was the right one. Someone who really loved me and not someone who was using me... Ha-ha, what a joke!'

Seb's face hardened. 'So he took your virginity...?'

'Yeah, we made love three hours before we got to the club. The policeman knew the drugs weren't mine—he even admitted it to me—but they were on me and he had to arrest me. Joe told me while he was laughing at me for getting arrested that he'd just wanted to bag and bed "the virgin rebel". That's what he called me.'

Seb swore, low and slow. 'I swear I'm going to rearrange his face.'

'I'm over it—over him. I really am.' Rowan managed a

small smile. 'But it wasn't the best night of my life. I was reeling. I'd had my heart kicked around by the boy who had just taken me to bed—the whole experience of which, sadly, was not nearly as brilliant as I thought it would be—'

'Bad?'

Trust a man to get distracted by sex, Rowan thought as she rocked her hand in the air. 'Meh…'

'Meh?'

'Not good, not bad—and I am *not* discussing my first sexual experience with you, Hollis. Jeez! Do you want to hear this or not?'

'Keep your panties on… So you went off to jail…'

'I had been there for a day or so and I was so scared, terrified. Another young girl had been arrested for something—I can't remember what. Her mother came to the jail, and when they wouldn't release this girl her mother came into the cell with her and just held her until she *could* be released. I wanted that like I've never wanted anything in my life.'

Rowan swallowed and took a deep slug of her wine.

'I just wanted my mother to love me, to support me, to hold me while I sat in that corner. And I knew that she wouldn't. Ever. That hurt more than anything else. So when I got home I thought I would test my theory; how far could I push her until I got a reaction out of her? I never got much of one. My dad screamed and raged and tried to lay down the law but my mum switched off. Until the day I wrote my finals. I came home and she and I had a…discussion.'

'About…?'

Okay, so this was something that she'd never told anybody. Not even Callie. 'My life, my plans. I told her I wanted to go overseas and she immediately agreed. Said it was the first sensible sentence I'd uttered all year.'

'What the…?'

'She said that it would be good for all of us—mainly

her, I think—that I went. I heard the subtext in her speech; she'd had enough of me and her life would be that much easier if I were out of her face. So I packed my stuff, took the money she offered—she was the one who cashed in those unit trusts of my grandmother's—and caught the first plane I could.'

'God, Ro...'

Seb ran his hand over his face and felt sick. They'd all known that Ro and her mum bumped heads, known that Peter was her obvious favourite, but they'd never believed— not for a second—that their relationship had been that broken. Okay, his mother wasn't a saint, and she'd left and it sucked, but she hadn't constantly been there, physically present but emotionally unavailable.

Rowan's staying away from Cape Town made a lot more sense now.

'I'm so sorry,' he muttered, knowing his words were inadequate and stupid after so much time.

But he didn't know what else to say—how to convey how angry and...sad he felt. Because, unlike him, Rowan had needed to be nurtured and shown affection, to be bolstered and boosted. She'd needed affection and love and affirmation.

Bile roiled in his stomach as the waitress placed their burgers in front of them. 'I should take you home...let me take you home.'

Then he felt Rowan's hand cover his, her touch comforting him when he should be comforting her.

'Your mind is going into overdrive, Seb. I'm fine now and I've learnt to live with it. I'm way over Joe Clark and him screwing me—figuratively and literally. As for my mum...she is what she is. I've grown up...'

'But you'd still like a relationship with her?'

'I'd love a relationship with her. So I'll see her, say my sorrys if that's what she needs to hear, and try again.'

He turned and stared down into her face. Oh, dear God, he could fall for her; tumble for this brave, beautiful woman with midnight in her eyes.

Seb shook his head, trying to replace emotion with rational thought. He was just feeling sorry for her, feeling guilty because he hadn't pushed hard enough, dug deep enough to find out the truth about her before this. He'd always known that there was more to Rowan's story, more to Rowan.

Besides she was leaving...*soon*. And he had no intention of letting anyone else leave with his heart again.

Mothers...jeez. The million and two ways they could screw you up.

Rowan popped a chip in her mouth and chewed thoughtfully. 'I really want to go to that antiques market, Seb.'

Seb picked up his knife and fork, looked at his food, and put them down again. He really didn't feel like eating.

'What?' he asked, his mind still reeling. He digested her words, understood them and frowned. 'Are you playing me?' he demanded, innately suspicious of her cajoling face. 'Are you making me feel sorry for you to get what you want?'

Rowan chuckled. 'It's what we woman do. You're smart enough not to fall for it.'

'Brat.'

'Let me try something else.' Rowan batted her eyelashes at him. 'If you take me I'll let you charm me out of that dress.'

Seb looked her up and down and slowly grinned. 'I'm going to charm you out of that dress anyway, so no deal.'

Rowan twisted her lips to hide her grin. 'I *can* resist you, you know.'

Laughter chased the shadows out of Seb's eyes. 'No, you can't. I can't resist you either. Eat—you're going to need the energy.'

'Is that a threat?' Rowan asked silkily.

Seb picked up her hand, turned it over and placed an open-mouthed kiss into the palm of her hand. Rowan shuddered and lust ran up and down her spine when he touched the tip of his tongue to her palm.

'Absolutely it's a threat,' Seb said, before attacking his burger.

Seb cast another look at Rowan as they walked down the steps to his car, parked by the front door earlier, and thought about walking into that cocktail party with her hand in his. Her dress would be enough to have the older men choking on their drinks, their wives raising an over-plucked eyebrow and any man below sixty sending approving looks at her stunning legs, from thigh to the two-inch silver heels she had absolutely no problem rocking.

She was gorgeous, with her wild hair pulled back into a casual roll, minimal make-up and a coral lipstick that perfectly matched the red of her dress. She looked fresh and sexy and he was already anticipating the end of the evening, when he could strip it off her as he'd promised. Which was insane, since they'd made love just over an hour ago and again this morning. And twice last night after they'd got back from visiting that antiques market, where Rowan had tried to persuade him to buy a silver cigarette case he didn't like and certainly didn't need.

'It's old and it's valuable. You could double your money,' he remembered her insisting.

'It might be old but it's ugly,' he'd replied, not telling her that he earned more money in fifteen minutes than he'd make on the hideous case.

He'd offended Rowan's horse-trader instincts for about a minute—until another pretty object had caught her attention and their brief argument had been totally forgotten as she'd engaged stallholder after stallholder in conversation.

It had taken them for ever to visit every stall—which

she'd had to do. She was so charming, easily drawing people into conversation and melting the sternest or shyest heart there. She had a natural warmth that just pulled people to her, he thought as he drove down the driveway.

'You look…God…amazing, Ro,' he said, turning left into the road.

'Thanks. You don't look too shabby yourself. I like that suit.'

Rowan placed her hand on his thigh and he could feel her warmth through the fabric of his black suit. He'd teamed it with a white shirt—no-brainer—but Rowan had swapped the tie he'd chosen—black—for a deep blue one he'd never worn in his life which, according to his sexy date, deepened the blue in his eyes.

He'd liked her choosing his tie… Seb sighed and reminded himself yet again to get a grip, catch a clue.

She. Was. Leaving.

As in bye-bye, birdy.

Next week.

And he was getting goofy because she was picking out his ties.

Get over yourself, already, Hollis.

Rowan's fingers dug into his thigh. 'Seb, stop!'

He slammed on the brakes. 'What? Jeez!' He looked past Rowan, down her parents' driveway, and saw Heidi and Stan standing in the driveway, pulling bags out of their sedate sedan.

'Oh, crap. Your parents are back.'

'Looks like it.' Rowan bit her lip and lifted her hand as her parents swivelled around to see who was idling at the bottom of their driveway. She turned and looked at Seb, her heart in her eyes. 'It would be so much easier if you just drove on.'

Seb touched her cheek with his thumb. 'I'm right behind you, babe.'

'Well, at least I'm looking my best,' Rowan quipped in a small voice as he turned off the engine.

'You look fantastic,' Seb said as he left the car, walked around and opened the passenger door for Rowan.

Heidi and Stan walked down the driveway to greet them.

'Seb, hello!' Heidi called as Seb took Rowan's icy hand in his. 'We're back—as you can see.'

'Stan…Heidi.' He placed his hand on Rowan's back and pushed her forward. 'So is Rowan.'

'Mum…hi, Dad.' Rowan stepped closer, reached up and brushed her father's cheek with her lips, leaned in for a small hug and then turned to her mum. Seb clenched his fist when Heidi pulled back and Rowan's lips brushed the air about two inches from her cheek. She couldn't even kiss her, hold her, after nine years apart?

What the…?

Who *was* this woman? Had he ever really known her? Had he been so blinded by the fact that she was there every day that he thought she was marvellous for that alone? No, he'd seen her interact with Peter—loving, kind, affectionate.

His heart clenched for Rowan as she stood back and straightened her shoulders. 'You're both looking well.'

'How long have you been home?' Her father took her hand, held it tight. 'It's so good to see you. You look beautiful—so grown-up.'

Rowan smiled. 'Seb and I are going to a party. I arrived about two weeks ago…I needed to come home unexpectedly. Seb's been helping me out.'

Heidi lifted her eyebrows and pursed her lips at Seb's hand, resting on her hip. 'Seems like he's been doing more than helping you out. Strange, since you could never stand each other before.'

Seb started to speak, but Rowan gripped the hand on her hip and he got the message. *Shut up, dude.*

'I've grown up, Mum.'

Heidi looked her up and down. 'Your skirts certainly haven't.'

'Mum! Nine years away and all you can do is gripe about my clothes?' Rowan snapped.

'Well, I think you look gorgeous, Ro.' Stan jumped into the conversational bloodbath. 'Absolutely terrific.'

'Well...' Heidi folded her arms. 'I'm tired, and you two are going to be late for wherever you are going. Maybe you should be on your way.'

'Heidi!' Stan protested, and Seb's temper simmered.

'We'll see her again,' Heidi said. 'Tomorrow. Maybe.'

Stan sent Rowan an apologetic look and Rowan stepped into his arms and gave him a longer hug. A hug Seb was pleased to see that he returned. He kissed her head before they stepped apart. 'I'll see you in the morning, Ro. It's good to have you back, darling.'

Rowan nodded and held onto Seb's hand with a death grip. 'See you then, Dad. And it's good to be back. Night, Mum.'

'Goodnight, Rowan. Sebastian.'

Seb pulled Rowan back to the car and opened the passenger door for her, helped her in. When he was back in his seat he placed his hand on the back of her neck. 'You okay, Ro?'

'Sure.' Rowan shrugged, her eyes on her parents, who were walking into their house. 'Situation normal. My mum cool and uninterested; my dad the buffer between the two of us.'

'She called me Sebastian. She's never called me that.'

Rowan managed a smile. 'It's because you're sleeping with me. She thinks you can do better.'

'Then she's an idiot.' Seb dropped his hand and started the engine. 'I need a drink. A couple of them.'

'Me too. Lead me into temptation, *Sebastian*.'

'Buzz off, Brat,' Seb shot back, but he kept his hand on her knee the whole way up the coast to the cocktail party.

In Seb's bedroom, much later that evening, Rowan slipped off her dangly silver earrings and dropped them onto Seb's credenza, next to his wallet and keys. 'Jeez, who would've thought I would run into Joe this evening at the cocktail party? I mean, heck, this is a big city. What were the chances?'

'Fairly good, I'd say, since he's reputed to be one of the most up-and-coming young businessmen in the city and it was a Chamber of Commerce function.'

'Up and coming dipstick, more like it,' Rowan muttered. 'Thanks, by the way.'

'For...?'

Seb shrugged off his jacket and Rowan could see the residual annoyance in his eyes. She knew that Seb had wanted to clock Joe, but he'd just cut him off at the knees with one burning look when he'd tried to engage them—her—in conversation.

'For sticking close...for not letting him near me.'

'My absolute pleasure,' Seb muttered, taking a step towards her. 'Why are we talking about him and why aren't you kissing me?'

'An epic fail on my part,' Rowan admitted, putting her hands on his waist.

'Damn straight,' Seb replied.

Rowan lifted her mouth to his, touching those surprisingly soft lips that could kiss her so tenderly but could also utter soft, deadly words that could strip hide. But he was only tender, only affectionate with her. He tasted of the whisky he'd sipped earlier, and as he opened his mouth to allow her to explore further she sensed a change in him.

This wasn't just about sex and pleasure any more, about maximising the moment. This kiss and the lovemaking that would follow were about making memories, capturing tastes and feelings that would sustain them when they separated.

Seb lifted his head and his deep, sombre eyes held hers as his hand travelled down the back of her neck to the zip of her dress. He pulled it down, one tantalising inch at a time, his fingers touching the skin beneath until the fabric gaped open to her buttocks. Using one finger, he pushed the fabric off one shoulder and then the other, until the dress fell in a frothy puddle over her feet.

Seb shoved his fingers in her hair and gently pulled the pins out, winding her curls around his hand before allowing the weight of her hair to fall down her back. Bending down in front of her, still fully dressed except for his jacket, he lifted one foot and deftly undid the ankle straps of her shoes. His fingers lightly caressed her ankles before he sat back on his heels and allowed his hands to drift up her calves, to explore the backs of her knees, the tops of her thighs.

'You are so beautiful,' Seb said, placing his forehead against her thigh.

Rowan frowned as she stroked his head. He sounded sad, she thought. Scared. As if this was just becoming a bit too much for him, a little too intense.

No, that was how *she* was feeling...

'Seb? Are you okay?'

'Fine,' Seb said, his words muffled.

He placed an open-mouthed kiss on her right knee and Rowan felt the familiar rush of heat, the tightening of her chest. How much longer would she feel like this? The intensity of their lovemaking couldn't last for ever—it never did. Then again, they didn't *have* for ever. They only had next week and then she would be gone. But she would enjoy every nerve-tightening second while she had the chance. She owed it to herself to do that.

Rowan stepped back, reached down and lifted Seb's tie, pulling it apart and allowing it to hang against his white shirt. Her fingers slipped between his neck and his collar and she snapped open the top button and then the next. Sinking to her knees, she placed her mouth on that masculine triangle at the bottom of his throat and inhaled deeply. God, she loved his smell.

Her fingers opened the rest of the buttons, and she shook her head when he tried to undo the clasp of her lacy bra.

'No, not yet,' she whispered. 'Let me play. I need to touch you, know you, taste you...'

'Why?' Seb demanded hoarsely.

Rowan bit her bottom lip as their eyes collided. 'So that I can remember every detail of you.'

'We could do this for a while yet, Ro. Nobody is making you go.'

Rowan shook her head as her hands slid over the bare skin of his sides. 'That's just sex talking, Seb. We both know that this can't last—won't last. You don't want a full-time lover and I can't stay in one place. We know this, Seb.'

'I just can't imagine not doing this any more,' Seb muttered, his face in her neck.

'Right now, I can't imagine going.'

Rowan pushed the shirt off his shoulders, stood up and pulled him to his feet. Small hands undid the snap of his suit pants and pushed the fabric off him, so that he stood naked in front of her, his erection hard and proud. Rowan ran her thumbnail down him and he jumped in reflex.

'Sit on the bed,' Rowan told him.

Rowan sat on the edge of his knees and her hands flowed over his broad shoulders, explored his tattoo and ran over the ridges of his stomach. 'I'm going to miss you when I go. I didn't think I would, but I know that I will. Lean back on your hands.'

Seb obeyed and tipped his head back. He stared at the

ceiling, his chest rising and falling rapidly. 'Don't just slip away without telling me,' he said, his voice vibrating. 'When you say goodbye, say goodbye. Don't sneak out.'

Like your mother did, Rowan thought. 'I promise. When I know I'm going, so will you. I promise to say goodbye properly.'

Rowan stroked her hand over his lower abdomen, moving her hand into his thatch of hair, down his penis and around to cup his balls. She felt him tense, relax, then groan.

'You're driving me crazy, Ro.'

Rowan was enjoying the power she was wielding, having this fantastically smart, sexy man under her control. It made her feel immensely potent to feel his reaction to her, to know that he was surrendering to her, trusting her to take care of him.

'I need to be inside you,' Seb groaned, launching himself upwards.

Rowan slipped off him and knelt in front of him, her fist encircling him, hard, warm, pulsing madly.

'Ro, don't. I won't be able to stop. I need you so much as it is,' Seb begged, his eyes wide in the dim light of the room. 'I won't be able to wait for you.'

'You can owe me…' Rowan smiled wickedly before her lips encircled him. She knew she'd won when his hand burrowed into her hair and his back bent over her head…

Was it so bad that she wanted him to keep a few erotic memories of her as well? Rowan certainly didn't think so.

CHAPTER TEN

'WELL, WELL, WELL...look what the cat has dragged in.'

Rowan thought she was still dreaming when she heard the gravelly voice—thought she was having a hallucination from too much sex and too little sleep when she saw Callie sitting at the dining table in the kitchen at Awelfor, blonde hair in a ponytail and her bare feet up on the corner of the table.

Callie?

'Callie!' Rowan screamed.

'Ro!' Callie shouted back as Rowan bounced forward and flung her arms around her best friend's neck, nearly toppling her off the chair.

Callie's arms wrapped around Rowan's back to return the hug, but when Callie's hand landed on her bottom Rowan lifted her eyebrows, then her head, and looked into Callie's green eyes.

'Are you copping a feel? Because if you are I have to tell you that you're not my type,' Rowan said, leaning her butt on the table, where Callie still had her feet.

'Just checking that you're wearing panties and haven't turned into a total slag while you've being bonking my brother.'

Callie grinned and Rowan's heart turned over. She and Seb shared that same smile—why had she never realised that until now?

'Coffee. I need coffee.' Rowan hoisted her bum off the table and wandered over to the coffee machine. She stared at it helplessly. 'Dammit, I hate this thing!'

As Rowan reached for the instant coffee she felt Callie shoulder her aside. 'Hasn't His Majesty shown you how it works?'

Rowan shrugged. 'He normally makes it for me himself; if he's not here I settle for instant.'

'It's not rocket science, BB.' Callie showed her what to do, and within a minute Rowan had made herself her first cappuccino.

'Awesome.' Rowan sipped and headed back for the table, sitting down before she started peppering Callie with questions. 'Why are you back? What happened to your Yank lover? Your appointments in LA and Vancouver?'

Callie quickly answered and then flipped the attention back to Rowan. Placing her face in her hands, she eyed her. 'You're glowing. I've never seen you glow.'

'Good sex.'

'I have good sex all the time and I never glow.' Callie's eyes radiated concern. 'What are you doing, Ro? Have you thought this through? Has Seb thought this through?'

Rowan sipped her coffee before sighing. 'I don't know… I can't speak for Seb—you know that he doesn't wear his heart on his sleeve. As for me… I went into this thinking it was just about sex, that I could control this…craziness I feel for him.'

'And can you? Did you? Have you?'

Rowan stared into her cup and wondered what to say. 'I have to, Cal. I can't do anything else but control it. I'm leaving. I have to leave.'

'Why?'

Rowan frowned at her. 'What?'

'Why do you have to leave? Who says that's the rule?

You've never been swayed by arguments about what one is "supposed" to do. So why do you now have to leave?'

Callie's verbal punch landed in her stomach. But if there was anyone she could be totally honest with it was Callie. 'Because staying is far too scary.'

'Why, sweetie?'

Rowan took a deep breath as her eyes filled with tears. 'Because I could love him, Cal. Really love him. But I don't know if I could love him enough to stay, to give up my freedom.'

'You'll never know if you don't try,' Callie pointed out.

'I'll never hurt him, or myself, if I leave before this takes on a life of its own,' Rowan said. 'I can leave now, but if this goes any deeper—if I fall in love with him—I'll be ripped apart when it ends. And it always ends, Cal.'

'Just don't leave without explaining to Seb exactly what you're doing,' Callie warned her, and Rowan remembered her promise to Seb the night before.

'I won't, Cal.' Rowan ran her finger around the rim of her cup and blew air into her cheeks. 'So that's where I am—emotionally, mentally. But I have no idea what Seb is thinking. He's probably not interested in anything more than what we have.'

'You guys really should talk more and bonk less,' Callie grumbled. 'Where *is* His Wonderfulness?'

'Still sleeping.' Rowan looked self-satisfied. 'I kind of wiped him out last night.'

'Blerch.' Callie shoved her fingers in her ears. 'Too much information.'

'Then I don't suppose you want to know about the lady kissing your dad on the cottage balcony at the moment?'

Callie slapped her hands over her eyes. 'No! What is *wrong* with you people?' She spread her fingers and looked at Rowan. 'Please tell me that she's older than us for a change.'

'A little older.' Rowan laughed. 'Okay, a lot older.'

Callie slowly lowered her hands. 'How much older? Five years? Ten?' she asked hopefully.

'Try thirty.' Rowan grinned.

Callie turned around and through the kitchen window looked at Annie, who was standing in Patch's arms and laughing up at him. In the morning sunlight they could see the fine lines around her eyes, the lack of tone in her arms. But her face was radiant and Patch's face reflected her happiness.

They looked like happy-ever-after.

'Oh, my, I think I'm going to cry,' Callie said, her words soaked with emotion. 'I think my daddy might be in love.'

'Crap on a stick,' Seb said from the doorway. 'That's all I need to hear. I'm going back to bed.'

Callie jumped up, snaked her arms around Seb's waist and squeezed. 'If I have to watch them play tonsil hockey so do you. Hey, big bro'.'

Seb dropped a kiss on her blonde head as he tucked her under his arm. His two favourite women in the room, and Ro was making him coffee. At least he hoped she was— though he thought that he needed it intravenously injected for the caffeine to have any effect soon.

Rowan walked to the fridge to grab a carton of milk and Seb had to hold Callie tighter to keep from reaching for her. Not necessarily to start anything—he was wiped!—but he just wanted to touch her, connect with her.

This was ridiculous, he thought. He'd never wanted to be close to someone before, had never sought out female company, yet he wanted to be closer to Rowan, needed to spend time with her outside the bedroom. He wanted more than sex. He needed...*time*, he decided. He just wanted more time.

Her parents were back and, judging by the looks she was sending towards their house, he could see that she was nervous about a repeat of last night's dismal performance. Seb stepped away from Callie and took the cup Rowan held out to him. He wanted to discuss her parents with her, see where she was mentally, and reassure her that he would go next door with her if she needed him to.

'Any chance of breakfast?' Callie asked brightly.

'Pancakes and bacon?' Rowan quickly responded with the suggestion of their favourite childhood meal—the only one that they could ever cook with any success.

'Whoop!' Callie bounced up again—Tigger on speed—and yanked open the freezer, looking for bacon.

'Top left?' Seb suggested, dropping into a chair and placing his bare feet up onto the seat next to him. *Coffee, kick in, please.*

He watched in resignation as Callie and Rowan fell into conversation as if they had seen each other yesterday, and tuned out automatically when they started discussing Callie's latest boyfriend in case he heard something he'd rather not…

Like the fact that Callie was having sex. Which he did not need to know. *Ever.*

Seb sighed into his coffee. He loved his sister, but he cursed her returning to Cape Town right now. He was selfish enough to want Rowan to himself for the little time she was in the country.

'Anyway, he was spectacular in the sack, but he couldn't hold a conversation with a stump.'

He saw the look Rowan sent his way, caught the teasing glint in her eyes because she knew how uncomfortable he felt hearing this stuff.

'Spectacular in the sack? Tell me more.'

'If you do, I'll beat you,' Seb interrupted, and changed the subject before they ganged up on him. 'Have you done any work on your netsukes, Ro? Anything?'

'Some.'

'Hallelujah.'

'There's no need to be snarky.' Rowan gently smacked the back of his head.

'You took two weeks to find out information I could probably have found in an hour. If that,' Seb retorted. 'I think snarky is called for.'

'I hate a bragger.' Rowan flicked his shoulder and Seb caught her finger and tugged her closer.

'That's not what you said last night,' Seb said, his voice silky as his brain started to fire on all cylinders.

Callie cracked an egg into a bowl and pulled a face. '*Eeew!* Gross! TMI, thank you. Tell me about these net-sukes so that I can push the thought of you two out of my head.'

Seb kissed Rowan's finger before letting her go.

Rowan wrinkled her nose as she opened the bacon. 'Well, they definitely aren't stolen. I found out that much. The four netsukes stolen from that gallery aren't anything like the ones I have, except for the subject matter.'

'Well, that's a relief.' Seb leaned back in his chair. 'So, what's the next step?'

Rowan pushed her hair behind her ears. 'I spoke to Grayson again, and he's scheduled a trip to London in ten days. If I can meet him in London he'll look at them and make me an offer.'

Seb fought to keep the dismay off his face and out of his voice. Ten days. She'd be out of his life in ten days. No, that didn't sound right.

Rowan carried on speaking and he forced himself to concentrate.

'I've some money to contribute to the airfare back to London, but—' she picked up a dishcloth and pulled it through her fingers in agitation '—I'd have to pay you the balance when I get to London, after Grayson has paid me. Is that okay with you?'

Seb managed to nod. Nothing was okay about this situation. Wanting to get closer to her, not wanting her to go, imagining her in his bed, in his life, for many more days, weeks—years, a lifetime... *Dammit!*

Seb watched her fry the bacon and thought it was deeply ironic that he'd been so on guard with his previous girlfriends, constantly batting off their attempts to get closer, and yet Rowan had pulled him in without making any effort at all.

He wanted to be with her and it was all self-imposed; he wanted to be with her, spend time with her, purely because he thought she was so damn wonderful. By not putting any pressure on him she'd untied the knots—the fear and concern over commitment—little by little by herself.

Was this what love felt like? He didn't think so. Who fell in love in two weeks? That was crazy! But he had had to admit that he was ass-deep in something. Something beyond lust, beyond attraction.

You just need some time alone to think this through, to be logical and practical, he insisted to himself. When she gave him some time to catch his breath he'd work it through, put the various components of what he was thinking into their proper boxes and he'd understand.

He needed to understand.

Seb tipped his head back and stared at the ceiling. She had to go. She would run because she needed to be free...

His heart wanted to flop at her feet and beg her to stay.

His brain told him he'd be okay—that things would go back to normal, that he'd plug the holes she'd made. Eventually. Maybe.

'Hey, you lovebirds! Stop snogging!'

Seb jumped at Callie's yell and saw his sister leaning across the sink, her face to the open window. 'You guys want pancakes? And, Dad, is she going be my new *mummee*?'

Rowan's eyes brimmed with mirth as she turned to look at him and his breath caught in his throat.

'Your sister—so shy, so bashful. She really should learn to put herself forward more.'

Rowan, her head reeling, carried the dinner dishes from the formal dining room to the kitchen and placed them on the counter for Seb to pack them into the dishwasher.

She'd had coffee with her father the morning after they'd returned home and then she'd waited two days for the invitation to dinner that her father had assured her was forthcoming. When it had never materialised, she'd bitten the bullet, called her dad and asked whether they'd like to have Sunday brunch with her and Seb.

It had been an unmitigated disaster.

Rowan felt Seb's arms around her waist, felt his solid frame against her chest, and the tears that she'd ruthlessly suppressed floated up her throat. 'I'm not sure whether to laugh or cry,' she said, her voice wobbly.

'At which part?' Seb asked, his lips just above her ear. 'There were many highlights. Your lack of a formal education, the fact that you are no better than a vagrant, your criminal past...'

'I'd heard all those before.' Rowan pushed her hair out of her eyes. 'What I *didn't* know was that they are putting the house on the market and moving to the UK to be closer to Peter when he goes there. I thought that Peter was planning to remain in Bahrain. Did you know that he was moving? He's your friend.'

Seb's arms dropped as she wiggled out of them. 'We don't talk that often, Ro. A bi-annual call to catch up—that's it. So, no, I didn't know about his move to the UK.'

'And his girlfriend? Did you know that she's six months pregnant?' Rowan heard the shrill demand in her voice and knew that she was not going to be unable to keep back the tide of emotion that was threatening to engulf her.

'No, I didn't know.'

Rowan moved a pile of plates from one stack to another, dumped the cutlery in an oven pan. 'Well, if that's not a huge bloody clue that they no longer consider me a part of this family then I don't know what is. I never thought it could still hurt this much.'

'What, Ro?'

'Knowing that I am, categorically, on my own,' Rowan whispered.

She'd always had this little dream—one she took out only occasionally and let it fly—that she was the beloved daughter, the fun sister, that she would have a relationship with her mother that was normal, loving…involved.

Well, their prosaic announcement earlier had detonated that fantasy into a million bloody shards. Every one of which was embedded in her heart.

'You're not on your own. You're part of us. You've always been part of us,' Seb stated, his voice calm and reasonable. Steady.

God, she wished she could climb into his steady and rest awhile. But she couldn't—wouldn't. Whatever they'd had was at an end. Her ties were cut with her parents and she should cut them with Seb as well. While she could.

They would be friends, would some day look back on the madness that had been their affair and smile, knowing that it had been a marvellous interlude in time that was pure fantasy.

'You are part of us,' Seb repeated.

Rowan shook her head. She wasn't—couldn't be. If she couldn't be accepted by her own family, how could she expect to be part of theirs? Especially after being away for so long. And what would that mean while she was on the road? The occasional call to Seb? To Patch? E-mails? Facebook?

It didn't work. She knew this.

Seb's hand drifted over her hair, a touch of pure comfort, and she jerked her head away. She had to start stepping back, start preparing herself to leave.

Practically she needed to get London to sell the netsukes, to bolster her bank account. To repay Seb.

Emotionally she had to pull away, to put some distance between them before he did. She couldn't bear it if he rejected her too—and he would. He'd made it very clear that what they had was a brief fling. He'd said nothing to make her believe that he wanted her to stay.

The realisation that a big part of her really wanted to stay terrified her.

'Oh, I took a call for you earlier, while you were in the shower,' Seb said, stepping away from her and leaning against the opposite kitchen counter.

'From..?'

'Melanie? Melissa?'

'Merle?'

'That's it. She said that you spoke to her the other day about organising her wedding?' Seb picked up an orange from the fruit basket and dug his fingers into the skin, pulling the peel away.

'She's Annie's niece and she wants a Moroccan-themed wedding. Since I've been to Morocco, Annie thought I could do it.' Rowan closed her eyes. 'I'd love to do it; I have all these ideas running through my head.'

'When is it?' Seb made a pile of peel on the dining room table.

'Three months' time.'

'So do it,' he suggested blandly.

Rowan blinked as she tried to process his words. Stay here for another three months? Was he insane? 'What are you suggesting?'

'Stay here with me. Do the wedding.' Seb pulled a seg-ment from the orange and popped it into his mouth.

'Are you mad? That's the most illogical, impractical, stupid suggestion you have ever made!' Rowan's voice climbed with every decibel. 'I have to get to London to sell the netsukes!'

'Planes go both ways,' Seb pointed out in his cool, prac-tical voice. 'Go to London. Come back.'

'I need to travel,—to keep moving, Sebastian. To be free!' Rowan shouted. 'I can't stay here.'

'Have I put a ring on your finger? Asked you to stay for ever? No. I've suggested that you stay for another three months, to do something you obviously want to do and obviously enjoy. I thought that you could stay here with me, which you seem to enjoy as well. Or am I wrong about that?'

'I thought that this was a fling...'

'And I thought you were good at change!' Seb snapped back. 'If you were anywhere else in the world would you stay?'

'Yes, but—'

'Then why can't you stay here? For a little while longer?'

'Because you haven't thought this out! Because you're feeling sorry for me, wanting to protect me, wanting to help me out of another jam! This is an impulsive offer that you are going to regret when you've thought it through and you'll wish that you'd never opened your big mouth. I don't want to be something you regret, Seb!'

'You wouldn't be.'

'Of course I would, Seb! I'm great for a fling but I'd drive you mad long-term. I can't stick to anything. I'll waft from job to job, get involved in one project and then go off at a tangent to explore something else. I'd pick up stray people and stray animals and bring them home. I'd fill your home with crazy objects that you'd hate and colourful fabrics that would hurt your eyes. I'd turn this place upside down! Drive you nuts.'

'Just leave the War Room alone.'

Rowan didn't hear him, so intent on listing every reason why she couldn't stay. 'And I'd feel hemmed-in, constrained. I'd feel frustrated and then I'd get bitchy—and then I'd start planning trips and then I'd get depressed because I'd know that I couldn't leave you like—'

'Like my mother did.'

Seb's eyes had hardened and Rowan swallowed. Dammit, why had she compared her leaving to his mother's? If he could survive that, it would be easy to wave *her* goodbye.

Just tell me that you love me, Rowan silently begged him, *that this is something more than just sex and I'll be prepared to take the risk. Tell me that I am important to you, that I mean...something. Throw me a bone here, Seb. Persuade me to stay.*

Seb didn't say a damn word.

Rowan scrubbed her hands over her face. 'I'm going to get some air. This is going nowhere.'

'Good idea. But while you're out there think of this.' Seb dropped the orange, placed sticky fingers and hands onto her face and held her head still while he ransacked her mouth.

Tongues clashed and collided—frustration and fury combined with lust and confusion. His hand on her butt pushed her into him, so that she could feel the long, solid, pulsing length of him against her stomach, and under her hands his heart thumped and rolled.

Seb yanked his mouth away from hers and looked at her with wild eyes. 'Yeah, think of that, Rowan. And then tell me you can just walk away from it.'

Rowan held her fingers to her lips, still tasting him there as he stormed out of the kitchen. She heard him thunder up the stairs and the door to his bedroom slam shut.

She would think about that—of course she would!—but she knew that thousand-degree kisses and fantastic sex wasn't enough long-term. Because falling in love with him properly would kill her if he didn't feel anything more than fierce attraction for her. She didn't know if she could pick up the pieces of her life again when he told her that he was tired of her, that it wasn't working, that he'd had enough.

She'd been the second best child, the not-up-to-par daughter, and she wasn't prepared to be the almost-good-enough-but-not-quite, good-for-the-short-term lover.

She wasn't prepared to play guessing games with her heart.

CHAPTER ELEVEN

ROWAN, NOT KNOWING where else to go, slipped through the gate into her parents' garden and headed to the north-east corner, to the mini-orchard, overgrown and neglected. In this place, between the peach and apricot trees, she and Callie had played, out of sight of both houses. It was a place where they could pretend, talk, wish, dream. Well, Callie had talked and she had dreamt.

God, she wished Callie was here. Callie would help her sort through her confusion.

'Rowan?'

Rowan spun around and hastily brushed the tears off her face. Her mum stood in front of her, looking deeply uncomfortable. Rowan held up her hands in defeat. 'Mum. What now? Why are you here?'

'I saw you streaking across the lawn, knew where you were going.' Heidi ran her hand through her still-black hair. 'Your father just tore into me, said that I was cruel to you.'

Yeah. Well. Duh.

'He thought I'd told you about Peter, about selling, moving. He thinks that we correspond regularly.'

Rowan tipped her head. 'Why did you let him think that?'

Heidi shrugged. 'I wanted to avoid an argument. I don't like arguing, conflict, trouble.'

'And I was trouble from the day I was born,' Rowan said bitterly.

Heidi didn't argue and Rowan cursed as pain slashed through her.

'Just go, Mum. I can't deal with you now.'

'When you were so sick, when you nearly died, I thought I would die too.'

Heidi's voice cracked and Rowan thought that she'd never heard her mum's voice so saturated with emotion.

'I was so scared… I don't think I've ever prayed so hard and so much. I loved you with every fibre in my being and the thought of losing you was too much for me to bear.'

What the heck…?

'When you recovered I suppose I…I retreated from you. I vowed to protect you, but I didn't think I could go through that again so I pulled back.'

Heidi must have seen something on Rowan's face because her lips twisted.

'I'm not good with emotion like you are, Rowan. I can't embrace it. I'm steadier when it's at a distance, when I am in control. Peter didn't demand that from me. You did.'

'So you pushed me away?' Rowan said, her voice flat.

Heidi nodded. 'People like us—me, your father, Peter, even Seb—we're intellectuals. We are brain-based not feelings-based. You were—*are*—all feelings. All the time. You need to touch, taste, experience.'

That was true, Rowan admitted.

Heidi nodded. 'I know you think I was cruel, encouraging you to go overseas, but I knew that you needed to. To taste, experience. Though I did think you'd come home in a year or two, settle down into a degree, get it out of your system.'

'Don't start,' Rowan warned her.

'I didn't think it would take you nine years to come home.' Heidi twisted her hands together. 'It's easier when you're not here. I can push the guilt away. But looking at you, so beautiful...'

'Mum.' Rowan placed her hand over her mouth.

Heidi straightened her shoulders and tossed her head. 'As for this...thing...with Seb...'

Oh, jeez, she really didn't want her mum commentating on her love-life. 'Mum, I don't feel like I want to hear—'

Heidi interrupted her. 'You need to leave. Because the two of you—'

Rowan growled in frustration. *Stop.* Maybe she did want to hear what she had to say. 'What, Mum?'

'The two of you spark off each other,' Heidi said, flustered. 'Anybody with half a brain can see that. But you're going to hurt each other. You are too different, worlds apart. It's not built for long-term... Love isn't enough.'

We're not in love, Rowan wanted to tell her. *Not quite. Not yet.*

Heidi kicked a branch at her foot. 'I suppose we'll have to get this area cleared if we want to sell.'

'Mum! We were talking about Seb and I! Tell me why you think we could never work.'

'Because you are too irrational, too impulsive for him to live with long-term, and his inability to be spontaneous would drive you mad. He wants someone steady and settled and you want someone exciting and unstructured. You'd kill each other.'

'So you don't believe in the theory that opposites attract? That love can conquer all?'

Heidi shook her head. 'It doesn't—not in real life. In books and in the movies, maybe, but this is your life—his life—and it's not a movie and it's not a book. Save yourselves the heartache, Rowan. I know you and I know Seb. This will blow up in your faces. You'll get hurt. And, believe it or not, I actually think you've been hurt enough.'

Rowan, reeling from having such an intense conversation with her mother, sucked in her breath. 'Why are you telling me this now?'

'Because I have failed you in so many ways, so many times. I should've tried to understand you better, loved you more, held you more. Drawn you closer instead of pushing you away. I failed you. But—' Heidi's voice cracked. 'But if I can save you some heartache, some pain, maybe you can start to forgive me. Maybe I can start to forgive myself.'

Heidi wrapped her arms around her middle and Rowan saw that her eyes were wet. She couldn't believe that her mother, who never cried, was crying over *her*.

She was nearly out of earshot when Rowan finally forced the word through her own tear-clogged throat. 'Mum?'

Heidi turned.

'I'm often in London. I have a house that I'm renovating there. Maybe we can meet, just you and I? Have tea, some time together. Maybe we can find a way back to each other?'

Heidi took a long time to answer and Rowan thought that she'd lost her. Again.

'I'd like that, Ro. I'd really like that.'

Rowan was relieved that Seb's bedroom was empty when she reached it. She immediately went to the spare room, dragged her backpack out of the cupboard and hauled it back to his room.

Somehow her clothes had found their way into his walk-in closet. Panties in his sock drawer, shorts next to his T-shirts. When had they migrated there? Who'd placed them there? Seb...? Seb had put the washing away. Hell, she'd been so busy bartending and arranging parties that she'd never got around to doing much laundry anyway. Seb had just done it quietly, with no fuss.

Shirts, shorts, jeans. Shoes? Red cowboy boots, trainers, pumps, flats. They all stood on the shelves in his shoe cupboard, along with her sparkly silver sandals. Rowan bit her lip as she traced the design on the front of one shoe; she loved these shoes but she wouldn't take them. Like the coral dress, like Seb, she had to leave them behind.

The box containing her netsukes sat on an open shelf above the shoes and Rowan stretched up and pulled it down. She lifted the lid and furiously unwrapped the little statues until she found the one she was looking for—the one of the Laughing Buddha with mischief in his eyes.

She wouldn't be selling this one—wouldn't take it with her. This was Seb's—her gift to him. She'd planned on keeping it herself but, like her, he'd fallen in love with it the first time he'd held it. It didn't matter that it was probably the oldest and most valuable of the collection. Nothing much mattered now. She placed it on the shelf next to a pile of his T-shirts, where she knew he would see it.

She was leaving and she had a new life to make. Her mum was right. They would eventually decimate each other. While she had the right to take chances with her own heart, she didn't have the right to play fast and loose with his. With anyone's. It was better to be on her own, responsible for only herself...

No risk of being hurt. Of hurting him.

'Running again, Brat?'

Rowan turned and looked at Seb, who had one shoulder plastered against the wall, his eyes shuttered.

'Packing.' Rowan kept her voice even. 'We both knew that I'd be leaving once I saw my folks.'

'Yeah, but neither of us thought that we'd be burning up the sheets a day later. That changes things, Rowan.'

'It's just sex, Seb. You can find it anywhere.'

Rowan yelped when Seb streaked across the room, gripped her arms and glared at her.

'It is not just sex! Get it?'

'Then what is it?' Rowan demanded. 'And let me go. You're hurting me.'

Tell me. Tell me that you need me to stay. Give me something to work with, to take a risk on.

Seb dropped his hands and then threw them up. 'It's something! I don't know what it is, exactly, but we'll never find out if you don't stop running!'

Something? Something wasn't enough. Not nearly enough.

'I'm leaving. I'm not running!' Rowan shouted. 'And I never said I'd stay! Besides, what would I be staying for? Another couple of months of sex? What do you want from me, Seb? Can you tell me?'

Seb raked his hand through his hair. 'No. Maybe. Not yet. I haven't thought it through.'

'You see, that's the essential difference between you and me. It has to make intellectual sense to you and it just has to feel right to me.' Rowan sat on the edge of the bed.

'Does it feel right for you to stay?' Seb asked quietly.

'Yes! But the problem is...'

'What?'

Rowan lifted pain-saturated eyes to his. 'This time I know that it's smart to leave. That, no matter how right it feels to stay, I have to listen to my brain. Because this time I can't trust my heart.'

'Why?'

'Because you'll break it. And I'll break yours. We have the ability to do that to each other,' Rowan said in a quiet, determined voice. 'If I walk—run—leave now, we can avoid that. You can't give me enough of what I need for me to consider staying. I don't want to hurt you, and God knows I don't want you to hurt me. Let me go, Seb, please. It's for the best. You know it is.'

'All I know—*feel*, dammit!—is that you are running as fast and as far away from me as possible. But I've never begged a woman for anything in my life and I'm not going to start now.'

Seb walked over to his desk, shoved the chair so hard that it skidded across the floor and bent over his computer. His fingers skipped over the keys and ten minutes later—the longest ten minutes of her life—he turned back to face her.

His face and voice were completely devoid of emotion. 'I've booked you on a flight to London, leaving tonight. I've ordered you a taxi. It will be here in an hour. I'm sure you won't mind spending the afternoon in the airport. It's what you do, isn't it?'

'Seb, I'm doing what I think is best for us,' Rowan protested, trying once more to get him to understand.

'And where does what I want, what I need, what I think is best, come into it? All I'm asking is for some time, Rowan! A slice of your time so that we can work out what we want to do. We've been together for nearly three weeks! We're adults. Adults don't make snap decisions about the rest of their lives, about whether they're going to get hurt or not. I want time with you—time that you seem to be able to give to mountains and monasteries, temples, sights and cities but not to me!' Seb roared. 'So, really, take your excuses about doing what is best for us and get the hell out of my life.'

Seb slammed the lid of his computer closed, sent her another fulminating, furious look and walked out of the room. Instead of slamming the door, as she knew he wanted to do, he closed it quietly. Its snick was the soundtrack to her heart cracking and snapping.

Crap; she was *so* screwed.

'You look awful, darling.' Grayson Darling looked at her across the table in the English tea room and then at an original artwork just beyond her head. 'Love that painting.'

'Gray, I've drunk the tea, eaten the scones…can we talk netsukes now?' Rowan demanded, in a thoroughly bad mood. Then again, she'd been in a bad mood since she'd left Cape Town two weeks ago and it was steadily getting worse. Having to spend two hours with Grayson, making small talk over high tea, was just making her feel even more cranky—which she hadn't believed was possible.

She needed to do this deal with Grayson; the money she'd made arranging those parties and bartending was almost finished and she was sick of sleeping on a friend's pull-out couch.

She needed money. Fast. She'd played this song to death; hopefully after today she wouldn't have to hear it again.

Grayson wiped his fingers on a snow-white cloth serviette and sighed dramatically as he pulled the box towards him. 'Where is the charming Rowan I enjoyed so much?'

Back in Cape Town, with her heart. With Seb. Seb… Her heart clenched. She missed him so much—missed her heart, which had remained behind with him. Without it she was just existing, just skating.

She didn't skate. She didn't exist. She *lived*. It was what she did. But no longer. Not any more. Not without Seb. She'd thought that she'd been so clever, leaving Cape Town before she fell in love with him. But love, she realised, didn't stop to count the miles between them and had snuck inside her anyway.

'Oh, Rowan, these are wonderful,' Grayson said, appreciation in every syllable as he lined up the netsukes between them. 'Fantastic composition, brilliant condition. But you're missing one… Where's the Laughing Buddha?'

'It's not for sale.'

'Of course it's for sale; it's the jewel of the collection.' Grayson looked at her in horror. 'It's the one I want.'

Seb's the one I want… Okay, stop being a complete drip, Dunn, and concentrate. 'Sorry, Grayson. I gave it away.'

Grayson closed his eyes and shook his head. 'Dear God, you are a basket case. Get it back.'

'It's gone. Move on. Make me an offer on these,' Rowan demanded, exhausted.

She watched as Grayson examined the netsukes again and allowed her mind to wander. She recognised the light of acquisition in his eyes and knew that within a day she'd be a couple of thousand pounds richer than she had been when she'd emptied her bank account a month ago. Good grief, had it only been a month? How could so much have happened in so short a time?

Forcing her mind away from the path it travelled far too frequently straight back to Seb, she tried to make plans on where to go from here. Back to Thailand or west to Canada? Or home to Cape Town.

Every cell in her body reacted when she thought of Cape Town. She didn't want to go anywhere else. She wanted to go home, to Seb.

Being deported and being broke had catapulted her into a situation where she'd had to slow down, move beyond the good-time surface and come face to face, heart to heart, with another person. With Seb. And she'd loved what she'd found. She'd resisted it, resisted love, with everything she had, and it was hard to admit that freedom didn't stand a chance against not having Seb in her life.

She loved him. Just loved him with every atom in her body. He was her freedom, the next world she had to discover, understand. He was what had been missing from her life, what she'd been searching for all over the world.

And he was right. She ran when she most needed to stand and fight.

'Fifty thousand and not a penny more for all of them,' Grayson said.

Rowan blinked, smiled and held out her hand. 'Deal. When can I have the money?'

Grayson looked horrified. 'Rowan, dammit, you are supposed to negotiate! Haven't I taught you *anything*?'

'I know you're low-balling me, Gray—' Well, she did now. 'But I don't have the time to argue with you. How much do you have on you?'

'Ten thousand. Okay, I'll give you sixty,' Grayson muttered. 'I'd feel like I was robbing you if you took less.'

Rowan held out her hand. 'I'll take the ten and you can transfer the balance into my account as per normal. Maybe by then you'll realise that you are still screwing me and up the offer again.'

Grayson sent the netsukes a greedy look before pulling out a money clip from his jacket pocket. 'It's entirely possible.'

Rowan took the cash from his hand, stood up and dropped a kiss on the balding crown of his head. 'Thanks. Enjoy.'

'If you ever want to sell the Laughing Buddha I'm your man.'

Rowan shook her head. 'I'll tell the new owner, but he won't sell it.'

'Gave it away…sacrilege.' Grayson gestured to the pile of food still on the table. 'Where are you shooting off to in such a hurry? We've hardly made a dent in the food.'

Rowan grinned at him. 'Home. I'm going home.'

Dusk was falling and it looked as if someone was randomly sprinkling lights over Scarborough as the sea darkened to cobalt and then to midnight-blue. It was Seb's favourite time of the day and, pre-Ro, he had often spent this half-hour at his desk, whisky in his hand, just watching the transition from night to day. With all the lights in his office off, his staff, who were still at their stations in the War Room, knew better than to disturb him.

Seb took a sip of his whisky, felt the burn and was grateful he could feel anything.

Since Rowan had left he'd felt numb. And that was when he wasn't feeling lost and sad and crap. He was feeling opposed to thinking and he didn't like it at all. This was why he didn't get emotionally involved; this was why he kept his distance.

He was a walking, talking cliché. Drinking too much, thinking too much, wishing too much. Finding things to do so that he didn't go to sleep, because she was there in his dreams and it hurt too damn much when he woke up, rolled over and realised—again—that she wasn't there.

He just hurt. Full-stop.

The lights flashed on overhead and he lifted his hand against the glare. 'What the…? Dad?'

'Drinking in the dark is a new low, even for you,' Patch said cheerfully, sitting in the chair on the opposite side of the desk. He gestured towards his half-full glass. 'Got another of those for your old man?'

Seb pushed the glass across the desk. 'Take this one. I'm going to hit the gym and try and work out my frustration.'

'Horny?' Patch joked, but his eyes were serious.

Seb couldn't find the energy to pretend. 'Just sad.'

'You do have it bad. Have *her* bad.' Patch sipped the whisky, put his ankle over his knee and looked at his son. 'I thought she'd be the one to get hurt, yet you are taking a pounding.'

'Yeah.' That summed it up.

'I'm going to marry Annie,' Patch said, and Seb's head snapped up.

He was wallowing and his father was getting married? What the—?

'She doesn't know, and I haven't said anything, but she's the one. I just want to be with her for ever. I know it in here.'

He thumped his heart. 'So do you, if you'd stop thinking so much and take a chance.'

Jeez, he'd tried. His father didn't know that he was the one who'd asked her to stay, to give them some time, so he briefly explained the situation.

Patch sent him a pitying look. 'So you asked her to stay... what did *that* mean?'

'Excuse me?'

'Did you tell her that you love her? That you want to be with her?' Patch demanded.

'No. I just asked her to stay, to give me time to think. I just wanted time to figure it out,' Seb protested.

'And if she'd given you that time and you'd decided that you didn't love her? What then? Where would she have been then?' Patch demanded. 'What reason did you give her to stay? Why would she stick around, running the risk of getting closer to you, when she knew she could get heart-slammed at the end of it?'

Seb dropped an F-bomb and his head. 'I didn't think about it like that.'

'What is the one thing Rowan has been looking for all her life, Seb?'

'Uh...'

'Love, acceptance, a place and a person she can belong to. How can somebody as smart as you not know this?'

He wasn't smart with people. He never had been.

'So, what are you going to do about it, Seb? Are you going to track her around the world like you do your mum? Never making contact and making yourself miserable? Or are you going to reach out and try and make this work?'

Seb felt the slap of Patch's words. 'What? Whoa, back up! Do you think I *should* contact my mum?'

Patch sighed. 'I think that you either have to or let her go. Callie and I, we're reconciled to the fact that she is out of our lives. We're over it—over her. You? Not so much. I think it would be healthier if you either had a relationship with her or if you cut ties completely. No man's land is no place to operate from. Same with Rowan. Either take a chance or let her go. Don't be half-assed about it.'

'Jeez, Dad. Why don't you just let it rip, huh?'

'I'm trying. Get Rowan back, Seb, or get a grip! Just, for all our sakes, stop moping!'

And that was his dad's verbal boot up the ass, Seb thought. He took a deep breath and ran his hand over his head. 'I don't know where she is. I presume she is still in London.'

Patch rolled his eyes. 'You've been tracking Laura since you were sixteen and you're telling me you don't know where Rowan is? That you can't find out where she is going? What do you do every day, Seb? Get on that bloody machine and found out!'

Seb grinned, jumped to his feet and headed for the computer across the room. Within minutes he'd plugged in the necessary code and the result flashed up on the screen.

Holy hell… Were his eyes playing cruel tricks on him?

He felt Patch at his elbow. 'What? What's the problem?'

Seb pointed to a line on the screen. 'Do you believe this? Am I seeing things?'

Patch's hand gripped his shaking shoulder to steady him. 'No, bud, I don't think that you are.'

Rowan cleared Customs and Immigration and stood in the middle of the arrivals hall, staring at the mobile in her hand. *Seb Hollis*, it said. *Seb Hollis. Dial me, dial me. Just push the green button.*

She'd thought that asking him for a favour all those weeks ago would be hard, but it was nothing—*nothing!*—compared to the terror she felt now.

Please love me. Please keep me.

Yeah, as if she was going to come right out and say that!

No, she'd figured this all out. She was going to be rational and unemotional; she'd say that they had something worth exploring, that she would stay if he wanted her to, give them time to work it out.

She would not be the gibberish-spewing, sobbing, crazy, wildly-in-love person she knew herself to be. She would be sensible if it killed her—which it probably would, if the terror didn't get her first.

What if he refused to come and get her? What if she had to bang down his door to see him? What if…?

She was driving herself over the edge. *Just dial the damn number!*

Seb took five rings to answer. 'Seb? It's me.'

'Rowan.'

Rowan heard the tension in his voice and felt her stomach swoop to her toes. Oh, this was much, much harder than anything she'd ever done before. *Courage, Dunn. This is your do-over, your second chance. You're going to regret not doing this, so do it!* 'I need a favour.'

'Another one?'

'It's the last one, I promise.'

'Uh huh.'

Before her vocal cords seized up she forced her words out. 'Can you come pick me up? I'm back and I'm at the airport. And I need to talk to you.'

'Yeah. Okay. Stay where you are. Sexy jeans, by the way,' he said, before abruptly disconnecting.

What the…? She was taking the biggest chance of her life and he was commentating on her jeans? How would he know what she was wearing anyway? How *could* he know…?

'Really sexy jeans. I like the way they hug your butt.'

Rowan spun around and there he was…large, solid, *there*…right in front of her. Dear Lord, he was there. Rowan lifted her fist to her mouth and bit her knuckle hard. The pain reassured her that he wasn't a figment of her imagination, that he was real.

So damn real. As real as the hand that now covered the side of her face.

'Breathe, Ro.'

Tears that she'd sworn weren't going to fall ran down her face. 'You're here.'

'I'll always be here, if you let me,' Seb told her, his eyes radiating emotion.

'How did you know...? How? My flight? I only decided yesterday to come back...to come home.' Ro gripped his shirt and hung on. As long as she held him he couldn't disappear on her. 'How?'

'I keep telling you that I could track you on the moon if I wanted to. When are you going to believe me?' Seb placed his hand on her hip and pulled her closer. 'Come here. I need to touch you—all of you.'

Rowan burrowed her face into his neck, inhaling his scent, trying to climb inside him. One strong hand held her head there, another wrapped around her lower back, pulling her as close as possible. They stood there for many minutes, just holding on.

Maybe, just maybe, he'd missed her as much as she'd missed him.

'Can I come home, Seb? Can I come back?' Rowan asked when she eventually lifted her head, forcing herself to meet his eyes.

Seb placed a gentle kiss on her mouth before pushing a curl behind her ear. He stroked the pad of his thumb across her cheekbone before dropping his hand back to her hip.

'You *are* home. You *are* back,' Seb replied. 'And, frankly, it's about bloody time.'

They didn't speak much on the way home, but Seb's hand on her knee reassured her that they would—that they would find a way to move forward. She placed her fingers on top of his and her heart turned over when he smiled at her. Was that love she saw in his eyes, on his face, or was she just imagining it?

She was probably just imagining it… Yes, he was happy that she was back, but there was no point in jumping to conclusions. She was just setting herself up for a fall. It was enough—it should be enough—to know that that she loved him, that she was home, that she had to take every day as it came and treasure the time she had with him.

She felt Seb's fingers widen under hers, stretch, and then he patted her knee. 'You were gripping my hand so hard I lost all feeling. Relax, Ro, we'll sort this out.'

'We will?'

Seb sent her his cocky grin. 'Damn straight. I'm not letting you go again without a fight.'

Rowan looked puzzled. 'I thought that *was* a fight.'

'That wasn't even close,' Seb assured her. 'Now, put your hand back on mine, try not to stop the blood, and relax. We're going to get home, have a glass of wine and talk it through. Like adults. In a reasonable, mature fashion…'

They had crazy monkey sex instead. On the stairs…

They walked into the house and Seb closed the front door behind him and dropped her rucksack to the floor. 'I'll take this upstairs later. Do you want a glass of wine?'

Rowan shook her head. She didn't want anything. She just wanted that mouth on hers, that skin under her hands, him inside her.

'Ro? Water? Juice? Food?'

Rowan shook her head again and Seb looked at her, puzzled. 'Okay. What *do* you want?'

'You. Just you. Right now. Right here,' Rowan whispered.

And, while she craved his touch, she didn't expect him

to immediately back her into the wall, his mouth covering hers and his hands everywhere. On her breasts, on her butt, her thighs, skimming her face, in her hair. It was as if he was rediscovering her, re-exploring her, touching her for the first time.

And she needed him to feed off her as she was feeding off him. She shoved her hands up and under his T-shirt, pulling it over his head so that she could touch his stomach without the barrier of cotton, run her hands over his chest, up his neck.

'Do you have any particular attachment to this shirt?' Seb demanded, his voice hoarse in her ear.

'Uh? What? No.'

'Good.' Seb grabbed each side of her shirt and ripped it open, scattering buttons over the floor. 'Much better,' he muttered, shoving the sleeves down her arms and letting it fall to the floor.

A finger hooked the cup of her bra away and his mouth covered her nipple as lust swirled and whirled, hot and fast.

Underneath love quivered and sighed, hoped and dreamt.

'I missed you so much,' Rowan said as he unhooked her bra and threw it over his shoulder.

'This place was like a morgue without you. Get those jeans off,' he muttered, his fingers busy pleasuring her breasts.

'Get yours off too,' Rowan retorted as she wiggled the fabric down her legs.

'For you? Any time.' Seb shucked his jeans along with his boxers and stared down at her, his heart in his eyes. 'You are so beautiful, Ro. I'm so glad you're home.'

'Me too.' Rowan sighed, placing her fingers on his cheek. 'Now, why don't you show me how glad you are by—?'

Seb's mouth cut off her words as one hand hoisted her thigh, his other hand pulled aside her panties and he thrust into her, hard and deep, filling her body, her mind and heart.

Seb. There was only Seb—would only be Seb.

'Ah, *now* I'm home,' Seb said into her mouth. 'You're my home, Ro. Only you.'

Later, after they'd made love again in his bed, Rowan sat on the love seat in the window of Seb's room and was thankful that he'd said that he needed to run downstairs for a minute.

She needed that minute. She needed more than a minute. To catch her breath, to allow her brain to catch up with her body.

She was trying to be brave, trying not to worry, but her brain was now in hyper-drive, red-lining with worry. Had nothing changed while she was away? Were they just going to fall back into what they'd had? When were they going to talk, work this out, as Seb had suggested in the car?

And what, exactly, did his 'working it out' entail?

Rowan released her bottom lip from between her teeth as Seb walked back into the room, carrying a large tray. His boxer shorts rode low on his hips and his 6-pack rippled as he walked over to her.

'Stop looking at me like that or you'll be back on that bed so fast your head will spin,' Seb said as he placed the tray on the cushions next to her.

'Promises, promises,' Rowan replied, and frowned when she looked down at the tray. A bottle of champagne she could understand, and the two glasses, but the set of keys that looked like a carbon copy of his house set and a keyless car remote had her puzzled. There was also a red jewellery box on the tray...

A jewellery box? Oh, dear God...

'You're not proposing, are you?' she asked, in a very high, very nervous voice.

Seb laughed. 'Not today.'

Phew!

'Then what's all this?' Rowan asked as Seb sat down, keeping the tray between them.

'We'll get to the box eventually, but first…it's time to work it out, Ro,' Seb said, popping the cork on the champagne and pouring her a glass.

He handed it over and poured his own glass.

'Why did you come home?' he asked her bluntly.

Rowan licked her lips. 'I missed you.'

'I missed you too. And…?'

Rowan stared at the bubbles in her glass. If she said these next words she could never take them back. They would be out there for ever…and she was okay with that.

'I love you. I do… I never expected to, never wanted to, but I do. So I thought I'd come home, tell you that and see how you feel about it.'

Seb just looked at her, his glass halfway to his mouth.

The moisture in Rowan's mouth dried up and she swirled some champagne around her tongue to get it to work. 'Feel free to give me a reaction, here, Hollis.'

'I feel pretty good about it. I thought I'd have to drag those words out of you with pliers but you've astounded me again.' Seb reached across the tray, kissed her gently and ran his thumb across her trembling bottom lip. 'I love you too, by the way. In every way possible and in lot of ways I thought were impossible.'

Ah… *Aaaahhhhh!* Rowan's shoulders fell down from her ears and her cheeks deepened. Relief, hot and strong, pulsed through her.

'Good to know… My mum says that we will destroy each other. That we are too different, diametrically opposed.' Rowan thought it was important to tell him that her mother rated their chances as less than nil.

'Your mother talks a lot of crap,' Seb said mildly, play-

ing with her fingers as he sipped his champagne. 'We'll be
fine. Yes, you'll turn my life upside down, but as long as
you leave the War Room and my hackers alone you can do
whatever you want. And if you go too crazy I'll pull you
back in. In the same way, if I get too stuck in my head,
you'll bully me out of it. We're good for each other pre-
cisely because we are so different.'

'I've been independent for so long and I'm worried that
I'll get restless, feel hemmed-in.' Rowan also felt it was
important to warn him. Maybe staying in one place would
be enough for her, being with him would be enough, but
there might come a day that she needed to fly, just to know
that she could...

'I know.' Seb gestured to the tray. 'I've thought about
that. So, first things first.' He held up the set of keys. 'Keys
to your house—this house. I don't want to hear any more
of this "your bedroom" and "your house" rubbish. This
house is as much yours as it is mine. Replace the furniture, paint the walls—do whatever you want; just treat it
as yours, okay?'

'It's not mine.'

'Rowan...!' Seb warned.

'Or yours, or Patch's. It's Yas's, as we all know. And
whatever I do I'll have to put up with Yas yapping on about
it, so I'll think long and hard before I go mad. You might
not care, but she will.' Rowan took the keys and bounced
them in her hand.

Seb grinned. 'All true, but I'll back you if comes down
to a fight.' He lifted up the credit-card-type key. 'Keyless
car key. We'll share the Quattro until I get you something
else to drive.'

'You can't buy me a car!' Rowan squeaked. 'I have
money. I can buy my own car. I sold the netsukes.'

'Thanks for mine, by the way. I love it. It's kept me from
going insane these past couple of weeks.' Seb tossed the

key card into her lap. 'Are we going to argue about money and stuff for the rest of our lives?'

'Are you going to love me that long?' Rowan asked, her hands on his knees.

'Planning on it.'

Seb picked up the jewellery box and tossed it from hand to hand. Rowan saw fear flash in his eyes.

'Giving you this is hard for me, but I know that it's necessary.'

Rowan frowned, took the box, flipped open the lid and saw that it was a credit card. He was giving her a credit card? What on earth...?

'There's enough money there to buy you ticket anywhere in the world, any time you want to go. Enough for you to book into any hotel you want to, buy what you want to. It has a heck of a limit in that it doesn't *have* a limit.'

'Seb. Why are you giving me a credit card? I don't understand.'

Seb licked his lips. 'It comes with a couple of conditions.'

'I'm listening.'

'I'll pay for everything, but you have to promise to say goodbye, to tell me that you're going. No walking out. And you can't use it after we've had a fight. You have to give us—me—a chance to work it out before you run.'

Tears tumbled. That was fair. God, that was so fair. She nodded furiously. 'Okay.'

'And you have to promise me that you'll always come back, because if you don't I swear I'll find you and drag you back home. I love you. It took me nine years to find you and I am not letting you go again.'

'Oh, Seb.' Rowan used the heels of her hands to swipe away her tears. It was such an enormous gift, such a demonstration of how well he knew her, how much he trusted her.

'Is that a deal, Brat?'

Rowan nodded. 'Deal.'

'Good. I told you we could work this out. Do you love me?'

'So much!'

'And I love you.' Seb's eyes brimmed with all the emotion he usually tried so hard to suppress. 'So explain to me—again—why you aren't over here, kissing me stupid?'

Rowan sighed as she moved into his arms. 'Another very epic fail on my part. Must try harder.'

* * * * *

LET'S TALK
Romance

For exclusive extracts, competitions
and special offers, find us online:

MILLS & BOON

THE HEART OF ROMANCE

A ROMANCE FOR EVERY KIND OF READER

MODERN

Prepare to be swept off your feet by sophisticated, sexy and seductive heroes, in some of the world's most glamourous and romantic locations, where power and passion collide.
8 stories per month.

HISTORICAL

Escape with historical heroes from time gone by. Whether your passion is for wicked Regency Rakes, muscled Vikings or rugged Highlanders, awaken the romance of the past.
6 stories per month.

MEDICAL

Set your pulse racing with dedicated, delectable doctors in the high-pressure world of medicine, where emotions run high and passion, comfort and love are the best medicine.
6 stories per month.

True Love

Celebrate true love with tender stories of heartfelt romance, from the rush of falling in love to the joy a new baby can bring, and a focus on the emotional heart of a relationship.
8 stories per month.

Desire

Indulge in secrets and scandal, intense drama and plenty of sizzling hot action with powerful and passionate heroes who have it all: wealth, status, good looks…everything but the right woman.
6 stories per month.

HEROES

Experience all the excitement of a gripping thriller, with an intense romance at its heart. Resourceful, true-to-life women and strong, fearless men face danger and desire - a killer combination!
8 stories per month.

DARE

Sensual love stories featuring smart, sassy heroines you'd want as a best friend, and compelling intense heroes who are worthy of them.
4 stories per month.

To see which titles are coming soon, please visit

millsandboon.co.uk/nextmonth